HELP. . . .

The skier lay motionless on her side.

As he walked toward her, the girl moved, groaned.

Her white hood fell back, off her face. He stared down in disbelief.

No! It was not she! *It was the wrong one!*

Through the swirling snow, she saw the glint of the knife in his fist. She looked with puzzlement into his eyes. "Help . . ." she pleaded. Her voice trailed away as the rage in his face swept over her. She opened her mouth in horror.

A black roaring filled his ears. She had seen him. She would recognize him, tell someone. She would ruin everything he had planned . . . years of waiting.

He knelt by her and raised his arm.

"No!" the girl screamed.

Ellen Ryp, a native New Yorker, has worked as an editor and a creative director. *Deadly Bonds* is her first novel. She and her husband live in Manhattan.

DEADLY BONDS

ELLEN RYP

WARNER BOOKS

A Warner Communications Company

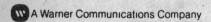

To the memory of my parents, Jacob and Belle Stern.
And for Emanuel.

CHAPTER
1

He had planned for everything except the snow.

The first damp flakes brushed down from the skies, blowing across his cheeks, tickling his eyelids. Cold, white feathers that steadily thickened until they dimmed the late-afternoon sun. Crouched at the base of the narrow gorge, one boot trailing over the rocks into the icy mountain stream, he spat out a fluff of snow that blew onto his lip. At his side lay the three red warning flags.

She would come soon. She would be alone. She always skied down the hazardous cutoff, leaving the others to bounce over the moguls of the main trail. He would recognize her as soon as he saw her. But she would not know who he was. He felt for the knife in the pocket of his tan parka. He would tell her—in one exulting moment he would tell her who and why . . . just before. . . .

The sky darkened through the shifting grey curtain of flakes. He moved his foot out of the water and gathered the flags closer to his huddled body. Listening intently, his thick lips parted to sharpen his hearing, he waited for the shush and slide of her skis.

Shouts rose from the slopes. Whoops of girlish laughter muffled by the now-heavy fall of snow.

"I can't see a damned thing!"

"Not that way, you dummy!"

"Over here! Follow me!"

Skis swished through the deadened air. He struggled up the side of the cliff to peer over the top. *Damn!* A pack of them were coming down Piz Wolfram together. Which one . . . *which one was she?*

He shook his head and squinted through the icy flurries that prickled his face. Three—no, four of them. Screaming and laughing, streaming down the trail, their orange and yellow and green and blue ski jackets flashing through the mist. A pole flew up, tethered to a flailing arm, as one of the girls tumbled in a splash of snow. But she was up quickly, sweeping off after the others, curving away from the cliff as she raced down toward the base of the trail.

She would not be coming! The thought panicked him, then turned to fury. The waiting, the planning, and she would not come!

He slumped to the base of the gully, snow frosting on his eyelashes, capping his bare head. His breath exploded in smoky puffs. Down the hill to his left, the brightly colored backs of the skiers receded, their shouts and bursts of laughter growing fainter. He hugged his shoulders and rocked against the side of the sheer embankment. He would wait. Tomorrow, or the day after. However long it took, he would get to her! His thick purplish lips flapped with the silent mouthing of rage.

Then he heard the distant sibilance.

He tensed and held his breath. The wind soughing through stands of evergreen? Again, the sound, this time closer. He raised up, but saw nothing through the driving white clouds. The steep slope rising off to his right at the top of the embankment was hidden by a blank wall of falling snow only a few meters away. But he was sure he heard it—the unmistakable tap of pole against ski, the faint breathing of fiberglass through freshly fallen powder.

Suddenly, a ghostly white figure burst through the curtain of flakes, trailing smoky tendrils of snow. He recoiled in shock and fell to his knees on the red warning flags. With a cry, the white figure hurtled over the lip of the embankment, flew over his head, and crashed in a clatter of skis and poles in the rocky stream at his feet. Then all was quiet in the thickened air except the trickling of icy water through its pebbled bed.

He pressed his back against the side of the cliff, his breath a rasping sob in his throat. The skier lay motionless on her side in the rocky shallows. The furred hood of her white ski jacket was twisted to cover her face. One white-panted leg was bent under the other, the safety binding snapped open to release the ski. Already flakes of snow were clinging, coating, building up on the outstretched figure.

So . . . so, finally. . . . He waited until his body stopped heaving. Then he rose on trembling legs and pulled the knife out of his pocket. As he walked toward her, the girl moved, groaned, rolled her head out of the water. Her white hood fell back off her face. He stared down in disbelief.

No! It was not she! *It was the wrong one!*

The girl moaned again, opened her eyes, and blinked against the falling snow. She smiled weakly up at him.

"Broke—something," she panted. "Please. . . ."

He stood over her, not moving.

"Need help . . . please . . . get someone. . . ." She tried to move, but cried out with pain.

He looked down at her, his mouth working with fury, not saying anything. *The wrong one!*

"Oh, please. . . . Get . . . help. . . ." the girl gasped. Through the swirling snow, she saw the glint of the knife in his fist. She looked with puzzlement into his eyes. "Help. . . ." she pleaded. Her voice trailed away as the rage in his face swept over her. She opened her mouth in horror. Her eyes began to slew wildly.

A black roaring filled his ears. She had seen him. She would recognize him, tell someone. She would ruin everything he had planned . . . the years of waiting. . . .

He knelt by her and raised his arm.

"No!" the girl screamed. She clutched at the ski pole strapped to her wrist, swung desperately at him. The pole caught his arm, and the knife flew into the snow as he struggled for balance. Numbed by terror against the pain, she tried to back away, braced on her elbows, but the flash of his bare

fist caught the side of her face and snapped her head back against a rock. She did not move again. Flakes of snow drifted into her open mouth and clung to her lashes.

Laboring against the driving wind, he dragged her by the shoulders till her head was half submerged in the icy stream. He pressed her face into the water. His mind raced in a frantic circle. No one would know . . . a skiing accident . . . she could never tell. . . . He was safe, free again to do what he had to. . . .

The minutes passed.

Finally, he pulled her out of the water and dragged her to the base of the embankment. Snow had already covered the red flags, and he had to feel around beneath the powder till he found them. They must be replaced before he left. Panting, he hauled himself to the top of the cliff and jammed the sticks into the snow, several meters apart, along the lip. The flags snapped in the wind. A light dusting of white brushed over their slick surface. Down below, a mound of snow was beginning to form over the still, white figure.

This weather would hold for days, he knew. Time . . . he would have plenty of time. . . . She would not get away from him. He always knew where to find her. And he had planned for this, just in case. The note he had prepared was still in his pocket. . . .

CHAPTER
2

Carla Temple leaned back against the oversized pillows with a tiny growl of satisfaction. One year, one whole year of denial that had only made the pain worse. She must have been crazy!

She smiled as she listened to Michael splashing in the bathroom. Everything had been perfect, just as she had planned. The same suite at the Hotel Chesa Monteviglia where they would slip away for afternoons of privacy a year ago, the champagne icing in its sweating bucket in front of the fireplace, the bowl of purple and green grapes, the creamy Swiss chocolates that Michael loved—all perfect, especially Michael.

The late afternoon light drifted faintly into the room. Carla stretched and fluffed out the curly, blue-black nimbus of her hair. She wore it short now, and its darkness emphasized the natural fairness of her complexion. She was paler now, too; the last of her outdoor glow had vanished months ago. But there was still a crackling vitality in her face that complemented its delicate beauty. When she smiled at someone, a warm, open smile that crinkled around her eyes, it was greeted as a gift.

Carla was smiling now, waiting. She checked her watch and glanced through the airy curtains at the snow driving past the windows. It was building up, blowing almost horizontally now, much stronger than when she had looked an hour ago. And the wind—it sounded like a major storm. She would have to get back soon. Oh, but not too soon!

The heavy white *plumeau*, which no well-dressed bed in the Alps would be without, lay on the floor where it had slid. The room was warm. Carla shifted languidly against the sheets. She hadn't forgotten the blissful freedom of lolling through stolen afternoons with Michael, the excitement of loving and rushing apart. They were so much alike—their youthful energy, their driving competitiveness, their successes, achieved with such dash and bravura. . . . Carla had never felt so comfortable with a man as with Michael. No, nothing forgotten, only postponed. . . .

She smoothed the single light sheet that covered the length of one leg. The column of her other leg rested on top of the bed, shapely and strong and glowing in the rosy pulse of the firelight. Her graceful body lay undraped, rising in classic proportion from the shiny curls of the dark triangle below her stomach to the pink buds that rode the high lift of her breasts.

As always, she was at ease with her body. Now, tingling with pleasure, she clasped her hands behind her head and waited.

The sound of flowing water stopped.

"Michael?" she called to the closed door. "More champagne! Hurry, hurry. I'm dying of thirst and I'm too lazy to move. What are you doing in there so long?"

There was a muffled clatter from beyond the door. Michael emerged from the bathroom. He was fully dressed again in his sleek brown and tan belted jumpsuit. His dark hair was wet and slicked back from his handsome face.

Carla frowned, puzzled.

Michael clumped across the room in his high plastic ski boots and sat on the edge of the bed. Without a word, he reached for her.

"What—?" she began, but his mouth covered hers. Anxiety replaced her surprise, and she pushed at his strong shoulders until he released her. "Where are you going?" she sputtered. "I have plenty of time. I thought we'd have the whole afternoon together."

His dark blue eyes slipped away from her. "Can't. I only stopped by to say hello, you know, see how you're doing. It's been so many—uh, so long, and I wasn't far from Fernstaad." He turned toward the sound of the wind outside. "Really lousy conditions for this time of year, aren't they?"

Carla pressed her lips together. "It's just a storm. You've been here for a while, then?"

"Well, around. For a little while. I didn't want to leave without seeing you."

She moved farther away from him on the bed. "I thought that's why you came here—just to see me, so we could be together after all this time."

"Absolutely. And I'm glad I did." He looked down and stroked the gleaming leg on the sheet. "Lady Lightning," he murmured. "You're more beautiful than ever, you know that?"

"Oh, cut the crap, Michael!" Her eyes sparkled with hurt. She flinched from his touch and pulled the sheet up over her breasts.

Reluctantly, Michael met her gaze. She *is* more beautiful, he thought, and he felt a fresh stirring in his groin. Unbearably lovely—*except*. . . .

Carla shook out the dark curls that haloed her head. She said, more softly, "It's not a forbidden subject, you know. We *can* talk about it. At least, I can."

Michael stood up and sighed. "Gotta go."

"So I see. Okay, you don't have to say it—*I* will. You're used to perfect, right? Only winners, the gold-medal kind, and that's not me. Not anymore."

"No, no," he protested. He stretched out a hand toward her, but she pulled away and shook her head again.

"I know you too long, and too well. So . . . where are you off to?"

He turned and walked to the window. For a moment, he was hypnotized by the snow whipping past, building into high drifts on the balcony outside. He turned back to her. "A bunch of us, we thought we'd go to Yugoslavia, test the runs there. We're taking the night train from Zurich. . . ." His voice trailed away.

"A bunch?" Carla asked. "Would that include Rosa Marcheliers?" At the name, Michael shrugged. "What did I tell you? Only gold medal," she said.

"Why do you want to stay here, anyhow?" he challenged. "Why don't you go home? Look, your parents asked me to try to change your mind."

"Ah, is *that* why you came? Why didn't you say so? Why did you let me make the reservations here—and all this?" Her arm spread to encompass the room, the champagne and fruit, the bed. "If you only came as a messenger!"

"I didn't plan this. You did. You made all the arrangements. I would have come to see you at Marlowe. But when I got here, when I saw you, I couldn't help myself. I'm sorry, Carla."

"I'm sorrier." She turned away from him. "Okay, you've delivered your message. You might as well go."

Michael moved from the window and hesitated, his tall, athletic body slightly slumped. Then he returned to the bed and stood looking down at Carla. "You really should go home, back to the States. You don't belong here anymore.''

"Yes, I do!" she snapped. "I live here, I work here, this is my home now. And if you think I'd_go back to be smothered by my parents' sympathy—and their money, which wouldn't buy anything I care about—well, you don't know me at all. And you forget, *they're* the original lovers of perfection."

Michael shuffled uncomfortably. "They only worry about you. It wouldn't hurt to let them look after you for a while."

"Oh, yes it would! It would hurt very much!" Anger flashed from Carla's eyes. "To vegetate and let everyone wait on me? To sit around waiting for my trusts to ripen and drop into my lap, waiting to turn into my mother or my spoiled aunts? *Unbearable!*"

"You're making a big deal out of—"

"Am I? At least *here* I'm doing something useful. No one cares who I am—or was. And no one gives a damn about my exalted family! I do my work, and as long as I do it well, I'm treated just like everyone else." She hugged the sheet tighter to her body and glared at him.

Michael sighed. "Stubborn."

"That's how I survive. Please, I wish you'd leave now!"

"Let me take you back to Marlowe," he said. "The snow has gotten really bad."

"I know my way around Fernstaad better than you. I'll get home under my own steam, thank you. Just *go!*"

He didn't argue too much longer.

After Michael left, Carla lay in bed, breathing deeply to calm herself, as her training had taught her. *Not one little whimper out of you, not one tear. I forbid it! What did you expect, anyhow?*

Outside, the wind howled.

Minutes passed. Finally, Carla threw off the sheet and swung her legs to the floor. She picked up the hotel phone and called for a taxi. Then she reached under the bed and pulled out the heavy brace and the metal crutches that she had tucked out of sight two hours ago.

CHAPTER
3

The Swiss town of Fernstaad rises from the shore of Lake Clemenza up the snowy slopes to a peak 3,200 meters high. In February, the height of the season, the lakeside village is a bustling carnival of elegant hotels, discos, luxurious boutiques, and one of the most celebrated coffeehouses in Europe, the *Konditorei* Klaus. Eating, shopping, and partying are as important as skiing in Fernstaad.

At the grand hotels, an archaic protocol is observed. The staff lovingly whispers the guests' titles in greeting: "*Buon giorno, Principessa.*" "A good run today, Count Markoff?" On the steep white face of the hills, the chalets of the seriously rich nestle in isolated beds of evergreen. At 1,600 meters you can spot deer in the woods bordering the walking trails, suddenly frozen into alert statues as they wait for you to pass before resuming their munching. Up here in the crystalline air, the hiss of skis, the shouts of children, the laughter of a skier hang-gliding on the updrafts, carry for miles and deceive your sense of distance.

The winter sun is bright and strong as it sparkles on the Alpine trails; skiers must guard against sunburn. Except for the occasional storm that locks in the valley for days, snowfall is a nighttime occurrence. The days shine blue and clear, with only a wisp of cloud in the sky.

The wire of a cable car rises above the west slope, passing over the dormitory built for last year's Olympic races, before it reaches the top of the giant slalom. A funicular railway curves up the east slope to Corsetti, and a second cable car system carries skiers farther up to Piz Wolfram, the highest run, at 3,100 meters.

The midpoint of the funicular is just outside the study hall windows of the Mary A. Marlowe School for Girls. All day long, trapped inside the massive stone building that was formerly a tuberculosis sanitorium, the students stare dreamily past their Latin declensions and watch the creaky minuet of cars passing on the divided rails. Sun glitters on the snowy hills beyond, winking, beckoning. The girls long to peel out of their blue-and-grey uniform skirts, their white blouses with thin ribbon ties, their crested school blazers, and jump into flashy ski overalls. At three o'clock they will be freed to the slopes.

Monitoring the study hall, Carla Temple dreams along with her students. Metal crutches rest against her chair; the brace on her left leg is beginning to burn her skin. Carla will not be freed to the slopes this afternoon. Or tomorrow, or next week. Or maybe never. Whatever encouragement the doctors offer, she feels as helpless as she did a year ago, after the accident. A freak twist on the course, a blur of snow and spiky trees, and Carla Temple, of the noted Rhode Island banking Temples—the flashing Carla Temple, favored to win the giant slalom—was out of the running forever.

Now she teaches English at the exclusive Marlowe boarding school, preferring to serve out her indefinite sentence in Switzerland rather than return to the States and the suffocation of unwanted sympathy. Waiting for the doctors' promised release, she understands better than any of the other teachers at Marlowe the girls' prisoner mentality. Carla is twenty-three, not much older than the oldest seniors. She is their favorite, their confidante, the black-haired beauty whose makeup the girls copy when they experiment alone in their rooms. And on any day of the week, her restlessness is more than a match for theirs.

Running is not allowed in the halls at Marlowe. But when three o'clock comes, the long corridors turn into a frantic course. The girls brake for the other teachers, slowing to a parody of sedateness, only to charge off again as soon as a stern back is turned. Carla they dodge nimbly. The seniors, her fifth-floor charges, fly in and out of their rooms half dressed, wailing over lost gloves, begging and borrowing scarves, goggles, sunscreen lotion. A narrow terrace on the south face of the building connects all the rooms on that side. Here, where tubercular patients once lay bundled under blankets in their deck chairs, nymphets in bras and panties race back and forth to other rooms, risking chill, detention, or worse punishments. By three-fifteen, the halls are quiet again.

Carla swings along on her crutches to her suite at the end of the corridor. She would not believe that her athlete's grace is striking even as she balances herself between the ugly metal poles. She will remove the hated brace, exercise her leg for half an hour, and bathe before she corrects the students' papers for tomorrow. The routine is endless.

At night, after a noisy meal in the communal dining room, after evening chapel and several hours of homework, the girls will settle into exhausted sleep. Then the teachers, and the building staff, and, lastly, Carla, who wrestles nightly with insomnia.

The temperature drops to minus twenty degrees Celsius. The old building breathes in heavy hibernation as it huddles against the roar of the wind outside. Floorboards, joints, the ratchets of the ancient cage of the lift creak as they adjust to the cold. Usually the night is black and clear over Lake Clemenza, hung with a white moon and a court of diamond stars. But tonight, the storm that came howling across the mountains like a ravening animal two days ago drives the snow to blot out the night lights. Only a fuzz of moon hovers over the valley. Below, in Fernstaad, the wealthy international sporting crowd jams the bars and discos. Some will last all night, until the moon fades and the first water bird wakes.

At four o'clock old Sleepless, the night watchman at Marlowe, reaches the fifth floor on his rounds. He pads down the carpeted hall, following the yellow beam of his flashlight and smiling to himself. He knows how terrified the girls are that a nighttime call to the bathroom will trap them there when he passes. He opens the door and sweeps his light over the stalls. *Got one.* A single stall door is shut. No slippered feet show below, but inside a girl is huddled on the seat, legs up, shivering in the cold and waiting to track his passage down the hall to the back stairs. He closes the door and moves on.

None of the girls knows that his real name is Johann. But Sleepless knows their names, even if he can't always put them together with their faces. A careless monitor left the files unlocked one night, and, although all records are kept in English by the American headmistress and her colleagues, he read them and understood enough.

Fifth-floor seniors. Sleepless ticks off their names to himself as he passes their doors. First, the haughty English girl, daughter of an earl or something royal. Acts like she's going to marry the prince, she does. Then the big blond girl, one of the few Swiss students at Marlowe. Sleepless has a small retirement account in the Fernstaad branch of her father's bank. Farther down the hall, the slim Saudi Arabian who looks so much younger than the others. He pictures the dark girl with eyes like sloes who climbed timidly out of the Rolls-Royce that first day, followed by her father, the sheikh, so trim in his Western clothes. *Ach*, all that lovely Arab oil, and still so shy.

Sleepless continues his tour down the hall. He pauses outside the next door, listening for telltale noises. That one, the French girl, she should be more careful. If she gets caught with one of the other girls in her room at night, she could get herself expelled. Such a way to behave! he clucks to himself. And such a pretty girl, too! Nicole Robineau, daughter of Dr. Pierre and Dr. Monique Robineau of Strasbourg. Sleepless saw her parents on television when they won the Nobel prize. For medicine, the reporter said. Sleepless wishes he could talk to them about his back; his own doctor just shakes his head and shrugs, and the back goes on hurting.

He swings his flashlight across the hall. Behind the nearest closed door is Bianca Gioianni, daughter of José Luis Gioianni of Buenos Aires, offices in Bogotá, Milan, and

Frankfurt. The Gioianni name appears on sides of beef at the butcher's, on dashing sports cars, and on many other things Sleepless has never been able to afford. The Gioianni girl looks just as dashing and expensive, too.

In the room beyond is Bianca's best friend, Mindy Parson, American, daughter of the actress, Dianne Denford, and the writer, Grantley Parson. Sleepless knows Mindy well enough; she's the bouncy redhead who is not at all timid. Frequently, she has raced past him when caught out at the bathroom in the middle of the night. She looks like her glamorous mother, whose movies Sleepless enjoys. California must be warm, he thinks, good for his aching back.

Opposite Mindy's room: Sophie Karas, the new student who arrived at the beginning of the term. Sleepless doesn't know very much about her; her records were not in the files he saw. But he knows she is sad and very homesick. He has heard her crying as he passed her door at night. She is not in her room tonight. She has run away again, for the third time, disappeared the day the storm began. Everyone will worry till they have word that she has arrived home, wherever that is.

Behind the last door, Miss Temple, poor thing, cries out through her dreams as Sleepless passes. He pauses at the foot of the tower stairs and flashes his light up the steps. The closed door at the top is the apartment of Miss Grimsby, owner and headmistress of the Marlowe School. Her Grimness, the girls call her. The thought makes Sleepless chuckle to himself as he clumps down the back staircase to the fourth floor.

It is Bianca Gioianni who receives the first note. She finds it in the pocket of her ski jacket after an afternoon of skiing and gobbling pastries and ice cream at the *Konditorei* Klaus.

The note is handwritten in shaky script on Marlowe School stationery and sealed in an unmarked envelope. It has just two words: *"Daughters die."*

CHAPTER
4

Sergeant Kellhorn circled the room, idly fingering the spines of books in the bookcase, the few decorative objects, the photographs on the end table next to the leather couch. Miss Grimsby sat behind the neat desk in her study. She had barely looked up from the papers in the small manila folder that was open in front of her when she had greeted him.

This was not the first time the young detective had visited the Marlowe School, nor the first time he had been in the headmistress's study. But on his previous visits he had always accompanied Inspector Neumayer, and had not felt free to explore as he would have liked. Now he moved around the room without haste, allowing the silence to build between them. Miss Grimsby finished her reading and sat quietly, her hands folded on the polished wood surface of her desk. The manila folder lay closed to one side. She, too, could wait. Years of dealing with the intractable young had given her immense patience, an aura of repose that some found threatening, others comforting.

At last, the detective finished his tour and came to rest, settling on the couch opposite Miss Grimsby's desk.

"Coffee, Herr Kellhorn, or perhaps you would prefer to have a schnapps against the cold?" She spoke in English, though her German was fluent, but she omitted his title. The offer was obligatory—a courtesy she always extended to her old friend, Inspector Neumayer. She would not underscore too heavily her annoyance that he had sent a subordinate, instead of coming himself. She expected the young detective to decline, and she was not mistaken.

Hans Kellhorn crossed his leg over his knee to brace the notes he was studying.

"Has the girl ever been missing this long?" he asked, moving without preamble into the subject of his visit.

Miss Grimsby slid the manila folder closer and opened it again, though she did not consult the scant pages inside. She was familiar with all their particulars. "No. Three days is the longest it has taken her to reach Athens before. The last time I spoke to Mr. Karas's secretary on the phone, less than an hour ago, he told me she still hadn't arrived."

"And this is four days since she disappeared?"

"As you know." Her eyes crackled with the light of sapphires, a cold blue light.

He would not be intimidated. "Just to review, then. Sophie Karas was last seen on the high run at Piz Wolfram, Monday, at four-thirty in the afternoon—" A muscle twitched briefly alongside Miss Grimsby's mouth. "—just before the storm began. Is that correct?" Miss Grimsby nodded. "The other girls expected her to meet them at the Klaus, but she never appeared?" Again, a curt nod. "The ski patrol has been searching the trails since Monday night when you called, but so far, it doesn't look like there was an accident. Of course, with the storm continuing, it has been too difficult. Now that the weather is clearing, there is still the possibility. . . ."

"Sophie Karas is an excellent skier, and very prudent," Miss Grimsby said. "She doesn't take chances—at least, not on skis. But, of course, you must continue to search."

"We'll send Shockman out with a patrol; he's our best man. I take it you think the child has run away again."

"I've been over this with Inspector Neumayer already. Perhaps you should check with him."

Sergeant Kellhorn recrossed his legs. "I have—indeed, I have. You will indulge me? Just a few more questions? I promise I will not take too much of your time. I can believe you must be very busy—and not a little upset."

They looked at each other, silent for a moment. Miss

Grimsby's handsome head rode high on her graceful neck. Today she looked older than her years, older and faintly haggard. The fair, grey-streaked hair that capped her head with short waves seemed dull in the light of the early afternoon sun that streamed through the windows of the study. Even her delicate porcelain complexion looked duller than usual. She was a handsome woman, although a shade too thin, with startling blue eyes and a generous mouth. But in appearance and manner, sexually neutral. How American she is, Sergeant Kellhorn thought in a leap to illogic that ignored the color and variety, the great pot of the unmelted that made up that vast country.

Miss Grimsby did not flinch under his scrutiny. She was used to men conjecturing about her, about her sexuality; she had learned to live with the impudence. Even from a puppy like this pompous young detective, with his dandyish Swiss manners and Swiss obsession with precision. How did he presume to know how she was feeling?

The air grew heavy with unspoken intolerance until Sergeant Kellhorn roused himself.

"The last time Miss Karas disappeared, was it in the afternoon, on the slopes, like now?" he asked.

"No. She slipped out at night, after the watchman's late rounds. It must have been around four in the morning. Johann, the night watchman, had just checked the outer doors and didn't realize until later that one had been unlatched. She made her way down the mountain to the Fernstaad station and caught the early train to Zurich." How frightened the child must have been, how terribly alone, Miss Grimsby thought. "We didn't know she was gone until morning chapel, when attendance is taken."

"And, of course, no one on the train paid any attention to her," Kellhorn said.

"There are always troops of young people in skiwear traveling back and forth on the trains at all hours during the season. Fernstaad, Chur, Zurich—it's like a traveling house party through the Alps."

"So she made her way to Athens from Zurich, taking trains all the way."

"That's what she told us later," Miss Grimsby said. "She had a change of clothing with her, something lighter, and she just left her ski clothes in a public bathroom when she reached warmer weather."

"And she had enough money with her?" he asked.

They all have enough money, Felice Grimsby thought, all the girls. Too much money for the little good it does them. "Yes," she answered.

"When did this happen?"

"It was early in January, not long after the girls returned from Christmas recess. Something Sophie read in the papers about her father may have upset her—she didn't say. There was some story about his getting married again. It wasn't true, but I believe Sophie must have seen the article and taken it badly."

"So she reached Athens in three days, traveling by train," Sergeant Kellhorn said. "And that was in January. What about the first time?"

"November. In the afternoon. It was a Sunday. Her class had been on an all-day hike to Sils Mariana. Sophie came back to Fernstaad with them, but did not show up for dinner that night." The facts, so simply stated, could not convey the terror Miss Grimsby had lived through that day, and the days following, until Mr. Karas's secretary called to say the girl was safe at home.

"Frau Grimsby," Kellhorn began, delicately using the polite *frau* instead of *fräulein*, "may I ask why you took the child back, twice, when she was so unhappy here? And such a risk? Surely you were aware of the responsibility?"

Again, the tiny twitch of a muscle near her mouth. Miss Grimsby did not answer.

"I believe," the sergeant continued, "that Miss Karas is the daughter of Panayotis Karas, is she not? A man of limitless wealth. Perhaps there was some—ah, arrangement . . . ?"

Miss Grimsby thought back with distaste to that January afternoon in her study, her interview with Pan Karas when he brought Sophie back to Marlowe. For once he had come himself, instead of sending the girl with his secretary or a housekeeper. A phalanx of his aides waited outside in his limousine; his private jet waited at the Fernstaad airport. He was on his way from here to there, his meeting with her just another deal, to be concluded as quickly as possible. He paced the room restlessly, bargaining as if he were haggling over the price of a new fleet of tankers. Miss Grimsby had tried to suppress the ugly word she had heard some of her more snobbish students use so often: *Eurotrash*. Sergeant Kellhorn was right; Pan Karas had made her an outrageous offer of money. Her answer was succinct:

"Mr. Karas, you are aware that the tuition at Marlowe is one of the highest for any private secondary school on the Continent, perhaps higher than for comparable schools here or abroad. We have ample funds for providing the best education possible, and generous endowments from our alumnae. As a businessperson, you may wish to be assured that there is also a satisfactory profit." She did not add that her own personal assets, partly inherited, the rest carefully accumulated over the years, were in a comfortable seven figures. He probably knew that, anyhow. Her eyes snapped at him with contempt. "Your offer is unnecessary, and most unwelcome."

Pan Karas raised a hand and said, with an ingratiating smile, "Come, now, you are a reasonable woman. What can I offer that you *would* welcome?"

Miss Grimsby took a deep breath. "I am sorry. I am very fond of Sophie, but I cannot take her back, under any circumstances."

Mr. Karas leaned heavily on her desk. "She has promised, I have made her swear an oath on the soul of her dead mother that she will never run away again!" *Heaven help her!* Miss Grimsby thought. Pan Karas sprang to life again, rushing across the room to throw open the door.

"Sophie! Come here!" he commanded.

The slight girl rose from the hard bench in the hall where she was waiting, hunched and weeping, and came obediently into the study. Her father slammed the door shut and led her to Miss Grimsby's desk. "Tell her," he said, "just as you told me."

"I—I promise—I won't do it again. I s-swear I won't ever. . . ."

"On the soul of your mother," her father prompted.

"On the soul of my m-mother, I won't run away again, never. I promise."

Miss Grimsby looked at the red-eyed girl standing so small, head bowed, in front of her. She looked at Pan Karas, puffed up and breathing heavily, as if he had just concluded the final argument of a sale.

Miss Grimsby sighed. "All right, Sophie. I believe you," she said. "Say good-bye to your father now and go up to your room. I will come up to see you shortly, before dinner."

Miss Grimsby returned her attention to Sergeant Kellhorn, whose question still hung in the air. "Yes," she said softly. "Yes, there was an 'arrangement,' as you put it." But not one made of francs or dollars or drachmas—not one that you, with your small Swiss mind, would understand.

The young detective idly calculated a hypothetical sum in his head and was satisfied with his acute judgment of human nature. Money changed hands, money changed minds. He nodded with understanding.

"There is another possibility we must not overlook," he continued. "The girl may have been kidnapped. I am sorry to suggest this, but there is always the danger of extremists, ransom seekers, even international terrorists, looking for attention. That is a constant threat in Fernstaad, to residents and visitors alike. A community like this, with its population of rich and important people. . . ." He waved his hand ruefully, but Miss Grimsby did not miss the edge of pride in his voice. "Sophie's father is a most prominent person, a man of international reputation, highly visible, would you not say?"

"Many of my girls have parents of great wealth and prominence. Sophie Karas is just one of them." Just one of the children in my care who are victims of emotional desertion, she thought. One I have failed with.

"Nevertheless, Panayotis Karas. . . ." His voice trailed off as they both considered the volatile Greek, a man who played as hard as he dealt, whose personal and business exploits were constantly splashed across the papers by a sensationalist press. Yes, highly visible. "I will be calling Interpol in Bern, just to see if there is any information that might be helpful."

"No. Please. I do not wish to attract any attention, not yet, if we can avoid it," Miss Grimsby said. "I have not been able to reach Mr. Karas personally, he is off sailing someplace. But his secretary has already advised him about Sophie. We expect her to reach Athens very soon. I prefer that you wait a bit, to spare us all—Sophie included—any unhealthy publicity."

"Of course. It is most important that we are discreet. Have no fear." Sergeant Kellhorn consulted his notes once again. "The girl was wearing a white ski outfit when she was last seen, is that correct?" The headmistress nodded. "Isn't that somewhat dangerous? To allow your students on the slopes dressed in white?"

Miss Grimsby's chin rose. "I have forbidden it. Unfortunately, I cannot always control the girls' wardrobes. Sophie's white outfit was new, a gift from her father." She did not bother to conceal her disgust at the stupidity. "I don't think she had it long enough even to put the insignia on." Sergeant Kellhorn looked puzzled. "The school insignia," Miss Grimsby explained. "We have iron-on patches for the ski jackets. I insist all the girls wear them. I like them to be identified as Marlowe girls, even when they are not wearing their uniforms or are away from the school. Even the teachers wear them on their ski jackets, and I do, too."

"You enjoy our local sport, then?" He tried to keep the amusement from his voice as he contemplated this stiff, unbending woman in flashy ski clothes, whipping down the snowy slopes.

She smiled, reading his thoughts. "You can't live in Fernstaad for twenty-odd years without at least giving it a try." The speech patterns of her students often slipped out.

Hans Kellhorn unfolded his legs and lifted out of the couch. As he started toward the door of the study, Miss Grimsby rose to accompany him, less out of politeness than out of discomfort at sitting through the long, disturbing meeting.

"I will be in touch with you," Kellhorn said. "And please let us know the minute you have any word from Athens."

"Certainly," Miss Grimsby said, opening the door. "You will give my regards to Inspector Neumayer? I trust I will be hearing from him, as well." She extended her hand in the manner of one performing a minor but disagreeable duty.

Just as he was leaving, Kellhorn turned. "One more question. Do you plan to take Sophie Karas back when she is found?"

The foolishness of the question almost caught her off balance. As always, she controlled her reactions, even paused to consider the suggestion. I should never have taken her back the second time, she thought. I was mistaken to think I—Marlowe—could make a difference to such an unhappy child. I cannot be mother and father to these girls; I can only give them the discipline, the stability, that may make them feel more secure. I must protect the others from this kind of—disruption. Still, something about her touched me . . . too much. . . .

"No," she answered. "Sophie Karas will not be coming back to Marlowe."

CHAPTER
5

Through the open door, Carla studied the two men in white lab coats as they, in turn, studied her X rays. The films were clipped to view boxes mounted on the wall above the screen of the CAT scanner. Snatches of conversation floated into the examining room.

"Emergency surgery. . . . Rebroke the bone to break out the callus that formed. . . . Exercising the quadriceps. . . ."

She lifted herself gracefully onto the paper-covered examining table and sat swinging her legs over the side. She was so used to the brace that both legs felt of almost equal weight. Outwardly, she looked relaxed, but inside she was seething. Another one, she thought. Damn Dr. Leitner. He had called in another consultant.

She leaned on one hand and ran the other through the rich black curls that framed her face. Her eyes, a light mystic grey with an aureole of deep purple, flashed impatience. Her bowed mouth, with its full, dimpled lower lip, pouted, heightening her kitten's look. Her dainty beauty was hypnotic, and often distracted people from the down-to-earth intelligence with which she usually viewed the world. Lately, Carla's world was a discouraging terrain. This leg is *old* already, she thought angrily. I'm sick of the waiting, the promises. . . .

The muttered consultation in the scanner room continued. "Not unusual in cases like this. . . ."

She knew exactly what her "case" was: the nonunion of a compound fracture of the tibia and fibula, and so *what*? After almost a year, she didn't think she could take being grounded much longer.

Dr. Leitner snapped off the lights of the view boxes, and the two men walked into the examining room.

"So, child, *wie geht's?*" The white-haired doctor smiled down at Carla.

"You tell me," she said. "I've been ready for the slopes for months. You're the one who's holding me back." She could almost feel the spray of cold powder on her face, the bite of her skis into the hard-packed run as she whipped around the gates of the slalom. "I think you're deliberately keeping me out of commission to give the local girls a chance."

"Soon, soon," the doctor laughed good-naturedly. "Let me present my new associate—Dr. Sunderson, Miss Temple."

The tall blond man in the lab coat stepped closer to the examining table, his hands clasped formally before him, a professional smile on his lips. Carla looked at him coldly, registering his age—early thirties, she thought—but oblivious to his fair, blue-eyed handsomeness.

"*Guten Tag, Herr Doktor*," she said politely.

His smile warmed from mechanical to human, and he felt a sudden catch of breath as he looked into her exquisite, slightly slanted eyes. My god, she was lovely! He didn't miss her almost feline irritation as she regarded him, but he was as transfixed as he had been when he was a teenager and all females dazzled him. His professional manner drained away in a rush.

"Johns Hopkins, class of seventy-eight," he said. "Born in Kansas City, American as apple pie, and I'm afraid that's what my German sounds like. It's a pleasure." He extended his hand, his strong features lit up with genuine delight. "I've heard impressive things about you, and your family, of course."

Carla let him take her hand, but she turned a questioning face to Dr. Leitner.

"Eric—Dr. Sunderson—is joining the clinic as my associate, permanently, we hope. He is one of the most gifted young specialists in orthopedics in your country, my best student when I lectured there, *ach*, so many years ago, yes, Eric?" He beamed at the younger man. "I mean to persuade him to stay here with us."

"If he can get me back on skis in a month, I'll help you, Dr. Leitner." Carla turned to the young doctor who still held her hand. "How about it, Dr. Sunderson?"

He released her hand and straightened his back, all professional again.

"Let's have a look." He undid the brace on Carla's left leg and began probing with strong, sure fingers. Carla looked down at his sun-streaked hair and tried to keep the spark of hope from igniting inside her. She had been disappointed too many times before. So many specialists, so many tiresome examinations, so much time lost. She felt like a permanent fixture at the Leitner Clinic.

Dr. Fritz Leitner was one of the kindest people Carla had ever known. She had given him her heart and her confidence almost from the minute she came swimming up out of the currents of anesthesia-induced unconsciousness after the first operation. There he stood, hazy to her barely focusing eyes, looking down at her. His hand held hers as he murmured in his guttural German to soothe away the awful pain, to re-assure. Without him, she believed she would have sunk into a permanent depression. But that was so long ago, and other operations had followed, and more pain. By now, she had spent so much time at the clinic that she could walk the corridors blindfolded.

The Leitner Clinic, in its grey stone fortress at the end of one of the steep streets of Fernstaad, was world-renowned for the sophistication of its staff in treating the trauma of skiing injuries. Like the Spanish physicians in the bull-crazed town of Pamplona who have become masters at repairing the damage caused when horn meets human flesh, the doctors in the Alpine town of Fernstaad had that special skill that comes with repetition in practice. Carla trusted them, Dr. Leitner especially. But still . . . still the brace, and the crutches, and the endless exercises that didn't change anything. . . .

The first accident was a nightmare. Swerving around the gates, driven by the clock she was racing, perhaps she let her concentration break for a second as she dug her skis against the grooves and ridges of the rutted run. Maybe she was too thrilled by the speed, or how proud of her Michael would be. Suddenly, she felt her leg twist and saw the course tilt. She heard the hideous snap just before the pain possessed her. Then she was down, writhing in agony. Just before she fainted from the shock and loss of blood, she saw it—the jagged, splintered edge of the tibia which had burst through its wall of muscle, pierced the skin, and torn through her ski pants. It was a sight that still visited her tormented dreams, even after all these months.

Then Dr. Leitner came, with his gentle patience, and her parents descended on her, badgering her to return with them to those miraculous specialists who would "fix everything" immediately, and then the terrible pain, and the corrective surgery that followed the first emergency operation. . . . And still the brace, and still the crutches. . . .

"Of course, if you've grown so attached to it, you can keep it," Dr. Sunderson was saying, smiling.

"Wh-what?" Carla said, her attention snapping back.

Both doctors were smiling at her now.

"I agree with Dr. Leitner," the young doctor said. "You don't need the brace anymore. The union looks good, and I think it's time you got back on that leg again. What do you say? Ready to give it a shot?"

"You mean—walk on it?"

"That's what it's there for."

"What if I break it again?" She remembered the second accident, fracturing the leg again almost a week after the cast came off, the terror and helplessness, the despair that closed in on her again.

"Don't make any plans," Dr. Sunderson said. "You're going to take it real easy for a while. Some ultrasound and heat-pack treatments, and I think you should start swimming therapy. There's a pool in Fernstaad you can use, isn't there?"

Carla turned to Dr. Leitner for confirmation. He beamed at her the way a man looks at his favorite granddaughter.

"The leg is ready, child, and so are you."

"What about my crutches?"

"Ugly as hell," Eric Sunderson said, "don't you think?"

Carla started laughing, hugging her shoulders with delight, and for the next ten minutes, as they discussed her exercise and therapy schedule, she continued to break into broad grins that made her look like the doll of every little girl's happy dreams.

When she left the clinic, unsteady and leaning on the cane she had borrowed for security, she was still smiling. Her left leg, without the encumbrance of the hated brace, felt so light it made her even giddier. Limping through the snowfall, still thick and driving for the third day, she climbed into the Marlowe station wagon that was waiting for her outside the clinic. She was too thrilled to enjoy the enchanted scenery, or to make the usual polite conversation with Kurt, the school handyman and chauffeur, as they drove up the long, winding road to Marlowe.

They pulled up at the imposing stone entrance to the school. The girls outside playing in the snow began gathering around her, squealing when they saw her without the brace, exclaiming in a mix of languages that was like music to Carla. Their excitement trailed her up to the fifth floor, and she felt as if she had done something momentous, like beating the clock for a new record.

She walked unsteadily down the hall to her suite—carefully, very carefully—leaning on the cane, feeling the strangeness of her feather-light leg.

Near the end of the fifth-floor corridor, Mindy Parson was standing outside Bianca Gioianni's door, arguing with her. The girls looked disturbed, and neither of them noticed that Carla no longer had her brace or crutches.

Oh, the storms of adolescence, Carla thought, the total self-absorption. Like little Sophie Karas, who never stopped to think about the anxiety she caused every time she ran away. Then Carla noticed the plain white envelope Bianca was clutching and felt immediate sympathy. A lover defecting, she surmised. By mail, at that. Life must seem an endless parade of cruelties to these young girls. She hoped they would never know the true pain of being abandoned in the midst of desperate need.

"Go ahead, ask her." Mindy shoved her friend.

"No, I won't!" Bianca whispered. "It's just a stupid joke. I wouldn't have showed it to you if I thought you would take it seriously."

Carla stopped opposite the girls. "Waiting for me?" She smiled encouragement at them—the handsome dark-haired Bianca, with her Italianate beauty, and the lovely redhead, Mindy, whose puckish charm made her the most popular girl in her class.

"No, Miss Temple," Bianca said. Her hand jerked back almost involuntarily, hiding the envelope behind her back.

"Hey, look at *you!*" Mindy cried, and the two girls were

on her, chirping and chattering and asking when she could ski again, and how *wonderful!*

Limping back to her room, Carla thought that whatever was on their minds, they'd come tell her when they were ready. They always did.

CHAPTER
6

The party surged in and out of the bars of Fernstaad, picking up celebrants like a snowball fattening itself as it rolls downhill. The weather was clearing, the midnight snowfall dwindling as the storm lumbered out of the valley to blow itself out on more southerly slopes. Tomorrow, Friday, would be clear.

The skiers were rowdy with cabin fever. Three days of exile from the runs had left them with an overstock of energy. They hooted and tumbled against each other as they roared through the lamplit, snowbanked streets. Sables, fitch, and fox flapped around leggy bodies. Fur-lined parkas were unzipped to cool the alcoholic fever. Horsy plumes of vapor rose into the night with their laughter, and the air rang with a motley of languages.

Shortly after one in the morning, they hit the Lolita Bar. Colored neon lights glinted through the smoky haze of the front-room bar, striping their faces red, green, purple. The insistent beat of a rock combo assaulted them from the back room, where shadowed figures jerked through the current notion of dancing.

"Oooh, lovely! Wanna dance," Anneliese Zuecher said.

"First, wanna drinky!" She minced to the bar, swaying in time to the music.

Anneliese was not dressed in glossy fur or flashy jumpsuit like the others. Instead, she was wearing her darkest, drabbest ski parka. She had pulled the hood over her light-blond hair hours earlier when she crept out of Marlowe and made her way down to Fernstaad. This was the outfit she saved for her special weekly missions. She had carefully pinned a dark kerchief into her breast pocket and draped it to conceal the obligatory school insignia. She wasn't going to risk being recognized as a Marlowe girl. Not that there was much danger of that. Anneliese Zuecher was tall, almost six feet in her highest heels, and looked years older than a high school senior should. She had a lovely, serious face and wide-open, cornflower-blue eyes. She also had a sense of purpose that usually made her prudent. But tonight was the second night she had slipped out to find Claude, and her failure two nights in a row was making her reckless.

Moving through the rainbow of lights in the Lolita Bar, Anneliese slid onto a stool and leaned toward the bartender. "Champagne, *bitte*." She shook out the silvery curtain of her hair and looked around the room. *Where the hell was Claude?* She had waited for him for an hour at the Rizzo Club, drinking more than she should have. Frustrated, she had stepped into the rest room and pulled out the small glassine envelope. It was her last, dammit, and the kids at school were already bugging her. *Where was that bastard?* She did two lines in the privacy of the commode and checked the bar once more before leaving.

She felt better outside. Head back, long hair tumbling over her shoulders, she stood with mouth open to catch the drifting snowflakes. She was laughing to herself when the party roared past and scooped her up on the way to the Lolita.

Seated on the bar stool, Anneliese smiled angelically at the bartender as he twisted the cork out of a split of Mumm's. She felt great. All was well. Claude would come soon. Any minute now, and she'd be on her way back to Marlowe with her treasure hidden in an inside pocket of her parka. She'd buy more than usual tonight, if Claude had it; she was sure she had spotted some potential new customers at school. More money, more fun for her.

Anneliese had been dealing cocaine at Marlowe for two years now. Laurent had been her regular supplier for most of that time, and she knew she could count on him for good stuff—nothing that had been stepped on so often that the rush was only mental. She was just a gram dealer, less than an ounce a week, but Laurent had never let her down. So when Laurent moved on to a fresher pasture in the Alps two weeks ago and turned his Fernstaad business over to Claude, Anneliese was sure she could trust him, too. Sweet Candyman Claude. Sometimes, in her druggy haze, she thought he looked familiar. But then, everyone did when she was high. Claude wouldn't let her down tonight. He knew it wasn't easy for her to get out of Marlowe each week. Well, easy enough—if she waited until Sleepless had passed through the silent and dark fifth floor and then scooted down the back stairs while the night watchman was checking the fourth. The outside kitchen door was her escape hatch, and the only hard part was slipping back in again. But she had mastered the art of loiding a lock with a plastic strip, and she'd never been caught before. So why worry?

No worrying, she told herself as she sipped from the tulip glass of sparkling wine. Easy, cool, just like her father. Her oh-so-respectable father, Hermann Zuecher, who was totally calm, as a proper Swiss banker should be. But Anneliese had always liked to listen at closed doors. So, even when she was a child, she had known his real occupation: international arms dealing. He was secretly supplying weapons and material to anyone with the money and motivation to play— Russians, Saudis, Iranians, even Chinese. The dignified Herr Zuecher was in the center of one of the biggest illegal arms-trading operations in the world. In fact, he *was* the center. Small or large, it didn't matter—ugly Uzis and Kalashnikov assault rifles, tanks and fighters, more and more sophisticated missiles—everything was arranged behind the closed doors of Herr Zuecher's private study, behind the library of their great Zurich home. Where Anneliese liked to hide and listen. Tense phone conversations, coded language, the subtle pressure of hard deals—Anneliese had heard it all, and it had excited her. She wanted to play, too.

She was playing now, and feeling very happy. Another sip of champagne, and Claude would be there.

"Oooh-ooh-ooh," Anneliese sang in a cracked alto, trying to pick up the music from the back room.

The man on the next bar stool turned to look at her. The Lolita's colored lights ran bars across his face, masking his features. She could tell he was older than the usual crowd at the Lolita, but sexy, and she liked the way he stared at her with partly opened mouth. She flashed him a twenty-lumen smile.

"Wanna dance?" she trilled. Her face was a detail from a Botticelli canvas, almost sexless with cherubic charm. The man smiled back at her. "Dance?" She shimmied on the bar stool.

"Come on, darling," Claude said smoothly as he slipped up behind Anneliese and tried to insinuate himself between the two at the bar. "You don't want to bother the nice man."

"Oh, where *have* you been?" Anneliese's voice was loud and slurred. "I've been looking for you—for days, for weeks!" She turned, swaying unsteadily, glass in hand. A slight collision of arms sent fingers of her wine sloshing onto Claude's parka and splashing the fur-lined ski jacket of the man on the bar stool next to her.

"Shit," Anneliese said as she watched the two wet stains spread. She lifted a paper square from the bar and tried to wipe both men's jackets, one after the other. The insignia on her breast pocket flashed beneath the fluttering kerchief pinned there for concealment.

"Stop that!" Claude hissed at her. "No harm done," he said quickly to the man. He gripped Anneliese's arm, set her glass firmly on the bar, and lifted her to her feet. "Come on. You're making a pest of yourself. Sorry, sir, an accident." Claude's face was placid in the striped lights, but his grip was hard as he yanked her away from the bar.

"I was here last night looking for—"

"Shut up! Don't say another word until we get outside. Zip up your jacket."

"I brought enough mon—"

"*For crissake!*" Claude dragged her into the icy air and around the corner of the Lolita to a shadowed recess of the building. He stopped and jiggled from one foot to the other, breathing out bursts of steam.

"Listen, Laurent didn't do me any favor sticking me with you. I don't need a loud-mouthed, stoned schoolkid spoiling the trade here. You hear me?"

The air was sobering. Anneliese's eyes, level with Claude's, returned to focus. She lifted her chin and scowled into his heavy-featured face.

"I'll take an ounce this week. New business, what do you think of that?"

"I think I can do better without you," Claude puffed. "You go around attracting attention, I'll end up locked away the rest of my life. How old are you—fifteen, sixteen? Go find another source, sweetheart. You're more trouble than you're worth."

Anneliese began to peel off the franc notes she had pulled from her pocket.

"An ounce, more—whatever this is good for," she said.

"What's that, your allowance?"

"Mine and everyone else's. Well, do you have it?"

Sniffing, shrugging, Claude counted through the five thousand dollars' worth of Swiss francs that Anneliese handed him, then passed her several glassine envelopes.

"You'll be here next week?" she asked, pocketing the bags.

"Next time, I see you stoned and coming on to the tourists, or making any noise, I don't know you."

"But I know *you!*" She pulled up her hood, tucked her hair out of sight, and zipped her parka. "Next Thursday, okay?" She stepped out into the snowy road and began her winding climb back up to Marlowe.

Claude stood in the shadows and stared after her, frowning.

Breathe the cold air. So clean, so delicious. Such a feeling of freedom. Or was it power? He felt a strange revival of pleasure that he remembered from long ago.

He had enjoyed it, killing that girl. It surprised him that it made him feel so good. He thought he was here to find *her*, just the one. But the satisfaction lingered. He wanted to do it again. He had been thinking about it since the thrill rushed through him that day in the snowstorm. Another one. Why not? Wouldn't it be better if *she* sensed the danger first? If she could feel it coming closer? Wouldn't it be more satisfying if she was *afraid?* Yes, he wanted her to know *terror* first.

He stomped through the snowy streets toward the edge of town. The air was bracing. He loved Fernstaad at this hour, three in the morning and people still partying. A playful group of celebrators passed him, whooping and lurching toward the next bar. He ignored their shouted invitation and kept going. The party at the chalet where he was a houseguest would be just as wild and noisy. He had decided not to return there tonight. He would go to the small room he had rented, instead. He needed to be alone to think.

He wanted to think about schoolgirls. How innocent and obvious they were, what a thin layer of pretend sophistication they wore. Like the tall Swiss girl, full of bounce and arrogance. It would be easy—hardly sporting . . . but it would give him pleasure. And then *she* would begin to suspect. How long before she became infected with fear?

Fat, drifting flakes of snow were still falling on his bare head when he reached the end of town. The packed cluster of buildings dwindled into a scattering of small houses at the outskirts where Fernstaad gave way to piney woods that bordered the highway to Chur. In addition to staying at the chalet, he had taken a tiny, cramped room in one of those isolated houses on the slopes. That was where he kept his papers, his true passport, those few things he had decided he would need when he had first made his plans. When was that? A month ago? Two? He had forgotten. It was when the invitation first came to his home, with a welcome to stay in the chalet of a friend of a friend in Fernstaad. *Fernstaad!* The very Swiss town that was *her* home! A chalet whose host he did not know—someone who didn't even know his real name, only one of his several aliases. A host who certainly wouldn't care about the hours he kept. He would be free to go about as he pleased, to do what he had always known he'd have to do one day. That invitation made him realize it was at last possible. He simply needed to make new plans now.

He trudged up the now-empty road, enjoying the quiet night. The town was divided into two sections, *Bad* and *Dorf*. His small rented room was in the home of the Breitels on a hill above Fernstaad *Bad*. Herr Breitel, blind since birth, and his aged mother sometimes rented that room to the overflow of visitors during high season. Not too often, though. The house was too far from the action, from the lifts to the slopes, the guest room too gloomy to attract the young students on ski vacation. Anyone not needing absolute privacy would have made arrangements for more fashionable lodging. Breitel and his mother didn't even bother filling out the required guest cards for the police on those rare occasions when they rented the room. He felt safe. No one would ever find him there. And old Pindar Breitel was so obviously glad to have the extra francs and rappen that he didn't ask any uncomfortable questions. Not that he could have. They had no real common language between them. Their simple conversations were brief and stilted, and only took place when the lonely old man was especially hungry for company.

Company! He snorted the word in a white cloud, into the icy air. Would Breitel be so eager to befriend him if he knew *why* he was there? He had firmly rebuffed the blind man's overtures from the start. His comings and goings were *his* business. That his bed was not slept in for several nights each week, that there were days when he didn't appear at all, was no affair of the Breitels. All they needed to know was that the money was good and he paid in advance. He would not have anyone hovering over him, spying, interfering. No one would ever do that to him again!

So good to be free. Walk quickly. Breathe the cold night air. So quiet. He hoped old Breitel wouldn't wake when he came in. Tomorrow would be clear. Things to do. *She's not far from me now. Soon.*

CHAPTER
7

Sleep eluded her. It was more exhausting to fight it, so Carla threw off the *plumeau* and sat at the edge of her bed.

Three-thirty in the morning. She had been listening to the bells of the church clock in town as they tolled the quarter hours through the night. Had she slept at all? She yawned and adjusted the straps of her nightgown. The cold hit her.

Shivering, she slipped into her white cashmere robe, reached for the cane at the side of the bed, then decided the hell with it. Barefoot, cautiously, she crossed the thick rug of her bedroom to the tall double windows overlooking the town.

It was still snowing, but very lightly. Below, Fernstaad lay peaceful in the hollow of the slopes, sparse night-lights twinkling in the dark. Carla sat on the window ledge and pulled her robe closer. Light from a faint moon outlined her brow and cheek in silver.

Michael. Where are you now?

Elvina would know. She could phone and find out. One of her mother's many fashionable friends, Elvina, the Gräfin von Wetzlar, dominated Fernstaad's social life from the hub of her great chalet, and she made it a point to know everything that was happening, from one end of the Alps to the other. The gräfin was very fond of Michael—of most young men —and he often stayed at her chalet. She would know where he was. Maybe he was still there, maybe he hadn't left for Yugoslavia, after all. The snowstorm might have changed his plans. Carla could call Elvina and—

34

—and what?

And make an ass of herself, that's what. Invite the gräfin to patronize and pity her. Is that what she wanted? And what would she do even if she found out where Michael was? Call him? Pursue him? No, Michael was gone, and nothing Carla had done was responsible. A momentary loss of control, a devastating crash—and everything she cared about was lost. Michael had left her because he wanted to, not because she had chased him away in anger. Nothing she could do would bring him back. Oh, it hurt!—the knowledge that she had no power to change a thing. All she could do was learn to live with it.

She felt an icy tingle on her cheek. It was wet. She swiped angrily at her tears and hugged her robe tighter.

Start learning. It's late enough.

The church clock tolled four. Carla leaned closer to the window and looked out into the dark night. The hell with Michael and the hell with broken legs! The hell with middle-of-the-night self-pity. There were much more serious problems to worry about.

Like that poor runaway child, Sophie Karas—still missing. God knew where she was or what had happened to her. Carla and Miss Grimsby had searched her room that evening looking for letters, a diary, for any clue that Sophie was not heading for Greece. There was nothing. Surely Sophie would be able to reach Athens unaided; she had done it twice before. Maybe she was safe at home already. Then why hadn't Mr. Karas's secretary called the school to let them know? He had called so promptly those first two times. Could Sophie have gotten sick somewhere along the way? Maybe she was lost in a strange town, helpless or hurt.

A flash of fear knotted Carla's throat. So many terrible things could happen to a young girl. . . .

No! Tomorrow, we'll hear.

Slowly, she rose from the window ledge and peered out one last time at the dancing snowflakes.

Sophie. Where are you now?

CHAPTER
8

Usually, it is small boys who find dead bodies. Drawn by a primordial urge to explore, they tramp through dark woods, penetrate rank caves, follow the course of a stream, uncovering secrets along the way. Usually, it is small boys who stumble across the awesome grotesque life leaves behind when it departs.

Usually, but not always.

On Friday, the sun bloomed fiery and white over Fernstaad. The first melt began to trickle under the mounds of snow that had grown to over two meters in height during the storm. Concussions of sound waves boomed on distant slopes as the Rack Rohr cannons set off small slides of unstable snow to prevent larger avalanches. The powdered pistes came to life again under a steady crawl of T-bar lifts, cable cars, and funiculars. Mingled with the joyous shouts of the skiers was the persistent gurgle of the melt.

Seated at her desk on the first floor of the Marlowe School, Miss Grimsby was tethered to her phone, oblivious to all the excitement outdoors. In three increasingly strained conversations with Mr. Andreas, Pan Karas's secretary, she learned that Sophie had still not reached Athens. Assurances were given, promises made—communication would be kept open around the clock.

The SOS Wolfram still combed the pistes, clutching powerful walkie-talkies with a range of forty kilometers, but there was no trace of the missing girl.

On Friday night, the *Kantonspolizei* sent up another helicopter to sweep the slopes again with its searchlight, just in case.

On Saturday, the sun continued to blaze over Piz Wolfram. The flow of melting ice swelled the streams to a rush of water down their steep slides. Wading through the slush along one pebbled bank, Filomena trotted after her big sister, Ada. The faded blue jacket she had inherited from Ada, who had worn it after Brigitta outgrew it, flapped loosely around her body. Water seeped into her boots as she waddled into the bubbling stream to pluck out its smoothest stones. Their mother, a chambermaid at the Hotel Chesa Monteviglia, had ordered them home early that afternoon to their chores. When you are seven and nine, such a command is an invitation to dawdle.

A glint of light caught Filomena's eye. A shaft of metal was poking out of the lacy crust of melting ice. The broken tip of a ski pole? The rusty side of a can? She squatted for a closer look—and found treasure. *A knife!* Long and tapered, with a thick black leather band around its handle, its metal tip catching the sun with a wink.

Filomena glanced slyly at Ada. Her sister was several meters downhill, bending to gather pebbles at the edge of the stream. No, she hadn't noticed the knife. Filomena inched around on squatting legs to block her sister's view. With a small mittened fist, she broke the crust of icy snow and slowly retrieved the weapon. She knew enough to be especially careful; knife cuts hurt—and, besides, if she had to explain a wound, her secret would be lost. Here was something she did not want to share. Straightening, her back still to Ada, she brushed crumbs of caked snow off the blade—very gently touching the sharp metal with mittened hands, her body hunched to hide her actions. She pulled off one thick, woolly mitten. Slowly, she tucked the knife inside, blade first. She wrapped the loose fabric around it twice for better protection, sucking air with a hiss through her clenched teeth as if she could feel the blade's bite. The length of the leather-covered handle protruded. Unzipping her jacket, she slid the knife between the outermost layer of bulky ski sweaters and the jacket's padded lining. Quickly, she zipped up again and patted the hardness inside. The thought of what might happen if she slipped and fell did not intrude on her excitement.

"*Ooooh!*" Ada gasped.

Filomena whirled. "I didn't. . . ." she began a guilt-ridden denial, but Ada was not looking at her. Her sister stood, back turned, in the shadows near the rise of the cliff where the sun had not yet melted all the snow. Ada's hands were at her sides, her back rigid, her head dropped so far forward that the teeth of her zipper pinched her chubby chin.

"What is it?" Filomena called. A finer treasure? The worm of envy stirred in her. But Ada did not answer. "Let me see." Filomena hurried to her sister's side, one hand pressed to her body to keep the knife inside her jacket from slipping.

Ada's eyes were riveted to a mound of snow against the steep bank of the hill. An arm in a sodden, grey-white sleeve stretched out to the swollen stream. The small hand at its cuff was waxen, its fingers curved upward like the clawed petals of a poisonous flower. A tiny pool of water was caught in its palm, winking like an evil eye as the light struck it. At the top of the mound, a distorted face seemed to blink through its mask of ice.

The two girls stared down in silence. "*What??*" Filomena whispered at last, nudging her sister. The touch brought Ada to life as if she had been struck.

"*Mamm-a-a-a!*" Ada shrieked. She wheeled and started to race down the streambed. Filomena, caught up in her sister's panic, followed breathlessly, splashing through the water, her hand pressed against the knife as she jogged.

After an army of men had tramped through their small apartment, after all the questions had been asked, after all the hysteria and busyness had passed, Filomena was relieved that her mother did not scold her for losing a mitten. Her treasure was safely stowed among the few grubby possessions she hid under her bed. She slept with deep satisfaction that night. Only later would the nightmares come.

CHAPTER
9

"Carla, would you please stay a minute longer?" Miss Grimsby asked.

Carla stood aside as the rest of the Marlowe teachers filed past her, stunned and silent, and out the door of the headmistress's office. Even the irascible old Mme. Guinet, the French teacher, had nothing to say in the face of the tragedy.

Carla had known something was terribly wrong when the detective from the *Kantonspolizei* arrived in the middle of dinner and led Miss Grimsby from the table. Then the hastily called staff meeting and the request that they all forgo whatever plans they had for that Saturday night and remain on the premises. And then the shattering news.

Sophie Karas had been found. After almost a week of agony, waiting to hear that she had reached Athens safely, the police had dug her frozen body out of the snow at the base of a cliff. She hadn't run away, after all. She had been in Fernstaad all the time, killed in a stupid skiing accident! The girl's death was heartbreaking. The shock to Marlowe would be terrible. Carla understood that Miss Grimsby was wrestling with both grief and fearful responsibility.

"I'm so very sorry," Carla said. "What can I do to help?"

"I was going to ask *you* that. I'm afraid you'll be in for the worst of it. Sophie was on your floor; her friends will be the most upset."

"She didn't really have any friends," Carla said. She moved cautiously on her borrowed cane and sat on the couch opposite the headmistress's desk. "The girls resented her. They thought that every time she ran away, we were much stricter with them, with all of them. Not true, of course, but that's how they saw it. And they felt that you never would have taken her back if her father weren't Pan Karas."

"Oh, how ridiculous!" Miss Grimsby snapped. "As if their own parents were any less prominent! No, it's not a question of imagined favoritism. I think they just found someone to pick on. I've seen that happen over the years. There's always some poor girl elected to be the scapegoat for every frustration. I never take it seriously, since it changes from term to term. Still, I believe that Sophie's death will be most painful for your girls, friends or not."

"I'll be prepared. I can handle them."

"I'm sure you can. Well, I only wanted to alert you. We may as well get this over with." Miss Grimsby rose from her chair behind the desk. "Everyone should be assembled in chapel by now. The sooner we tell them, the better. I imagine the news will be all over Fernstaad by tomorrow, and I don't want the students to hear it from anyone else."

"Is there anything special I can do to help?" Carla repeated her offer as she stood.

"Yes. You can promise to come to me if you're having trouble, and I don't mean only with the girls. I know how wonderful you are with them. But your own feelings . . . I expect this—this accident has been particularly difficult for you."

"Please, don't worry about me." Carla pushed away her concern. "Will the police be needing me for further information?"

"It's possible, but I doubt it. I've tried to reach Inspector Neumayer and I expect him to return my call, maybe later tonight. I'll let you know if he wants to talk to you. Do you have to cancel any plans for this evening?"

Carla looked at her, surprised, then turned away quickly. "No, no plans."

Miss Grimsby nodded. The two walked to the door together, Miss Grimsby exiting first. In the hall, she straightened her shoulders, lifted her head, and started down the corridor toward the school chapel. Carla followed, admiring the older woman's control, fighting back her own turbulent emotions before they could swamp her.

CHAPTER
10

Inspector Rudi Neumayer sat at the edge of his rumpled bed, stretched, and began his morning routine of coughing. For ten minutes he hacked violently, spat into a handkerchief, rubbed his aching stomach muscles, and doubled over with new spasms as he tried to clear a conduit to his lungs. When the last spasm subsided, he lit a Camel and inhaled deeply. How Margarethe would have scolded, nagged him if she were still alive. How he missed her.

Two years—was it already two years? A long time not to care about anything. During that time, the beef had built up on his body. But he was a big man and had learned to carry it.

Rubbing his head, he padded to the small kitchen of his apartment and set a pot of water to boil. Sunday. Today is my *verdammter* birthday, he thought. How the hell did I get to be fifty-seven? The last time I looked, I was forty-eight, everything was possible, Margarethe was finally content. So was I, only I didn't notice at the time. Time. I thought it stretched out forever before us. *Us*. I thought we finally had our lives back again, our privacy. Children grown, responsibilities ended. Just the two of us, together.

The water boiled down in the pot to less than a cup. He

poured it over the brown crystals of Nestlé and watched the foam form and spill over the top of his coffee cup. Through his kitchen window, he could see the great peaks of Fernstaad gleaming in the distance, washed by the sun. He belched gently, almost a sigh. A slender, laughing ghost came and pressed against his back. He could feel her snuffling playfully into his neck, her slim arms winding around his girth. *Wrap me up and take me away. There's nothing left for me here*.

The phone rang. The laughing ghost fled.

His four children were scattered, but this would be Elena, his eldest, no doubt. Calling to wish him happy birthday, to find out if he had had enough for breakfast, to make sure he was still alive. His dearest child, living happily with her husband and children in London, worrying about him long distance.

He roused himself to sound cheerful as he picked up the phone.

"Neumayer," he said out of habit.

"Kellhorn here. Sorry to disturb you so early, sir."

"That's okay," Neumayer sighed. Why would Kellhorn call him, early *or* late? He was always so busy making sure he would get to handle everything himself, alone. "Something?"

"Just routine." His voice said it wasn't. "An accident at the Marlowe School—to one of the girls. A bad accident, I am sorry to say. The girl went over a cliff coming down from Wolfram during the storm last week. Probably Monday late. She's dead. Possible broken neck. The medical examiner is working on her now."

"Ah, poor thing." Inspector Neumayer sank into the chair next to the phone and scrabbled through a pack of Camels. "Who was she?"

"Daughter of Pan Karas."

"Jesus!" Neumayer blew smoke out between his teeth. So that's where the child was. She hadn't run away after all.

Kellhorn filled him in on the little they knew so far. Neumayer listened, mostly in silence, occasionally making a note on the pad next to the phone. A reel began to unwind in his head, as it always did—his own private movie. Wind whipping the snow off the peaks . . . dense grey mist . . . a small, solitary figure hunched over skis, curving through the mist in her—

"What was she wearing, Kellhorn?"

"White—pants and jacket."

Neumayer clicked his tongue, and the reel continued. A white specter, barely visible now through the snow, sliding in slow motion toward the edge of a cliff . . . the shock of empty air beneath her skis— Something was wrong.

"Why wasn't the cliff flagged?"

"It was," Kellhorn said. "She should have seen the flags, even through the snow. The drifts never got higher than three-quarters up the poles, and if she went over the cliff Monday, when the storm started, they would have been visible from a pretty fair distance."

"So." Neumayer cradled the phone against his shoulder while he sucked flame into a fresh cigarette from the stub that was almost burning his fingers.

Two little girls had found the body. No, they hadn't touched it. It was mostly buried under a drift against the side of the rise. Pan Karas would be arriving in Fernstaad tomorrow. By then, he hoped they'd have the autopsy report. Why hadn't they notified Neumayer yesterday when the body was found? It was just routine, sir; all was in order. He, Kellhorn, had everything under control. Only—

"Something bothering you, Kellhorn?"

"Someone. That headmistress at Marlowe—Grimsby. She insists on talking to you. I've told her that this is all too unfortunate, that accidents like this do happen now and then."

"How very comforting," Neumayer growled. Kellhorn ignored it.

"She knows that everything possible was done, but even if we had found the girl immediately after she was reported missing, it would have been too late. She seems to have been killed instantly by the fall. Anyhow, Grimsby wants to speak to you. Could you give her a call sometime today? We're all busy enough without having to deal with a pack of hysterical teachers."

"*Frau* Grimsby," Neumayer corrected with irritation.

"And I have never known her to be hysterical in all the years she has been here in Fernstaad. Certainly she is entitled to all the cooperation we can give her. In fact, I think someone should be there when Mr. Karas arrives tomorrow. That won't be easy for anyone."

Sergeant Kellhorn sniffed audibly. Neumayer braced himself, resigned.

"I'll need a car in twenty minutes. I'll be going straight to Marlowe, and then I want to see the site of the accident. You said it wasn't far from the funicular rails? Fine. Call the *Bergbahnen* terminal and tell Chief Kuhn that I'll be there later this morning. Tell him I'll want the cars slowed when we get near the site. I'll be able to slip off and walk the rest of the way over the slopes. It will be faster than taking the car."

"We took pictures of the girl before the SOS Wolfram moved her," Kellhorn said. "Very clear shots. There's hardly any point in checking over the location now. It's been badly trampled by my men"—*his* men?—"going over it thoroughly, just to be sure. We photographed the whole sequence of digging her out and strapping her to the sled. The SOS boys are badly upset over this one." Neumayer breathed in too quickly, and a coughing spasm began. He covered the mouthpiece and turned his head. Kellhorn continued. "I'll leave a set of the pictures on your desk. Sir? Are you okay?"

"I'm fine," Neumayer gasped. "Why don't you just send the photos with the car? And let Chief Kuhn know the nearest rail point to the accident. I might as well look it over myself after I leave Marlowe. That's all, Kellhorn."

"Very good, sir. If you think—"

"And Kellhorn—"

"Sir."

"I said every cooperation, and I mean just that."

"Sir?"

"A school full of young girls, a violent accident— The parents are going to make it harder for everyone. Not just Karas—the rest of them will be asking questions that have no answers. The Marlowe School has become an institution in Fernstaad, and I want to see it protected."

"Of course. I agree," Kellhorn grunted. "Perhaps I should join you at the school? I can pick you up myself in half an hour . . . ?"

"No, I think it would be best that I go alone. You see if you can get the medical examiner to speed up his report. I'd like to have it today, if possible."

"Sunday?"

"So it is. I'll see you later."

Neumayer was already into a fresh cigarette when he hung up.

It was worse than Carla had expected. Last night, after chapel, had been a nightmare on her floor. The girls had first greeted the catastrophe with disbelief, denial, even a measure of guilt—hadn't they been bitching all week about the problems Sophie caused for them every time she ran off? Then the news penetrated, and the specter of death gripped them. Keening through the hall, the girls rushed hysterically from room to room, bursting into fresh tears with each visit. Finally, Carla called them all into her sitting room to let them express their anguish. She had calmed them little by little, reassuring them that the accident was freakish—*that they were safe*. It was very late before the floor quieted in sleep.

Now Carla followed the girls into the stark interior of the town church for the Sunday morning worship that the school required. Only this Sunday there would be a hastily arranged memorial service for Sophie Karas. Her body would be flown far from the cold white snow that had entombed her briefly, to rest in her own sun-washed homeland. But today, the ritual of formal separation would be held, for whatever comfort it might bring.

Carla walked down the aisle to the front of the church. She felt conspicuous because of her limping gait and the cane that gave her security. There was always a shifting cast of tourists in Fernstaad, always someone new to stare at her. She would have preferred to sit with the other Marlowe teachers, but Mindy Parson beckoned, silently pleading for Carla to join her. She slid into the pew next to Mindy and composed herself for the ordeal ahead.

* * *

Rudi Neumayer climbed the steps from the courtyard to the front door of the Marlowe School. He felt a great heaviness in his legs. The bells from the *Evangelische* steeple down in town were just tolling the hour. Ten o'clock. The Sunday services were beginning. That explained the eerie stillness inside the front hall of the school. Neumayer had never been there on a Sunday at that hour. He was used to a swirl of young girls flurrying around him, twittering like the tiny *Schneefinken* in the larch trees outside. Now, with all the girls and most of the teachers in church, the building was uncomfortably quiet.

"Rudi." Miss Grimsby stepped out of her office, hand outstretched. "Thank you for coming. Please, come in." She spoke tiredly, in English.

"I don't know how I can help you, Felice, but you know that anything I can do—" He paused to let her pass in front of him into the study.

"Of course. I'm very grateful." She settled him on the large leather couch opposite her desk and turned her back to pour a cup of steaming coffee from the tray near the window. She stood as straight as ever, but there was a sagging in her neck and shoulders that made her seem shorter, somehow slumped into herself. She handed him the coffee and sat next to him on the couch. A cup of strong English breakfast tea, already cold, rested on the end table at her elbow. She picked it up, trying to still the rattle of china.

"This has been particularly painful, Rudi. I keep thinking that if I hadn't assumed the child had run away again, I might have been able to—" She turned her head from him. "—prevent her death."

"No, no, that's foolish. The preliminary report is that the poor girl was killed instantly by the fall. Kellhorn says it seems to be her neck—"

"Kellhorn!" She set her cup down with a clatter.

"He's a good man, Felice, doing his best."

Miss Grimsby folded her hands in her lap and leaned back, staring blankly ahead of her. "I'm sure you're right. I'm sorry, Rudi. I've had over a dozen phone calls from parents, last night and this morning. From terror to outrage, and several levels of shock in between. I can't say I blame them.''

"You've talked to Karas?"

"No, just to his secretary, Mr. Andreas. Sophie's father will be flying in tomorrow." She looked down at her hands, now clenched so that her flowered skirt bunched in her lap.

"I'll be here when he arrives," Neumayer said, setting his cup on a table. Miss Grimsby nodded. He wanted to reach for her hands, but instead, he hefted himself back into the couch. "How did the other parents find out so quickly?"

Felice Grimsby turned her brilliant sapphire eyes on him and spoke like someone reciting critical policy.

"The girls may call their parents whenever they wish. I insist on that as their right. I have no wish to make a prison of Marlowe, although, God knows, they feel that way anyhow. Certainly, we try to discourage them from excessive phoning, and they're not allowed to call during classtime or scheduled activities. But it makes them feel better to know they have access to their homes when they really feel a need.''

Neumayer bobbed his head quickly, not so much in agreement but because he found himself flinching in the face of her intensity.

"The senior girls were especially upset last night," Miss Grimsby continued. "Even if Sophie wasn't very popular, she was their classmate and shared their floor. There was a line of them sobbing in the hall outside the administration office last night, waiting for the phones. I imagine there is an orgy of grieving going on in the town churches right now.''

The mourning of the young. . . . Neumayer thought of his own Elena when she was a red-cheeked youngster, of their fluffy puppy Luli who slipped his leash one day on the slopes and was caught by the treads of a giant snow cat smoothing out the pistes below Piz Wolfram. The mourning of the young may pass quickly, he thought, but it is total and unremitting while it lasts. Another terrible reel began to unwind in his head: the puppy Luli dashing across the slopes, young Elena chasing after him over the iced and slippery track, the grinding machine coming closer, the silver teeth of its treads chomping at the snow. . . . What if *she* had slipped? He shuddered and shook his head to stop the picture. Reaching to the end table, he plucked up an old framed photo of Miss Grimsby and her family and studied it without really seeing it. Miss Grimsby stirred next to him, and he pulled himself back.

"I can't bear to think of Sophie lying in the snow all that time," she said.

"She was beyond feeling, Felice," Neumayer said softly.

"Yes, but I'm not." She rose and carried her teacup to the table near the window. "More coffee?" He waved no. "You see, all the while, I thought she had broken a promise. I think I was more disturbed about that than worried for her. I never believed she was in serious danger—only that she had run off again."

"So did we all."

"I know, but I find it very hard to forgive myself for losing trust in her. She did not deserve that from me. Young people need to feel trusted." Neumayer replaced the photo silently; no words of comfort came to him. "Why did it take so long to find her?" she asked.

"The storm, the high drifts." He shrugged helplessly. "Apparently she was hidden in a gorge next to a stream, impossible to spot. I'm going there now, as soon as I leave you. But I don't think I'll have any better answers for you. I came as an old friend who wants to help. I am sorry, but it is not very likely that I can give you any professional aid. This has just been a tragic accident that no one could have prevented. Please believe I wish it were otherwise."

"Why didn't you call me last night?"

He shifted uncomfortably. "I just found out this morning."

"Kellhorn again!"

"Try to be fair, Felice. You usually are. Kellhorn has been very concerned and handling everything with care, I know. And tact. That's just as important, I'm afraid. We will help you, any way we can."

She crossed to his side as he rose and took his large hand in both of hers.

"Dear Rudi, there's not much that can be done, but I do thank you. I won't keep you any longer." She walked him to the door of her study, her arm linked through his. "Mr.

Karas should arrive here sometime before noon tomorrow. If you could possibly—"

"I'll be here."

CHAPTER
11

The *Kantonspolizei* car was waiting patiently.

Out in the fresh air on the steps of Marlowe, Neumayer dived into his pocket for a cigarette. Felice had never asked him not to smoke, but he always felt constrained in her presence. He drew on the cigarette with a fierce nicotine hunger. One day he would quit, just as he had promised Margarethe.

Before the car deposited him at the funicular terminal in town, he studied the photos of Sophie Karas for the second time that morning. They were no less pathetic for being familiar.

He climbed the damp steps of the *Bergbahnen* and squeezed his bulk into the narrow cab at the front of the funicular car. Next to him at the controls was a young man he didn't know, gap-toothed and athletic-looking in his dark-blue uniform. He introduced himself as Willi and said they hadn't known when the inspector was coming so they had continued their scheduled runs. That left Artur, who knew the point closest to the accident site, in the upslope car, but the two drivers could switch places at the midpoint.

Bells rang in the control box outside. Willi leaped out of the cab and signaled back. Behind him in the three angled compartments of the funicular car, the noisy, colorfully dressed skiers were packed together, stomping impatiently in their heavy, astronautlike plastic boots, clacking their skis in their eagerness to be out on the slopes. Willi slid back into the cab next to Neumayer, closed the doors, and waited for the gears to grab the car. Slowly, they began the ascent.

Five minutes later, nearing the midpoint, the car started to slow down. Neumayer could see the bright blue front of the descending car as it emerged from a tunnel up the mountain. Stretching up to meet it were the shining arms of the divided rails.

Willi opened the cab door and leaned out, holding a bar inside with one hand. Neumayer could hear the skiers exclaiming at the unexpected slowing, feel the tension of their fear that the machine was about to fail, to roll backwards down the hill, faster and faster, till it crashed in splinters at the base of the mountain.

Ahead, a blue-uniformed figure swung out of the cab of the descending car, one hand clinging to the inside, the other arm outstretched. As the two cars passed each other, Willi was gone in one graceful jump, and Artur, clutching at the bar inside the door, struggled into the cab and plumped himself in front of the controls next to Neumayer.

"Gruezi!" Artur said pleasantly, puffing slightly. "Such a fine day! Better to be up the hill than down, eh?"

"My friend, you're getting too old for such stunts."

"And you?" Artur laughed, patting the bulge of Neumayer's belly. "Maybe it is better I should jump off first when we get where you're going and help you out—what do you say?"

"Don't try it," Neumayer smiled. "I don't want to see you racing after an empty cab all the way to the top." He squinted at the bright sunlight glistening on the white slopes surrounding them. "How long before we get there?"

Artur's face was instantly serious. "I'll slow us down again in another three minutes. That's closest to the place. A terrible thing, isn't it?" They rode in the silence of their separate thoughts for the next few minutes.

Neumayer slid out of the cab, stumbling slightly as he scrambled away from the rails. He signaled to Artur, who leaned worriedly out of the front of the car as it moved slowly

up the curved track. Artur pointed with a stiff arm across the
snow and disappeared inside. The funicular picked up speed
and was already far enough away to look like a child's toy
before Neumayer had caught his breath.

He set off on the short trek to the accident site. He was
conscious of the gloriously pristine air, the beauty of the
majestic slopes rising all around him, of having grown so
soft he was laboring through the higher drifts.

He had no trouble finding the gorge. A small gathering of
curious skiers and hikers had found it already. Some merely
slowed on their downhill run as they passed; others were
bunched against the guard ropes along the lip of the cliff,
peering down. Corporal Trivella, his skis resting in the crook
of his arm, stood to one side of the group, waiting.

"Kellhorn sent me," Trivella said as Neumayer approached. "In case you need any help."

"Let's clear off the sightseers, to start with." Neumayer
slipped under the ropes and slid to the bottom of the cliff.

The gorge was in deep shadow. A stand of snow-heavy
pine trees blocked the sun. The ground was trampled into
sullied slush alongside the swollen stream. Icy water rushed
down its course, gurgling and grinding away at the larger
stones in its path, smoothing the chips into gleaming pebbles.

Neumayer shivered in the damp chill. He turned his back
to the stream. Mounds of snow, gouged marks at the base of
the cliff, showed all too clearly where Sophie had been dug
out. A faint, packed depression in the snow remained. All
around him, the ridged tracks of boots ranged along the bank.
He stared at the trampled site, losing track of time. He began
to record its details as they meshed with the photos he had
studied. A new, even more pitiful movie started winding onto
a reel in his head. Margarethe was the only one who knew:
In all his years with the *Kantonspolizei*, he had never gotten
tough enough, not deep inside; no callus protected him. He
clutched the collar of his jacket closer around his neck.

Moving slowly, Neumayer stooped to sift a handful of
snow that caught his eye. Nothing. He walked the length of
the bank to the point where the stream burst out of the narrow,
pine-topped rise. Then back to its downslope end.

The squawk of a walkie-talkie sounded from the top of the cliff.

Trivella called down to him. "Kellhorn, sir. He wanted to know if you had arrived."

Neumayer moved back up the bank. "Tell him I've seen enough. I'll be coming down soon."

Trivella spoke into the black box in his hand, then called out again. "Should he send the car for you? It's about a kilometer to the nearest point in the road."

"I'll walk. It's less than that to the Jutta Steps, and down is always easier. I'll see him in about forty-five minutes. No need for you to stay any longer, either. Just carry on, Trivella."

The corporal transmitted his message and bent to adjust his skis. When he looked again, Neumayer was a round, brown-jacketed ball wobbling and sliding against the white snow down the slope.

To his horror, he had overslept. The faint bells from the *Evangelische Kirche* far across town woke him with a start as he remembered where he wanted to be. Breathlessly, he splashed water on his face, dressed hurriedly, and ran out of the house, one arm jabbing into the flapping sleeve of his tan parka.

Breitel and his mother had already left for church. Roman, he knew. He would not risk going there, nor would he risk riding on a public bus. He hurried up the long street that wound from *Bad* to *Dorf*, trying not to call attention to himself by running. When he reached the church, he stood for a minute on the steps to catch his breath and brush crumbs of snow from his pants. Above him, chiseled over the door, was the only adornment on the building's severe facade: glowing gold-and-blue lettering proclaiming, *Soli Deo Gloria*. With passion, he thought of *her*, maybe just on the other side of the door. Hunger to see her made him tremble.

The bells of the steeple clock were tolling the three-quarter hour when he slipped inside and squeezed into a crowded pew at the back of the church.

The airy, whitewashed interior was as plain as the outside.

It shone with the same cold light as the mountains—a comfortable habitat for people who live mostly in snow. He unzipped his parka, breathing rapidly through open lips as he waited for the disruption of his entrance to subside. He willed himself to become absorbed by the others as an anonymous part of a group. His eyes roamed the church, searching.

All was white and the silver of cold steel. Sleek steel organ pipes rose to the ceiling. A tall steel cross stood more than a meter high on its low wooden platform. The only touch of color was a large tub of flowers, and they were almost swallowed up by the intimidating white. He began to perspire, but was afraid to remove his parka. Before him were ten crowded pews on both sides of the center aisle. He scanned the backs of heads, certain he would recognize her.

The service was almost over. Usually, it was as plain as the church. But this Sunday's worship was punctuated with girlish sobbing.

". . . the cruelest of tragedies. This lovely young girl, friend and schoolmate of many of you here today, taken so soon from your midst, from a life filled with promise. . . ." The black-robed pastor, looking like a brother monk of Martin Luther himself, spoke from his simple wood pulpit, conjuring up an impossibly perfect Sophie. His guttural Swiss German echoed through the church, setting even the youngest children, who could not understand him, to weeping. Even some of the vacationers from the elegant hotels who had stumbled, exhausted with hangovers, into church were red-eyed and sniffing into their exquisite linen handkerchiefs.

Sophie. So that was her name, he thought. When had they found her? Sophie Karas. Was she related to Pan Karas? They called it an accident. Good.

In a corner of the third pew, Carla Temple sat, surrounded by Marlowe girls. Mindy Parson was on her right, head drooping, her bright red curls hidden beneath a black lace shawl. Carla could see from the corner of her eye the sheen of tears on Mindy's cheek. She was grieving soundlessly—feeling guilt, perhaps, and regret, but above all, genuine pain. Carla reached around and hugged Mindy to her, causing the girl to gasp in an uncontrollable sob. On Carla's left, Nicole Robineau sat silent and rigid. Beyond her, Anneliese Zuecher sniffed and twitched restlessly.

He could not find her. His skin crawled at the thought that she might be there at that very moment, so close, and still he did not see her. Maybe she was with the Romans in their huge modern church up the street. But he would not follow her there. He squirmed with fustration.

". . . to accept with grace the inevitable will of God. . . ."

He was not listening as the minister's sermon wound down. Suddenly, the organist played a sonorous D-major chord announcing the final hymn, and the congregation rose to its feet.

"*Alle Menschen müssen sterben*. . . ." They began to sing the rich four-part harmony of the Bach chorale, so touching in its simple major mode, with its plaintive verse. It was a familiar hymn, but for once he thought of its words so calmly greeting death. "*Every mortal soon must perish, every living creature, too*. . . ."

He ducked his head as he slid out of the pew and left the church. He would not be caught in the bustle of their leaving.

". . . *like the grass must fade and wither*. . . ."

The singing followed him down the sunny street and mingled with the steeple bells tolling the hour. He had failed to recognize her today, although she might have been there. But he did have one satisfaction. The tall Swiss girl; he had seen *her*. So inviting. Yes, he had plans for her, too.

Outside on the front steps of the church, Nicole Robineau stood together with the red-eyed Mindy.

"At least I'm not a hypocrite," Nicole said in lilting French cadence.

"No, just a simple bitch."

"I never liked Sophie and I'll be damned if I'll pretend now, just because she's dead."

"I'm not pretending anything." Mindy let her black shawl slide off her head. "I feel sick, perfectly rotten."

"Nobody's perfect, *chérie*. But you do look rotten!"

"Oh, knock it off!"

"You said yourself that Sophie just made trouble for the rest of us. Every time she ran away—"

"Well, she wasn't running anywhere this time."

"So?" Nicole challenged.

"So, what's eating *you?*"

Nicole shrugged. "Getting my period, I guess."

"Go take it out on someone else."

Mindy looped her shawl around her neck and ran down the steps. Farther up the street leading to the Catholic church, Bianca was waving to her. Nicole watched them meet, saw the outbreak of new tears as they hugged each other. Then they turned, sniffling, in the direction of the *Konditorei* Klaus.

A hot chocolate fix, that's all they need, Nicole thought. Then: *Damn! Why do I feel so mean? All that wailing in church made me want to claw someone! No, it made me hungry! Oh, hell!*

"Wait for me!" she called.

Standing just outside the church door, Carla watched Nicole rushing after Mindy and Bianca as they strode up the snowy street. She had overheard the conversation on the steps and felt an extra twinge of sympathy for Nicole—for what her sharp tongue concealed.

Carla had met the girl's parents once, when Nicole was recovering from pneumonia. They had actually torn themselves from their laboratory in France and come to check on the unexpected malfunctioning of their child. At least, that's the way it had seemed. Carla was told it was the only time they had visited the school, including when Nicole had first been enrolled. Robots would have been better parents, Carla thought. The good doctors Robineau behaved like strangers with their daughter, indifferent ship's passengers thrown together for a short time, clicking and glancing off each other like polished marbles. They were older than most of the other parents, and intensely private. They didn't look at you when they spoke, and they didn't speak very often, either. Not even to Nicole. Occasionally, at dinner, they burst into rapid-fire French, bristling with technical terms. It was a relief when they left Marlowe a few days later to return to the Bas-Rhin, to their beloved laboratory in Strasbourg. And that was before their Nobel prize. They must be even more ghastly now!

There was an uncomfortable sense of recognition that Carla acknowledged whenever she thought of Nicole Robineau's parents.

So they remind you of your own parents. So what?

Carla saw Nicole catch up with the other girls and disappear with them around the corner of a building.

So, it ain't easy.

CHAPTER
12

It was getting harder, Nicole thought.

She pushed into the crowded *Konditorei* Klaus behind Mindy and Bianca. She was relieved to be in such a cheery atmosphere after the grim church service for Sophie. Besides, she had her own problems to solve.

Now he wanted her to bring another girl, to make it a threesome—or was he planning a foursome? Who the hell could she ask? Who was totally game for anything? She had never confided in any of the other girls. Would they be shocked? Not everybody got their kicks making that kind of racy home movie. Besides, it was getting a little rough. *Merde!* It had started out as fun, and now. . . .

She shrugged out of her jacket and followed Mindy and Bianca inside.

The steamy warmth and luscious odors of the coffeehouse enveloped the girls. They stopped and stamped the packed snow off their boots. Mindy and Bianca hung their parkas on top of the mounds of neon-colored ski jackets on the hooks that lined the entrance wall. Nicole, who hadn't brought a purse, had zipped her money into her jacket pocket, so she folded her parka over her arm, instead of hanging it with the others. She stood in deep thought.

Maybe she could ask Anneliese. The big cow was always looking for a new thrill. But she was so loud, and usually half stoned. Nicole wondered why Miss Grimsby or Miss Temple hadn't caught on yet. Especially now that Anneliese had started dealing to the younger kids. No, Anneliese was a risk.

Who else, who else?

"Hey, wake up, Nicole!" Mindy said. "You look upset. Don't tell me it finally hit you—about Sophie. Come on, there's nothing we can do about it. Go see if you can get us a table. I'm starving."

Fast recovery, Nicole thought. She walked through the vestibule into the back, while Mindy steered Bianca off to the front counters.

The front rooms of the *Konditorei* Klaus were ringed with counters filled with cakes, pastries, sandwiches, and tiny plates of eggs and salads arranged like flowers in aspic. If you were not hungry enough to order a meal at the tables inside, you could pick up your own snacks in the front and bring them to a table, where waitresses would take your order for drinks or ice cream. All day long, ravenous skiers in boots that made them waddle like ducks clumped back and forth carrying plates, squeezing into seats at the small, over-crowded tables in the back. You sat wherever you could find a place, no matter who else was at the table. Mostly, you ignored strangers. But sometimes, unexpected friendships flowered in the warm holiday atmosphere. Like last month, when Bianca found herself "in love" and exchanging passionate letters with a handsome university student in Darmstadt whom she had met when he was on a ski vacation in Fernstaad. Nicole and Mindy had even helped Bianca compose a letter to him in the Klaus just two weeks ago.

Bianca. She would be perfect. She looked so sexy, and her boobs were the envy of the school. Perfect typecasting, except that Bianca was all show. The only thing she knew about sex was what she read in the endless stream of romance novels she gobbled like whipped cream. How could anyone survive on so much goo? Sometimes it was hard to stomach her innocence. Besides, Nicole knew about Bianca's father. He was one of the most powerful men in South America, and so devoted to preserving his little girl's virginity that he'd probably put out a contract on the poor Darmstadt student just for writing *letters*. If he ever found out. Take that, pen pal! God, no, Bianca was unthinkable.

Who else?

Three people were just getting up from a table at the back window. Nicole rushed over to claim their seats before anyone else could. She waited as they gathered up their belongings from the mess on the table, expecting that the man in the fourth chair would leave with them. He sat unmoving, staring through his dark, wraparound sunglasses out the big window overlooking Lake Clemenza below. The sun blazed on the glass, almost blotting out the lake's icy stretch and the steep glacial mountains that rose from the opposite shore.

"Bitte?" Nicole said politely, pointing to the vacated seats. It was simply good form to ask.

The man turned slowly and looked up at Nicole. She couldn't see his eyes flicker as he noticed the Marlowe insignia on the jacket over her arm. He smiled pleasantly and beckoned her to sit down.

Nicole settled herself and tilted the other two chairs in toward the table to indicate that they were taken. She ignored the waitress, who bustled up to clear away the dirty dishes of the previous occupants, and she ignored the man, even though she could sense he was studying her from behind his dark glasses.

She turned to the window and considered her problem again.

Okay, who then? Who would turn him on?

Mindy, probably. *Everybody* liked Mindy Parson. The bouncy redhead, with her healthy California good looks, was just naturally popular. Besides, she was an eerie copy of her famous mother, Dianne Denford. Now *that* would be a kick for him! Having the beautiful, leggy actress in his very own blue movie—well, a fuzzy carbon, but close enough. He'd love it! Except Mindy would never agree to it. It was one thing for her to buy a few bags from Anneliese now and then—Nicole knew she did—but rough sex in front of a camera . . . ? Forget it!

Still, the idea tickled her: "Now playing, *Nympho School-girls in the Alps*, starring Dianne Denford—sort of. . . ."

Nicole smiled to herself. The man was looking at her with open appreciation. Just to ward off any attempt at conversation, she turned and fussed in the pocket of the jacket she had hung over the back of her chair.

Think! Who else?

Maybe she should just tell him to forget it, she wasn't interested anymore. It was boring, and it was getting too heavy. Last week, he had tied her hand and foot to the bedposts, like an animal waiting to be skinned. It hadn't been fun—in fact, it had been a little scary. Not that he'd ever really hurt her. He was crazy about her, he kept telling her. Wasn't that part of the thrill? That had made it even more exciting—the whirring of the camera, the danger of being found out. . . .

What the hell! Why not? Why didn't she just ask Katharyn?

"Stop brooding and look what we've got!" Mindy stood over Nicole and set down two loaded plates. Behind her, Bianca balanced another two. It looked as if they had enough sandwiches and pastries between them for the entire senior class at Marlowe.

Mindy smoothed her green ribbed sweater over her trim body and sat enthusiastically. Bianca followed, spreading the plates among them on the table.

"Didn't you get us anything to drink?" Bianca complained. She caught the waitress's eye, and all three girls ordered hot chocolate *mit Schlagsahne*. Soon they were sipping and chewing and happily gossiping about everyone else at school.

"What do you think of Katharyn?" Nicole asked casually, reaching for another tea sandwich.

"Ah, *Lady* Katharyn," Bianca said.

"Why do you ask?" Mindy said.

"No reason, really. What do you think of her?"

"The exalted daughter of *Lord* Sunynghame," Bianca said.

"The snotty only child of the seventeenth earl of who-knows-where, and who cares?" Mindy said. "Why do *you* care?" She bit into a rich pastry.

"I'm only asking," Nicole said.

"She's the best student in our class," Bianca said.

"She's the busiest dyke on our floor," Mindy said.

Nicole looked quickly at the man. He was staring out the window again. He probably didn't understand a word they were saying.

"You taking a poll?" Mindy asked, licking her fingers.

Nicole sipped her hot chocolate. *In a way*, she thought. *That's just what I'm doing*. No question about it, Lady Katharyn Sunynghame was a pest, but a useful one. She'd bet she could get her to do anything she wanted. Yes, she'd ask Katharyn to come with her the next time. Maybe even tonight. That would please him.

Satisfied, Nicole dropped the subject and turned to Bianca. "Did you bring the letter?"

And then the three girls gave their full attention to the flimsy blue airmail sheet as Bianca read aloud the latest passionate declarations from Darmstadt.

Schoolgirls! The man squirmed and cupped his twitching crotch beneath the table. Any one of these would be perfect, too. He signaled the waitress and paid. As soon as the bulge between his legs subsided he rose, plucked his tan parka from the back of his chair, and left with a small nod at the girls.

They did not notice him go.

CHAPTER
13

"That's the third time today you have mentioned Carla Temple," Dr. Fritz Leitner said as he walked down the corridor at the Leitner Clinic. His hand lightly tapped Eric Sunderson's shoulder and he chuckled. "I think I can make a preliminary diagnosis, Doctor."

"She's an interesting case," Eric replied blandly.

"So? A case? You did not perhaps notice that she is also a most enchanting young woman? No, of course not."

Eric smiled and held the door for the older man as they entered his office.

"I do admire her courage," Eric admitted. "And the way she caught on so quickly to the exercises I showed her. Even when they hurt, she didn't complain. You know, Fritz, that's rare. This past year must have been hell for her."

Dr. Leitner sat at his desk and motioned Eric into a chair. He sighed and nodded. "A beautiful young athlete at the height of her power—*tch*, it was a tragedy. But she works very hard to make it better, and I see so much progress I am encouraged. She has a good attitude, I think. That will help her."

"She makes you care, doesn't she."

"I always care," Dr. Leitner said gently. "But you are right, Carla is special to me." He looked at his watch and rubbed his hands briskly. "Now, back to work. . . ."

The two men turned to the patients' records piled on Dr. Leitner's desk. It was Monday, the day to go over the new crop of weekend accidents and review the older cases. For

61

the next hour, they discussed the charts, adjusted the treatments, standard and experimental, confirmed or revised their prognoses.

Shortly before noon, Eric stood by the view box studying a lighted X ray. "Compound fracture of the tibia and fibula. Very similar to Carla Temple's, only this boy—"

"That's the fourth time," Dr. Leitner said.

"What?"

"The fourth time you have mentioned Carla. And all before lunch."

Eric dropped back into his chair, amused at his own transparency. "Well, what do you prescribe?"

Dr. Leitner shrugged. "This is not my specialty, Eric. No prescription. But I give you a suggestion: Call her tonight. Simple, yes?"

Eric shook his head. "I think it's too soon."

"For you or for her? Oh, I know what *you* went through before you came here. That's past now, isn't it? I think Carla would enjoy hearing from you. Especially now, after that terrible accident at the school, that poor child killed skiing. You saw her when they brought her in, didn't you? Before she went to Dr. Lüthi?"

Eric remembered the small, distorted face, the body in sodden ski clothes, as he pronounced her dead and ordered her removed to the medical examiner for autopsy. That had been a tough one.

"I think you might make Carla feel better," Fritz Leitner broke into Eric's thoughts. "Certainly you can call, even as her physician. You could ask how the new exercises are going. I know she is planning to start her swimming therapy this afternoon at the big pool in town. So there, you see, you have a good excuse, if you need one."

Eric jumped up again and returned to the view box.

"Let's get back to your specialty," he said, smiling. "Yours and mine. I think we're both better at bones."

But even as they resumed discussion of the X ray on the view box, a compelling idea planted itself in Eric's mind and kept popping up to distract him for the next few hours.

CHAPTER
14

Carla stroked across the length of the pool, exhilarated, as if she were in competition again. She had already completed the series of exercises Dr. Sunderson had taught her. Standing in the shallows of the large, square pool, hands braced against the slippery tiles, she had slowly lifted and twisted and stretched her leg in the diminished gravity of the water. As always, she concentrated in her usual disciplined way as she followed the boring routine. Around her, children laughed and splashed. The inflated orange water wings wrapped around their arms made them look like stubby little angels.

The exercises were finally finished. Now she was free to feel the power of her body again. She flung herself through the water, heady with a sheer physical joy. Motion . . . speed . . . power! How long had it been? Her arms stretched, her chest heaved, her long body streaked through the water. *Years . . . it feels like it's been years!* She began imagining racers on both sides. *Faster! Winning fast!* But no, she wasn't imagining it; someone *was* pacing her, stroking off to her right for the past three laps. She stopped at the deep end, treading water. A handsome head bobbed up at her side, water sheeting from his blond hair.

"Is this a house call, Dr. Sunderson?"

"Eric, please," he smiled. "Dr. Leitner warned me you'd probably overdo it your first day, so I thought I'd drop in and check on you."

"What a nerve!" Carla said, but she was smiling, too.

"Actually, I love swimming—did a little racing in college. This is just time off for me, a bit of R and R."

"So soon? Is Dr. Leitner wearing you out already?"

"Think you could use your influence? Put in a good word for me, get him to ease up?" he said seriously.

Carla laughed and splashed at him. Eric's hand rolled down his face to squeegee water from his eyes.

"Hey! Want to race?" she challenged.

"You wouldn't have a chance! No, Carla, I think you've done enough for today. I know how eager you are, but you do have to take it a little slower."

"You mean, patience?"

"You got it."

"I hate that word!"

"Come on, get dressed. I'll buy you coffee and you can teach me some German."

They sat in the glassed-in café on the balcony overlooking the pool. Below, fountains splashed and children ran shrieking through the spray. Their wet swimsuits rested in bags at their feet, next to Carla's borrowed cane. Carla's wet hair had formed a halo of dark, glistening ringlets around her face. She tilted her head and snuggled her chin into the high collar of her soft, white turtleneck sweater.

"Thanks," she said, her grey eyes shining with mischief.

Eric stirred a cube of sugar into his coffee. "What for?" he asked warily.

"For not taking my arm when we got out of the pool. For not trying to steer me like some kind of—of—cripple."

"You were doing fine on your own."

"But you wanted to, didn't you? I could feel it."

He looked at her severely. "Not because I think of you as crippled. I know better than you how well you're doing. I wish you had half the confidence I do. If I felt like taking your arm it was only because—I felt like taking your arm. You looked so pretty climbing out of the pool."

"Like a mermaid, I'll bet! I'm fat as a seal and all out of shape."

Eric laughed. "I like the shape you're into." He reached across the table to touch her fingers before she curled them away from his hand. "How about having a little faith in your doctor, what do you say? You'll be trading in that cane for your ski poles sooner than you think."

"Is that a promise?"

"Professionally speaking, cross my heart and spit twice."

"I hate medical jargon!"

"How do you feel about dinner, then? Do you hate that, too?"

"Not as much as lunch—at least, lunch today." A shadow had driven the playfulness from her face. "We had an accident at the school—well, on the slopes. One of the girls was killed during the storm last week. She lost her way and went over a cliff."

Eric did not want to tell her that he had done the preliminary examination of the body. He said quietly, "I know. I'm very sorry."

"Her father came to—get her. Today. While we were at lunch. We could hear him bellowing all over the school. It was awful! He's Pan Karas, you know?" Eric nodded. "He started yelling about not having given permission for an autopsy, then ended up—well, crying, only it sounded more like barking. It must have been hell for Miss Grimsby." She caught his sudden frown. "Headmistress at Marlowe," she explained. "I've never seen her so upset. She took him into her study while we were having lunch upstairs in the dining room, but we could hear him all the way up to the second floor."

Eric was silent.

"Don't you want to say something like 'accidents happen'?" Carla couldn't explain why she felt suddenly angry at him, why there was a quaver in her voice.

"I'm listening," he said simply.

"Sorry. . . . You see, the girl was on my floor, she was one of the seniors I was responsible for. We thought she had run away again—she'd done that twice already. But she was *dead*, all that time! I don't know why I feel so responsible, I just don't know. Sixteen—oh my God, she was only *sixteen!*"

"And you're only twenty-three."

"Twenty-four in a couple of weeks," Carla said dully.

"I know. I've seen your records, remember? Okay, you're almost twenty-four and you've had an accident, a skiing accident, and you're alive. You're going to heal and be well and live as you did before. This girl had a skiing accident, too, but it killed her. What are you thinking, Carla?" She looked at him, her eyes swimming. "That *she* should have survived, not you? That there was some sort of cosmic trade? *Her* life instead of yours?" She gasped, and the tears spilled over. "You *do* know better than that, don't you?" Carla dug into her pocket for a handkerchief. "Don't you?"

He watched her cry it out. She turned her head to the glass that separated the balcony from the pool below. Only Eric could see her shoulders shaking, see her nod and finally sag with relief.

It was brief. When she turned back to him, there was a weary smile on her face.

"Better?" Eric asked.

"Dumb. Very dumb," she said, swiping at her nose.

"Very," he agreed. "A temporary lapse, I think. Here— a fresh handkerchief, large economy size."

She plucked it out of his hand and blew. "Do you always get so personal with your patients?"

"Only the homely ones. Gives them confidence."

"You *do* think you're pretty smart," she said.

"Not too shabby."

"Not too modest!"

"Is that good or bad? . . . That's better. I like to see you smile. Do it again."

"Never," she said, smiling. "I'm too hungry. Oh, I really *am!* Your exercises just made me ravenous!"

"Let's go."

"Where?"

"What's that place—the Klaus? The hot spot of the Alps. How about it?"

Carla considered the suggestion. "It's a school hangout, but I don't suppose we'll run into any of the girls at this hour."

"Great," Eric said. "You can take me, and I'll get you anything they can put whipped cream on."

"How about a pizza?"

"You got it!"

Bundled up in their parkas and scarves and heavy boots, they pushed out of the doors of the *Hallenschwimmbad* and stood at the top of the steps, breathing the icy air. Eric let Carla go first. Slowly, she negotiated the snowy steps. He felt her concentration as she placed the cane and stepped down carefully after it. When they were halfway through town and could already see the gingerbread facade of the *Konditorei Klaus* up ahead, Carla moved closer to him and lightly slipped her arm through his.

CHAPTER
15

The medical examiner's report was on Neumayer's desk when he returned from the Marlowe School that afternoon. He lumbered into his chair and stared at it balefully. He would be glad when this file was closed.

Eleven typewritten pages were neatly stacked before him. Old Lüthi must be getting long-winded in his old age, Neumayer thought. The M.E.'s reports were usually much shorter.

He struck a match to a Camel and hunched over his desk, rubbing his temple. The scene at the school had drained him. He had admired Felice's control, but he knew what her seeming calm had cost her. At one point, he thought they would have to call a doctor for the raging Pan Karas. The worst came when the shining wooden coffin was slid into the truck for the ride to the Fernstaad airport; both Neumayer and Karas's secretary, Andreas, stood ready to restrain him. Neumayer was grateful that the schoolgirls were upstairs in the dining room on the other side of the building at the time.

He yawned and tried to ease the ache out of his shoulders. At last, he dragged the pages of the report to him and began to read:

Anatomic Diagnoses

1. Drowning with severe pulmonary edema, congestion, and (L) pleural effusion, 50 cc

Neumayer snapped to attention in his chair.

2. Fractures, (R) tibia and fibula
3. Contusion, (L) parietal-occipital scalp
4. Contusion, (R) jaw

   Cause of death—drowning
   Manner of death—pending

"What the hell . . . ?" Neumayer exploded. He reached for the phone, his face darkening, but thought twice and resumed his reading.

The body is that of a well-developed, well-nourished female weighing 50 kg, measuring 160 cm, and appearing the stated age of 16 years. Received on the body are the following articles of clothing:

1. A water-soaked white nylon ski parka with a furred hood. Multiple vertically oriented dirt streaks are apparent on the back.
2. Water-soaked white nylon ski overalls. . . .

Neumayer picked up a pencil and began making notes in the margin. He had missed lunch, and now his stomach growled for attention. He dug a Lindt pistachio bar out of a drawer and munched as he smoked. The report continued:

> The neck is symmetrical. The breasts are firm and rounded. The thorax is well-expanded. The abdomen is flat. The external genitalia are normal adult female. There is no rigor mortis. There is livor mortis involving the back and posterior aspects of the neck and lower extremities. . . .

He read for another fifteen minutes, then reread, underlining and making notes that only he could decipher.

> The lungs are voluminous, overexpanded, and retain their size and shape after removal from the thorax. The Ⓡ lung weighs 950 g and the Ⓛ weighs 1,125 g. Rib impressions are visible on the pleural surfaces bilaterally. In addition, there are focal and confluent subpleural hemorrhages bilaterally. . . .

Neumayer's half-eaten chocolate bar lay in its crumpled foil on his desk. He was stopped again by the final words of the report:

> Comment: This young woman was injured while skiing, and drowned in a mountain stream. Final classification of the manner of death awaits further investigation.

When he had finished his fourth cigarette, he stacked the pages together and centered them on his desk.

There was an unfamiliar signature on the report: "U. Freimann." Why hadn't Lüthi prepared it himself? Neumayer picked up the phone and dialed.

"Dr. Lüthi, *bitte*." He listened to the ring of the M.E.'s extension, a bulge of flesh protruding between his scowling brows.

The operator came back on the line. "That phone is not being answered. Can someone else help you?"

"Get me Dr. Freimann."

He tapped his pencil on his notepad as the phone rang. "Freimann."

A woman? "Uh, is this Dr. U. Freimann?"

"Dr. Ursula Freimann. Who is this, please?"

"Inspector Neumayer, *Kantonspolizei*. I was trying to reach Dr. Lüthi."

"He is at a conference in Zurich. You are calling about the Sophie Karas report?" Her voice was clipped, no Swiss accent to muddy the consonants of her educated German. She sounded young.

"When do you expect him back?"

"Next Tuesday. It was I who performed the autopsy on Sophie Karas. I will answer any questions you have. I expect you have questions?"

"Should I?"

"If you are calling in reference to some other matter, kindly tell me what, please? I am Dr. Lüthi's assistant, in charge now while he is away. How may I help you?"

She must be new. Neumayer was sensitive to the warning that here was someone with no time to waste on pleasantries.

"Dr. Freimann, I know you must be very busy. I am indeed calling about the Sophie Karas report. You are not surprised?"

"No. I was told that this was an accident victim. You have seen that I did not certify the manner of death as accidental. I was expecting your call."

"I do have questions. Apparently, so do you. It might save time if you were to tell me first what prevented you from a positive conclusion on the manner of death." If it had been Lüthi, Neumayer would have asked his questions directly. Now he wanted to know what this crisp-voiced woman had concluded on her own. "Anything in my notes that you haven't covered, we can discuss later."

"Certainly," she said. Neumayer wedged the receiver between his ear and shoulder as he pulled a match out of its wooden box. "You will notice on page two—" She must have had the report on her desk in front of her, waiting. Neumayer dropped the still-flaming match into his ashtray and hastily flipped to the second page. Dr. Freimann continued without a pause. "—there are vertical streaks of dirt on the back of the jacket. I found this odd, considering that the young woman had fallen from some height to a relatively flat surface below. I have studied the photographs of the SOS Wolfram, as well as the body. This did not seem consistent with the kind of marks I would have expected on the clothing."

"The girl might have slipped farther up the hill and slid down toward the edge of the cliff till she fell over it. Isn't that possible?" Neumayer said.

"Yes. But I would have expected to find different fractures and contusions. Slightly different, but significant."

"Couldn't the dirt marks have come from a previous fall?"

"Yes. Did they?"

"I don't know," Neumayer said.

"Then I consider it something unexplained. Just one point. Now, if you look at page three—" Neumayer exhaled a puff of smoke and quickly, obediently flipped the page. Dr. Ursula Freimann was beginning to remind him of his daughter, Elena. "—where I have described the livor mortis. That's the settling of blood that occurs after death."

In spite of himself, in spite of the subject, Neumayer smiled. "How old are you, Dr. Freimann?"

"Thirty-one," she bristled. "How old are you?"

He laughed. "Very old," he said, "since this afternoon. No offense, *Frau Doktor*. But I have been reading autopsy reports for longer than you have been alive. I do know what livor mortis is."

"Good. No offense taken, *Herr Inspektor*. It will go faster if I don't have to explain too many of the technicalities. In this case, the livor mortis indicates that the body was on its back for some time."

"Yes?"

"I did not find this consistent with the cause of death— drowning. That's another point to be explained. Now, on page seven—"

"There is no doubt that the child drowned?"

He wanted to hear her defend it herself. She did, with a

patient recapitulation of the condition of the lungs, then went on from where he had interrupted her.

"Page seven, point B, item two—you will see I have indicated that the stomach contained approximately two hundred cc of turbid, watery fluid and small quantities of sand. In a drowning, some water would have been swallowed, as well as inhaled into the lungs. This, too, is quite consistent with my determination of the cause of death."

Consistency guides her; the lack of it sets up warning flags she won't ignore, Neumayer thought. He had never articulated the idea to himself, but that was exactly the path he followed in his own reasoning.

Dr. Freimann continued her explication, point by significant point. When she was done, Neumayer had no additional questions—not about the report. Only about everything else.

"You will want to speak to Dr. Lüthi," Dr. Freimann said. "Shall I have him call you when he returns next week?"

"Dr. Lüthi is one of my oldest friends in Fernstaad. I always like hearing from him. But I will probably call him myself, so you needn't bother asking him."

"Of course. I have already left a copy of the Karas report on his desk."

"You did a fine job, Dr. Freimann." He paused, but she did not respond. "It is you I would like to speak to if I think of any further questions. Will you be available, or are you planning any trips yourself?"

"I will be here."

"Thank you."

"*Bitte*," she said crisply. He heard her take a sharp breath and thought she would say something else. But she exhaled slowly and said, "So, if there is nothing more for the moment, I will say *auf Wiedersehen, Herr Inspektor*."

After he hung up, Neumayer spread the pages of the report in a fan in front of him, then stacked them, aligned them with a tap on his desk, clipped them together—playing with them as his mind gripped one thought after another, like a gymnast climbing the parallel rungs of a laddered wall. He had an instinct for timing. He had asked Dr. Freimann everything except her opinion. She would have resisted today, insisted that she dealt only in facts, not conjectures. But he did not believe that. He would call her again, probably tomorrow. Meanwhile, he must consider those facts. What had seemed to him tragic but orderly was turning into a puzzle with ominous undercurrents.

CHAPTER
16

Carla stood with Eric outside the *Konditorei* Klaus. The air was colder, as the afternoon sun was fast disappearing behind the peak of Piz Wolfram. The slopes were speckled with skiers making one last run before twilight closed in. Purple shadows chased them down the mountain.

"Are you tired?" Eric asked.

"I'd better not be," Carla said. "I've got a pile of work waiting for me before dinner, my punishment for goofing off all afternoon. I enjoyed it, though. I'm glad we ran into each other at the pool." She stepped away from him, feeling a little awkward. It seemed inappropriate to offer her hand in a formal parting shake, but she was eager to leave—and he seemed just as eager to linger. "So . . . thanks for keeping me company—"

He moved closer. "I'll take you back to school."

"Please, no!" she said. "There are two empty taxis waiting right across the street. I'll be fine."

"Taxis? No class! I was going to hire one of those big fancy horse-drawn sleighs with all the bells and the furry lap robes. You could arrive in style."

"And spend the rest of the week answering questions from a bunch of nosy girls? No, thanks! Besides, I've taken enough of your time today. Your other patients will all be having relapses by the time you get back to the clinic.''

The mention of the clinic triggered a professional response. Eric started explaining what Carla should do if her leg felt sore from the exercises, repeating himself to make sure she understood, insisting that she call if she had any pain. It was unnecessary, she told him, the leg felt fine, and besides, he had told her all this last week.

A trio of handsome women in fur emerged from the coffeehouse behind them and crossed the snowy street to the taxis. They drove off in the first one.

''Let's wait for their husbands to come out,'' Eric said. ''They'll take the second car, and you'll be stuck with me and the horses.''

''What makes you think they're married?'' Carla asked, smiling as she hailed the remaining taxi.

Eric looked at her in mock seriousness. ''The length of their furs, of course. And the elegance of their face-lifts. They all want to look like you.''

Don't encourage him, Carla warned herself.

The taxi driver had noticed Carla's cane and maneuvered across the street, tires crunching in the snow as he stopped in front of them.

''I don't believe you,'' Carla challenged. ''You couldn't tell that those women had face-lifts. You hardly saw them.''

''Maybe not. But I know they'd like to look like you.'' He held the taxi door open for her. ''As for me, I'm happy just looking *at* you.''

Oh-oh, Carla thought. She settled in the car and leaned out toward him. ''Well . . . thanks again.'' She couldn't stop herself; she held out her hand. ''It was lovely.''

''For me,'' Eric said, not releasing her.

Don't.

She pulled away and closed the door. She knew he was watching as they drove off.

Carla paid the driver in the courtyard and noticed, as she mounted the front steps of Marlowe, that the tiredness had finally reached her. It was a good feeling, though. Inside the school, she stopped to pick up her mail and phone messages from the row of mailboxes off the front hall. Standing there, she considered the afternoon. She had to admit that she hadn't felt so wonderful in a long time. Well, maybe last week, with Michael—at first. Before the day turned into a disaster. But now, after the hours in the swimming pool, and then with Eric at the Klaus, she felt positively *healthy*.

She lingered in the hall and began flipping through her messages. Some school notices; a letter on her mother's heavy, oyster-white stationery; another note from her mother's friend, the Gräfin von Wetzlar, urging her to come to the soiree at her chalet tomorrow evening—how many times would Carla have to say no before the gräfin gave up?—and finally, the monthly statement from her Fernstaad bank, advising her of the latest transfer of funds into her account. Again, no matter how often she said no, it could not cut off the flow of money that she didn't need or want.

Carla sighed and turned to her phone messages. There were two. The first was from Eric. He must have called the minute after they parted at the Klaus. She laughed as she read the note:

"Long time no see. Dinner tomorrow?"

He certainly knew how charming he was. This time, however, Carla had no intention of making a fool of herself over another self-satisfied, overconfident man. Eric was new in Fernstaad. He'd soon find himself a proper playmate. As far as Carla was concerned, he was Dr. Leitner's associate, assigned to her case, and their relationship would remain strictly business. She wasn't going to get hurt again.

The second message was from Rudi Neumayer of the *Kantonspolizei*, asking her to return his call as soon as possible.

She took the lift to the fifth floor. The hall was quiet, as the girls had not yet come back from the ski slopes. Miss Grimsby had been firm about not restricting their skiing; it would have been an artificial response to the recent tragedy and it wouldn't have helped anyone. Carla agreed with the headmistress's reasoning.

She settled at the desk in her sitting room and dialed the number of the *Kantonspolizei*.

"Ah, Miss Temple. Thank you for calling," Neumayer said. "I won't take much of your time. I just want to ask you something about Sophie Karas. Frau Grimsby didn't know, but perhaps you do."

"I'll be glad to help, if I can. But I have to admit that I didn't know Sophie very well. She was extremely shy, and she hadn't been here long enough to get used to me. She never confided in me, if your question is personal."

"No, not exactly. I wonder if you know whether she had a previous accident on the slopes? A bad fall, perhaps, sometime in the past months?"

"I'm pretty sure she didn't," Carla said. "She was a good skier, very cautious, and also, a little babyish. We would have heard about any bumps or bruises. Sophie had a habit of rushing to the school nurse with every sniffle or paper cut."

"So," Neumayer drew out the word. "And you never saw her come back from the slopes with dirt streaks on the back of her white ski parka? As if she had tumbled and slid some distance?"

"What white parka?" Carla asked. "Sophie used to wear some sort of dark fur vest over her ski sweaters. Brown mink, I think. I once asked her if she was sure it kept her warm enough."

"I see," Neumayer said. "So you never saw her in a white ski outfit?"

"I would have stopped her if I had. That's against school regulations. It could be dangerous," Carla said.

"I understand the outfit was new. She might have been wearing it for the first time, the day of the accident?" Neumayer prodded.

"It's possible. I usually see the girls when they leave for the slopes. But I was—uh, down in Fernstaad visiting someone last Monday, the day of the storm. Sophie might have slipped out wearing it that day. Oh, lord! Is that how they found her, in a white ski outfit?"

"Yes, but don't be upset about it, my dear," Neumayer

said. "It had nothing to do with the cause of her death, I promise you."

"Maybe if I hadn't—" Carla began.

"No, no," Neumayer interrupted. "Believe me, there is no reason to think the accident happened because of what she was wearing. But I must ask you, did Sophie Karas seem disturbed in any manner around that time?"

Carla shook her head as she thought. "Actually, on the contrary, I thought she was a little more relaxed and friendly. I remember thinking that she was finally adjusting."

"Well, I thank you for your help," Neumayer said. "I won't keep you any longer. You will call me if you think of anything else?"

"Of course," Carla said.

Neumayer leaned forward and laid a heavy paw on the autopsy report on his desk. *So, Dr. Ursula Freimann, there's your answer*, he thought. *No previous fall to explain the marks.*

A sickening alternative began to form.

CHAPTER
17

The harsh bell jangled. Carla's arm shot out and pounced on her alarm clock. Unwittingly, she had surrendered to a sensual dream and was drifting through it in limpid pleasure when the bell shocked her into a half-awake state.

The bell rang again, urgent and irritating. Not the clock. It was the telephone at her bedside. She was awake now, and grumpy. She snatched at the phone.

"Yes?" she mumbled into the receiver.

"Good morning. Did you sleep well?"

"I don't know," Carla said. "I'm not finished yet. Was that a professional question, Eric?"

"I'm flattered that you recognized my voice."

"What time is it?"

"Time to think about dinner," Eric said. "You didn't return my call yesterday. Do we have a date tonight?"

"Good God, it's not even seven!" Carla said, reading the time on her digital clock. "What are you doing up so early?"

"So late," Eric corrected. "I'm just finishing work—a tricky case kept me here all night. I thought I'd catch you before you got busy and I got comatose. Are we on for tonight?"

Carla groaned as she sat up in bed. "Oh, no, sorry, I can't."

"Other plans? Okay, how about tomorrow?"

"Look, Eric, I don't think it's a good idea for us to—"

"Sure it is," he interrupted. "You're American, I'm American—that makes us practically related. And I'm a stranger here in town, ma'am."

Carla thought it through in the brief silence. "I have an idea. Today is Tuesday. A friend of my mother's always gives a grand party every Tuesday during the season. She's Elvina von Wetzlar, the Gräfin von Wetzlar, and she has a huge chalet on the mountain. She's been inviting me ever since she and the graf arrived."

"Graf? Gray-fin?"

"Count and countess. But don't worry about it. I hear the parties are very lively, and you might enjoy yourself. I'll call and get you invited. I'm sure they'd love to have you."

"Fine. What time should I pick you up?"

"I won't be able to make it," Carla said firmly. "But you'll have a good time. Wine, women, and song—as close to a Roman orgy as you'll find in the Alps. No one feels much like a stranger after one of the gräfin's soirees. Actually, they're supposed to be rather wild, but I'm sure you can take care of yourself."

There was another silence. Then Eric said quietly, "I don't think so, Carla. That wasn't what I had in mind. But I appreciate the offer. Maybe some other time . . . maybe you'll feel more sociable when you're steadier on that leg. Meanwhile, you take good care of it.'' Eric's voice was lighter now. ''I'm getting attached to it, you know?''

''I'll call Elvina, anyhow. In case you change your mind,'' Carla said. ''You ought to go, Eric, meet the really beautiful people of Fernstaad.'' Did it come out as sarcastically as she thought? She recovered crisply. ''Anyone can tell you where the von Wetzlar chalet is. I'll make sure you're expected.''

He didn't respond.

''So . . . I'll be seeing you at the clinic,'' Carla said.

Did I mean to do that? Carla thought after she hung up. Did I really mean to do that?

CHAPTER
18

Anneliese Zuecher had run short sooner than she expected. Word had spread among the younger girls, and her supply was almost exhausted over the weekend. She barely had enough for herself, and it was only Tuesday. She'd certainly be able to connect with Claude on Thursday, but why wait? She knew where to find him tonight. Everyone who was anyone—*and* his dealer—would be at the regular Tuesday soiree at the chalet of the Graf and Gräfin von Wetzlar. Anneliese would be there, too.

If you could not afford Fernstaad in season, if you did not have entrée to its feverish social life, you could always go to St. Moritz or Gstaad or Kitzbühel. Anneliese was sorry that her parents hadn't found a school for her in one of those relatively relaxed ski towns. She hated Fernstaad and the inflated, titled self-importance of its winter population. The skiing was, of course, the best in the Alps, but the rest of it was a drag. Especially the von Wetzlars' parties, which she had sneaked into before. It wasn't worth the effort—leaving Marlowe bundled up for the walk through the snow, dragging evening clothes with her, since the gräfin insisted everyone dress, and changing in one of the outbuildings—but Mindy Parson had talked her into it last year, and Anneliese had gone several times after that on her own. That was where she first met Laurent. He was a regular at the von Wetzlars', he told her. And it was Laurent who introduced her to a new recreation—cocaine. It was an exciting first, and it made life at Marlowe a little more bearable. And certainly more profitable.

Laurent had moved on, but Candyman Claude was on hand to keep things going. Anneliese was sure she'd find him at the chalet, so she made the effort.

Sneaking out of school tonight was no problem. The mile-long trek across the slopes was pleasant in the bright moonlight, even burdened with the bundle containing her evening skirt and shoes. Leaving her warm ski clothes in a pile in the corner of the stable to the rear of the chalet, Anneliese shivered through the snow and entered a side terrace door.

The von Wetzlar chalet had more than forty rooms. It rode high on a slope overlooking Lake Clemenza, surrounded by walls of graceful larch and pine trees. It was an unlikely Alpine structure, since the graf and gräfin had extended the original harmonious building years ago. They created five terraced levels, adding a greenhouse, a stable, and three pools, one that flowed from outside to a tiled indoor court hung with plants and bubbling with fountains. Anneliese passed through this steamy court and stopped to check the naked pink bodies laughing and splashing in the pool.

No Claude. It didn't surprise her. There were better places here to do business. She watched a plump young woman, body glistening and rosy from the heated water, climb up the pool's ladder, squealing, breasts bobbling as she ran across slippery tiles, pursued by two paunchy men. Although the gräfin would not tolerate guests arriving in casual après-ski, she did not seem to care how many of them peeled during the evening.

What a nuisance, Anneliese thought as she fluffed out her full, ankle-length, black-and-green-paisley evening skirt. She straightened the collar of her long-sleeved white silk blouse, smoothed the wide green silk cummerbund, and looked around restlessly. She felt definitely uncool in her Goody-Two-Shoes outfit, but it did make her look older. Blending in was important.

A whining sound rose above the noise from the pool. Sitar music, the Gräfin von Wetzlar's latest passion. Wobbly tones filled the entire chalet, transmitted through an elaborate audio system from the music den, where a darkly earnest and very cold sitarist from Bombay sat cross-legged on cushions and thrummed an endless, quivering nonmelody. Anneliese twitched uneasily, as if a cloud of mosquitoes had surrounded her. She bent to adjust the heel straps of her black suede sling-back shoes.

"May I help you, my dear?"

The voice at her ear dripped with sexual intimacy. The hand that gripped her elbow touched her breast and remained there.

"Hey!" Anneliese snapped upright and pulled away. She did not recognize the face.

"I was afraid you might lose your balance," the man said. His smile was sweaty with forced innocence. "It's so nice to see you again."

"Do I know you?" Anneliese could not identify the man or his accent.

"We've seen each other before," he said vaguely. "Perhaps we haven't been introduced formally. Permit me." He bowed slightly. "Barone Ugo di Raspoldini-Sant'Agata. I am called Mookie by my friends. You will tell me your name, and then *we* will be friends."

Ah, yes, Anneliese thought. The Barone. *Mookie*. She looked down into the confident face, heavy and perspiring in the heat of the pool court. Here he was, in full evening dress, lurking around the spectacle of nudity. He was the one. She had heard his name when she was listening outside Nicole

Robineau's door. She had learned of the extracurricular activities he conducted regularly for her classmate. Nicole must be crazy! Katharyn, too. Anneliese had been eavesdropping last Sunday when she heard Nicole pursuading that snotty British bitch to join her. Fun? Kicks? With someone whose turn-on was schoolgirls, the younger the better? How could anyone let this letch with the ludicrous name touch her? In front of a camera, too? Apparently, the honorable Lady Katharyn Sunynghame had as strong a stomach as Nicole.

Anneliese backed away from the barone. "I'm meeting someone. I'm sure he's looking for me."

"Don't you think he'll wait? For someone as charming as you? Come, you mustn't be so shy. Let me get you something to eat, and we can become acquainted. You haven't told me your name."

"It's late," Anneliese said, plucking at the cuff of her sleeve, embarrassed to discover she wasn't wearing her watch. "Please, excuse me." She turned and started to walk away, hoping that she sounded as cold and dismissing as she meant to, that her height and her prim dress gave her a dignity she wasn't feeling.

The barone closed in behind her, linking arms. She jumped at his touch.

"Now, where are you going?" he said smoothly. "Won't you let me look after you? You must be hungry, my dear—and cold, after walking outside in such light clothes."

Good lord, he had seen her sneak in the side door! What would he do, have her thrown out? He sounded so sure of himself.

She shook off his arm and tried for politeness. "I'm quite fine, thank you. Excuse me, I really must go."

She strode off across the dry outer tiles surrounding the pool. She sensed that he was not following, but it was only temporary relief. Behind her, the barone laughed easily. "Maybe later," he called. "I'll find you."

Damn Claude! How could she shake the barone and look for Claude at the same time? He was making her work too hard, just for a few bags. If she didn't see him soon, she'd get herself another connection. She was beginning to feel too desperate. What she needed now was another hit.

She patted the pocket of her skirt as she passed the dressing rooms and left the pool court. One bag left. Her last. It was almost empty, but it was more than enough to satisfy, to give her that sparkle that was like nothing else. Enough to calm her down. She'd find someplace private and do it all. Or should she save some, just in case? What the hell—all. As soon as she felt better, she'd go looking for Claude.

The drone of the sitar trailed her. She skirted the noisy main kitchen that opened to a huge buffet and glanced in at the crowd around the tables. Claude was not there. She sniffed with momentary hunger, then decided she had more important things to do. She wandered down a wide hallway paneled in dark wood. A man and woman holding loaded plates of food and sloshing wineglasses brushed past her, calling loudly to friends behind her.

Isn't there anyplace quiet in this whole chalet? Anneliese wondered. She remembered that there was a large gaming room at the end of the hall. She could see that its massive carved-wood door was closed. Did that mean the room was empty? She stopped before the door and listened for sounds inside. It was impossible to hear anything over the sound of the sitar. Without knocking, she entered.

The only light inside came from the blaze in the great stone fireplace. It undulated on a shadowy couple entangled on the billiard table. The woman's shapely legs glowed against the dark fabric of the man's dinner jacket. He knelt before her, trousers dropped to his knees, his shoulders encircled by those long shiny legs, as the couple bucked and gibbered breathlessly on the table.

"*Oh!*" Anneliese cried.

The man raised his head, studied her for a brief instant, then smiled lewdly. He motioned for Anneliese to come closer.

She snorted in disgust. She had recognized him. Awkwardly, she backed out of the gaming room and closed the door behind her.

Inside, Wieprecht, Graf von Wetzlar, laughed and returned to his pleasures.

Anneliese scurried down the hallway and turned the corner. She was so distracted she almost did not notice Claude standing on the steps at the end of the hall. He was talking quietly to two men; their three bodies were leaning in toward one another. A surreptitious exchange of small items was taking place at thigh level. When Anneliese recognized him, she called out and rushed forward.

Claude straightened and scowled at her. He stepped away from the men and came quickly down the stairs to meet her.

"What are you doing here?" he snapped.

"Looking for you, and going crazy!" she snapped back. "I've run out. I need—"

"God, not now! Not here!" He turned her by her shoulders and inched her back down the hall.

"Stop pushing me!"

"Quiet!" He looked around, thinking quickly. "Do you know where the greenhouse is? The other side of the chalet, one level down?" She nodded. "Wait for me there. Don't go anyplace else until I see you. Understand?" She nodded again. A man passed them in the hall, on his way to the pool. Claude waited until he was gone. "And don't talk to anyone on the way, either. I'll be there in about a half hour. Are you listening?"

"Yes, but why can't you come now?" She fixed him with her child's cornflower-blue eyes.

"Because I'm busy, okay?" His teeth were clenched, and he breathed in angrily. "I'll come as soon as I can. Go on, now." Claude gave her a small shove. "Go." He turned back to the men on the stairs.

Anneliese found the small corridor off the main hallway. She hurried, fearful of being spotted by the barone on the prowl. She had already decided that if the dreaded Mookie touched her again, he would feel her knee—where it would hurt most. The sitar music accompanied her down the steps of the corridor to the glassed door of the greenhouse. She twisted the handle and entered the heated chamber.

A spectral blue light washed over her, leaching the color from her lips and eyes. She closed the door behind her. The music stopped, at last! In the welcome silence, Anneliese strolled down one of the long aisles, bordered by benches of opulent flowers. There were the graf's prized orchids, angular and ugly, thousands of them, and masses of bushy greenery. She walked slowly to the back of the greenhouse until she found an open spot on a bench. She brushed crumbs of earth to the floor, then sat facing the glass outer wall.

Gradually, her eyes grew accustomed to the acid blue light. She reached into her pocket and pulled out the bag of coke. She concentrated on her preparations. Then, quickly, she did two lines. *Quickly, quickly.* She smiled as she felt her pulse begin to race, her blood pressure take off. *Here come the rockets!* She inhaled deeply and watched the blue vein in her wrist leap. Outside, the night was a dark blank wall beyond the glass panes. She stared out, contented, fingering the glassine envelope. Still plenty left inside. Now that she had found Claude, she definitely didn't have to save any of it. *Keep it up, up, up!*

She had a sense of time skipping. . . .

Anneliese wriggled on the hard bench. How long had she been there? What time was it? Two in the morning? Three? Jesus, she'd have to start thinking about getting back to school. The bag in her hand was empty now. She crackled it into a ball and dropped it to the floor. She felt too heavy to move. Besides, Claude . . . soon. . . . She slipped off the straps of her shoes and swiveled sideways, raising her bent legs to the bench and hugging them closely. She rested her head on her knees and began to breathe deeply.

A noise at the front of the greenhouse woke her. Someone else was inside. A man. He had stumbled against a bench and knocked over a plant. Anneliese heard him swear softly.

"Claude?"

There was no answer. She squinted in the distorting light at the man coming toward her down the long aisle. He was holding out something small in the palm of one hand.

"I've brought you something you're going to like," he said.

CHAPTER
19

It was early morning when Inspector Rudi Neumayer swerved the *Kantonspolizei* car into a skiddy U-turn and stopped in front of the medical examiner's office.

He had not forgotten that Dr. Lüthi would still be at the conference in Zurich—until next Tuesday, that crisp young woman, Dr. Freimann, had told him. Nevertheless, he greeted the receptionist in the outer office of the M.E.'s lab and casually asked for his old friend. As he expected, he was referred to Ursula Freimann.

Her office was small but neat. Neumayer's sensitive nose twitched at the sting of chemicals that hovered about the room. Seated across from Dr. Freimann, on the opposite side of her tidy desk, he studied her as she returned one large green folder to a filing drawer and pulled out another.

When she had met him at the door, he was surprised to find her appearance so dainty, in comparison with her brusque manner on the phone. Actually, the daintiness was more a matter of size than of grace. She was short, with a small, tight body that was compact and muscular, like a pony's. He enjoyed watching her move—she had an easy efficiency, no wasted gestures. Her light-brown hair was sun-streaked and cut short in a straight and shiny cap that followed the contours of her well-shaped head. Her face was broad across the cheek-bones, the clear brown eyes widely spaced, which gave her an almost exotic look, except that there was an unexpected spattering of freckles across her nose. She looked like an earthy young boy who ought to be out skiing or chasing a soccer ball. It was vaguely incongruous to see her dressed in a starched white lab coat, to realize that she was a highly competent pathologist.

Neumayer began an apology—a casual visit to his friend, Dr. Lüthi. He had forgotten about the Zurich conference. He certainly would have called first, rather than intrude on Dr. Freimann's busy schedule. . . .

"I expected to hear from you," she said, silencing his explanation. Without waiting for him to ask any questions, she opened the green folder on her desk and said, "As long as you're here, what troubles me especially about the Karas girl's death is the position of the body when it was found—"

She certainly wasted no time getting to the point.

And, yes, that had been nagging at Neumayer, too. He wanted to hear her construct the puzzle herself, to see how it meshed with his own thoughts.

"—not *in* the water, but only *near* the stream, at the base of the cliff. In fact," she flipped through the pages in the folder with strong, square-tipped fingers. "Ah, here they are, the photos taken by the SOS Wolfram." She slid them across her desk. "I must take into consideration all the information I receive. You will see from those pictures that the body is on its back, completely out of the water. Now, that is a fairly shallow stream, even when swollen by melting snow. At its height, the water would still not have enough depth or force to throw a body that far beyond its banks. And, at the time I estimate death—by drowning, you will remember—the water would have been quite low, and all but frozen."

Neumayer halted the film that threatened to start unreeling in his mind. His own mental movie, bubbling up again. But he did not want to be distracted now. He waited for Dr. Freimann to continue.

"I don't think there is any question that the accident occurred at just the place where the body was found, yes? On the first day of the storm?"

Neumayer nodded agreement. He looked down at the glossy photos, at the tragedy forever captured by the unflinching eye of the camera.

"I thought not. You see, the melt that began several days after the storm might have carried her farther downstream, but there is not much possibility that she could have drowned any farther up the streambed. The trees are too thick along the top of the cliff there, for a very long stretch—the pictures show that clearly. She would have crashed into them at any point above this spot. They would have stopped her. No, the only place she could have gone over the cliff is right here." She jabbed at the photo on the top of the pile. "But I do not see how she could have plunged off the slope and drowned in that stream, and still have come to rest on her back at the base of the cliff."

There it was, just as Neumayer had been worrying it himself. And he had not succeeded in untangling a single thread yet. Did Dr. Freimann have anything to add?

She did. "Then, there are the marks on the head and jaw, equally violent, so neatly front and back—"

"What are you suggesting, Dr. Freimann?"

"I offer no suggestions. I am simply explaining several inconsistencies that prevented me from certifying the manner of death as an accident."

"Do you think the girl could have been moved—let's say, after she fell over the cliff, when she was already dead?"

"That would be consistent with the vertical dirt streaks on the back of the jacket and overalls, but I am not prepared to conclude so with any certainty."

"You are very cautious with your conclusions. Are there so many other explanations for the marks on the clothing, the location of the body as it was found?"

"I am sure there are other possibilities that I am not aware of. I do not waste time guessing. I only know what is possible and what is not."

Neumayer pushed the photographs back across the desk and watched the young woman return them neatly to their place in her folder.

"What do you propose to do?" he asked her.

"I have already done it. My report is as complete as I am capable of making it, and I have given you my further opinion." She spoke the last word with what Neumayer felt was slightly frosty contempt. "I doubt that I will have any-thing else to add. But Dr. Lüthi may—"

"I have a daughter your age," Neumayer interrupted. Ur-sula Freimann looked at him politely, waiting for the point. "You remind me of her."

"Oh? Is she a physician?"

"No—a mother, a wife, a daughter. Still, you seem very much like her, so logical and precise. I am quite old-fash-ioned, Dr. Freimann. I believe that young women should be protected. And young girls. And children."

"Of course." She sat straighter in her chair. *What a strange man. What is he rambling about?*

"Never mind," Neumayer said. "I am most grateful for your time. And for your opinions. If you have any further thoughts, I would appreciate hearing from you."

"Certainly," she said hastily. "That is my function." She closed the folder on her desk and started to rise.

The phone at her elbow rang.

"Freimann," she said into the receiver. "Yes." She flicked her eyes at Neumayer. "He is still here. Just leaving, in fact. Certainly." She handed the receiver to Neumayer across the desk. "Sergeant Kellhorn," she said.

"Yes?" He listened for a minute, then stood abruptly. "Since when? Ummmm. Has she ever done this before?" He turned his back to Dr. Freimann to give himself the illusion of privacy. "I know how nervous they all are, but there's no point in jumping to conclusions. The girl will probably turn up soon with some foolish explanation. Tell Frau Grimsby I'll call her as soon as I get back. Tell her I said she shouldn't waste her time worrying—she should just think up some suitable punishment." He patted his pocket for his cigarettes. "Dammit, Hans, we don't know that. I don't want you up-setting that woman with any wild conjectures. Just say I'll call. I'm leaving now."

His departure from the pathologist's office was accom-plished with distracted politeness.

Ursula Freimann stared at the door through which Inspector Neumayer had just exited. Smoke from his cigarette still trailed in the air. His tense conversation still hung in the room. Obviously, there was more trouble at Marlowe. Another girl missing? Another accident? Did it have anything to do with the death of Sophie Karas? Now, what made her think that? She wasn't paid to make wild conjectures. She shrugged it off as unproductive. Her own responsibilities were quite enough.

She started to replace the green folder marked *Karas, Sophie* in her desk drawer, then hesitated. The Karas girl was only the third autopsy she had performed since coming to Fernstaad. Everything about it made her prickle. Maybe it was because she had expected it to be so simple: the violence of a tragic accident, but with everything else in order. Then, bit by bit, one thing after another seemed out of place. There were more questions than answers. She was experienced and thorough; she treated her instincts not with trust, but as doors that must be opened so that what lay beyond could be explored.

Still, others were experienced, too, more than she. All that was asked of her was that she report her findings, what she had *seen*. And, when pressed, as Inspector Neumayer had done so very transparently, she could point to those doors and let others do their own exploring. If she had been in Fernstaad longer, if she had known Dr. Lüthi or Inspector Neumayer better, she might have discussed with them the thoughts that caused her to tingle anew as she started to slide the Karas file into her drawer.

Hanging from the drawer's metal runners was a large compartment marked *Accident*, and just beyond, a very slim folder labeled *Homicide*. She hesitated. Had she really done all that might be expected of her?

At last, she lodged the green folder in the compartment marked *Pending*. She closed the drawer with a metallic clunk, locked it, and tucked the key into the pocket of her starched white lab coat. Then she left her office and returned to the laboratory.

Carla was in Felice Grimsby's office two days later when Inspector Neumayer called. The man who took care of the plants at the von Wetzlar chalet had discovered the body of a young girl in the greenhouse. Identification was required, but, from the description, this was surely the missing Anneliese Zuecher. She was wearing evening clothes, but a bundle containing ski boots, ski pants, and a parka was found outside in a corner of the stable. The parka carried the Marlowe School insignia.

"What hap— How did she die?" Felice Grimsby sagged at her desk and pressed her eyelids. Carla rose and came over to her, face white, understanding the unheard half of the conversation.

"I'll have to say it bluntly, my dear," Neumayer said. "Preliminary examination suggests drugs—an accidental overdose. There was enough to kill five of her. We'll know better after the autopsy. At the moment, it looks like her first experience with, uh, intravenous use—an experiment that went wild."

"Rudi! Intravenous? Was it *heroin*?"

"So it seems. We're listing it as a self-administered overdose, tentatively."

"What was she doing at the chalet? Anneliese wouldn't have any reason to visit the von Wetzlars. I never approved an invitation from the graf or the gräfin. No, you must be wrong." Miss Grimsby shook her head violently. "The girl had no permission— *Heroin!* No, it couldn't be Anneliese—"

Neumayer's voice was kind, but there was an undercurrent of steely tension. "Felice, you may be right. The ski clothes could belong to someone else. No connection, possibly. But I need your help. We'll have to have a positive identification. Maybe you could send the teacher who first reported the girl missing—Carla Temple, wasn't it? I know her. There's no need for you to do this, Felice. You don't have to come."

"Where is—the body?" The tremor almost choked off Miss Grimsby's words.

"At the medical examiner's office. I'm here now. I'll be sending a car to Marlowe immediately. Would you please have Miss Temple meet me here as soon as possible. I'll be waiting for her."

There was a long silence.

"Hello? Are you there?" Neumayer said. "Felice?"

"I'll come myself," Miss Grimsby said quietly.

Carla insisted on accompanying the headmistress. They did not speak during the ride to town, nor as Rudi Neumayer gently led them into the back of the M.E.'s lab. Standing over the sheeted body, both women nodded simultaneously as the cherubic, sleeping face on its pillow of golden hair was revealed. Carla stepped back quickly, feeling the salty sting in her eyes. Miss Grimsby hovered over the dead girl until Neumayer wrapped a strong arm around her shoulders and turned her away.

Carla left them alone together and walked out into the bracing sparkle of the sunny day. The mountains thrust proudly into the brilliant blue sky, a sky as blue as the once-vivid eyes of the dead girl inside. Two of them—two of Carla's young students, dead in two weeks. Senseless accidents that had ended two beautiful young lives. One of them in circumstances too sordid to accept. It was almost as if a plague had descended on the school, an attack. Nothing like this had ever happened at Marlowe, in all its distinguished history. Carla felt the pain and horror in equal measure. Then a sudden, childish thought struck her: *Accidents come in threes*. She was appalled at the silliness of the superstition. Then, suddenly, she was terribly, deeply frightened.

CHAPTER
20

For the second time in his short tenure at the Leitner Clinic, Dr. Eric Sunderson had been called on to pronounce a young girl dead. The formalities in Fernstaad required that even an obviously deceased person be removed first to a center of medical treatment before being transferred to the medical examiner's laboratory. The constant danger of skiers and hikers suffering from catastrophic hypothermia on the frozen slopes dictated immediate transfer to a hospital where equipment was available, in case a flicker of stubborn life remained to be fanned awake again.

That was not the case with Anneliese Zuecher. She had been found in a heated greenhouse, no frozen condition concealed a living spark within her body, and he had pronounced her dead and sent her on her way. The second Marlowe student in two weeks.

Dr. Leitner knocked on his office door late that afternoon and entered, carrying a bottle of slivovitz. He grunted as he lowered himself into a leather easy chair and held up the bottle.

"You will join me in a schnapps, Eric? Good plum brandy, good for old bones on cold days."

"Is that medically sound, Doctor? Treating bones with brandy?" Eric rose to fetch two glasses.

"So, then, good for old, weary hearts—young ones, too." Dr. Leitner poured, lifted his glass with a tired "Prosit!" and swallowed in one gulp. Eric inhaled the fumes from the colorless liquor and sipped. "We do not usually lose so many young people in Fernstaad. I thought you should know that. Two girls, two accidents in that many weeks, it is not so common."

"I didn't think so," Eric said. "This one looks like an accidental suicide, anyhow. I'm pretty sure it's a heroin overdose. I told Inspector Neumayer. He'll have the M.E. confirm it, of course."

"What made you conclude that?" Fritz Leitner asked.

"The condition of the body—and the clothes. The girl was wearing a long-sleeved white blouse. There was recent blood on the sleeve. It had leaked through from inside the elbow, and that cuff was unbuttoned. I rolled it up. She must have jabbed herself fiercely, more than once. Left arm. No other track marks, though. I imagine that's where a right-handed person starts experimenting." He drained his glass and winced. "Hard drugs, for Christ's sake!"

"Today's tragedy." Dr. Leitner held out the bottle, and Eric accepted a refill. "I wonder what they will find to abuse themselves with tomorrow, these idiotic children. I begin to lose patience with the pain they cause themselves and those who love them." The bottle clunked against his glass as he poured himself a large measure. "So, did you happen to see the girl at the party Tuesday night?"

Eric's hand hovered, his glass halfway to his lips. "What?"

"Anneliese Zuecher. At the von Wetzlars. You were there, without Carla, I understand."

"How did you know that?"

"Elvina," Fritz Leitner sighed. "She rushed here this morning, after they removed the body from her greenhouse. Her nerves, she insisted. I must give her something extra strong. I've been treating the gräfin for more years than I want to remember, and I've never known anyone with steadier nerves. She is made of iron, is that how you say it? Always, I tell her I am giving her such a strong prescription she must be careful of the side effects. What I give her wouldn't put a baby to sleep." He shook his head, amused. "She is one who babbles, very devoted to gossip. So I know that Carla Temple arranged an invitation for you to the chalet. And I know that you were there, but Carla was not. Should I ask a personal question?"

"Do you have to? I was bored, so I went. Alone. I didn't really want to, but it seems that Carla isn't interested in the pleasure of my company." Eric meant to sound casual, but his voice was dull with disappointment.

"Please, don't be upset, my friend," Dr. Leitner soothed him. "She may not be ready for you—or for anyone. I know her well, by now. She is stubborn. She will want to choose her own time. But I believe you can help her in many ways, not just as a physician. I believe she can help you, too. And I think you are still interested, yes?"

"I think you are right, and very nosy," Eric said, smiling.

Dr. Leitner touched his nose and laughed. "Oh, yes, I am."

"And I also think you stick up for Carla too much."

"No more than I would for you." They did not look at each other during the small silence that followed. "Well, more slivovitz? Good. So, did you enjoy the party? They are very fashionable, the graf and gräfin. Did you have a good evening?"

"No, I did not," Eric said.

"That is too bad. I hoped you might have met friendly, interesting new people there."

"Very friendly. Not very interesting."

Dr. Leitner nodded. "And you did not meet the girl, Anneliese? She was not actually invited, and Elvina is upset that she was there. You didn't see her during the evening?"

"No. It's a very large chalet."

"It is," Dr. Leitner agreed. "Pity. Although I don't know why I say that. Even if you had met her, what could you have done that would have changed anything?"

Eric stared into his glass, both hands wrapped around it. "Nothing," he said.

Fritz Leitner shifted in his chair, his voice rising to lighten the conversation. "You are off this weekend? Do you have any plans?"

"I thought I might hike to Sils Mariana. But if you think you'll need me, I'll stay in Fernstaad."

"No, no, you go and enjoy yourself. Although Sils Mariana is not a very lively town, I think. You could have a better time here, if you tried."

Eric didn't miss the older man's obvious train of thought. He smiled pleasantly at him. "I suppose you mean I should call Carla again. You don't give up, do you?" Dr. Leitner shrugged. "Well, neither do I, I promise you."

CHAPTER
21

He had to get into the school.

He had spent most of the night thinking about it.

When Pindar Breitel knocked on his door Sunday morning to find out whether he was coming down for breakfast, he was still sunk in fitful sleep. He started, then fell back on the rumpled sheets. The light hurt his eyes. His sluggish body refused to move.

He called out to Breitel that he would have breakfast in town later, not to bother about him. He closed his eyes again, but the jolt of adrenaline had already jarred his system and driven away sleep. He began to review the satisfactions—and the frustrations—of the past week.

She had been so willing, the big Swiss girl. He had found her in the back of the greenhouse, dozing, just coming down from her drugged high and eager to try something new. Silly fool! She had watched him cook up her very last kick, watched impatiently as he prepared the tiny syringe that would send her on her way, her light hair brushing his hand as she bent to see him tie off the blood flow through the artery of her arm. She had hardly protested when he jabbed her, hard, more than once in that soft flesh. He couldn't help himself, he was so excited. What did a last flash of pain matter to her, anyhow? She was gone very quickly.

It was all so satisfying. He had been careful, too—he had worn gloves, and wiped everything clean before leaving it in the dirt of the greenhouse floor. He had even thought to inject her left arm. Although she was not wearing a watch on her left wrist to guide him, he thought she was probably right-handed, as most of the population is. Yes, he wanted it to look like a self-induced death, at first. He was sure that *she* would begin to question and worry soon enough.

Ah, there was the frustration: The Swiss girl wasn't the one he wanted to punish. And since she had been an unexpected opportunity, he had not prepared a note to slip into her pocket, to be found later on her body and continue the ripple of fear that would surely grow to terror before he was finished.

He did not want to wait any longer. He had spent the night considering various plans, testing each for signs that they were just nighttime fantasies. He had to get into the school. Now he thought he knew the way.

He was familiar with the building. He had studied the outside of the school yesterday afternoon when he hiked down the slopes and walking trails from Corsetti. The huge old building that housed the Marlowe School dominated a hill two thousand meters above Lake Clemenza, overlooking Fernstaad *Dorf* below. It had nine doors. A furtive sweep around the exterior told him they were all solidly equipped with locks and bolts and grilles. All except one—the door from the kitchen. It was the last door he discovered, after circling the school.

A flight of stone steps led down from the almost hidden second-story kitchen door to a rank of large garbage pails nested in a hollow below the building. Hidden behind a thick stand of larch trees, he watched a sweating kitchen worker lug pails down the steps and empty them into the large containers in the drifted snow. The door looked newer than the building. It was wood-framed with squares of mullioned panes in its upper half. He could not see through the glass when the door was closed, but the worker had left it open. Inside was a brisk march of white-garbed kitchen assistants moving through a fog of steam. They called to each other in Italian, laughing as they carried heavy copper pots, gesticulating with ladles and giant whisks. The door had only one lock.

He would enter the building at night. If he could not pick

the lock, he would break a pane of glass and reach inside. One of Frau Breitel's thick kitchen towels would muffle the sound. He would be prepared, now that he knew where to find her. Through slits of narrow windows, he had seen the back staircase. Several flights of steps wound up from one of the heavily bolted outer doors, all the way to the top floor. He knew her room, too. He had seen her on her balcony. She was dreaming idly as she stood at the railing, looking out over the hills across the lake. It was only a glimpse; she had turned quickly and stepped inside, but he knew it was she. Just as he had known twice before when he saw her in the *Konditorei* Klaus.

Wide awake now, he jumped out of bed. Excitement and a morning need to urinate had stiffened his penis. He scurried to the bathroom, plans churning.

Fifteen minutes later, he returned to the bedroom. He was freshly shaved and showered, his fingernails scraped moon-white clean. His hair was wet and slicked back from his high temples. His eyes sparkled coldly as he knelt at the side of his bed.

Reaching under the frilled dust ruffle, he pulled out his light canvas suitcase. It was stuffed with wrinkled shirts and worn underwear. He had thought he would be leaving sooner. Now he might have to ask Frau Breitel to do his laundry. She had certainly offered often enough since he arrived. Each time, he had thanked her and declined. But the thought of having to wear dirty clothes—that was how he thought of them, though nothing was really soiled—made him wild. Yes, he would ask Frau Breitel tomorrow—if he failed again tonight.

But he would not fail. Not this time.

He dug under the crumpled shirts with squeamish distaste. A large, metal-tabbed envelope lay at the bottom. He pulled it out, closed the case, and shoved it back under the bed.

Seated at the rough pine desk near the bedroom door, he removed several pages from the envelope and smoothed them on the desktop. He wanted to lock his door, but it had no such closing; privacy was not a feature of the Breitel guest house. At least they respected his need and did not intrude too much. Briefly, he thought of wedging a chair under the doorknob, but he knew they would not enter without at least knocking.

He spread the creamy pages in front of him. There were three left. He had believed he would need only one. Now he was glad he had saved the rest. A raised insignia in shiny black ink formed an imposing crest on the upper right corner of each page. Centered at the top were shiny raised letters:

MARY A. MARLOWE
School for Girls
7557 Fernstaad

He had found the stationery that first day in the *Konditorei* Klaus, several weeks ago. He had not been in Fernstaad very long. He had seen the girls across the room, recognized the school insignia on their parkas, and moved closer. There they sat, the three of them, hunched over the large window table, giggling, noisily interrupting each other as they laughed over a letter they were composing. Sheets of stationery were scattered among the ice cream glasses and plates on the crowded table. What was so funny? What dirty girlish prank were they up to? Then a trio of teachers from the school had entered. Who knew why the girls were in such a flurry to conceal their composition? With tiny squeals, they scooped the pages off the table and into their laps. Four sheets had fluttered to the floor unnoticed, and he had retrieved them after the girls had left the Klaus. Three sheets remained.

He picked the cleanest and began to write:
"Daughters die."
Tonight.

CHAPTER
22

The joints had made Nicole and Katharyn hungry. Nicole had slipped into Katharyn's room after midnight for a smoke, but mainly to talk to her about the barone. She had been sick all week, thinking about the horror of that night with all of them together. Mookie had brought along another man, and with Katharyn there and the second man egging them on, it had been disgusting—and terrifying. Nicole did not want to do it again.

Moonlight seeped into the room. Nicole sat cross-legged at the foot of Katharyn's bed, sucking in smoke, trying to sound not too prim, trying to conceal her self-disgust. She ducked her head so that her long hair almost hid her face. See, it had gotten all too boring and messy.

Katharyn argued. She didn't mind. She found it wild and exciting. That they had both been degraded, that the sport was dangerous and threatened to get seriously out of hand at any moment, did not trouble her. If Nicole wanted to have done with it, Katharyn would go alone next week.

They had smoked two joints apiece, and Katharyn began to stroke Nicole, to calm her and change her mind. But they were both too tired to play. Without meaning to, Nicole had fallen asleep in Katharyn's bed.

Now they were uncomfortably awake. It was four-fifteen and freezing. They had flung the windows wide open to dispel the cigarette smoke, and the frigid night air filled the room. They were cold and very hungry. Neither of them had any food in their rooms. They decided to risk a furtive trip down to the kitchen. First, they'd have to wake Mindy and get her key.

The contraband key was the prized possession of the fifth-floor seniors. The school kitchen was now locked every night, ever since it was determined that Anneliese Zuecher had slipped out of the building through that door. Mindy had taken the key from Miss Grimsby's desk drawer one day while everyone was at lunch and made a copy in Fernstaad that afternoon before returning the original. It might become a pain keeping track of who had it last, but in times of desperation, it was a lifesaver. This was one of those times.

It took some persuading to convince Mindy, grumpy with sleep, to dig the key out of its hiding place. She finally did, and then, pulling on her long, fleecy yellow bathrobe, she decided to join them.

"We'll need your flashlight, too," Nicole said.

"Pests!" Mindy said, but she grabbed it from a drawer and followed Nicole and Katharyn to the door.

The fifth-floor corridor was dark and quiet. One dim light shone its jaundiced glow over the bathroom door near the end of the empty hall. The steady *thuck-tock* of the tall standing clock was the only sound. They peered out into the shadows.

Katharyn stepped cautiously into the hall, with Nicole close behind her. Grumbling, Mindy tightened her robe against the cold. "This isn't worth it!" she hissed, but she scurried after the others.

When they were almost opposite the bathroom door, Mindy stopped and clutched Nicole's shoulder.

"Listen!"

"Oh, Jesu!" Nicole said.

"Sleepless!" Katharyn said. Her face was pale in the frame of her sleek dark hair. "The bastard's coming up the front steps!"

They jostled each other as they flew into the bathroom.

The unmistakable lumpish tread of the night watchman sounded from the hall outside—a heavy shuffle coming closer and closer, like a sound from a horror film.

The girls dived into the cubicles, locked the doors, and

plumped down on the closed seats, tugging their feet up out of sight.

The footsteps stopped outside. The bathroom door swished open. A bright beam of light threw sharp white angles on the floor inside the cubicles. A softer flare lit the ceiling. The light swept back and forth along the floor and paused. Then, slowly, it backed away and went out as the bathroom door opened and closed again with a sigh.

"Don't move!" Mindy commanded softly in the dark. "Wait till he's gone."

Outside in the hall, Sleepless sighed, echoing the closing door. So, what was going on? Some new mischief? He had never caught *three* of them before. He was sure he heard muffled giggling inside the cubicles. What were they up to in the middle of the night?

He turned and started to clump down the hall toward the back stairs. He did not understand young girls; he never had. Why were they always laughing and shrieking? Or else crying noisily? He found it easier to accept their sadness than their hilarity. Life was most often lonely and full of grief, he knew—like for that poor child who had been killed skiing two weeks ago. Such a tragedy! And the crazy one, poisoning herself to death just for fun. *Schrecklich!* He had helped carry her hastily packed trunk down the back stairs only yesterday, as girls screamed through the hall, "Man on the floor!" They were laughing, even then, when only the day before they had been draped in gloom. Yes, he could understand their grief, but he was baffled by their merriment. *Mein lieber Gott*, what was so endlessly funny?

Well, he would be especially alert tonight. Who knew what those three were up to? He hoped they would not make some kind of mess, something he might be blamed for not preventing. He hoped there would not be more trouble. God forbid, another accident!

He started down the steps. The sharp beam of his flashlight swept over the banister supports, making shadowy arms beckon on the stairwell walls. He muttered to himself as he descended. First, he would finish his rounds. Then he would come back up and check the fifth floor again.

* * *

Felice Grimsby could not sleep. Her bed had become a prison where dark thoughts trapped and assaulted her. She felt that control was being wrenched from her by some force she could not comprehend.

How could anything so monstrous have happened to her girls, to *her*? She was so protective of them. Her mind resisted the reality. The death of two senior students in such a short time—and one in such a shocking manner. Drugs! It stunned her that someone had so corrupted one of her girls. Now, two of them dead! No, it must be some kind of grisly mistake. She would think of other matters, of her daily responsibilities. She must. The school, the girls, needed her to be strong.

She lay in the dark and concentrated on breathing evenly.

Still, Felice Grimsby could not sleep. For almost a week, her nights had been a torment of insomnia. This was unusual for her, after a lifetime of being a heavy sleeper, but she was not going to worry about herself. That wouldn't help. She did not believe in sleeping pills. She believed in self-discipline. If she could not will herself into sleep, she knew that, eventually, her body would overcome her agitated spirit and seize the rest it needed. Meanwhile, she would not fight it. She turned on her bedside lamp and reached for her reading glasses. The leather-cased clock on her night table said 4:45. Wearily, she lifted a book from a small stack next to the clock and opened it to the marker. The *Lettres Choisies de Mme. de Sévigné*, had been a favorite of hers since her school days. She would find a temporary refuge from her troubled thoughts in the seventeenth century with that brilliant, aristocratic woman of letters. She buried herself in the French text.

A thump sounded from the corridor below. It came from the foot of the tower stairs that led to her rooms. Or possibly from the back staircase opposite them.

Miss Grimsby's tower apartment was reached from the end of the floor. None of the girls, nor Miss Temple, would pass that way at night. It must be Johann, the night watchman. He must have dropped something.

Miss Grimsby listened intently. This past week, she had

grown used to hearing Johann's heavy steps coming down the hall. She wondered how she had missed him tonight. She must have become too absorbed in the marquise's delicious court gossip, that was the explanation.

Another sound drifted up the tower stairs. Muffled giggling and the sibilance of shushing. Alert now, Miss Grimsby closed her book on its marker and sat up. Her breath came lightly as she strained to hear.

What now?

The rustling continued below. She swung her feet into her slippers and pulled on the quilted bathrobe that lay at the foot of her bed. Visiting between rooms was strictly forbidden after lights-out, and this sounded unmistakably worse. More than one girl was down there, at the end of the hall near the back stairs. The penalty for leaving the floor and roaming the building at night was a term's suspension, if they were caught.

Then another thought struck her: What if they were trying to sneak out of the building, *like Anneliese!*

Electrified, she rushed across the carpet from her bedroom into her sitting room. Normally, she would not have interfered. It was the teacher on each floor who was responsible, and she had total confidence in Carla Temple. But nothing seemed normal anymore. This might be simple mischief-making. But it also might be something much more dangerous. The girls would have to be stopped. If she caught any of them on the back stairs, she would have to suspend them. They'd probably miss graduating next term. She hated the thought, but she was driven by fear. And, besides, the rules were for everyone's protection. Lenience in anything other than extraordinary circumstances would compromise the discipline of the whole school.

She seized the doorknob to let herself out of her suite at the top of the tower stairs.

Then she heard the door of Miss Temple's room open below.

Like Miss Grimsby, Carla had been unable to sleep. The noise of the girls in the hall signaled trouble. Her responsibility. Grabbing her cane, she hurried out into the hall. She saw a faint light disappear quickly down the back stairs.

Damn those girls! What were they up to now? Something sick, like Anneliese? Had they forgotten so quickly?

Furious, she leaned on her cane and limped down the corridor.

Even if it were only innocent foolishness, they could get themselves suspended for the rest of the semester. Didn't they want to finish and be on their way? Most of the seniors were going on to college. Couldn't they understand what suspension from Marlowe now could do to their plans? God, what ninnies! Okay, which ones were about to screw up? Mindy, she bet herself. Maybe Nicole, or Bianca, too. What in the world were they up to, making such a racket in the middle of the night? Fortunately, Miss Grimsby was a deep sleeper. If Carla could catch the girls before Sleepless or one of the other teachers did, she would hustle them back to their rooms and give them all hell in the morning.

She stood at the top of the stairs and looked down. The fast-vanishing light flickered two flights below. In between was darkness. Carla pulled a small flashlight from the pocket of her bathrobe and tried to juggle both the cane and the light in one hand. This isn't going to be easy, she thought. She transferred the cane and the flashlight to her right hand and leaned heavily on the banister with her left. Placing the cane on the first step, she started down.

At the top of the tower stairs, Miss Grimsby relaxed her grip on the doorknob. Good. She would not have to interfere now and possibly challenge Miss Temple's authority. That feisty young teacher would handle the situation with intelligence and a minimum of fuss. Miss Grimsby would be spared a great unpleasantness, and so would the girls.

She returned to her bed and to the Marquise de Sévigné. She would stay awake reading until she was sure that Carla Temple had everything under control.

Standing in the dark behind the open door of the library, Sleepless watched through the crack as two girls padded quickly by, shushing each other as they ran. He could not tell who they were, but he knew where they were headed. For the kitchen, of course! It would not be the first time a student had raided Herr Blumen's freezer, although he had never caught anyone. Well, tonight they were out of luck. The kitchen door was locked tight. He had checked it himself.

Should he step out right now and scare them back upstairs, or wait till they discovered the locked door and returned quietly to their rooms? Scaring them would be fun, but he did not care to listen to their shrill, girlish screeching. Others would hear and come, and there would be a nasty fuss. Still, he should not let them run around the building like this. He could find himself in trouble if something happened.

He stood there, vacillating. Just as he was about to turn on his flashlight and challenge them, a third girl ran shivering past the library door. Ah, yes—*three* of them, he remembered. What a lot of noise they would make if they saw him! He would wait.

There was a rustle of whispering, then a faint clink of metal on metal. Sleepless scratched the stubble on his chin. *Himmel!* Did they have a key?

He heard a tumbler clink, then the sound of a door opening. Now, *here* was trouble. He stepped out into the hall. It was empty. The door to the kitchen was open, still swinging on its hinges at the end of the corridor. Sleepless took a deep breath and hurried toward it.

Carla had tracked the girls down to the second floor and seen them turn to the right. By the time she reached the landing, she was exhausted. Her leg throbbed terribly. She rested for a minute, leaning against the banister. That was enough exercise for one day—or night. She would take the lift back up. As soon as she caught up with those idiots who were so determined to get themselves in hot water. They must have gone to the library. What irony! It was a constant effort to get them there for their schoolwork. What was the sudden attraction, at almost five in the morning? Well, it didn't matter. They could not get past her now.

She would not give them any boring lecture tonight. Just

make sure they got back to their rooms as quickly and quietly as possible. By morning, they would already have anticipated what she would say to them, and she could make it short and sweet. Their own guilt would do the rest. She only hoped they would not be upset about making her follow them on her cane down those five flights of stairs. That extra bit of guilt she would not accept from them.

She moved slowly, painfully, down the corridor. The library door was open, but so, to her amazement, was the door to the kitchen. How had they managed *that* trick? Still, it made more sense than a raid on the library. Anyhow, hungry or not, their little escapade was finished.

Suddenly, she heard a crash and the tinkle of broken glass.

A girl screamed.

A man grunted heavily, *"Gott im Himmel!"*

Two of the girls ran out of the kitchen into the hall, panting and swearing, their eyes wide. Nicole was first, Katharyn close behind her.

"Jesus, Miss Temple!" Nicole cried when she saw Carla.

"Get upstairs, *quickly!*" Carla said.

"Someone. . . .broke in!" Nicole gasped. "In the kitchen!"

"What?"

"From outside!" Katharyn said.

"Mindy's in there—and Sleepless!" Nicole said.

Carla stared at Nicole for a second, then took a step toward the kitchen. She almost collided with Mindy, who burst out of the door, screaming, "Someone's coming—"

"Move it!" Carla ordered, jabbing her finger at the stair-case.

Katharyn and Nicole scrambled for the stairs.

A violent crash rang from the kitchen, the clanging of heavy pots and pans tumbling to the floor . . . the sound of a body falling. A man groaned.

"Sleepless!" Mindy said. She hesitated at Carla's side.

"I said, *go!*" Carla gripped Mindy's shoulders, turned her toward the stairs, and shoved.

"No!" Mindy moved back and stood, heaving, next to Carla.

Carla glared at her in frustration. Then she realized that her cane was vibrating on the carpeted floor, the tremor in her arm traveling its length.

"Idiot!" she whispered.

Mindy shook her head again and moved closer.

Then there was silence. Only the rasping of their breath. Their eyes were fixed on the kitchen door. They both shook uncontrollably, and blood pounded in their ears. But they heard no further sound from the kitchen.

At last, Carla moved. Placing a trembling hand on Mindy's shoulder, she began to back down the corridor, pulling the frightened girl with her. Step by stealthy step, they passed the library, moved along the rows of locked office doors, past the glass-walled dining room on their opposite side, listening fearfully.

The lift was there on the second floor. *Thank God!* Carla signaled Mindy with a silencing finger across her lips and slowly started to open the door. It creaked. She gritted her teeth and sucked in air. Tugging the door wide, she pushed Mindy inside and hobbled in after her. She punched the button for the fifth floor. Slowly, the inner door slid closed.

They stared at each other, wide-eyed, as the lift rose. Neither spoke.

When the door slid open at the fifth floor, Mindy raced out and held the outer door for Carla.

"They were outside the kitchen!" Mindy whispered, gasping. "On the steps."

"You're sure?"

"We heard them break the window in the door—"

"How many?"

"Don't know! Sleepless came in—"

"Go to your room," Carla said.

"What are you going to do?"

"Now!"

Moving as quickly as she could, Carla steered Mindy to her door and waited till she was inside. Then she swung herself in long, rolling strides down the hall. Breathless, she reached her own room and closed the door behind her. She hopped the last few steps across her sitting room, leaning on the cane with both hands, and sank into the chair at her desk. Her hand was shaking violently as she seized the phone and dialed. It seemed like ages before she heard the answer at the other end of the line:

"*Kantonspolizei.*"

CHAPTER
23

The building was ominously quiet. Nothing was moving. The minutes flashed by silently on Carla's digital clock. She was conscious of a sweaty itch all over her body. The feeling grew into acute discomfort until, at last, she couldn't stand it anymore. She hurried into her bathroom for a thirty-second shower, then flung on jeans and a heavy sweater without bothering with underwear. She sat tensely in her sitting room, straining to hear any strange sounds in the hall, listening for the crunch of tires outside. Needles of pain stabbed her leg, and she massaged it with trepidation.

Finally, she heard cars speeding up the road from town. She grabbed a ski parka, just in case she had to direct the police around the outside of the school. Leaning heavily on her cane, she left her room and took the lift downstairs.

The *Kantonspolizei* car swung into the courtyard first. It was followed immediately by the ambulance from the Leitner Clinic. When Carla opened the front door, four men were leaping from the vehicles. Light snow drifted down; the ground and the cars were already thickly dusted in white.

It was shortly before six. The sky was still the indigo of night, though a faint glow showed on the horizon. Most of the school was still asleep. In the dark predawn, the men rushed up the front steps. One medic rolled a wheeled stretcher; the second carried cases of equipment.

"Corporal Trivella, ma'am," the first officer inside identified himself. "Miss Temple?"

Carla nodded. Without speaking, she led them to the back, into the kitchen.

The sight was shocking.

Felice Grimsby was kneeling on the floor, surrounded by a junkyard of giant copper pots and splintered wood. Dish towels and curtains fluttered in the wind blowing through the shattered window in the kitchen's outer door. Snow had built up at its base. Miss Grimsby was cradling the inert body of the night watchman, stretched out in the chaotic mess of the floor. Her quilted robe glistened with blood.

"He's alive, he's breathing," she said dully as the men rushed in. "I haven't moved him—or touched anything too much."

"*K-k-k-k*. . . ." Sleepless rasped.

Miss Grimsby looked around and saw Carla.

"Oh, thank goodness! I thought something had happened to you, too!"

Gently, Carla helped her to her feet. The police and the men from the ambulance took over.

"How did you get here?" Carla asked the headmistress. "Do you want them to give you something?" She was alarmed at the woman's paleness.

"I'm fine," Miss Grimsby said, waving away the suggestion.

They stood together, Carla clutching her parka for comfort, and watched the medics work over Sleepless. The policemen ranged around the kitchen, making notes as they checked the damage in the room. Trivella, the senior officer, approached the two huddled women.

"A few questions, Frau Grimsby?"

"In my office," she said. "Come with me, Carla. They'll want to talk to both of us." She gave a brief glance at the night watchman, at the medics manipulating him—bracing, splinting, inserting tubes, trussing him, like busy chefs preparing a side of beef. Then she motioned for the policemen to follow her. She was steady and erect in her soiled robe, steadier than Carla, as they walked down the hall.

Inside her office, Miss Grimsby opened the drapes covering the tall windows. The sky was growing lighter, the snow tapering off. She stood silently looking out for a moment.

A second *Kantonspolizei* car pulled into the courtyard, the whirring of its tires muffled by the snow on the ground.

"I'll bring them in," Carla said. She left the office and headed back to the front door.

Somewhere in the building, a phone rang faintly. Who would be calling at this hour? she wondered. The ringing continued, unanswered, as she walked the length of the corridor. It must be the school's night line. It was set to ring at the switchboard in the secretary's office, and there was an extension in Miss Grimsby's tower rooms. Neither phone was attended now.

Carla opened the front door. Sergeant Hans Kellhorn strode inside, rubbing his hands briskly.

"They're in Miss Grimsby's office," she told him.

"I know the way," he said. He walked past her toward the corridor. "Someone should answer that phone."

"Of course," Carla said. She detoured to the switchboard. Yes, it was the night line. She lifted the receiver.

"Marlowe School," she said, almost a question.

"Hello? Carla? Is that *you?*"

"Who—Eric?"

"Thank God I got you!" Eric said. His relief was evident, and it surprised her.

"What are you doing on this line?"

"I've been calling your direct number. No answer. You sound awful. Are you all right?"

"Yes, of course," she said. "Why—what made you call me? It's so early. We've had a terrible accident here. Did you know?"

"Yes, I heard. Your headmistress called for an ambulance. Something about the night watchman. They told me she mentioned your name, too. I thought *you* had been hurt."

"No, no, I'm okay. Scared stiff, and the leg is pretty wobbly. But I'm all right."

"What a relief!" Eric said. "Sorry, but I've been imagining all sorts of things. I've been terribly worried about you. What happened there?"

Carla told him. About the girls in the hall, the trek down the dark flights of stairs, the crash in the kitchen . . . and Sleepless, and Miss Grimsby, and the police, and the blood all over. . . . It rushed out in a babble, and Eric had to interrupt her several times to understand.

"What about the watchman?" he asked finally. "Is he—did the medics say anything?"

"He's alive, I think. Unconscious."

"What about your leg?"

"Hurts, but it's working."

"Is the ambulance still there?"

"I haven't heard any cars leave yet," Carla said. "Why?"

"I want you to come to the clinic. Now. So I can have a look at you, too. Come in with the ambulance. Will you do that, Carla?"

She stiffened at the phone. "I don't need to be babied. I'm just a little sore, but otherwise, it's no worse than your exercises." It *was* worse, but she didn't want to admit it. Not to Eric. "Besides, they need me here. I'll have to see the police first. Where are you, anyhow? At the clinic? Already?"

"Yes. I just got here," Eric said. "And I want to check you as soon as possible. Can you get in later this morning?"

"Maybe. I'll see. Listen, it's nice of you to worry about me, but I'm a big girl, and I can ask for help when I need it." She caught herself. "Oh, damn! That sounded all wrong. Forgive me! I'm just upset."

"Upset, and a little nutty," Eric said, but his voice was patient. "Don't be stubborn, now. Come let me have a look at that leg. I don't make house calls anymore, you know."

In spite of herself, Carla laughed. "Okay, I'll come as soon as I can get away. Promise. And thanks for caring, Eric. I mean that."

She felt better after she hung up, but exhaustion was creeping up on her. She limped slowly back to Miss Grimsby's office, wishing she could just get into bed and sleep for a week.

Miss Grimsby was seated behind her desk. Most of her bloodied robe was mercifully out of sight. When she saw the pain in Carla's eyes, the effort it took to control her steps, the headmistress became concerned—and quite firm. Carla must go immediately to the clinic and have Dr. Leitner or someone see to her leg. It was only sensible. She was to go in the ambulance right away. If there was nothing wrong, she'd be back in time for her first class. And the *Kantonspolizei* could talk to her later. Miss Grimsby insisted. No arguing. Just go.

Two against one, Carla thought. But the way she was feeling, it seemed like a good idea. She picked up her parka, which she had left in Miss Grimsby's office, and allowed Corporal Trivella to escort her to the waiting ambulance. He helped her into the front, and she was grateful to be spared having to sit with the unconscious man already lying in the back.

On the road down to Fernstaad, they passed a third *Kantonspolizei* car racing up to the school. Carla recognized the scowling bulk of Inspector Neumayer wedged into the front passenger seat.

So, who's minding the store? she wondered, as she watched the sun rise through sparkling motes of snowflakes that sprinkled down on the sleeping town.

A storm of activity erupted as soon as they pulled up at the emergency entrance of the Leitner Clinic. The medic in back with Sleepless jumped out before the ambulance stopped rolling. More people in white coats rushed from the building. An attendant held a plastic IV bag high in the air as he ran beside the stretcher. When Sleepless was wheeled through the doors, Carla saw Eric, waiting just inside. He huddled over the stretcher, his hands moving over the still form, gave hasty orders, and disappeared. He had not noticed her, bundled in her parka in the front seat of the ambulance.

How easily he takes charge! How tall and strong he

looked—and calm, almost loving, as he touched the unconscious man. Carla flushed with the stirring of an unwelcome emotion. With disappointment, too. She probably wouldn't see him now. Some other doctor—maybe even Dr. Leitner, if he was there—would come to look her over. Eric would be too occupied with Sleepless. No, she would not see him, after all—and she hadn't realized till now that she had been looking forward to it.

She climbed wearily out of the ambulance. The medics had left her alone to attend to their emergency, knowing that hers was a more or less routine visit to the clinic. It was more fatigue than anything, she hoped, but she was aware that it was considerably more than routine. Her leg reminded her by buckling slightly as she walked inside.

A snappy nurse led her to an examining room and told her that someone would be in to see her very soon.

Carla tugged off her parka and let it drop onto a chair. She sat on top of it and looked around tiredly. The room was a chilly white; there was no place to rest her eyes. They burned and teared at the same time. She rubbed them and yawned with deep gulps. The examining table was rock hard, she knew from long experience, but what the hell! She hopped over to it, lifted herself up, and stretched out with a groan.

Ten minutes later, the nurse opened the door.

"Dr. Sunderson knows you're here. He'll be in as soon—"

She saw that Carla was asleep and breathing deeply. She backed silently out of the room.

"Soon" turned into another half hour. The nurse had advised Dr. Sunderson that his young patient was sleeping peacefully, in no apparent pain. When Eric was finally able to leave Johann Bächli to the care of others, he first changed out of his spattered white coat into a fresh one before entering the antiseptic examining room where Carla waited.

He thought he had never seen a sweeter sight.

Carla lay on the examining table, one arm hanging limply over the side. Her head was slightly turned into the cushion of her tousled black curls, her lips parted in sleep like a rosy flowerlet. Her heavy white ski sweater rose and fell with gentle, rhythmic breathing. She looked impossibly beautiful and vulnerable. He stared down at her, tenderness relaxing his strong features. Then he felt a flash of agonized memory. Yes, he had seen that sight before, many times. When he would tiptoe into his little Jenny's room at night and watch the sleeping child with a mixture of awe and fierce possessiveness. He shook his head. He had promised himself long ago that he would not torture himself with the unchangeable. And Carla was not a child, but a beautiful and desirable woman. There was nothing weak or dependent about her; she would never need him as Jenny had. Still, looking down at her, he had a wild sense of possession, like someone who has captured a sleeping creature in its helplessness.

"Carla?" he said softly. She smelled of fresh talcum powder.

"Mmmmmmm." She turned her head away, eyes still closed.

"Wake up, honey." He lifted her hand to relieve the pooling of blood in her fingertips. It was so soft! He smiled at her with pleasure. "Time to shine."

"Mmmmmmm . . . Michael?" she mumbled. Her body stirred sensually in sleep.

Eric released her hand and stepped back. *Who? Michael?* He felt an irrational moment of jealousy before he stopped himself. What had he been thinking? He had no rights here. Carla's life, past or present, belonged to her. Why wouldn't she be sharing it with someone? That would certainly explain her lack of response to him. Fritz Leitner was crazy to encourage him. He'd tell him the next time the subject came up—if it ever did. He'd try to prevent that. End of discussion. He was a physician and he was here to do a job.

He moved back to the table.

"Such laziness!" he said cheerfully. "Sleeping the whole morning away. Come on, Carla, time to get up!"

Carla awoke, momentarily disoriented. When she saw Eric standing over her, she realized where she was—and why. She sat up on the table, groaning with stiffness, and slid her legs over the edge.

"Hello, there." She smiled at him dreamily and couldn't

repress a deep yawn. Then she was suddenly wide awake and peppy. "Well, here I am, just as the doctor ordered. Hello, Doctor. Am I cured? Can I go now?"

"How are you feeling?"

"Exhausted." She rubbed the back of her neck. Worry crossed her face. "Oh, how is Sleepless—Johann Bächli? Will he be all right?"

"He's fine, for the moment," Eric answered evasively. He crossed the room and picked up Carla's charts from the medical cabinet. Carla noticed that he was walking stiffly, favoring one leg.

"What happened to *you?* Are you limping?" she asked.

"What? Oh, this." He slapped his leg. "I was in Sils Mariana and decided to take some skiing lessons—where no one knows me. Pride, I guess. I haven't mastered the three-point landing yet."

"No kidding! For a minute, I thought you were mimicking me," she said with a twinkle. "You wouldn't tease, would you?"

"Never! Okay, let me have a look at you now. I'll want some new X rays, but first, I'll see what you've done to yourself. Stand up and slip off those tight jeans."

Carla lifted herself off the table and undid the button at her waist. She started to pull down the zipper, then stopped with a gasp. She wasn't wearing anything underneath! The hasty shower that morning, the way she had flung on her clothes without thinking, came back to her in a flood of confusion. Her hands fumbled, her face flamed. The right words wouldn't come.

"What's the matter? Zipper stuck?" Eric asked. "Hey, what's this? You look embarrassed! Come on, I'm a doctor. I've seen ladies' undies before."

Carla ducked her head. "No undies," she muttered, furious at herself. "I was in a state this morning. I just threw on anything. Forgot the amenities. Look, why don't I just come back later. I'm fine, really."

Eric hesitated. "I'll send the nurse in with a gown," he said. "If Dr. Leitner's here, he can look at you, if you'd be more comfortable. Just don't go away. The sooner someone examines that leg, the better. Trust me.''

Carla watched the door close behind him. *Trust me.* She considered the phrase. *Actually, I think I do.* It amused her that Eric had looked even more embarrassed than she felt. And it worried her, too, that she was finding him more and more appealing.

She left her sweater on and carefully wrapped the prim white gown the nurse brought her twice around her waist. Her pulse quickened when she heard the knock on the door.

Dr. Fritz Leitner entered, wagging a scolding finger at her. Despite her disappointment that it was not Eric, she was relieved to see her old, dependable friend. And elated when he finished his examination half an hour later.

"I could kiss you!" Carla cried. "I could simply hug you to death!"

"Oh, ho!" Dr. Leitner said, beaming with flustered delight. "And how do I deserve that?"

"No further damage, you said. Just a little muscle strain. You're sure, aren't you?" She swung both legs out from the examining table to compare their minute differences, and then let them dangle again from the edge. Worry and relief chased each other across her face. "It feels so awful. But you meant it, didn't you?"

"Don't think I give you permission to do that again. It isn't even two weeks since you stopped wearing the brace. I expect you to be more sensible, child. So many flights of stairs! What were you thinking of?"

"Other responsibilities," she said quietly. "They seemed more important at the time." She tugged at the high neck of her bulky white ski sweater. The room was much too hot, and she was much too anxious.

"So," Dr. Leitner said. "You have to use your own judgment, of course, but I want you to realize that you have been very fortunate. I don't think there is any further harm to the leg, but there could have been."

He turned his back and flipped through the heavy sheets of X rays he had taken fifteen minutes earlier. He had already looked at them outside the examining room and given Carla the happy news. But now she squeezed her hands into tense fists, fearful that the elderly doctor would spot some new problem he had overlooked.

"Hmmm, hmmm," Dr. Leitner sang tunelessly as he clipped one of the thick, dark X rays to a small view box near the table. "No, nothing changed. Good, yes, that is very good." He removed one sheet and began studying another. "Have you stopped breathing, Carla?" he said over his shoulder. "For that, I give you permission."

Carla laughed. "May I get dressed now?" She reached for her jeans, which she had left folded at the foot of the table.

There was another knock at the door.

"Yes, come in," Dr. Leitner called. "Ah, Eric. Here, have a look at these." And to Carla: "I just want Dr. Sunderson to see how pretty your bones look, even if you are not treating them very kindly."

"Hello, again." Eric gave her a brief, professional nod and looked up at the fuzzy skeletal section that glowed from the light of the view box.

Carla felt herself tense again. *Damn! I thought I already passed that test. Don't let him find anything!*

The two men put their heads together and conferred over the X rays. Carla was aware that she was staring at Eric's back, admiring the flare of his broad shoulders. A swimmer's shoulders, an athlete's body, almost. Heat flushed her cheeks, and she looked down. Her bare thighs looked terribly white all of a sudden. With what she hoped was artful casualness, she draped her jeans across her legs. A small chuckle escaped as she considered her belated modesty and her not-very-subtle subconscious longings.

Neither man paid any attention to her.

"I'm satisfied," Eric said to Dr. Leitner. "How about you, Fritz?" The older man nodded. Eric crossed to the examining table. "Mind if I have a look?" He leaned down and pressed his strong fingers into Carla's left calf, causing her to wince.

"Tender, hunh? It'll feel worse tomorrow, I'm sorry to tell you, but there's nothing to worry about."

Carla clutched her jeans tighter to her lap. "Um, Eric—?" she began. Even with Dr. Leitner across the room, she wanted to say something light, something graceful, about why she had refused his invitation last week. But what? Why had she put him off so coldly, even going so far as to arrange an invitation for him to the von Wetzlars, when she didn't really think he'd enjoy himself there? She tried again. "Eric—?"

"Relax," Eric said. "It's Dr. Sunderson today." She looked down at him, puzzled. He broke into a warm, crooked grin. "I'm kidding, of course. But you look so jumpy, I just want to reassure you. I'm not going to bite, you know."

Too bad, she thought, and grinned back at him. But Eric had already straightened and was returning to Dr. Leitner and the X rays.

"You can dress now," Dr. Leitner said, "and come to my office. I want to give you a prescription—"

"And the rest of that lecture you started, right?"

"I'll leave that to your compatriot—yes, Eric? You speak her language. Maybe you can convince her to show more respect for all my hard work on that leg."

"Do my best. If you have a minute, Fritz, I'd like to talk to you about Bächli."

"Please, how is he?" Carla asked. "May I see him before I go?"

"Not today," Eric answered. "I'm afraid he's not well enough for visitors, still not coherent. He wouldn't even know you were there. It's better that he just rest."

Carla caught the slight shake of his head as he looked over at Dr. Leitner.

"Poor Sleepless," she said.

"Come see me as soon as you are dressed," Dr. Leitner said. "I want you to make another appointment for later this week."

With a brief nod at Carla, Eric followed the older man out of the examining room and closed the door behind him.

Carla exhaled a sigh of relief and hopped off the table. She dressed quickly and presented herself in Dr. Leitner's office, wondering if Eric would be there, too.

He wasn't.

Later, on her way out of the clinic, she looked around for him, but did not see him again.

CHAPTER
24

Inspector Neumayer strode up the front steps of the Marlowe School. It was his second trip of the day, and he was furious and frustrated. More trouble at Marlowe, and it could have been prevented. The one door at the school that was not wired with hidden alarms at night had been the target of prowlers. He had been very sharp with Felice that morning, but her own distress had checked his anger. Yes, the door had been newly replaced; yes, she had planned to have it wired; yes, she had waited too long. She should have insisted that the locksmith and electrician come immediately, but no one had ever tried to break into the school before.

It was so unnecessary, this new disruption, following so closely after the calamity of the students' deaths. They preyed on him, like a rat gnawing. Especially the death of Sophie Karas. Something was terribly wrong there. As for Anneliese Zuecher, his men would work overtime until they found out who had been supplying her with drugs. Schoolchildren, for God's sake! Horrible!

He ground out his cigarette in the slush at the top step. His eyes were red from lack of sleep, and grumpiness puddled in his belly. He always felt that way when he was ripped from a dream into which Margarethe had come whispering and laughing. She came to him so seldom now. The six o'clock call from Sergeant Kellhorn had sent her dancing beyond reach of his memory, and he had awakened with animal alertness. By the time the car brought him to Marlowe, the ambulance had already come and gone, passing him on the road up to the school. He had looked over the damage quickly, then left for the clinic to see about the night watchman. Maybe *he* could tell them something.

What old Bächli had mumbled at him in his stupor had been even more confusing than the break-in itself.

Now he was back at Marlowe for a more careful study of the situation.

Neumayer paused outside the front door and checked its wiring, even though he knew his men had been sweeping the building thoroughly all morning for other potential breach points. He grunted with grudging satisfaction and turned to scan the front grounds. The air was crisp and frosty. The early morning snowfall had washed the grounds a bright blue-white that twinkled ravishingly in the afternoon sun. Beautiful, he thought, and traitorous. It had obliterated all outside tracks of the break-in.

Below, in the school courtyard, two other *Kantonspolizei* cars waited next to his, one of them Kellhorn's. He hoped his abrasive sergeant was not antagonizing Felice. Nothing could be accomplished with bullying or impatience.

Inside the main hall, groups of young girls hurried back and forth during the afternoon break between classes. To Neumayer, they seemed visibly disturbed, hushed and unusually serious. He stopped at the open door of Miss Grimsby's secretary's office and announced his arrival.

"She's in with Sergeant Kellhorn and Madame Guinet right now," Lina told him. "She said to send you in as soon as you get here."

Neumayer removed his heavy down jacket and laid it on the bench outside Lina's office. Then he crossed the hall and tapped on Miss Grimsby's door. Without waiting for an answer, he entered.

An angular, grey-haired woman sat at the edge of the leather couch, waving her hands excitedly. ". . . always such a crashing and banging about below," she was complaining. "They have no consideration, those in the kitchen. I ask and ask to be installed on a higher floor, Madame. Who can sleep with always that clanging and banging so early in the morning?''

"Rudi, come in, please," Miss Grimsby said. Worry imprinted deep creases in her forehead. "How is he? Did you see him?''

Neumayer raised a hand to postpone answering and nodded slightly.

Hans Kellhorn was tucked into a corner of the big leather couch facing Miss Grimsby's desk, scribbling quick notes in his spiral-ringed book. He turned to his chief and made a slight gesture of rising before he returned his attention to the irate woman seated next to him. Mme. Guinet stopped her tirade abruptly and squinted at Neumayer.

"Madame Guinet, have you met Inspector Neumayer of the Fernstaad *Kantonspolizei*?" Miss Grimsby performed her introduction. "Rudi, this is Madame Guinet, our French teacher. Her rooms are on the third floor, opposite the back staircase. It seems that she heard the break-in this morning, or at least what followed after, when—"

"Every morning, it is not any different," Mme. Guinet interrupted. "That bedlam from the kitchen!" She pointed her irritation at Neumayer, even as she extended her hand to shake his. "I am telling this to Kalman here—"

"Kellhorn."

"But I do not think he believes me. He should pass a night with me and see for himself."

Neumayer caught the brief twinkle in Felice Grimsby's eye, but suppressed his own amusement. He settled into the couch on the other side of Mme. Guinet, polite attentiveness on his face. She was a tall, rather handsome woman, very much like his own mother. She was doused with violet cologne, and the heavy scent rose to cloud Miss Grimsby's office. Her white-streaked hair was rolled around an old-fashioned rat to form an untidy halo around her head. It was the way his mother had worn her hair, with wisps straggling out to catch the light and create a hazy aura. But there the resemblance ended. Mme. Guinet's small brown eyes were ferret sharp, and now they pierced him with anger. Her back to Kellhorn, she repeated for Neumayer her story of endless imposition and interrupted sleep caused by the inconsideration and rudeness of Herr Blumen, the chef, and his noisy kitchen staff.

"So it seemed no different, nothing unusual this morning?" Neumayer asked. He cast an uneasy glance at Hans Kellhorn, who had risen to pace the room. So touchy, that young man, Neumayer thought.

Mme. Guinet shrugged her reply. "Perhaps worse, who can say? Me, I am so used to the suffering. If it is terrible, so then it is sometimes *more* terrible. They are such clumsies—"

"*Was* it worse?"

Mme. Guinet puffed out air from between puckered, thin lips. "Yes, I think, maybe. But not so that I thought I must do something about it."

"What *did* you do?"

"I tried to sleep again." She raised her eyebrows at Miss Grimsby across the room. "As always."

"And did you?"

"*Certainement!* How else shall I be able to perform through the day with never enough sleep? I have adjusted myself."

"So you didn't think anyone was trying to break into the school?"

"Ah, *no!*"

Miss Grimsby rose from her desk. "Thank you, Madame Guinet. I am sorry we have had to interrupt your classes—"

"I have warned those girls that no one is to pass without they know the *subjonctif*—"

"Yes, of course. If Herren Neumayer and Kellhorn have no further questions?" They shook their heads. "Please return to your lessons." She walked the older woman to the door. "We can talk later about changing your suite to a higher floor. Maybe one of the fourth-floor apartments would be better. . . ."

When the door had closed behind Mme. Guinet, Miss Grimsby returned to the two men.

"I'm sorry. She's really an excellent teacher; her students are years ahead of their level. She's just—well, self-absorbed most of the time. She wasn't much help, I'm afraid."

Sergeant Kellhorn sank into the couch again and flicked at his trousers with annoyance.

"Please, Rudi," Miss Grimsby said, "how is Johann?"

"We don't know yet. I was at the clinic this morning—"

"Did you see him?"

"Only briefly. Dr. Leitner said he's out of immediate danger, but they won't know for some time how extensive the head injuries are. They've done a CAT scan. Nothing showed, but that doesn't mean there hasn't been serious damage to the brain. It could show up anytime."

"Poor Johann." Miss Grimsby sighed.

Neumayer turned to Kellhorn. "That's Johann Bächli, Hans. The night watchman here."

"It's already in my notes," Kellhorn said. "I arrived this morning while they were putting him in the ambulance."

"Was he able to talk?" Miss Grimsby asked Neumayer.

"Not—coherently." He shrugged out the word. "Some of what he said coincides with what we've already learned. The rest is hallucination. I think he is still delirious, and may remain that way for quite a while. Dr. Leitner couldn't be more specific about how long."

"I'll go see him later today," Miss Grimsby said.

"I don't think you should, Felice. Dr. Leitner was very annoyed at me for staying as long as I did. He probably won't even let you in."

"Fritz Leitner is an old friend. He'll understand, I'm sure. Johann has no family here in Fernstaad. I feel responsible— *I'm* his family."

Kellhorn cleared his throat. "Is there anything I should add to the files, sir?"

"Yes, what did Johann tell you?" Miss Grimsby prompted.

The story had been whispered to Neumayer in gasps by the bruised man. Sunk in his hospital pillows and tethered to hissing, flashing machines, he had plucked weakly at Neumayer's hand as he told his disoriented tale.

"He says he followed three girls down the hall and into the kitchen early this morning," Neumayer began. "They had a key to unlock the door."

"We know that," Miss Grimsby said ruefully.

"Yes, of course. He says they were carrying a large trunk."

"What?" Kellhorn's pencil hovered over his notebook.

"And Sophie Karas was lying on top of it."

"Oh, my God!" Miss Grimsby said.

"I told you he is having delusions. That's not all—"

"I certainly want to see him," Miss Grimsby said.

"Wait till you hear the rest. Johann told me that he remembers hearing the crash of the glass—someone outside breaking the windowpane in the door. He had just shined his flashlight on the three girls—they were in the ell where the freezer and several work counters are—when he heard the noise. He rushed out into the main kitchen, as fast as the old fellow could rush, I guess. He was passing through one of the aisles between the stoves and ranges when he turned his flashlight on the door."

"Did he see who it was?" Miss Grimsby asked.

"Yes," Neumayer said uncomfortably.

"You mean, he recognized the person?" Kellhorn asked.

"Well—" Neumayer hesitated.

"Who was it, Rudi?" Miss Grimsby asked.

"Johann says he saw *you*, Felice."

"Oh, dear!"

"It was a woman?" Kellhorn said.

"No, I asked him that. He said it was a man—he only spoke of one man, but there could have been more. We can't tell. The snow covered all footprints. Johann told me he saw a man, but then, a minute later, he said it was Frau Grimsby. He doesn't remember anything else after that."

"It's quite clear what happened," Kellhorn said. "No one ever got into the kitchen from outside. They just tried. The window glass was broken, but the door was still locked when Corporal Trivella got here. Your watchman must have frightened off whoever it was. Shining his flashlight, probably. It appears then that Bächli slipped as he was running past the stoves toward the door. He grabbed at the brace that supports the rack of copper pots hanging over the big range. To steady himself. He must have pulled it very hard as he fell. The whole thing came down on him."

Miss Grimsby closed her eyes and shuddered. "*Awful!*" she said. "There were more than fifteen giant pots hanging there. Some of them held over forty liters. It's a wonder he wasn't killed! I keep thinking of him lying there—"

Neumayer was twitching for a cigarette. He rose from the couch and crossed to the windows, hoping to subdue the urge. "You were the first to reach him, Felice. Quite a while before Trivella came. I know you explained everything to Sergeant Kellhorn, but would you tell it once again for me?"

She laced her fingers in front of her on the desk and nodded. "It was about five in the morning. I was in my room, at the top of the tower stairs above the fifth floor. I was in bed, awake, reading. Actually, I was waiting—listening, really."

"Waiting?" Kellhorn had flipped back in his notes and was following her account again. "All you told me was that you could not sleep and were reading."

"Well, I have a rather delicate situation here—"

"Please," Neumayer interrupted. He left the windows and slid a chair closer to Miss Grimsby's desk, positioning it so that he could sit with his back to Kellhorn, partly blocking the sergeant's view of the headmistress. "What were you listening for?"

"I knew that several girls had left the floor." She turned her icy sapphire eyes on Neumayer and continued, in a tone that promised she was ready for any challenge. "I won't go into that right now. I have a very sensitive matter on my hands." To Kellhorn: "But it's true, I couldn't sleep. I was reading. Then I heard the girls in the hall below. They were starting down the back staircase. I was going to stop them, but another teacher heard them, also."

Kellhorn had already inched over on the couch so that Miss Grimsby was again in his sight line. "That would be Miss Temple. Carla Temple."

"Yes. She's in charge of the fifth floor." Then, back to Neumayer: "She's a sensible young woman, very popular with the girls. They listen to her—most of the time. I was confident that she could stop any further foolishness without my intervention. I was just listening for the sound of the girls returning to their rooms. Of course, I had no idea Miss Temple was going to have to follow them all the way down to the second floor. I certainly would have gone after them myself. Miss Temple is—she walks with a cane, you know. An accident—'' Neumayer nodded. "I never would have let her strain herself like that.''

"What did make you go down to the kitchen?" Neumayer prodded.

"I heard the crash, all those pots. They must have made a terrible racket down below for the sound to reach me all the way up in the tower. This is a very old building, with thick walls and flooring. Most sound is muffled. But, even though the noise was faint, I could hear it through my closed door and I knew it came from the kitchen. I got up quickly and was just putting on my bathrobe when I heard the girls, running up the back stairs and down the fifth-floor corridor.''

"Did you know how many girls?" Neumayer pulled the pack of Camels out of his pocket and rustled its cellophane casing.

"Not then. Not right away. I didn't know how many had left the floor. It turns out there were three. But I knew that two of them had come back. I heard their doors closing.''

"You told me you heard all the girls return to their rooms,'' Kellhorn said.

Miss Grimsby straightened her trim, squared shoulders, and color flowed across her cheeks. "No, I told you I heard the girls coming back. Just 'the girls'—that was all I said.''

Neumayer raised a hand. "Okay. Two girls returned to their rooms. That was within a minute—two minutes?—after the crash?" Miss Grimsby nodded. "You heard two doors close, one after the other.''

"Yes. By then, I had crossed through my sitting room and opened the door at the top of the tower steps. I was listening very carefully because I wanted to be sure Miss Temple was back, too.''

"Where was the third girl?" Kellhorn asked.

"She had stayed on the second floor, outside the kitchen— with Miss Temple.'' Miss Grimsby paused in thought.

Neumayer reached into his other pocket and grasped a box of small wooden matches. "Go on.''

"Well, then, I realized suddenly that it couldn't have been more than five-fifteen in the morning—five-thirty, at the latest—and I knew something was very wrong."

"Yes?"

"The first of the kitchen staff doesn't arrive until six. Nobody should have been in the kitchen at that hour."

Neumayer rattled the matches in their box. "So you went immediately down the back stairs to investigate?"

"Not what you'd call immediately. I waited for another minute or two, expecting to hear Miss Temple, or the sound of the lift—something. I was getting terribly concerned. When I didn't hear anything—not a stirring anywhere in the building—I got my flashlight out of my desk drawer and started down the back staircase."

"That was foolish, wasn't it? You could have been in considerable danger. Why didn't you call the station right away?"

"Oh, goodness, Rudi, at the time, I didn't think there was anything to make a fuss about—just some schoolgirl mischief that might have gotten a little out of hand. Nothing like *this* ever happened before at Marlowe."

"So," Sergeant Kellhorn impatiently flipped a page in his notebook, "you were going down the back stairs at just about the time Miss Temple—ah, and the third girl—were coming up in the lift at the opposite end of the building. They returned together, I assume?" He was poised to scribble.

"Yes. I went down as quickly as I could. I never realized how dark those stairs are at night," Miss Grimsby continued. "When I got to the kitchen, it was totally black inside. Johann's flashlight must have shattered when the pots fell on him. I pulled the master switch and lit the whole kitchen at once—and saw him lying there. . . ." Neumayer popped a Camel into his mouth, then pulled it out again. "I called to him, but he didn't answer, didn't move. I thought he was dead. There's a phone on the wall near the door. I called the Leitner Clinic first. By the time I reached the station, they told me they had already gotten a call and Officer Trivella was on his way."

Kellhorn closed his notebook and stood up abruptly. "Well, that explains why Johann Bächli thought he saw you outside the kitchen door." Miss Grimsby and Neumayer looked at him. "He heard you, when you called to him."

"He was unconscious," Miss Grimsby said. "His eyes were closed, and he was bleeding heavily. I couldn't see any movement at all. He didn't say he heard me; he said he *saw* me. Isn't that right, Rudi?"

"Still, it would not be uncommon," Kellhorn persisted. "Patients in comas can often hear sounds around them. He just confused the information and concluded that, because he heard you, you must be near. And the only other person he saw, besides the girls, was whoever was outside the kitchen door."

"It's possible," Neumayer said without much interest. "I think I would ask Dr. Leitner his opinion. Bizarre hallucinations are common in people who have received violent blows to the head." He tapped the cigarette against a horny thumbnail.

"Rudi, could I speak to you alone?" Miss Grimsby said. She turned to the sergeant. "Would you excuse us, Herr Kellhorn? It's rather private, if you don't mind . . . ?"

Kellhorn sniffed and bobbed his upper body in a slight, tight bow. "Of course not. I intend to speak to Miss Temple again. I will ask your secretary to call her."

"Oh, she'll be in class for another twenty minutes. Do you think you could wait?"

"Certainly. I plan to re-examine the security of the locks, anyhow. I can do that first." He crossed the room swiftly, yanked the door open, and turned to Neumayer: "My men will find me if you wish to speak to me before you leave, sir." He nodded to Miss Grimsby and, dignity once more intact, closed the door softly behind him.

"Really, Felice, I expect you to be more cooperative. Why didn't you tell Kellhorn right away that there were three girls involved?"

"That's just the problem. I want to keep the details as quiet as possible. The rest of the school doesn't have to be told too much, do they? You see, I have a difficult decision to make." She sighed and pushed her chair back away from her desk. "By rights, I should suspend three senior girls—send them home to their families and delay their graduation for at least six months." She rose with a heaviness unusual for her and walked to the windows. Hesitating in front of the fragrant pot of coffee on the table, she turned to Neumayer again. He looked at her with sympathy, absently twirling the still-unlit cigarette between his fingers. "Do you realize what that means? They've all been accepted in their first-choice universities, starting next fall. If they don't graduate—oh, smoke if you want to, Rudi, but for heaven's sake, just stop fooling with that thing!"

Neumayer returned the Camel to its pack and the pack to his pocket. "How can I help you?" he asked patiently, tucking the matchbox away and crossing his hands over his belly.

"You see, I don't want to do it. I don't want to suspend those girls. They've been badly frightened as it is, and I think that's enough punishment. I don't believe they'll have the stomach for any more stupid pranks. If I give them a chance—let them stay and graduate—they'll be model students for the rest of the term."

"So?"

Miss Grimsby poured two cups of coffee without rattling the china. "The discipline of the school must also be considered. If the rest of the students think those girls got away with something—that's how they're bound to look at it—well, I'm afraid it will be very difficult to maintain order."

Neumayer accepted the steaming coffee and settled on the couch. "What do you want me to do?"

"Your Sergeant Kellhorn wants to speak to the girls, find out if they saw anything that might be helpful. He asked me for the names of the two he knew about, and I suppose he'll want the third one, too." She stood with her back to the windows, her eyes holding Neumayer's. "I haven't told him who the girls are, and I hope I won't have to."

"We'll need to speak to them, you realize."

"But why? They didn't see anything, they already told Miss Temple that. Why can't I keep this just a private school matter? Surely it was just a tramp who tried to break in—"

"We don't get many tramps in Fernstaad," Neumayer said, sipping his coffee. "Please look at it from my point of view. I can't pretend this isn't important—I must investigate it as thoroughly as possible. Besides, you won't be able to hide the girls' involvement. They'll tell their friends themselves.''

"I can prevent that." Miss Grimsby left her coffee untouched on the table and walked toward Neumayer. "I will make it a condition of their staying. Forcefully enough to impress them. Please, Rudi—"

"I'm sorry. We'll have to speak to them. And the sooner, the better.''

She stopped halfway across her study and looked at him for a long minute. Then she returned for her coffee and joined Neumayer on the couch. "Okay," she shrugged. "Then, *you* do it. No one else will have to know if you handle it yourself."

The appeal hung in the air.

"No," he said at last. "Sergeant Kellhorn has been responsible here, and I have great confidence in his ability. He'll understand your problem if you explain it. I myself will emphasize strongly the need for—some delicacy. You can keep it as private as you're able, we'll cooperate. But I won't push Kellhorn off the case or weaken his authority. I value him, my dear.''

Miss Grimsby took a deep swallow of coffee. "I really prefer tea," she said calmly. Then: "The girls are Mindy Parson, Nicole Robineau, and Katharyn Sunynghame.''

"Oh," Neumayer said, impressed.

CHAPTER
25

Dr. Ursula Freimann finished transcribing the notes she had taped during her autopsy of Anneliese Zuecher. She lined up the pages on her desk and sat back to consider them.

Were there any questions left? The cause and manner of death seemed clear—a self-injected dose of enough heroin to kill three of the girl, given her size and body mass. Was there anything she had overlooked, or was she now ready to certify the manner of death and send her report on to Inspector Neumayer?

She tapped her fingers on the pages. She wished Dr. Lüthi were here to consult, but he had extended his stay in Zurich for another week. She was on her own, as she usually liked to be. But still, she would have welcomed going over the details with her seasoned superior. She did not want another case with loose ends, like the Karas girl.

The body of Anneliese Zuecher had already been sent home for burial, but her clothes lay in a neat package on Dr. Freimann's desk. She would hand them over to Inspector Neumayer with her report. Just one more review before she released it.

She began to read.

At her elbow was the list of paraphernalia the police had retrieved from the von Wetzlar greenhouse. She checked it against her report as she read. It seemed complete for the fatal task—syringe, rubber tubing, envelope with traces of heroin, a deep-bowled spoon that was flame-blackened at the base, the debris around the body. The police had been thorough in their search. And thorough in supplying her with as much information as they had. They expected her to be just as careful. And she had. She had even checked to see whether the girl was right-handed, and would logically inject herself in the left arm during her first experiment. Comparing the development of the muscles of the right and left hands, Dr. Freimann concluded that she was.

What else?

She finished rereading her report and was satisfied. An accidental suicide—poor, pretty young thing!

She rose sadly and placed the pages on top of the package of the dead girl's clothes. She would ask Gertrud to send everything to Inspector Neumayer right away. If he had any questions, he would certainly call her. She glanced at the police list on her desk. That would stay here, to go into the files with copies of her report. She picked up the bundle for Gertrud and started to leave her office.

At the door she hesitated, frowning. *Where is it? Why isn't it on the list?*

She almost laughed out loud at herself. Of course it wasn't there. The police must have found it and simply not bothered including it. It was too insignificant. Still, the list was so detailed, carefully describing everything that had been found on or around the body.

Maybe you missed it.

She returned to her desk and looked down at the single sheet the *Kantonspolizei* had sent her, as if the words might have sprouted suddenly on the page.

Had it still been on the body—on the clothes, in a pocket? Surely the police had already checked.

Dr. Freimann unwrapped the package of clothing. Unfolding the long, black-and-green-paisley skirt, she slipped her hand inside the pockets, one after the other. Empty. Was there a small pocket in the wide cummerbund? No. Nor in the silk blouse with the bloodied sleeve that still gave off a faint perfumed scent. She knew she wouldn't find it in the bra and panties or the sling-back shoes, but she looked anyhow.

Maybe she ought to mention it to Inspector Neumayer, if he called about her report. Just to be sure. It wasn't logical. She knew that the elaborate von Wetzlar greenhouse had several taps that supplied water, but where was the box of matches or the cigarette lighter that Anneliese Zuecher had used to cook up her deadly heroin solution? Not on the body, not on the list. What, then, was the source of fire?

It was the kind of inconsistency that Dr. Freimann hated. But she had already raised questions about the death of Sophie Karas. Was she going to do that again? She could always delay her report. Or change it, pending more information.

Enough! Let it go.

She ruffled her shiny light-brown hair in a nervous gesture. Squinting with dissatisfaction, she gathered up the items strewn around her desk, rewrapped the clothes, and laid her report on top. She would send it as it was and speak to Inspector Neumayer later.

She left her office, carrying the bundle down the hall to Gertrud's desk. As she walked, a mocking chant began to hum in her head, keeping pace with her steps. A grisly, singsong nursery rhyme:

Where is the match that lit the fire that burned the spoon that cooked the soup that killed the girl that struck the match. . . .

No! *Dammit, no!* Not until she was completely satisfied.

Back at her desk, she dialed the *Kantonspolizei* and asked for Inspector Neumayer.

CHAPTER
26

At its height, the season in Fernstaad brings with it the annual infestation of jewelers and art dealers. Oozing and hustling their way into town, they home like pigeons on the great chalets. This year, as always, they paid special attention to the sprawling chalet of the Graf and Gräfin von Wetzlar. There they found their own favorite pigeon—Elvina, Gräfin von Wetzlar—a woman for whom nothing was too expensive, too ugly, or too ludicrous to acquire. The gräfin and the dealers were made for each other—to the great delight of her husband. Anything that kept his third wife amused relieved him of the burden and released him for his own pleasurable pursuits.

A brace of dealers, perspiring in anticipation, was just arriving at the chalet as Wieprecht, Graf von Wetzlar, was making his escape. They had been invited to lunch, which the graf thought was tacky and unnecessary. But he knew that Elvina enjoyed summoning them in pairs for a lengthy meal and watching them jockey for her attention. Along with their wares, they brought delicious gossip and vied with each other in trying to shock their hostess—something that was becoming more difficult with the passing of the years.

Today would be different. Elvina had her own shocking news, and she had been chattering it all over Fernstaad. *"A body in the greenhouse . . . a young girl . . . so tragic, my dears . . . I've been sick all week."* She went through town, from luncheon to tea to late-night supper, her can't-be-too-thin body sleek in pantsuit or evening gown, the glossy white fur of her Russian lynx wrapping her from chin to ankle in an aura of smoke that matched her stylish hair. Her eyes sparkled like a crocodile's. *"Accidental overdose . . . the police keep coming back . . . such a disruption, you can't imagine. . . !"*

The crowd at this week's soiree had been twice its normal size. Curious guests had tramped through the greenhouse and damaged some of the graf's most valuable orchids—those rare treasures he had gathered himself on expeditions to Mount Kinabalu, the lofty summit of Borneo. The graf was enraged. He now spent as much time away from the chalet —and the gräfin—as possible.

Passing Elvina's rooms on his way out, he heard her on one of her endless phone conversations: *"And the police, with their questions . . . and the medical examiner, holding up the autopsy report. . . . Yes, a terrible tragedy! Still, one must go on. . . ."*

Wieprecht, Graf von Wetzlar, nodded curtly to the two art dealers on the front steps of the chalet and waved his man into the smaller Rolls, the white one. A short ride to the funicular station, up by rail to Corsetti, and then the cable car to the top of the mountain. His goal was the fabled Crescent Club at the peak of Piz Wolfram. It was the only civilized place left in the Alps, he thought—and that included his own chalet. The club was more private.

The funicular ride to the Corsetti station went quickly. Waiting in line to board the cable car for Piz Wolfram did not. The graf shuffled his sealskin boots in the snow impatiently. Why did he have to wait behind all these *tourists*?

They should find another way up the mountain. Next weekend would be even worse. The town would be invaded by hordes descending for the great race, the *Fernstaader Skimarathon*. A week from tomorrow, Saturday, was the day of the amateur competition on touring skis, a celebrated annual event. Ten thousand skiers would line up at the eastern shore of Lake Clemenza to begin the charge—across the frozen lake, through the snowy fields, and down the slopes surrounding Fernstaad. During this brief weekend, athletes and revelers would take over the town as they did at no other time, except during the Olympics. His own chalet, huge as it was, would be bursting with houseguests.

He pulled up the collar of his dark mink coat and inched forward with the line, grumbling in his impatience.

At last, he was packed tightly inside the swinging red cabin of the cable car. He craned his neck as the door slid closed, looking for anyone else whose destination might also be the Crescent Club. He could usually find old friends from Le Rosey and Oxford, men whose titles were genuine, and no one bothered using them—except for the royals, of course. But everyone accepted into the Crescent Club had either a centuries-old style and nobility inherited with his great lands and wealth, or the fine gift of being entertaining—along with his great lands and wealth. The graf didn't see anyone he knew. Ruddy faces glowing with sun surrounded him, lips white with sunblock laughed, skis held at attention clacked as the car began to pull up its cable to Piz Wolfram.

They glided up the mountain, dipping low over the jagged rock that broke through the snow on the high peaks. Finally, the car came to rest at the Piz Wolfram station. The noisy crowd streamed out toward the sunny pistes.

"Hallo, Veep. Lunching at the club today?"

The graf turned toward the voice. It was low and sensual, but it carried over the jollity of the skiers around them.

"Mookie! I didn't see you for all this rabble. What luck! Yes, lunch, indeed, and I expect you to join me."

"Delighted," the barone said. The crowd parted and flowed around the two men in their path. "You've recovered, I see. Good man!"

"From our fun and games, yes. Not from dead bodies in the greenhouse."

"More than one?"

"No, no. Although, to hear Elvina tell it, we might just as well have a corpse in every room in the chalet. The police have almost moved in. I don't think there's a plant left in my greenhouse that they haven't poked into."

"Tsk, I heard. Sorry you've had such trouble." The barone took his friend's arm and started walking him to the low chalet that housed the Crescent Club.

Nearby, a leggy young beauty lost her balance and toppled in a splash of snow, her skis clattering as she fell. She lay there, laughing, her even white teeth gleaming through pink lips, lighting up her olive-toned complexion. The two men looked at her in silent appreciation, momentarily distracted.

"They get prettier every year, don't they?" the graf said. "Or are we just getting older?"

"Not you, Veep."

"Drugs! Why do they do it?" He looked at the dark girl, who had risen gracefully and was skiing toward the crest of a piste.

"Why do you?" the barone asked.

The graf turned to the barone, annoyed, then laughed. "I need it. Occasionally. They don't. But now, the *Kantonspolizei* are acting as if I've been supplying half of Fernstaad from my chalet. I tell you, the season is dead for me. I'm ready to leave, pack up and go. Elvina won't hear of it. She's been enjoying herself, for God's sake!"

The barone clucked sympathetically. "A shame, but I think I know the cure. Something like hair of the dog, you might say." He chuckled at his own dark, private joke. They were almost at the door of the club. His voice became more intimate. "So, Veep, those young girls, you enjoyed them?" The graf snorted lewdly in response. "I thought so. It's easy to get carried away, isn't it? But perhaps it was too tame for you. Maybe you would prefer a more—ah, satisfying kind of experience? Less restrained, shall we say?" The graf was alert, but said nothing as they walked. "I've seen films where the conclusion was most—dramatic. Do you know what I mean?''

The graf stopped. "Snuff films? Oh, come, now! They're just fakes. I've seen a few of them. Bad acting and a lot of raspberry syrup dripped around.''

The barone nodded. "You may be right. Still, they do have an element of excitement, don't you think?'' The graf did not reply. "Oh, well, if it doesn't appeal. . . .'' He nudged them forward again.

They had reached the door of the Crescent Club. Barone Ugo di Raspoldini-Sant'Agata held it open for his friend Wieprecht, Graf von Wetzlar. A rush of fireplace-warmed air welcomed them.

"What did you have in mind, Mookie?'' the graf asked as they crossed the threshold.

The barone leaned toward him and lowered his voice. "Well, I might be able to arrange a private, uh, party— someplace quiet, like Val Triazzo. . . .''

CHAPTER
27

"Heads up, Mindy,'' Carla said. "Don't stand there drooping like that. You look too gloomy to be believed. Come, sit down. I just want to talk to you.''

They were in Carla's comfortable sitting room waiting for the dinner bell to ring.

With a shrug, Mindy Parson crossed the room and flopped into the overstuffed easy chair Carla indicated. She busied herself by scratching at the boisterous flowers of the upholstery on one rounded arm.

She was already dressed for dinner; she had prepared herself early after she had received Miss Temple's summons in her mailbox. She had been losing weight during the past term—her girlish plumpness was finally melting away. Now her pleated blue-and-grey-plaid skirt was loose at the waist, and the crisp white blouse had slid up to hang over the waistband. The thin black ribbon tie drooped below her collar, and her crested grey blazer hunched at the shoulders as she slumped in the chair. She looked dull in her neutral school uniform. Even the rich red corona of curls that circled her head could not add a spark to her woebegone appearance.

"Okay, I get the picture," Carla said. "You don't have to lay it on so thick." Mindy cast her a sidelong glance. "I expected you to be relieved. You've just been given a reprieve. Doesn't that make you feel better?" Mindy sighed and continued to scratch at the patterned flowers. "I know. You've been answering questions till you're sick of it. Everybody's been talking at you all week. Well, now it's my turn. I promise I won't mention the words 'stupid,' 'childish,' or 'dangerous,' but you may feel free to."

Mindy raised her head and studied Carla. "Did *you* get us off the hook—with Miss Grimsby, I mean?"

"I think my recommendation had more to do with boiling in oil."

Mindy laughed weakly.

"Don't give me too much credit, Mindy. I was very angry, believe it!"

The young girl searched Carla's eyes. Their lovely, purple-ringed grey was light and clear, and Mindy could not tell if it was the snap of residual anger or a tiny twinkle of amusement that she saw. Miss Temple always looked so cool, it was hard to know.

"How's your leg?" Mindy asked, playing with her blouse tie.

"Don't tell me you've been worried?"

"Well—"

"It's fine. No harm done, although I can do without that kind of forced exercise in the future, if you don't mind." Carla rose and picked up her cane from the back of the desk chair. She smoothed her trim-fitting dress, a long-sleeved knit of bright lemon angora with a slim string tie at the waist, and crossed the sitting room to open a window. Mindy was aware that Miss Temple was limping a little more heavily today, and the thought depressed her even more. "Don't get up," Carla said from the window. "I want to talk to you—about my leg."

"Oh, Miss Temple, I didn't mean to—" Mindy straightened in the easy chair as Carla returned to her desk.

"That's all right," Carla stopped her. "You're not prying, if that's what you thought. No, this needs to be said, and I want you to accept it." She sat at the desk again and regarded the wary girl. "Mindy, you didn't follow my instructions that morning, outside the kitchen. I told you to go back up to your room. It was important that you do what I said, but you refused. That was very brave of you—I know how frightened you were—but it was also very wrong. You see, this leg slows me down, and it's a nuisance—but I'm not helpless." She emphasized every word. Mindy felt her chin tremble. "And I'm here to protect *you*, not the other way around. You were concerned for my safety when you should have been thinking about your own. That comes first, and that's my responsibility. You must never challenge it again. No sniffling, now. I want you to use your head. You know I'm right."

Mindy lifted her chin. "I couldn't leave you down there, alone—"

"Yes, you could have! How in the world did you think you could help me? If there had been even worse, more serious trouble, you would only have been in my way. I would have had to worry about you, instead of taking care of myself, which I'm very capable of doing. And if I couldn't have—well, that's *my* problem. Miss Grimsby hired me to do a job, not to burden her students with worry about me, or how I would get around. She's satisfied that my leg is no handicap to my functioning. *You* must be satisfied, too."

Carla leaned back in her chair and took a deep breath.

"Okay, I don't want to run this into the ground. End of lecture. Just remember what I said the next time you're tempted to try some heroics."

Mindy bobbed her head.

"Oh, and one more thing—thank you." Carla smiled, and twin dimples flashed alongside her mouth.

"Wow!" Mindy collapsed with relief against the cushioned back of the easy chair. "This week has been the pits!"

"I wouldn't say that at all. You don't realize how lucky you've been. Nothing terrible happened to you, although it certainly might have. And Miss Grimsby isn't going to suspend you. On the whole, I'd say you've had one of your better weeks."

Volatile as she was, Mindy grinned happily. Then she was instantly serious again.

"Did you hear whether they caught the guys who broke in?"

Carla brought her up-to-date, mainly to forestall any wild speculation or gossiping that was sure to take place when Mindy got together with her two accomplices; and also because Carla had always resented never being given enough information when she herself was young.

No, they hadn't caught anyone. No one actually ever got inside the school. Sleepless had frightened them away before he pulled the pots down on himself. That was the crash they had heard from outside the kitchen. The police did not know how many people had been trying to break in. The snowfall was heavy enough so that all tracks were gone. The only person who might have seen who was outside the kitchen door was Sleepless, and he was semiconscious and hallucinating, and couldn't remember anything helpful.

"Must have been some bums," Mindy said.

"In Fernstaad? Not very likely. Maybe a practical joke—some of those restless university boys houseguesting at one of the big chalets—"

"Yeah, a joke. Like that dumb note Bianca got. Some joke!"

The dinner bell rang. Carla reached for the square of checkered black-and-white silk neatly folded on her desk and began tying the scarf around her neck. She was tired and glad that she had gotten through the difficult meeting with Mindy without rattling either of them too much. She stood up, eager to have the girl gone now. Outside, doors slammed—the usual stampede not to be late to dinner was beginning.

"I just thought I'd mention it," Mindy said, rising slowly. "The note, I mean." Carla looked at her without comprehension. "Someone said they were going to kill Bianca."

"*What?*"

"Oh, that wasn't exactly what it said—"

"Mindy, what *are* you talking about?"

The flustered girl was quickly sorry. She did not want Miss Temple to make a big deal out of something silly, but still, it was bothering her. She explained about Bianca finding the note in the pocket of her ski jacket—that it hadn't been there when she had hung it up in the Klaus. Mindy didn't remember when, but it was sometime in the past week or two. The note didn't mention Bianca specifically, but it was real creepy—

"I'd like to see it. Can you show it to me?" Carla asked.

"Bianca tore it up and flushed it down the john. I wanted her to show it to you, but she was so pissed—excuse me. I mean, it really was weird—"

"What exactly did it say, Mindy? Think."

"Mmm, something about daughters. '*Daughters die*'— that was it!"

"That's all? No name or anything?"

"No. Just those two words," Mindy said, then volunteered that the note was on Marlowe stationery, without any address on the envelope, and must have been written by one of the kids playing a sick joke.

"Well, you're probably right, but I wish Bianca had saved it for me. Still, if it wasn't put into Bianca's mailbox or handed to her, if it was slipped into her pocket in the Klaus when she wasn't even wearing her jacket, it probably wasn't even meant for her. Maybe not for anyone in particular, either. Just a sick joke, as you said." Carla was caught between her own distracted thoughts and her desire not to stimulate the young girl's anxieties any further. "I wouldn't worry about it. Now, get going or you'll be late for dinner."

Mindy headed for the door, then turned. "You won't say anything to Bianca—that I told you, I mean?"

"Why not?"

Mindy shrugged. "She asked me not to."

"I'll see," Carla said. "Oh, and if you really want something to worry about, you can tell your coconspirators, and anyone else you like, that I'll probably be giving a quiz on *Finnegans Wake* tomorrow."

"You wouldn't!" Mindy cried. "You promised! You said we were reading it just to get a feel for the language. No tests, you said!"

"Yes, but I'm feeling mean. A couple of essay questions, I think. And if I do it, you'll be marked, and it will count on your final grade. No more discussion, please," Carla dismissed her.

Mindy pulled open the door and said, *"Shit!"* into the hall, slamming the door harder than she meant to but hoping that Miss Temple had heard her.

Carla had no intention of giving a test on *Finnegans Wake*. She didn't understand the book herself, and had said so to the girls when she first proposed that they read and discuss it together. It would take her days to formulate questions that might have any meaning for them. But she knew that the news of a possible test tomorrow would spread through the fifth floor, and the spontaneous combustion of panicked studying would keep the girls occupied tonight. They would be too frantic and busy to gossip around, at least this evening.

She straightened her scarf and picked up her cane. The pain in her leg was almost gone, but it felt weak. She was afraid of straining it. Suppose she did further damage . . . no, she couldn't bear to think about the possibility! She hadn't returned to the clinic that week—she felt sufficiently improved, with her exercises and the swimming therapy. But now she thought she ought to see Dr. Leitner. Or was she thinking about Eric? She hadn't seen him at the pool that week, to her considerable disappointment. Maybe he was still stiff from his skiing lessons. A compelling idea struck her: Why not teach Eric to ski? If he really wanted to learn, who better to teach him?

Don't be silly!

She wriggled her toes in her shoes, then bent lightly into

a slow-motion slalom twist. She could almost taste it—the rush of wind, the snow spray on her cheeks, the whip of the gates. . . . She leaned down and kneaded her calf. *Please, heal!* she whispered.

Then, on a sudden impulse, she added another whispered prayer: *Please, keep all our girls safe from harm.*

The dinner bell had already rung. Carla crossed her sitting room to the door.

The hall was almost empty as she stepped outside, only a few stragglers racing for the front staircase at the opposite end. Wrapped in her thoughts, she walked to the lift.

"*Daughters die?*" she mused aloud. That was pretty sick. She ought to mention it to Miss Grimsby. As if the woman didn't have enough worries already. Something else troubled her about the note, too—more than just what it said . . . something that eluded her for the moment. It would come to her. Then she would speak to the headmistress. No, better, she would call Inspector Neumayer at the *Kantonspolizei*.

A sick joke? It certainly wasn't funny—at all. . . .

CHAPTER
28

The outside of his thigh was still black and blue, bruised when he had stumbled, rushing in alarm down the kitchen steps. The tools in his pocket had done the damage—he had fallen on them—although he had been too excited at the time to feel the full impact. The pain had come later. He didn't mind the soreness as much as the fact that his leg looked so—dirty. If he were a believer in omens, he would say that his mission was threatened with failure. But he fought back such thoughts as a sign of weakness. Something had gone wrong, something beyond his control. And he still did not know what had happened.

Just before he broke the pane of glass in the kitchen door, he had peered into the darkness inside. Nothing was moving. The whole gigantic hulk of the Marlowe School was asleep, he was sure of that. But, suddenly, the bright light had flashed in his face, whiting out all vision. And then came the prolonged thunder of a crash that sounded deafening, even on the far side of the door. The noise blasted the stillness of the night and paralyzed him for an instant. Then, a guttural cry from inside had galvanized him into flight. Down the steps, through the snowfall, hugging the trees, he had fled across the spine of hill high above town that separated *Dorf* from *Bad*.

The first morning light was brightening the sky to swimming pool blue by the time he descended to Fernstaad *Bad*.

If he believed in portents, he might have given up. To fail again—the thought made him tremble. But he would hold to his purpose, *that* he swore. An injury had been done to him, and he would be paid. Those years of suffering, of being imprisoned within his own rage. . . . All the way down the mountain, he promised himself he would achieve the one satisfaction that had given his life purpose.

Quietly, he let himself into the guest house with the flimsy key the Breitels had doled out to him when he arrived. Silently, he crept up the stairs to his tiny, suffocating room. Gently, he eased himself into bed, naked after shedding all his sweated clothes. He would have bathed first, if he had not been so exhausted. And fearful. Pindar Breitel—the ears of the blind. They were a special sense, he knew.

Tomorrow, he would find out what had happened, what Herr Breitel knew. But first, he had to sleep. . . .

During the rest of the week, the news about the death of the girl in the von Wetzlar greenhouse overshadowed the attempted break-in at Marlowe as local gossip. The details were scrambled and embroidered, and he didn't know whether to believe the talk that the medical examiner's office was not completely satisfied. The pathologist, a young woman new in Fernstaad, might have found something—so the latest story went. *Impossible!* He had been too careful. He knew he hadn't left anything suspicious behind.

He did not want to stay in Fernstaad much longer. He had an open ticket on Swissair that would carry him home, but he wouldn't reserve his return flight through the Fernstaad office. He knew his name was in the airline's computer, accessible to anyone who might think of looking for it, but he didn't want to call attention to himself in town. He would finish his mission and leave Fernstaad by train for Zurich. There he was sure to get a flight, even at the last moment.

Meanwhile, he would make new plans.

And try not to be distracted again.

Ah, but those girls . . . those delicious not-quite-women . . . so soft and willing. . . . And there was this new possibility—

No! Stop it! That kind of thinking could prove too dangerous to his purpose.

His mind shifted.

What, he wondered, did the pathologist think she had found?

CHAPTER
29

"Absolutely not!" Eric was almost shouting into the phone. "Where did you get such a crazy idea?"

Carla sighed into the receiver. It had been a long day. "I didn't say *I* would be on skis. *You* would. You'd be the guinea pig, and I would just stand there and try not to laugh. No, I'm serious. I'd be glad to help you—I'd like to, since you're interested."

"Not that interested," Eric said. "I don't want you anywhere near the slopes. You could have an accident just as easily, tramping around in the snow without skis. Listen to me, Carla. I'm so happy that you called, I'd like to say yes to anything you ask, but not if it looks like trouble for you. Besides, I'm a little suspicious of your motives. I think you just want to use me as an excuse to get out on those hills again. Right?"

Carla removed a pinching gold earring and transferred the receiver to the undressed ear. "Wrong! This is purely a charitable gesture, no more than good manners, and I'm stung, simply cut to the quick, wherever that is, that you would doubt me."

"Are you finished?" Eric laughed. "Okay, I'm serious, too. Fritz Leitner tells me you haven't been back to the clinic all week. That's not smart. If you're waiting for an invitation, you've got it."

"I've been very busy here."

"No defense. Can you come in tomorrow?"

"On Saturday? Will you be there?"

"Waiting for you. If you can make it around noon, we'll have a bite at the Klaus afterward. Would you like that?"

"Yes, I would. But I did mean it, you know—about the skiing lesson. I'm really much stronger, and I think the exercise would be good for me. And I'll bet I can make a champion out of you."

It was Eric's turn to sigh. "When you come in tomorrow, I'll give you the full lecture, complete with charts and slides and fire and brimstone and—"

"Oh, excuse me, Eric. *Come in*," she called in answer to the knock on the door. Then into the phone again: "One of my students. I asked her to come see me after dinner. Gotta go. Till tomorrow."

She hung up and turned to the door as Bianca Gioianni entered.

* * *

Joke or no joke, it was too ominous to ignore. Carla wanted to know more before she spoke to Inspector Neumayer. As gently as she could, she pressed Bianca for information about the note.

Daughters die? Was she sure?

Bianca was obviously upset. She tried to shrug it off with an angry shake of her long, thick black hair. Finally, she confirmed that the note had said just what Mindy had told Carla.

"You could at least have shown it to me," Carla said.

"But why? I didn't want you to make a fuss," Bianca said with irritation.

"Is there something you're not telling me? Like, you know who wrote it? One of the young men on ski holiday in Fernstaad? I know you've made some friends in town, outside of the regular school curriculum." Bianca didn't respond, so Carla smiled encouragement and tried again. "Look, I'm not going to get you into trouble, if that's what you're worried about. But if you have any idea who put that note into your pocket, I wish you'd tell me."

"No! I haven't seen anyone since—well, there *was* someone, but he went back to school in Germany more than a month ago. Honest. I haven't talked to anyone in town for ages."

"Well, you're a very pretty girl. It's possible you may have attracted some attention you'd be better off without, and you may not even be aware of it."

"Oh, I'd know!" Bianca laughed, and there was a sophistication in her manner that convinced Carla she was very well aware of how easily she generated interest. "No, I swear I have no idea how the note got there. It must have been meant for someone else—a stupid joke on another person who was in the Klaus that day. It was mobbed, you know? Skis everywhere, a dozen jackets hanging on every hook— we were lucky to get our own back. That was the day of the big storm, a couple of weeks ago. Everyone came off the slopes early—you couldn't even see to the tip of your skis through the snow. We had to fight to get a table at the Klaus, it was so crowded. Miss Grimsby was there, too. We waved at her.''

''Who was with you?'' Carla asked.

''Mindy and Nicole and—*oh!*''

''Yes?''

''I was going to say Sophie Karas, but I remember now that she never came. That was the day she disappeared. Oh, how awful! We were all sitting there saying mean things about her— we thought she had run off again. When all the time, she was —lying there, at that very moment . . . the accident . . . *dead!*'' She burst into rapid Spanish, clearly a bitter self-accusation.

''Bianca! No, honey, you didn't do anything wrong!'' Carla went to the shaken girl and put a comforting arm around her shoulders.

It took some time to calm her. Carla had to listen to the accumulated pain about Sophie, then about Anneliese, and, finally, her fears for herself.

After Bianca left her sitting room, Carla was exhausted. A long day had become even longer.

Saturday morning, with the sun blazing on the Alpine peaks, Carla stood on her balcony and thought about her conversation with Rudi Neumayer a few minutes ago. When she told him about Bianca's note, he asked only a few questions, and those Carla couldn't answer. She was just repeating what Bianca and Mindy had told her. Inspector Neumayer had simply mumbled and thanked her, reminding her to contact him again if she had anything else to tell him. Carla didn't know how seriously he took the information.

She breathed deeply in the cold air. She heard a slight rustle above and looked up. Miss Grimsby was also enjoying the view, from the higher vantage of her tower balcony, leaning against the railing and staring out at the mountains across the lake. Their snowy bosom glinted with gold in the sunlight. It was a phenomenon that Carla knew usually delighted the headmistress: Sand from the Sahara, blown north by the violent sirocco of the desert, had been captured by the high peaks to dress themselves in glitter. It was a glorious sight. Carla would have liked to enjoy it, but she stepped back off the balcony into her sitting room, out of sight. She didn't want to intrude on the few minutes of peace Miss Grimsby might have found.

Also, she would have to hurry or she would be late. She was supposed to be at the clinic in less than half an hour.

She finished dressing quickly—and completely, this time. She was amused at herself for choosing her laciest, most feminine bra and bikini briefs—not because she expected them to be seen, but because they made her feel good. Ski pants, sweater, and parka were the proper outerwear, and she dressed in one of her most flattering outfits. She wore makeup today, but not too much. It's an appointment, not a date, she told herself. Still, one more spray of light cologne. . . .

At eleven-thirty, she walked down the front steps of Marlowe, just as Kurt, the school driver, was turning the station wagon into the courtyard.

When Eric walked into the examining room in his starched white lab coat, Carla felt a shiver of joy. She tried to suppress it under a lid of banter.

"Good morning, Dr. Sunderson. And how is your leg today? Better, I see."

"Don't distract me when I'm working, please," Eric said. "You now have the status of worst patient on the block, and I'm very angry at you." He looked at her with mock severity. Carla could see the matching spark of joy in his blue eyes.

"Okay, Doctor, then get to work. And leave the lecturing to the teachers." She dangled her bare legs over the table and studied his strong back as he bent over the sink to wash his hands. It struck her that she had always been attracted to men with powerful shoulders. An unwelcome thought of Michael flashed through her mind, a surge of pain and regret. She shook her head to be rid of it.

Eric didn't speak as he examined her leg, except to ask her questions about how it felt. He palpated the calf, turned the ankle gently, told her to show him how she did two of the more strenuous exercises, and helped her off the table to demonstrate her walking ability. It was all very professional, but Carla was intensely conscious of his touch.

At last, he was finished. He stood in the center of the room, nodding at her.

"What does that mean, that enigmatic nodding?" Carla asked. "That I'm perfect, I trust. My leg, I mean."

"Why stop there?" he laughed. "Okay, not bad for all the abuse and neglect you've given it. I hate telling you this because I think you'll take it as permission to go do something stupid again, but I would say you're almost healed. You won't be needing that cane much longer. Keep it with you, anyhow, for safety. And don't stop any of the therapy—the water exercises and all the rest. And, please, promise me you won't let a whole week go by before you come in again."

"It's only been six days," she protested.

"You're impossible!"

"Does that mean no lunch?" Carla teased. She judged his look as more than just a hunger for the delicacies at the *Konditorei* Klaus.

"Meet me in my office when you're dressed. I'm sorry, but it'll have to be a quick snack—it's hectic here today. But I've been looking forward to it."

"Johann Bächli—?" she began.

"I'll tell you at lunch," he said as he left the room.

Dressed again, Carla picked up her ski jacket and unzipped the breast pocket, rummaging for her comb. There was no need for primping; she already looked glorious. Her color was heightened by the exhilaration of seeing Eric again. Her hair looked exactly the same after she was finished with the comb, but she felt better. Contrary to her usual lack of self-consciousness, she carefully checked her appearance in a small mirror on the wall. Satisfied, she replaced the comb, zipped the pocket, and pressed it smooth, running her fingers over the raised fabric of the school insignia on the jacket's pocket.

The school insignia.

The Marlowe crest—she had never looked at it closely before. On the large grey-and-white fabric patch, a heraldic shield was emblazoned with a standing crane and dotted with fleurs-de-lis. Above the crest was a rampant boar. It was only a whimsical design, signifying nothing—a notion that years ago had caught the fancy of the school's founder, Mary Adeline Marlowe. It was part of the many accoutrements and traditions Miss Grimsby had inherited when she took over the school. A fussy, meaningless insignia, a crest that rested on a base formed by the word *Marlowe*.

That was what had eluded her the night before, when she had first learned about the note: No one in Fernstaad could mistake the insignia as random decoration. All the students wore that crest, and the faculty, too. It was large enough and seen often enough on the ski slopes and in town to instantly identify the wearer as coming from the school. Anyone who slipped a note into the pocket of a ski jacket bearing that crest must have intended it for a Marlowe girl!

Daughters die? she thought. Had someone actually meant to threaten Bianca? The train of thought continued: Sophie? . . . Anneliese? . . . the break-in Sunday night? *Oh, lord!*

She hurried down the hall to Eric's office, carrying her jacket, teeth clenched in agitation. She, too, had been looking forward to their lunch together, but now she had an even more compelling desire to see Rudi Neumayer. She wanted to show the inspector the very visible Marlowe crest on her own ski jacket, not that it wasn't already quite familiar to him. She had to know if he made the same connection she did. If she left now, she might be able to catch him before lunch. Eric would understand—she hoped.

She entered his office and found him still in his white lab coat, standing at his desk and scribbling on a prescription pad.

"Sorry, Carla, Fritz asked me to go check up on Johann Bächli. I'm afraid the old fellow isn't doing very well today. Rain check on that lunch?"

"Absolutely," she said, relieved. "There's something I have to do in town, anyhow, and I must take care of it right away."

"I have a prescription for you, a very mild muscle relaxant, just in case. Also, Fritz instructed me to give you a really forceful talking to, but I was saving that for our lunch. Now—"

"Now is definitely not the time. I promise I'll lecture myself all the way back to Marlowe, but I really have to go."

She reached for the prescription. He held it away.

"Whoa! You can't be in that much of a rush. First, our rain check."

They arranged for dinner the following week. Eric handed her the slip of paper, noting her distraction as she fumbled with her jacket.

"You look upset," he said. He moved closer, inside the aura of her scent. She looked up at him, then away. "Listen, is there something I can help you with?"

Carla hesitated. "Well, it's Sophie Karas—the girl who was killed in the skiing accident. I just—I'm not so sure it *was* an accident." The words came out slowly, as if she couldn't believe what she was saying.

He looked at her, startled. "Are you still tormenting yourself about that?"

"No, I mean it! I think it might have been—deliberate. And maybe Anneliese Zuecher, too."

"Carla, you've been listening to town gossip. You're too smart for that. The girl poisoned herself—she took an overdose of heroin. That's bad enough. Don't make it into something worse."

"I'm trying not to, but it just doesn't feel right. None of it. And now I'm afraid another girl may be in danger!"

Eric reached for her, held her shoulders as he searched her troubled grey eyes. "Why do you say that?"

"It's complicated. I just know something's wrong."

"Have you told the police?"

"Yes. I called Inspector Neumayer this morning."

"And?"

"He didn't really say anything. But I have to talk to him again, now. I'm going there, to the *Kantonspolizei*, before I go back to school. Please, Eric, I have to leave." She tried to shrug away from him, but he held her firmly.

"Okay, you'll feel better once he reassures you. But don't turn these tragedies into a galloping paranoia. Next, you'll tell me someone's out to get *you!*" She flinched and stared at him. "Sorry, bad joke. I just don't want you to get nutty about this.'' He released her with a sigh. ''You and Fritz are the sanest people I know in Fernstaad. It hurts to see you so—disturbed. I already told you I care, remember?'' He grinned at her boyishly.

She felt herself relaxing and responding. She smiled back, softness crinkling around her eyes.

''Go see your inspector,'' he said. ''And if you have any more fears like this, come tell me. Promise? I've got a strong shoulder for you to lean on.''

Carla laughed with delight and surprise. Had he been reading her thoughts?

Impulsively, she leaned toward him and brushed his cheek with lips as cool and soft as snowflakes. She heard the catch in his breath. He turned his head slowly, lips traveling till they found hers. He tasted tentatively, inhaling her fragrance, willing them both onto a different plane. She went suddenly soft and liquid inside, brushing her mouth against his, sipping delicately to test his heady new taste and texture. Hunger blossomed between them, and he pulled her close, pressing the small of her back, gathering her body into his. She let her jacket fall and slid her arms around his neck. Her slender fingers laced into his hair. They swayed together, exploring with mouth and tongue, each second a delicious revelation, their bodies moving to find the proper fit. A low murmur of need escaped from his throat, and she gave herself up to the warmth and wetness and pleasure of each tingling point of contact between them. Healthy, young, alive with vital greed, she searched his newness and found a perfect promise.

Finally, at some moment signaled by their initial satisfaction and a mutual urge to check in with reality, they drew apart. She looked up at him with moist, barely focused eyes. His breath was shallow; she saw his eyes questioning, waiting for her response. A slow smile spread on her face, and she tilted her head.

''More,'' she commanded, her voice husky.

''*Yes!*''

He bent to kiss her again, and they rocked rhythmically in an enveloping embrace that was calmer and more purposeful than before. They could be patient. There would soon be enough time. . . .

It was Eric who broke the spell and reminded them of their immediate responsibilities.

They parted reluctantly at the door of his office—Eric to attend to Johann Bächli, and Carla, trimly zipped in her ski jacket, to the *Kantonspolizei*. She didn't look back at him, although she knew he was watching her walk down the hall. He had cautioned her again not to let her imagination run wild about the girls. Excited as she was about him, it troubled her that he didn't take her more seriously; she didn't like him staring at her in such a perplexed way as he tried to brush away her fears. But, then, she hadn't really told him *why* she was afraid. That would have been wrong, a breach of privacy—the girls' and the school's.

She heard the bells of the *Evangelische* steeple singing the half hour as she pushed through the front doors of the clinic. One-thirty. She wondered if Inspector Neumayer would still be at the station, or out for lunch.

Then she had another sudden, uncomfortable thought: Maybe she had been wrong to tell Eric *anything*.

She stood inside the vestibule of the *Konditorei* Pappagallo, jacket under her arm, and scanned the dining room for Rudi Neumayer. He was seated alone at a corner table, utensils busy over his plate. When she approached, he rose and smiled in greeting. Her answering smile was perfunctory.

"I stopped in at the station," she said. "Sergeant Kellhorn told me you might be here. I hope I'm not interrupting—"

"Not at all. A very lovely surprise. You will join me, please?" He held a chair for her and reached for her jacket. She stopped him with a wave of her hand.

Seated again, he pressed a menu on her. To please him, she ordered a small salad and a pot of tea. He did not attempt to draw her into small talk. They sat in silence as the waitress removed the remains of his smoked eel and set down a gargantuan platter heaped with *saucisson vaudois* and mounds of golden *Rösti*.

"I'm delighted to have your company," he said, tasting the newly uncorked Dôle des Monts and accepting with regret her refusal to share in a glass. "But I think this is not a social call?"

She nodded and looked around, distracted by the midday clamor at the crowded tables of the café. To give her time to collect her thoughts, he addressed himself to the steaming sausages and potatoes on his plate.

At last, she began to speak in a tensely controlled voice.

He listened carefully, sipping his wine, asking questions in a casual way, now only picking at his meal but trying to avoid giving the impression that he shared her alarm. He studied the crest on her jacket when she urged it on him, nodded patiently as if he had never noticed it before, and made noncommittal noises to calm her.

By the time he steered her out of the Pappagallo into the snowdrifted streets, the wine and the tea were finished, but most of their food remained untouched on their plates.

CHAPTER
30

You did not tell Felice Grimsby what to do. When she wanted your advice, she asked for it. You knew that she would be selective about what she accepted or discarded, and there was never any point in arguing. But when you told her what *you* insisted on doing—what you felt was absolutely necessary—she did not waste too much time trying to dissuade you.

Rudi Neumayer had run through a range of suggestions in his head on Saturday as he sat with Carla Temple in the

Pappagallo, even though he knew that Felice would reject most of what he proposed.

No, there would be no general detention at the Marlowe School to keep the girls permanently on the premises. Nor would it be practical, or even possible, to remove the identifying crests from all the garments of the more than one hundred fifty students. It would not do any good, anyhow. The girls frequently wore their school uniforms to town and were easily identifiable—if not by their clothes, then by their manner. Besides, any change in the dress regulations would only set up confused speculation, possibly alarm. And, above all, there would be no closing the school for an unscheduled midsemester vacation. Neumayer's only victory was a small concession from Felice that left him far from satisfied: She would allow him to station guards at the school, as long as they were unobtrusive.

The week was new, and already Neumayer was tired. Alone in his office, he considered his options. He had already called headquarters in Chur on Monday, and his two requests had been filled. The first was for the police cards of all the hotel guests who had arrived in Fernstaad in the past four weeks. The cards were kept in town for a week and then routinely transferred to Chur for filing. Now that he had them back, Neumayer shuffled through them restlessly, not expecting much. His second request was for two guards— trained and armed policemen—to stand twelve-hour surveillance shifts at Marlowe. The men would wear simple watchman uniforms and be identified to the staff as replacements for Johann Bächli—a necessity since the old man's accident. Neumayer had already dispatched them, with Hans Kellhorn, to the school. Felice had not protested, either because she knew it would be useless, or because she actually welcomed their presence. She did make it clear that she was not happy about Kellhorn's presence, but that was as far as she went. So Kellhorn would now have his chance to speak to the three girls about the break-in.

Neumayer had lost count of how many times he had reviewed the autopsies of the two Marlowe girls. Yesterday, when a new question had occurred to him, he had called Ursula Freimann at the M.E.'s office. No, there was no envelope, no note in either girl's clothing. Only the items listed in the report.

This afternoon, he would call Interpol in Bern, unofficially. There was nothing he could tell them that would warrant their formal involvement, but he had an old friend there who frequently cooperated on a personal basis. Neumayer did not expect much help from that source, either, but he could not overlook any possibility. If what he now believed was true —that Sophie Karas, and possibly also Anneliese Zuecher, had been viciously murdered by a killer who was still out there, still planning another assault on yet another Marlowe girl—his task was brutal.

He hunched over his desk and worked his way listlessly through more of the registration cards. An innocent enough collection. The usual playboys and the women who trouped after them, a higher than usual gathering of hustlers and gentleman cardsharps. But there would be no registration records for the princes, poseurs, and world-class profiteers invited to the great chalets. No way of knowing who might have wangled an invitation from one of the more naive hostesses. Trendy rock stars, international movie celebrities, and the glitzy company they kept were beginning to show up more regularly in Fernstaad these days—especially in high season. Who knew what kind of menace followed in their wake?

Hopeless, Neumayer thought. He shoved the cards to one side and gathered up the morning reports from Kellhorn and his subordinates. Nothing special there, either. The standard range of small misdemeanors, a heavier load of minor accidents on the slopes, and shopkeepers' complaints. There had been a call from Fritz Leitner at the clinic, which had come while Neumayer was out to lunch. And yesterday's message, still unanswered, that Pindar Breitel had stopped by to visit with him, which the blind man occasionally did, out of loneliness and because Neumayer had befriended him over the years. Well, old Breitel would have to wait. Neumayer had no time for the courtesy of a kindly social call.

He picked up the telephone and was quickly connected to Fritz Leitner.

"More bad news, Rudi. I'm sorry, but we lost Johann Bächli this morning."

"Damn!"

"Pneumonia—we were getting it pretty much under control, but his heart simply couldn't take any more strain. He may even have had a stroke. I was planning another CAT scan as soon as his temperature came down, but he went too quickly."

"Was he conscious—before, I mean? Did you hear him say anything lucid?"

"No. Delirious to the end. We had him hooked up to so many tubes he wouldn't have been able to speak, anyhow."

"Nothing?"

"Nurse said she thought he was asking for Frau Grimsby, that was all—just before she and Dr. Sunderson connected him to the respirator. I wasn't there, Rudi. If you want to speak to them—"

"I may," Neumayer said. "I'm sorry now that I discouraged Felice from going to see him. A pity. It might have made both of them feel a little better."

"Oh, she was here. Yesterday. You know Felice when she makes up her mind about something. I let her in for a few minutes."

"Yes, I should have known." Neumayer laughed in a short burst that started a coughing spasm.

Dr. Leitner sighed.

"Rudi, I don't want to be hooking *you* up to a respirator someday."

"No lectures, Fritz," Neumayer said, catching his breath. "Have you told Felice yet?"

"She knows. She'll be here later this afternoon. She'll be making the arrangements for the burial. And you'll have our report tomorrow, probably late in the afternoon. Eric Sunderson—my new associate—will be preparing it. I don't suppose you'll need an autopsy on this."

"Would you mind?"

The question caught Dr. Leitner by surprise. He hesitated.

"No, of course not. But—is there something I don't know?"

"You know as much about this as I do. I just want to be sure I'm not missing anything. Bächli's accident was connected with the attempted break-in at the Marlowe School. That case is still open. I have to explore anything that might help."

"Naturally. I understand. I'll send him over to Lüthi, with a copy of our report, as well."

"Lüthi isn't back from Zurich yet—he's been held up on business," Neumayer said. "Could you send him to Ursula Freimann? I'll call to let her know."

"Certainly. Tell her she can expect him sometime tomorrow."

"I realize how busy you are, Fritz, but do you think you could do it this afternoon?"

Fritz Leitner did not miss the edge in Neumayer's voice.

"So? It is that important? Yes, I'll take care of it—myself, if necessary. You alert Dr. Freimann. Tell her Bächli will be there within the next two hours." Through the phone, Dr. Leitner could hear the crisp striking of a wooden match, the puff of ignited phosphorus. "Rudi, why don't you try a pipe, or even cigars?"

"Thank you, my friend. I shouldn't make you worry about me." Neumayer exhaled, smiling.

"Ah, it is just my nature. I've been doing it too long to stop now. Call me if you need anything else."

"I will."

Sergeant Kellhorn was experienced at interrogating witnesses and suspects and malefactors of any stripe that were likely to turn up in Fernstaad. There were subtle techniques of encouraging or intimidating, prompting whenever necessary. Each case was different, and he prided himself on his ability to manipulate any situation. But he sensed that he was not having great success at the moment with the young girls at the Marlowe School.

He had already spoken to two of the girls involved in the vandalism last week. The first was Nicole Robineau, then

Katharyn Sunynghame—one at a time. Neither had been any help. They were uncommunicative, weary, almost bored with the subject. He could understand that; they must have been answering questions from Grimsby and other school authorities for several days. But he found them so unresponsive that they seemed actually haughty. And their stories had added nothing to what he already knew. He was not looking forward to interviewing the third girl.

Kellhorn checked his notes. Mindy Parson. Just more time to be wasted.

He closed his notebook and leaned back in the chair behind Miss Grimsby's desk. The headmistress had let him use her study during the short break between afternoon classes. She was being very cooperative. She had told him that she felt her presence during the questioning might only further intimidate the girls, so she would not be there. However, she insisted that another teacher be present, and the logical person was Carla Temple, the young woman who had followed the girls on their nighttime escapade. Kellhorn had questioned her at the start, but had learned nothing that wasn't already in Officer Trivella's notes—except that the teacher seemed extremely uneasy.

Temple had gone to collect the Parson girl. While he waited, Kellhorn considered whether another approach might not be more profitable. Being stern had not accomplished anything with the first two girls. Perhaps he should try a more informal attitude. Yes, just a friendly chat. They were not criminals, after all.

He rose and tucked his notebook into his back pocket. He thought about removing his jacket, but decided against it. Casually unbuttoned would do. He might even loosen his tie. And they would sit together on the big leather couch, instead of facing each other across the open stretch of Grimsby's empty desk.

Kellhorn began to pace the study in anticipation. At the window table, coffee steamed on a hot plate. A cup in his hand, no notebook to make the girl nervous, would be a nice touch, he thought. He walked to the table, measured a generous spoonful of sugar into an empty cup, and poured. The first sip warmed him. He carried the cup to the couch and settled himself.

Old photos clustered on the end table next to the couch; they were the only sign of human clutter in the whole room. He admired a frame of rich blue and green enamel and picked it up for a closer look. Must cost at least a hundred, maybe a hundred fifty francs, he thought. It gleamed with the iridescent colors of a peacock. The photo inside was bleak by comparison—an old, faded black-and-white snapshot of parents with their two children. A young boy in shorts leaned against the knee of a seated man and scowled into the camera. Next to them sat a woman, cradling an infant and squinting at the sun. Could that be Grimsby's own family? Was the baby the formidable Grimsby herself? Kellhorn wondered. He chuckled at the doughy blob in the woman's arms and set the photo down.

A slight change of air pressure sucked the windows into their casements with a rattle, signaling Kellhorn that the door had opened.

Carla Temple shepherded a pretty red-haired girl into the study. She wore the standard neutral school uniform. Kellhorn shifted on the couch, watching them over its high back. Yes, he approved of the order and modesty of the Marlowe girls' dress.

"Come in, come in." He waved them closer. Carla performed the introductions as they crossed the room. "Nothing to be nervous about. Sit here, miss." Kellhorn patted the seat next to him. "I was just having a coffee. Would you like some?"

"No, thank you," Mindy said stiffly. She sat next to Kellhorn.

Carla touched the girl's shoulder to reassure her, then crossed the room and sat near the windows. Kellhorn had gotten used to the teacher's unobtrusive presence while he was talking to the first two girls and he paid no attention to her now.

"I won't keep you long," he said to Mindy. "Just a few

questions that I've already asked your friends. Did they tell you?''

Mindy nodded.

"Then you know there's nothing to worry about. You'll just tell me what you remember about that night, and then you can go back to your classes. Now, that won't hurt, will it?''

Mindy shook her head, serious and unsmiling. She looked quite composed, and Kellhorn wondered why he was taking such pains to reassure her.

"So, shall we begin? You and your friends were going down to the kitchen—?''

Mindy thought for a moment, then began her story with their avoiding Sleepless, with her being the last girl to leave the floor. The dark stairs. Following Nicole and Katharyn down to the second floor. The key that had unlocked the kitchen door. Then Sleepless, terrifying them so by shining his flashlight on them. Everything had happened so fast. The crash and tinkle of glass at the outside door. Sleepless turning his light away from them as they rushed out of the kitchen ell to the door.

"And you all ran out of the kitchen right away—together,'' Kellhorn encouraged. "As soon as you heard the crash.''

Mindy hesitated.

"Didn't you?'' Kellhorn asked. He was sure her friends had told him that, and Temple had confirmed it. All three girls had come flying out of the kitchen into the hall, seconds after the glass was broken. He wished he could pull out his book and flip to his notes, but he did not want to interrupt the girl.

"Well—I was carrying a large bowl of chocolate pudding, you see. I was in the middle of the floor, in the kitchen ell, holding the bowl. I couldn't just drop it. I mean, it would have made a terrible mess,'' she said reasonably.

"Yes?''

"So I ran back to the counter and set it down. When I turned around, Nicole and Katharyn were already gone. I ran out of the ell as fast as I could, through the kitchen and out into the hall.''

"Then, you were the last one out of the kitchen?"

Mindy nodded. Kellhorn looked over at Carla Temple, alert now in her chair near the windows.

"Did you see anything as you passed through the kitchen? Did you see—uh, Sleepless fall?"

"No, he was running past the ovens. He was just shining his light on the door when I came out of the ell." Kellhorn leaned forward, his mouth open, breath almost held. "I saw this arm coming through the broken pane of glass, a hand reaching for the doorknob inside. It was horrible!"

Her shiver was the first sign of emotion Kellhorn had seen since the girl had entered the room.

"Was it a man?" Kellhorn asked. "More than one?"

"I only saw one man."

"Mindy, you *saw* him?" Carla burst in. "Why didn't you tell me?"

Kellhorn raised a silencing hand but kept his eyes fixed on the young girl. "What did he look like?" he asked quietly.

"Surprised," she said, squeezing her hands in her lap. "I mean, I didn't really have a good look at him. I was so frightened, I just wanted to get out."

"Of course you did. But still, you saw a man's face. And you remember that he looked surprised."

"Well, I—I think so. It was very quick. I was running, you know. And those frames in the glass,—" She made an airy cross with both hands. "They were in the way."

"Was he dark, this man? Did he have dark hair—or maybe he was blond?" Tension had crept into Kellhorn's voice.

"I—don't remember." Her eyes darted to Carla in appeal. Carla rose and walked to her side.

"Did you think it was a young man?" Kellhorn asked. "Or old?"

"Oh, old—your age," Mindy said earnestly. "Maybe older, even."

Carla pressed an inappropriate smile from her lips and put her hand on Mindy's shoulder. "Take your time—just think for a minute. Anything you can remember will help Sergeant Kellhorn find him."

Mindy closed her eyes and shook her head slowly, concentrating. "There *was* something—it's peculiar, but I had this queer feeling that I knew him. Not really *knew* him. Just—I had seen him before."

Kellhorn's tongue flicked at his lip. He reached into his back pocket and pulled out his notebook. "In town?" he asked. "Did you see him in Fernstaad?"

"N-no, I don't think so. Maybe. It was all so quick, I can't remember. I wouldn't have thought of it if you hadn't asked."

"You mean the face was familiar," Carla said, "but you might not necessarily know his name?"

"In a way, yes. But maybe he just looked like someone else, or I met him somewhere without talking to him. You know, like in the Klaus."

"You said you didn't think you had seen him in town." Kellhorn was scribbling now.

"Oh—yes. I did say that. I'm sorry—I guess I'm just confused."

"Do you think you would recognize him if you saw him again?"

Mindy grimaced and shrugged with uncertainty. "I wish I could say yes. It's important, isn't it?" she asked Carla.

"It could be," Kellhorn answered for her. He closed his notebook and reached for the cup on the end table. The coffee was cold now, but he took a deep swallow. "I may even want to talk to you again. This wasn't so hard, now, was it?"

Mindy agreed out of politeness. She was no longer paying any attention to Sergeant Kellhorn. The look on Miss Temple's face worried her. How could such a dumb thing like sneaking into the damn kitchen have turned into such a mess?

Kellhorn stood up and began buttoning his jacket. "I don't think we have to keep you any longer," he said to Mindy.

Carla nudged the girl gently. "You can go now. If you think of anything else, we can talk later. Tonight, if you like."

"Okay," Mindy said, rising. "Uh, Sleepless—is he better now?"

"He's recovering very nicely," Kellhorn said. "He'll be back watching over you girls in no time, making sure you behave, you'll see."

Carla looked at him, surprised. She had assumed he already knew about the watchman's death, but obviously he hadn't heard yet. The call from Dr. Leitner must have come while Sergeant Kellhorn was out showing the two new security guards around the school. Miss Grimsby had told Carla sometime after lunch, and they had discussed the best way to tell the girls. Both agreed it would be better to wait.

"What's your next class, Mindy?" Carla asked quickly.

"French." Her eyes rolled up as if a guillotine blade hung from the ceiling.

"Oh-oh! Better hurry. Madame Guinet wouldn't accept an excuse from the president of the Republic himself! If you want to see me, just knock on my door before dinner, or after, if you like. I'll be there."

As soon as Mindy had gone, Carla told the sergeant about Johann Bächli. The latest death to hit the school, she said. Almost like an epidemic, didn't he think? Kellhorn laughed, a snort without mirth, and waved away the suggestion. Carla's face reddened. He was dismissing her as if she were being childish or superstitious, or worse, hysterical. Why, the man's own superior, Rudi Neumayer, had been much more sympathetic and understanding! *Was* she getting nutty, as Eric suggested? No, dammit, and she wasn't going to be patronized!

She was so angry that she left Miss Grimsby's office with only a curt good-bye to the sergeant—just left him standing there, ignoring her as he scribbled in his notebook.

It wasn't until later that Carla remembered she was having dinner with Eric tonight. She would leave a note in Mindy's mailbox, in case the girl wanted to talk to her. Tomorrow, they would both have more time.

CHAPTER
31

Filomena sat on the side of her bed in the tiny room she shared with her older sister, Ada, and felt very sorry for herself.

Everybody was being so mean to her today. Especially Mamma. It wasn't fair of Mamma to slap her this morning. Just because she was slow in getting dressed for school. Or maybe Mamma was mad that Filomena couldn't remember what happened to her other mitten. She didn't lose it on purpose. Why was everyone picking on her?

And crabby Ada was worse. After Mamma left their room, Ada *pinched* her, *hard*, to make her cry louder so Mamma would be even madder. It wasn't *her* fault that Ada pinched her. She was so mean, that Ada. And she *lied!* She promised Filomena she'd let her play with her special Signora Campana bride doll, her best doll, when they got home from school today. And now she wouldn't. She didn't even care about it anymore. She was just being mean. And she broke her promise!

"I hate you!" Filomena said to the empty bed next to hers. "I'm never going to play with you again. And if I get a new doll for my birthday, I won't even let you look at her. *You'll* be sorry!"

She sulked on her bed and wished that Ada would come into the room right now so she could tell her how much she hated her, how she'd get even with her someday. But Ada was outside playing with her friends. Filomena hated Ada's friends, too. They never, *never* let Filomena join them.

Nobody cared about her.

She felt the sting of salty tears in her eyes and a moist dripping starting in her nostrils. She bent down to pull off her slushy boots, then straightened and wiped her nose with one dirty hand, leaving a clownish smudge, like a mustache, across her face. She flung herself back onto her bed and began to think with relish of how sorry Ada would be one day.

But, soon, she grew bored with just lying there and thinking. What could she do now?

Suddenly, she remembered the box under her bed—her *treasures!* And, at the same moment, she remembered where her lost mitten was. Wrapped around that huge knife she found in the snow! That day Ada saw the awful face in the ice, the dead lady . . . when all the police came to their apartment and asked scary questions. Filomena shuddered. But her mitten—it wasn't lost at all! It was there under the bed, all the time!

Excited, she sprang from the bed and crouched at its side, reached below and tugged out her grubby treasure box.

Yes, there it was—right on top!

She lifted the knife out, very carefully, holding it by the thick black leather band that wrapped its handle. Slowly, carefully, she slid her mitten off the wicked-looking blade.

Mamma would be so glad!

Signora Luzzatto climbed wearily up the steps to her third-floor apartment, carrying the bundle of her work clothes as if they were bricks. The lift was broken again. Of all days, when she was long past exhaustion. How she hated *Skimarathon* week! The Hotel Chesa Monteviglia was already flooded with tourists, right up to its smallest spare room. It was punishment to be a chambermaid there during the *Skimarathon*. Not that she minded hard work—but this was slavery. Running all day long, mopping and cleaning, bring me this, bring me that. . . . She had not even had time to stop for lunch. And now she would have to go straight into her kitchen and start preparing dinner for her family.

She was grey with fatigue as she labored up the steps—and troubled by guilt. All day, she had felt miserable for having slapped Filomena that morning. The child could not help it if she was sometimes slow, if she lost a mitten now and then. Didn't all children do that? But Signora Luzzatto was so tired she had become ill-tempered and had struck out without thinking.

Poor Filomena—her baby! She was such a sensitive little girl, she cried about everything. She must be sulking in her room right now. Ada had told her, in the street downstairs, that Filomena was home. Well, Mamma would make it up to her baby. That new doll that Filomena wanted so badly—it was expensive, but she would buy it for her, for her birthday.

Signora Luzzatto stopped outside the apartment door and pulled out her keys.

"Filomena?" she called as she opened the door.

Inside, Filomena jumped as she heard the key turn in the lock and her mother's voice calling to her. Quickly, she threw her mitten onto the bed and started to stuff the knife back into her treasure box. Its razor-edged blade sliced cleanly through the soft tissue of her palm, biting into the palmar fascia just below the skin. The pain reached her a second later, along with the shock of seeing the neat line of red suddenly blooming in her hand.

At the door, Signora Luzzatto dropped her bundle and tore frantically into the bedroom when she heard Filomena's hysterical screams.

CHAPTER
32

"It's German?" Neumayer asked.

"Yes, sir," Corporal Trivella said from the door of Neumayer's office. "I thought you'd want to have a look at it."

He entered the room carrying the knife outstretched in his hand, balanced on a folded sheet of plastic in his palm.

"Good God! Quite a nasty-looking thing, isn't it? I thought little girls liked to play with dolls."

"Not this one, apparently. She gave her mother a pretty bad scare."

"Is the child all right?" Neumayer asked.

"Oh, yes. Nothing terribly serious. Her mother raced her to the clinic, and they bandaged her hand and gave her a shot. She'll heal quickly, the doctor told me."

"Are you sure about where this was found?"

"That's what the child told her mother. She picked it up at the edge of the stream—it was half-buried in the snow, right near the Karas girl—just at the time her sister stumbled over the body. Her mother brought the knife to the clinic with her, and they just sent it over."

"Well, let's see it."

Trivella laid the knife on his superior's desk and bent over it.

"You can see it's made in Germany." Trivella pointed to the markings on the blade.

The knife was twenty-seven centimeters long, a wide and flat-bladed weapon—a field knife, or survival knife, as it was usually called. It gleamed dangerously on Neumayer's desk. He reached out and turned it sideways to study the markings. It was a factory-made Carl Schlieper from Solingen, Germany, with the signature eye and sun rays on its steel blade above the half-serrated back. Its concave edge was honed to razor sharpness. Between the tip of the butt and the wide brass guard, the handle was wrapped several times in a long strip of black leather—not part of its original manufacture, but an embellishment by its owner. A small rectangle showed where a scrap of tape had held the leather. The tape was gone now, possibly lost in the snow, and the black strapping was beginning to unravel.

"It looks fairly new," Corporal Trivella said.

"Mmmmm," Neumayer said absently. He poked at it with one finger, turning it around again. Gently, he peeled back several turns of the loose leather strip to reveal the black cast metal of the handle.

"Do you think it was brought in from England or America?" The sergeant leaned closer, studying the English words on the blade just below the guard: "*Tempered, Stainless, Surgical.*"

"Not necessarily," Neumayer said. "I know this model. Standard for export. You could buy it almost anyplace in the world—at Kaspi's, for example, right here in Fernstaad. It comes in a black scabbard. I don't suppose that was found, was it? Did the little girl pick that up, too?"

"No, only the knife. She told her mother she carried it away wrapped in a mitten. The whole area around the stream was thoroughly combed right after the body was found, as Sergeant Kellhorn ordered. No one turned up any scabbard." He hesitated. "I believe there is some question about the Karas death—"

Neumayer looked up at the sergeant sharply.

"Well, I did see the autopsy report when it came in." Trivella shrugged.

"Good man," Neumayer nodded, "but I don't think we want too much notice paid to this case at the moment. Understood?"

"Yes, sir. Could there be a connection between the Karas girl's—uh, accident, and the knife?"

"It would only be guessing. There were no knife wounds on the body, as you know since you read the report."

"Shall I have the lab check it for prints?"

Neumayer hunched gloomily over his desk, his arms barricading the knife between them as if it were a skittish animal about to flee. Of all the things he did not have faith in, the chance of lifting significant fingerprints from found objects topped his list.

"May as well," he sighed. "But I think its owner has taken pains to avoid leaving any traces. Still, it's worth a try. The knife does look new, and it's an expensive model. Big, too. I don't think you could lose something like this without realizing it immediately. So, what prevented its owner from retrieving it?"

"Maybe he was in too much of a hurry—?"

"I was only speculating out loud. Here, take it. Let me know what you find."

"Sir." Trivella lifted the knife from Neumayer's desk by its plastic sling and wrapped it carefully.

After Corporal Trivella had left his office, Neumayer reached for the phone and called Heinz Kaspi, owner of the largest arms shop in Fernstaad. Because of its prime location in the center of town and its immense range of rifles, pistols, shotguns, and equipment for hunting, fishing, and archery, Kaspi's was Neumayer's first target.

Half an hour later, Neumayer had spoken to the owners of all three arms shops in town. None of them had any useful information for him. No one had any record of selling a Carl Schlieper knife of the dimensions Neumayer described in the past few weeks. All of them promised to alert their staff to get as much identification as they could on any customer purchasing or showing an interest in survival knives, or any other weapons that did not require official registration.

Well, that was that. All Neumayer had to do now was call the dozens of small stores that sold knives of any kind—even Swiss army knives. Gift shops, boutiques, drugstores, to-bacconists, newsdealers, even linen and ceramic shops. Almost every store in Fernstaad seemed to offer the tomato-red folding knives with their great variety of hidden cutlery, some models that included sharply honed blades just as serviceable as a survival knife. And he had to ask his questions carefully, without arousing suspicion.

Some things were possible. Some not.

"Found knives and missing matches," he muttered to himself.

Carla smoothed the heavy coat folded over her arm and knocked on the door of Miss Grimsby's office. Her hands were cold with excitement, but her face radiated inner warmth. She wore a swirly, rich red silk dress, flagrantly sexy with its low-draped bodice, which made the creamy curve of her shoulders and breast look edible. And her favorite perfume, Balenciaga's Quadrille, which Michael used to say made him dizzy. Let Eric handle *that* combination. This evening, there would be no more talk of the problems at Marlowe. Not tonight.

She fussed with her hair as she waited for the crisp "Come in" that was the headmistress's usual command. When she didn't hear any sound, she tried the knob. The door opened.

Miss Grimsby stood at the tall windows, looking out at the vibrant blue of evening that now claimed the mountains and softened their jagged contours. She did not move as Carla entered the room.

"I just came to say good night," Carla said.

"Oh, Carla!" Miss Grimsby turned from the windows. "Don't you look lovely!"

"I knocked, but I guess you didn't hear me."

"Come in, my dear. Are you going out for the evening? I didn't see you at dinner. Goodness, what time is it?" She looked at her watch.

"Eight-thirty. Yes, I have a date in town."

Miss Grimsby smiled but made no comment about the specialness of the event, as Carla had known she wouldn't. It was obvious to the headmistress from Carla's appearance—her dress, her high color, and the sparkle of her richly lashed eyes; the crackling electricity that she brought into the room—that this evening was, indeed, special. Miss Grimsby had never doubted that Carla would one day regain the natural interests of a woman her age, however long it took. She was much too healthy to remain a sexual recluse. Still, Miss Grimsby was pleased now. It had been a very long time in happening.

"I'm having dinner with Dr. Sunderson, Dr. Leitner's new associate at the clinic," Carla said lightly.

"Oh, yes. I've met him." Miss Grimsby's voice was pleasant, but the expression on her face had sagged slightly. She turned her head to the window again as she thought of the occasion of that meeting. It had been at Johann Bächli's bedside.

Carla shifted her coat to her other arm and looked with sympathy at the headmistress. She understood her distress, but it was painful to see this remarkably composed and confident woman looking so troubled. Miss Grimsby's unflappable calm, her quiet strength and impeccable judgment, were what gave Marlowe its richly deserved reputation as one of the finest secondary schools in the world. It was unsettling for Carla to see her this shaken. She tried to think of something comforting to say, but nothing came to mind.

The moment passed quickly, and Miss Grimsby turned back into the room, her head high. "Are you in a rush, or do you have time for a sherry?" she asked.

"Thank you, I'd love to," Carla said. "I'm not meeting Eric until nine, and the taxi won't be here for another twenty minutes."

"You could have had Kurt drive you," Miss Grimsby said. She bent to the low cabinet near the windows and removed a heavy, cut-crystal decanter and two delicate stem glasses.

"I suppose so," Carla said with a twinkle.

"Of course," Miss Grimsby smiled in response. "It wouldn't be very stylish to be ferried to dinner in town by a schoolbus, would it?"

Carla laughed at the woman's perception and laid her coat on the arm of the leather couch facing the desk. She rested her cane against the coat and waited until Miss Grimsby had handed her the sherry and settled in a straight-backed side chair. Then Carla sank into the comfortable corner cushion of the couch.

"I've been thinking about Johann Bächli," Miss Grimsby said, suddenly serious. "Brooding, I'm afraid. In some ways, his death has pained me more than the deaths of poor Sophie and Anneliese. Oh, don't misunderstand. I know that sounded cruel—young girls, an old man. Maybe 'more' is the wrong word. But I've known Johann since I first came to Marlowe. I was about your age then. He was the only person still left at the school from those days. Even Madame Guinet came later." She sipped her sherry, then placed the glass on the end table near one of the framed family photographs. "The funeral will be on Thursday, early in the morning. It will be private."

"I'd like to come," Carla said, setting her glass on the table next to Miss Grimsby's. "Would you mind?"

"I'd rather you didn't. Don't be offended. I've only asked

a few of the teachers—those who knew him the longest."
She mentioned the German teacher and the choral master,
and a few of the older teachers, such as Mme. Guinet, who
had known the old watchman for years. And, of course, Herr
Blumen, the chef, who had cried like a baby when he learned
of Johann's death. "I'd prefer to have your presence here at
school. Besides, your first class Thursday is at nine-thirty."
Miss Grimsby knew the schedule of every Marlowe teacher
by heart. "We may not be back by then. Please understand,
I need you more here."

"Don't you think some of the others would want to go,
too?"

"Perhaps. But I don't want too many of them leaving the
school grounds at the same time. I won't have the girls disturbed, and I have no intention of telling them about Johann's
death for a while. It would be too upsetting, so soon after
Sophie and Anneliese. It wouldn't make any difference to
Johann, anyhow. There aren't any relatives to pay respects
to. He was quite alone."

"I know," Carla said. "He thought of you as his family."

"This may surprise you, but it was mutual. That's how I
thought of him, ever since I came to Marlowe—old Sleepless,
watching over us while we slept, grumbling like a bear in
the halls at night. . . . Enough of that! I don't want to sound
sentimental." She reached for her sherry. "Still, I'm going
to miss him. I do feel the loss of—my oldest family."

"I thought *this* was your family." Carla waved at the
framed photos on the end table.

"They were. They're gone now," the headmistress said
simply.

"Oh," Carla murmured. The moment had become uncomfortable. For distraction, she picked up a handsome blue-and-
green-enamel frame and studied the old photograph inside—
two solemn adults, a scowling young boy, and a baby. "Were
these your parents?"

"Yes," Miss Grimsby said.

"And this is you as a baby?"

"No. I had an older sister, and a brother even older. They
both died before I was born. Automobile accident. I never

knew them. That's the only photo of them my parents had—at least, the only one I ever found. They weren't much for taking pictures—not until I came along. All the rest are of my parents and me. Not a very interesting collection, I'm afraid.''

"I love old family photographs," Carla protested, replacing the enamel frame on the table and picking up another. "Especially snapshots. My family's are mostly studio portraits. Talk about formal!"

"Yes, I can imagine," Miss Grimsby said. "I've seen them in the papers. Is it a large family? Do they all live in Rhode Island?" It was politeness, not prying.

"Oh, yes. Parents, two older sisters, and a brother, not to mention aunts, uncles, and cousins by the dozens—just itching for me to come home so they can all feel sorry for me." It sounded harsher than Carla meant.

"You may be wrong about that." Miss Grimsby smiled gently at her. "We're fellow New Englanders, you and I. Did you know that?"

"New Hampshire?"

"Yes. A small town on a big lake," Miss Grimsby nodded. "Sometimes I miss it very much. I haven't been back for almost three years, not since my mother died. She went six months after my father. They were very close." Delicately, she sipped the last of the wine in her glass. Carla realized that she had never had such a personal conversation with the headmistress before. Calamity had given them the intimacy of conspirators. "Well, let's not make ourselves too gloomy on such a lovely evening. Your taxi should be here any minute," Miss Grimsby said, glancing at her watch.

Carla finished her drink and stood up. As if in response, the yellow headlights of a vehicle swept across the windows of Miss Grimsby's office, and the crunch of heavily treaded snow tires sounded from the courtyard outside.

"Just a minute," Miss Grimsby said. "You'll want a set of keys to let yourself in later." She did not routinely distribute them to her staff. If faculty members planned to be out late, they could either collect the keys before they left the school, or ring the night bell and have Sleepless let them in. It was a small security measure she had always practiced, although now, nothing seemed very secure to her.

The headmistress went to her desk and pulled two large keys on a chain from the back of an unlocked drawer. Three more sets remained in the small tray where she kept them. She realized that anyone with access to her office during the day when it was not locked could just as easily remove the keys, perhaps even have copies made, without her knowing it. Foolish of her to think of it now, so late. If no other teachers needed keys, she would move the remaining sets to the massive safe in the corner of the room as soon as Carla Temple left.

Carla buttoned her coat and adjusted its soft wide scarf around her neck. Miss Grimsby handed her the keys. She tucked them into the flat red Hermès crocodile purse that dangled from her shoulder, then picked up her cane.

"You might meet the new night watchman when you come in," Miss Grimsby said.

"Herr Bittmar? I've already met him, in the hall this afternoon. He was in the process of charming Lina, if that's possible." Carla laughed as she thought of the sallow, grumpy secretary, suddenly behaving so flustered, almost kittenish.

"No, the night man is Herr Suter. You probably won't even see him." She walked Carla to the door and opened it. "Have a lovely evening, my dear."

"I wish I didn't need this chaperon." Carla waggled her cane.

"That won't be forever. Good night, Carla."

Miss Grimsby closed the door softly and waited with her hand on the doorknob. She had no intention of hovering anxiously over the self-reliant young woman. Still, the front steps could become extremely icy in the freezing night air. When, at last, she heard the car door slam outside and the tires scrunch as the taxi pulled out of the courtyard, she returned to her desk, removed the three sets of keys, and locked them inside the safe.

Now, was there anything else she ought to be doing?

* * *

The bruise had leaked across the outside of his thigh in a yellow-and-purple stain. It disgusted him to look at it each time he changed his clothes.

Minna Breitel had left the stack of clean laundry on his bed while he was out, neatly ironed and folded and sweet-smelling. He picked up the pile and buried his face in its softness for the joy of snuffling its clean fragrance. He patted the clothes as he carried them to the small chest of drawers in his room. *So soft!* He set the pile in a drawer, then hesitated. *So clean!* He could not resist the impulse to change his underclothes once again. The excitement, the tension, was stimulating a familiar compulsion. But he was aware of it; he could control it.

Still, to put on fresh underwear, just once more today.

He lifted out a clean pair of shorts and laid it on his bed. Like the rest of his clothing, it had been purchased on his arrival in Fernstaad—Swiss-made, like the shirts and heavy sweater he had splurged on. He had purged his warbrobe of any foreign labels that might identify him. Now he stripped off his clothes and knelt to retrieve the light canvas suitcase under the bed.

Inside the case, the large envelope containing the two remaining sheets of Marlowe School stationery rested at the bottom. Did he still need them? Or should he destroy them, as he had the last note he had prepared—the one that had gotten crumpled and dirty the other night outside the school? No, he would save them.

He stuffed the underwear he had just removed into the suitcase, on top of the envelope. Even though he was naked, he did not feel cold as he knelt by his bed. His room was fiercely overheated, like most houses in the wintery Alps. Then he pressed the clothes down, and a sudden chill gripped him. He had felt the slight bulge beneath the envelope, a reminder of still another problem to be solved.

The bulge was the black leather scabbard of the knife he had lost that day when—that day in the snowstorm. He remembered losing it; he remembered how. But why hadn't he searched for it? He was sure he had been so careful about everything that day. How could he have left without his knife? He could not go back to look for it afterward—he knew that as soon as he realized it was lost. But he could not remember why he had forgotten it in the first place, why he had left without it.

Not that it mattered. The knife could not be traced. He had bought it, together with the suitcase and several other necessities, at the airport in Zurich when he arrived. Even if it had been found, there was no way to trace it back to him. Still, it was gone, and he felt uncomfortable. He desperately needed to replace it, but he could not buy a new weapon in town. That *would* be dangerous. He would have to steal one. And not from the Breitels' kitchen, either. The shrewd old lady would know. But he had already decided where. And he was going there, anyhow.

The medical examiner's laboratory. He had seen it in a small side street during his wanderings through town. Even in the middle of the day, no one had entered or left as he stood silently and watched. When he returned in the evening, it seemed deserted. He was sure it would be empty at night, unguarded. He had to take the chance. Somehow, he must get into the files and find out what the M.E.'s report said, what they had found in the greenhouse. He'd be killing two birds with one stone, he thought wryly. But first, he must satisfy a more immediate need.

He closed the suitcase and replaced it under the bed. He would bathe himself clean, as clean as his fresh clothing. He crossed the small room and stepped into the bathroom.

Pindar Breitel could feel the restlessness of his boarder upstairs. He tracked the man's footsteps as he paced the room overhead. From the bed to the chest of drawers and back. An object was lightly slid a short distance along the floor, then back again. Bare feet padded into the bathroom. He was running the tub *again*.

The sounds were not the usual ones made by the guests he and his mother had housed over the years. Herr Breitel could not say for certain, but something was different about this one. His constant movement, the rushing of water in the bathroom at all hours, his disappearance for days at a time —it was odd. Breitel's mother had described the man, but he did not sound special in any way. Maybe his eyes—*Mutti* had mentioned the man's blue eyes more than once. Breitel did not like to admit it, but he had always had trouble imagining colors. Yellow, he thought he understood. It would be like the fire of the winter sun, so hot as it reflected off the snowy Alps. Green would be for the lush grass of the summer hills, and red for the summertime berries and flowers. But blue? That was confusing. The sky? The ski slopes in early evening? How was that possible? Snowflakes were not blue. How could so many different things change into blue? He tried to picture the blue eyes of the man upstairs as his mother had described them. All he could think of was cold, like the wall of icy air he stepped through when he went outside.

Breitel sighed with frustration. He wished he had someplace to go. *Mutti* always had her shopping. For him, the days were sometimes so long and dreary. Yesterday, he had stopped in at the *Kantonspolizei* to visit Rudi Neumayer, but the inspector was not there. The officers had been very busy, rushing about, almost brusque. He could not even stay to talk to some of the other men. They all seemed so preoccupied, and he did not like to be in the way. Funny that Neumayer had not called him. He usually did if he was out when Breitel came in. *Skimarathon* week must be causing much additional work for the *Kantonspolizei*. So *Mutti* had told him when she described the crowds in town. It must be worse this year than ever.

So tiring doing nothing. Maybe tomorrow he would wander into town and call on Neumayer again. Probably he ought to wait until after the weekend, when things were calmer. But it was only Tuesday—such a long time to wait. Maybe if he just stopped in for a few minutes, tomorrow or Thursday . . . ?

Dr. Ursula Freimann had never minded working long hours, or late at night. Like now. She was alone in Fernstaad and hadn't met anyone that she would have liked to spend her personal time with. Her work was far more interesting, anyhow, as she had always found. So she was not upset when Dr. Leitner's call came earlier in the afternoon: Inspector Neumayer was eager to have a report as soon as possible; would she be available? The case was briefly described, and she assured Dr. Leitner that she would take care of it whenever he was ready. She would wait at the laboratory. But later, when Johann Bächli's body arrived from the clinic, Ursula Freimann was surprised. What could possibly be the urgency about this subject?

Nevertheless, she began her careful preliminary preparations. She was hardly aware of the rest of the laboratory staff as they started to drift, one by one, out of the building at the end of the day. It wasn't until Gertrud knocked on the door of her lab to say good night and ask if Dr. Freimann wished her to lock up that she realized everyone else had already left.

"Yes, of course," she called out. "Please lock both the inner and outer doors. I've already started in here."

Neumayer would send a messenger to pick up her report later that evening, but there was a bell outside that she would hear, even through the thick, double-locked doors of the lab.

Dr. Freimann strode purposefully around the room, checking her equipment under the shadowless intensity of the bright fluorescent lights. The stinging smell of formalin and disinfectant soap, the gurgling of the active flow of water, were all comfortably familiar, even though she was not yet completely at home in the Fernstaad autopsy room. Her rubber-soled shoes made no sound as she moved along the tables and examined her tools: scissors and shears and scalpels; knives of all sizes, including one with a tremendous blade, sixty centimeters long; clamps and forceps and probes; ladles, handsaws, wire saws, band saws, and, incongruously, several pieces of kitchen cutlery that she had always found useful and had brought to Switzerland with her. She wore a light sweater under her surgical gown and plastic apron, even though the cool of the room was pleasant. She looked over the rows of wide-mouthed jars and varied scales and checked her portable dictating machine. Everything was ready.

She approached the table where Johann Bächli waited patiently, no longer sleepless.

From her very first years as a pathologist, Dr. Freimann had disciplined herself into a scientist's detachment. The body to be studied was not her kin; no human commonality connected them. It was a field of mystery into which she would cut a path, to probe, measure, and weigh until it gave up its secrets. Objective research without prejudice, nothing known until it was revealed. An almost abstract exercise from which she remained distant. But there were still times when she slipped over the edge of her aloofness and found the ghost of the living body waiting for her. She would see it clearly as the true wonder of form and function it was, a mirror of herself, a *being* that had once lived in intimate relation with others. Lover, friend, cousin, parent, or child—it insisted on its former humanity: *I was as you are now*. Then, at the very moment it claimed its kinship to her, it would flee, its final spark extinguished before her eyes. Then she would shake with shock at the terrible emptiness left behind.

Alone now in the antiseptic white of her laboratory, with only the chuckle of running water for company, Dr. Freimann looked down at the tragedy below, at Johann Bächli in his last relation to the living—to her. He would not protest when she violated his last privacy—there would be no defending himself. He was empty now. It was he who was aloof.

She stood for a moment, eyes closed.

Then she shook herself free.

Turning on her dictating machine, she began a meticulous external examination, carefully describing and recording her findings as she went. When she was finished with that initial exploration, she picked up a medium-blade scalpel with one rubber-gloved hand.

''I begin with a shallow Y incision,'' she told the machine, ''starting at the right shoulder, drawn down and forward across the clavicle to join the cut from the left shoulder, then down the midsternum and abdomen, alongside the umbilicus. . . .'' Later, she would transcribe this simply into, ''The body is opened with the usual Y-shaped incision,'' but, for the moment, she preferred to be as detailed as possible, especially in view of the police interest in the case. Also, she liked talking out loud in a continuous flow as she worked.

Several hours later, Dr. Freimann straightened and arched her back to relieve the ache that had crept into her shoulders. Her legs were tired, too, so she perched on a tall stool near a sink for a few minutes. Had she overlooked anything? She left her dictating machine running in case something occurred to her. But, no—all observations had been noted, all surface lacerations described, all weights and measurements recorded, all conclusions detailed. Her examination was complete, and there was nothing remarkable in her findings. The evidence of shock and pulmonary edema was present, but death had come from acute myocardial infarction. Johann Bächli's damaged heart had finally come to rest.

She rose and returned to the perforated metal bed on which the body lay. Seizing the near arm and leg, she was able to slide the body off and onto a trolley without much difficulty. She rolled it to one of the large refrigerator compartments that was kept at minus twenty degrees Celsius for long-term storage. When the final transfer was accomplished, she carefully gathered up a handful of her instruments and slipped them into the wire basket of the autoclave, where they would be steamed under pressure until sterilized. She hosed down the work area lightly, then peeled off her apron and gown and dropped them into the disinfectant soak. Finally, she snapped off her gloves. She still had another hour's work ahead of her transcribing her notes, she thought wearily.

Suddenly, she heard a sound outside the lab. It seemed to be coming from the hall along the row of offices that led to the reception area. But how was that possible? She was sure she had heard Gertrud lock the door to that hall after everyone had left. Maybe the noise was out in the reception area. Had Gertrud forgotten to lock the outer door on her way out?

Leaving her lab, Dr. Freimann walked down the hall, past the offices, and turned the sharp corner to the inner door. On the other side, just beyond its thick, full length of glass, the shadowy figure of a man hulked in the unlit reception room. He jumped back, as startled to see her as she was to see him.

Dr. Freimann approached the separating door for a closer look, but did not unlock it.

"*Ja? Was wollen Sie?*" she called through the thickness

of the door. "You are from the *Kantonspolizei?*" she demanded in her precise, clipped German.

The man came up to the door again without speaking. He was not in police uniform. His neck was hunched inside the collar of his heavy tan parka, face partly hidden. He pointed at the lock on the door.

Ursula Freimann shook her head.

"I can hear you through the door," she said. "What do you want? Did Inspector Neumayer send you for my report? Well?"

The man nodded slowly.

"It's not ready. You'll have to come back in another hour."

The man did not move. He shuffled nervously in the shadows of the dark reception room, but did not step away from the door.

"I told you, I'm still working on that report. How did you get in here, anyhow? I didn't hear the bell ring."

No response. Was the fellow deaf, or stupid?

"Listen, I'm very busy. Tell Inspector Neumayer that my report isn't finished yet. I'll have it for him in an hour. You come back then. One hour," she said, raising one forefinger as if she were speaking to a child.

"*Ich warte,*" the man said.

I wait? Dr. Freimann wondered if the man was simple, or if she was just hearing a cloddish idiom of the unfamiliar *Schweizerdeutschen* dialect.

"No, you can't wait. You'll have to leave now. You're not supposed to be here. You're just delaying my work. Why don't you go have a coffee at the Klaus down the street and come back in an hour? I'll call the *Kantonspolizei* and let them know I'm not ready. Go on, now." She waved at the outer door. "Go along."

She waited as the man turned slowly and walked through the reception room. He opened the outer door and lumbered through it, closing it behind him.

Ursula Freimann walked down the hall to her office. She would telephone Inspector Neumayer's office and explain to him that he would have to send the messenger again, later. Then she could get on with her report. She was very tired, and it was already much later than she had realized. She pulled out her keys to unlock her office. A sudden thought stopped her. She had better lock the outer door so that she would not be interrupted again in the middle of her work.

She retraced her steps and used her keys to let herself out into the reception room. She would speak to Gertrud on Monday about not closing up securely when she left at the end of the day.

Smothering a yawn, Dr. Freimann crossed through the dark room, her keys clinking in her hand. She reached for the door—then recoiled with shock as it burst open.

The man crashed heavily in on her. With powerful force, he spun her around and locked her neck in the strangling grip of the crook of his elbow. There was not even time to cry out—not that anyone would have heard her. The pressure on her trachea was closing her airway, stifling her breathing. She struggled fiercely, but she could already feel the dizziness creeping up on her. She dropped her keys with a ringing clatter. The choking pressure relaxed slightly. She tried to pull away, but was jerked back with a force that lifted her off her feet. A black roaring rose in her ears.

Holding her tightly, the man propelled Dr. Freimann forward, through the inner door, past the row of offices along the dimly lit hall, and into the gleaming laboratory.

CHAPTER
33

Carla raked the tines of her fork absentmindedly across the tablecloth and turned toward the door of the restaurant. It was the tenth time she had checked the people entering since the captain had seated her—alone—at the intimate table in the alcove. And at least the tenth time she had checked her watch. Nine-twenty now. The romantic music of the piano trio in the corner of the main room was beginning to grate. She sipped from her glass of white wine and wriggled restlessly in her chair.

When she saw the captain approaching, she read his message before he reached her table.

"*Bitte*, Fräulein Temple, Herr Doktor Sunderson is calling."

She followed the captain to the phone at his station near the front door, already prepared to sound gracious. She could almost feel the flowy red silk of her dress going limp as she walked.

Eric was abject in his apologies, and sounded as frustrated as Carla felt. He had been summoned into emergency surgery and hadn't been able to call sooner. He didn't know when he'd be able to leave the clinic—possibly in another hour or so. Would she please forgive him? And order dinner for herself? The captain had been instructed to bill him. He might be able to join her for dessert.

It was the least appealing suggestion she might have expected, but she called on her best manners and most mature understanding to decline with thanks and assure him she quite understood. Another time, when they could both enjoy the evening, she said. He would undoubtedly be tired, and she had an early class in the morning. Yes, she was disappointed, too, but it couldn't be helped. Tomorrow night? Why didn't he call later when he was free, or in the morning, and they would decide then.

He hung up after repeating his regrets and assurances, leaving Carla wondering about the social dependability of physicians. And also wondering what to do with the rest of the evening.

She certainly wouldn't care for a romantic dinner for one, and she didn't want to stop in at the Klaus or the Pappagallo dressed as she was. But she was definitely hungry. And too frustrated to want to return to Marlowe so early and risk having to answer questions if she ran into Miss Grimsby.

She stood at the captain's station, frowning in indecision.

A jolly party of diners descended from the upstairs dining room. One of the women recognized Carla and closed in on her with great enthusiasm.

"Carla, my dear! How wonderful to see you! My, don't you look splendid! And only a cane, now. Progress, progress!" She leaned to kiss the air next to Carla's cheek, then stood back, beaming. "How is your dear mother? I haven't seen her for ages."

Carla responded politely, wishing she had left already.

"Are you coming or going? We're on our way to Elvina's. Why don't you join us? All the riffraff in town are finding their way to her Tuesday soirees these days—too impossible, you know—but Elvina would be thrilled to see you. She speaks of you so often. Do come with us! Are you alone? Oh, that won't do! Come along, now."

Trapped, Carla persuaded herself that a rowdy evening at the gräfin's might just lift her gloom—and also her mother would be pleased to learn that she had performed a long-expected social duty. She retrieved her coat and allowed herself to be swept into the waiting limousine and up the mountain to the von Wetzlar chalet. The chatter at her side continued through the entire ride.

Sergeant Hans Kellhorn stood over the sink in his neat kitchen and arranged the dirty dinner dishes in fastidious order. His sleeves were rolled up, and the ties of his white linen apron were wrapped twice around his spare body. He would wash up first, then stroll down to the lake to watch the procession of midnight skiers coming down from Piz Wolfram with their candles. This was the official opening of *Skimarathon* week—a glorious spectacle that he looked forward to seeing each year.

But first, the dishes.

Order, symmetry, everything in its own precise rhythm and time. That's how he had done everything in his thirty-four years—methodically. His solitary life did not weigh too heavily on him. One day, he would find a woman with the same good taste and habits, or with the good sense to learn.

For the moment, he was content that he was a respected member of the *Kantonspolizei*, admired for his many skills. He felt that his powers of logic and deduction were superior, and he knew he was openly envied as a marksman of dazzling accuracy, a brilliant shooter who could handle any weapon within minutes of being introduced to it.

Considering the esteem he was accustomed to, Hans Kellhorn was quite irritated by his rude treatment at the Marlowe School. It was not just Grimsby—he was used to her haughtiness—but her teachers, as well. Like that nervous young woman, Carla Temple. Who cared *who* her family was? Fernstaad was crawling with people far wealthier— well, at least more prestigious. How dared she treat him so arrogantly? Did she really expect him to take her silly fears seriously?

He took a final sip of the Gigondas that had accompanied his steak dinner and rinsed the residue of béarnaise from the sauce bowl. Order, precision, cleanliness.

The sound of the phone rang over the running water. The unexpected, just as he always expected it.

"Kellhorn," he said briskly into the receiver.

"Neumayer here. Listen, Hans—" The voice was tense, breathing heavily; the use of his first name alerted Kellhorn that something unusual had happened—an emergency. He tightened his grip on the phone. "I'm at the M.E.'s," Neumayer growled. "I need you here right away. Someone got into the lab and attacked Dr. Freimann, Lüthi's new assistant. The ambulance is on its way—"

"Did he see who it was?"

"She. Dr. Freimann is a woman. And she's in no condition to talk."

"Dead?" Kellhorn asked.

"Still breathing, but barely. I don't know if she'll make it." Neumayer sounded exhausted, almost sick. "I'm going to the clinic with her, just in case. The lab is a mess. Really nasty, Hans. She put up quite a fight, it seems. I want you to see what you can find here. Bring two of the men with you, but watch them. I don't want anything that could be important to get messed up. That's why I'm calling you."

"Understood. But how was Dr. Freimann able to call you if—"

"She didn't. I stopped by the lab myself. She was working late, doing a report for me on Johann Bächli. I expected to hear from her when it was ready. She didn't phone, and didn't answer when I called, so I came by here on my way home. *God! Poor thing!*" Kellhorn waited while Neumayer blew into his handkerchief. "The outer door was open, not forced. She may have opened it herself. There's blood in the reception room, too, maybe tracks. But the real damage is in the lab. I tracked it up some myself. See what you can find."

"Right."

"No sense my locking up now. I'll leave it open for you. Get here as fast as you can."

"Yes, sir."

"And try to locate Dr. Lüthi. He's in Zurich—someone will have a number for him. I'd like him back in Fernstaad before the weekend, if possible—as soon as he can leave. This is bad, Hans, really bad."

"What would anyone be looking for in the morgue?" Kellhorn asked. "Do you think there's a connection with the Marlowe break-in?"

"Damned if I know!" Neumayer exploded. "We've never had anything like this before. A madman, a deliberate killer loose in town—"

Through the receiver, Kellhorn heard the faint, two-note shrilling of the ambulance siren, growing louder and louder, then cutting off abruptly.

"I'm leaving now," Kellhorn said.

"I'll check with you later." A slam of the phone disconnected them.

Neumayer had warned him, but still, Kellhorn was not prepared. The violence of the attack in the medical examiner's laboratory shrieked at him from every corner, a grisly tale. The place was a horror—overturned stools and instrument tables, stained metal and broken glass, scalpels glued to the congealing blood on the floor, white walls splattered red. He could see where the woman's body had fallen, the smeared tracks of the ambulance attendants who had lifted her to the stretcher and wheeled her away. How could anyone have survived . . . ?

Kellhorn picked his way carefully through the gore. The relentless light in the lab offered no softening shadows. The faces of his two men were ash green. He supposed that that was what he looked like, too.

As soon as one of his men had photographed the scene from all possible angles, Kellhorn went to work. Meticulously, he swabbed up blood samples, made sure they were correctly labeled by their position in the room, tweezed splinters of broken glass into envelopes, stalked the room, observing, collecting. A small, blood-splashed box lay on the floor, hidden behind an overturned table. A rosy droplet in one corner of the box winked at him cruelly. He stooped for a closer look.

It was a tape recorder, a small, portable dictating machine. The drop in the corner was not blood. It was a light. *The machine was on and running.*

Kellhorn slipped his hand inside a large plastic bag. Almost holding his breath, he reached out and picked up the tape recorder with a firm grip. Reversing the plastic mitten on his hand, he pulled it over the machine and gently sealed it. He found the proper switch and pressed carefully through the wrapping to turn off the recorder. Maybe they had something.

To anyone who has ever been to Fernstaad in season, the traditional midnight candlelight procession from Piz Wolfram to Fernstaad *Dorf* that ushers in *Skimarathon* week is one of the most beautiful sights in the Alps. People gather early all around Lake Clemenza for the best vantage. From anywhere in town, you can look up and see tiny fireflies of golden light spilling down the slopes, glowing against the blue-black of the mountains.

The senior Marlowe girls were allowed to take part in the procession—provided they were good skiers, and provided they had parental permission, and provided their grades were up to the mark, and provided they were not on detention for some violation of rules. . . . The provisions usually winnowed the list down to only a handful of girls. This year, with Mindy, Katharyn, and Nicole on detention—for some mysterious infraction they refused to discuss—only Bianca Gioianni and the shy Saudi Arabian girl in their class had made it.

Bianca had lost track of her classmate, Scheherazade, at the Corsetti funicular station. She felt only a little guilty. Mostly, she was relieved not to have a responsibility that might prevent her from sneaking in a little private socializing during the run. Maybe even some partying afterward. Scheherazade could make it back to school on her own.

In the clear, frigid air at the top of Piz Wolfram, Bianca held her lighted candle and skied to the edge of the piste. A tall, athletically handsome man she had noticed before on the slopes skied to her side and braked sharply.

"Ciao, bella! Dove sono le amiche?" He looked around for Bianca's friends, used to seeing them all together.

Bianca smiled up at him and returned his greeting in beautiful Italian, a language that was just as familiar to her as her native Spanish. She explained that her friends couldn't come, that she was alone, and, yes, she would love to have his company on the run down from Piz Wolfram. Introductions were brief—he was Renato Maag from Pontresina, and the luckiest man in Fernstaad to have found her without her usual chaperones.

Flattery given and accepted easily, Bianca edged closer to the lip of the piste and looked down the slope, alive now with dancing sparks.

"Just follow the lights ahead of you," Renato said, "and don't wander outside the flags. It's all been marked off, so keep to the trail. I'll be right behind you."

Bianca took a deep breath and plunged over the edge. A stinging wind pricked at her cheeks. She swooped in lazy arcs, moving slowly, alert to the dark shapes around her. She could hear the joyful shouts of the skiers, and the flickers of their candles guided her. Below the brilliant pool of light in the hollow of town drew her forward. Down and down . . . gathering assurance as she began to recognize the markings of the piste that she knew so well in full daylight: a stand of trees that signaled the halfway point to Corsetti; a deep gully not far off beyond the line of flags; the hikers' bridge farther down; the cleft that marked the funicular rails; the massive building of the Marlowe School. . . . With each turn, she was aware of Renato close behind her.

By the time she reached the base of the long trail, she was so thrilled she would have been glad to make the run all over again. She thrust her candle into the crusted snow to extinguish its flame and pressed her pole into the release spring of her ski bindings. Renato skied up to her, face wet from the snow spray, teeth gleaming with his exhilaration.

"Wonderful, wasn't it!" he said. Steam puffed out with each word. Bianca agreed. "I'm meeting my friends at the Lolita. Would you like to join us?" he asked.

She hesitated. It was late, but she felt a flood of energy that she knew would last for hours. She was in no rush to return to school.

"Well . . . sure! Just for a little while." She bound her skis and pole together and hoisted them to her shoulder as Renato stepped out of his. All around them, skiers who had exhausted themselves on the run lay sprawled in the snow— laughing, catching their breath, then struggling up to stream into Fernstaad for a celebratory drink. The clubs and bars would be mobbed tonight.

Bianca and Renato stepped into the road and joined the traffic.

As they passed a low embankment against which a handful of weary skiers rested, a man in a thick tan parka pushed himself awkwardly from his perch and staggered into the road. He was breathing heavily, although he wasn't wearing ski boots or carrying skis. He lurched forward and crashed into Bianca. The blow sent her toppling.

"*Aaaay! Bastard!*" Renato shouted. "*Watch where you're going!*" It was a toss-up whether he should beat the man to a pulp or help Bianca up. Chivalry won. He reached for her hand.

The man in the tan parka didn't stop to apologize. He continued up the road, weaving and pushing against the traffic that surged down off the slopes. Then he disappeared around a bend toward Fernstaad *Bad*.

Bianca stood shakily and stamped her boots in the packed snow of the road. "I'm all right, nothing hurts," she assured Renato. She brushed off her light-colored overalls and bent to retrieve her skis.

"Here, I'll take them," he said. He shouldered them with his own. "Are you sure you're okay?"

She took a few steps and felt no pain. "Yes, fine, thank you."

They fell into step together, Renato ranting about the behavior of the tourists getting worse every year.

Bianca shook out her long black hair and straightened her jacket as they passed under a light shining from its high pole at the side of the road.

"The bastard didn't even try to help you up!" Renato said. "I should have given him— *Hey!* Stop a minute! I think he *did* hurt you! Look at that!"

They stopped under the light and stared at Bianca's jacket. A bright smear of blood stained its front and trailed from the shoulder down to the elbow of one sléeve.

"*¡Dios mio¡*" she cried.

Bitch, bitch! Oh, God, it hurts!

The woman in the laboratory—she had slashed at him with one of her instruments and cut open his arm, right through his parka! He had taken care of *her*, though. That long kitchen knife—what was it doing in a lab? *That* had stopped her! Right into her back! He had it now, together with some of her ugly tools, wrapped in a wad of towels and zipped inside his parka. And he would use it again. But his arm, it throbbed so! And the towel he had tied as a tourniquet around it had not stopped the bleeding right away—not for such a long time. He was thirsty, terribly thirsty. And tired. He needed to rest. But he couldn't return to the chalet or his room at the Breitels' until he could get the pressure to stop the awful flow of blood. He had fled the lab, leaving the body of that bitch on the floor. Then the pain had seized him, making him dizzy. And the cold. He had to stop—*rest*.

He stumbled through the more deserted side streets toward Fernstaad *Bad*, clutching at the towel packed under his torn sleeve. He passed a dark, inviting alley. Hesitating for a moment, he slipped inside and huddled in a doorway. Slowly, he sank to the ground. Warm air from a cellar vent blew gently over him.

He had not expected anyone to be at the laboratory so late at night. Opening the outer door had been easy. But the shock of seeing the white-coated woman peering at him through the glass of the inner door had thrown his plans into momentary confusion. She seemed to be expecting someone, but he couldn't be sure. He didn't understand her German. Clearly, she wanted him to leave. But she stared at him with such suspicion. And she mentioned the police. Who did she think he was? He didn't like the way she studied him through the door. What did she know? Well, it didn't matter now. He had taken care of her. *He had to!* Now he would take care of himself.

Slowly, unwillingly, he fell into heavy sleep. . . .

When he woke, the steeple bells were tolling. Three-quarters after the hour. But which hour? He had lost track of time. *Where was he?*

Pain jolted him back, and he remembered the horror of the night. He tried to read his watch, but it was too dark. Gasping, he struggled to his feet.

He set off again, detouring to a higher road that wound along the side of the slopes at the base of the ski pistes. At night, those roads would be empty; no one would see him there. Suddenly, the lights on the mountain caught his eye—hundreds of them, shimmery specks in the dark, spilling down toward him! He looked up in wonder. *What was going on?*

Then he remembered: Tonight was the night of the candlelight procession. He must hurry! They mustn't find him when they reached the bottom of the run!

He was quivering with the cold, but he had to keep going, climbing up the steep road, hugging the banks of snow at the base of the trails. His eyes flickered upward, tracking the fireflies of light as they crawled closer and closer. He had never been so tired in his life.

Finally, he had to stop, just for a few minutes. He couldn't go another step.

He flung himself to the side of the road and sprawled on a snowbank. He would catch his breath, only for a minute or two. . . .

Sleep began to creep up on him again. . . .

He woke with a start. A tumult of skiers was pouring off the hills, converging on all sides of him in a riot of noise. What time was it? Oh, God, he had to get away!

Struggling up, he slid to the road and pushed against the crowd as he tried to move forward. Someone bumped him, and he almost fell. He regained his balance and kept going. He heard someone shouting—was it at him?—but he did not turn around. Pressing ahead, he staggered up the road toward Fernstaad *Bad*.

At last, when he had escaped the throng of skiers, he tried to clear his head so that he could review his plans. The cold was helping. He knew what he must do.

First, he would need antiseptic and bandages. The wounded arm was probably not as bad as it felt, but he must take care of it. He had seen first-aid supplies downstairs in Minna Breitel's roomy kitchen. He would take what was necessary and think of explanations later, in case the old woman noticed. Then, he must get himself a new jacket. He couldn't wear this one anymore. He thought he had seen a small clothing store on one of the side streets when he wandered through town several days ago. It was very private, isolated. He would go there tomorrow.

Yes, tomorrow—he would take care of *everything* tomorrow. . . .

Carla paid the taxi driver who had rescued her from an excruciating evening at the von Wetzlars and stood for a moment in the dark, watching the car curve out of the courtyard and disappear down the road. Behind her, the hulking expanse of Marlowe rose up and caught the moon's reflection in its blind windows.

Elvina had been at her gushy worst. The gräfin was one of the most ravishingly handsome women of her age, but when she opened her mouth, out poured toads and spiders. She was gossipy, insincere, and a compulsive meddler. She had taken possession of Carla and pushed her on every unattached male at the chalet—at least, those that she had no further interest in. She had gabbled nonstop, leaving Carla mute—the death in the greenhouse, the parade of morbid thrill-seekers to the chalet, her husband's total lack of sympathy for her suffering. Why, Veep had even abandoned her that very evening, off to his club with his phony barone crony, no doubt . . . but such a joy to see her at last, and she must promise to come more often.

Carla suffered in stoic politeness, wondering how she had ever gotten so desperate that she had inflicted this torment on herself. Finally, she shook off the gräfin and a persistent young man whose eyes danced with druggy energy and called a taxi for her escape.

Above, the black, star-studded sky was clear. The glow of the last candle-bearers weaving slowly down from Piz Wolfram caused a pang. How she wished she could be up there with them! Or, at least, watching the spectacle with Eric.

The chill stirred her, and she climbed the steps to the softly lit front terrace. Using the keys Miss Grimsby had given her, she opened the double locks of the heavy front door.

Inside, the school slumbered. The first-floor hall was heated, but the night air that seeped in was trapped by the marble floor and breathed off again as penetrating cold. The few night-lights were dim enough to leave the hall in umber gloom. Carla shivered as she passed a table lamp. Her shadow rose fuzzily, with bloated importance, up the far wall. The heels of her red suede evening boots rang in the silence. It depressed her to hear the uneven rhythm that emphasized her unbalanced tread.

She checked her mailbox—empty—and returned to the chilly hall to summon the lift. Its old cage creaked down slowly, the sound racketing in the hall. She leaned on her cane, impatient with the noise and the slowness, wishing she could take the stairs.

Suddenly, she heard a new sound.

Footsteps—coming from the long corridor to her left.

A looming shadow slid up the opposite wall.

She turned to see a light moving toward her along the corridor. Behind it was the figure of a tall man. Without meaning to, she gasped.

"Sorry! I didn't mean to frighten you," the man said in German as he approached her. He turned the beam of his flashlight to the floor. "You are Fräulein Temple?"

She nodded weakly. She hadn't realized that she had become so very jumpy lately.

"I'm Suter, the night man. Frau Grimsby told me you would be in late. Please excuse me if I startled you. I only came to check when I heard the lift. Are you all right?" His thin face registered concern. Close up, he was not as huge as his shadow had made him appear.

"I had forgotten you would be in the building," Carla said. She smiled with faint embarrassment. The lift bounced to a stop in front of them, and Herr Suter opened the door for her. "Thank you. I'm glad to know you're here."

"Till morning," he said, and wished her a good night as he closed the door behind her.

You simp! she told herself as the lift noisily pulled itself up to the fifth floor. *Making an ass of yourself over shadows!* Then she realized that she was not the least bit tired, despite the long day and the tedious evening. She was angry, in fact—at Eric, for disappointing her, and at herself, just for feeling angry . . . and childish . . . and spoiled. . . . *Enough!* She decided she would not go to bed right away. First, she would do her exercises, then take a luxurious hot bath with that wonderful pine oil they made right here in Fernstaad. Then a book—yes, she would read for a while, and maybe Eric would call. . . .

An hour later, the book she was reading slipped out of her hand. She gave up waiting for Eric to call and went to bed.

"Let me hear that again," Neumayer said.

It was almost three in the morning. The purple of intense fatigue was smudged in rings beneath the inspector's eyes. His jowls sagged, and an unhealthy yellow tinted his face.

He sat at his desk, across from Hans Kellhorn, and stared at the tape recorder between them.

Kellhorn rewound the tape to the spot he knew Neumayer wanted to hear. It was the third or fourth time now. Kellhorn himself had listened to the entire tape after he returned from the medical examiner's laboratory. The woman's voice was so calm, so precise and professional, almost casual as she described what she was doing: "*I begin with a shallow Y incision. . . .*" He had listened to the whole thing, marveling at the detail and organized explication of procedure that was like a textbook in its thoroughness. He had meant to wind the tape ahead, bit by bit, until he found something that might be important, but he had been drawn to the crisp German voice of this unknown Dr. Freimann, and fearful for her. He tried to imagine what she might look like. It mattered to him, personally, inexplicably, that the woman was still alive, that she was being cared for by Dr. Leitner and his team. He had seen them work miracles more than once before.

Now he wound the tape back to the long, empty silence that had followed the pathologist's dictation, and waited for the sounds of violence. Why had the doctor left the tape running? What had made her leave the lab? There was no clue on the tape. They heard her footsteps recede, then silence, until she returned with her attacker. That was what Neumayer was waiting to hear again.

They listened as the now-familiar scene came alive: the door crashing open, the deep grunting of a male voice, the sound of someone carrying or dragging a heavy burden, the choked gasp of the woman—"*Was . . . wollen . . . Sie?*"—then the frantic pursuit around the lab. Dr. Freimann must have broken free and run crashing around the room, overturning metal tables, hurling whatever she could seize at her pursuer. Glass smashed, instruments clattered to the floor, her breath came in sobs of panic and exertion. Then the man howled in pain, and they heard his shocked cry: "*Aaagh! God damn you!*"

"Again," Neumayer said, pointing to the machine.

Kellhorn pressed the rewind button for a second.

"*Aaagh! God damn you!*"

Without being ordered, Kellhorn pressed the button again. *"Aaagh! God damn you!"*

The men stared at each other across Neumayer's desk, barely listening as the tape continued. They would not hear the man's voice again—only his fierce grunt and the shuddering gasp of the woman, the sound of a limp body tumbling to the floor. . . .

They let the tape roll, through the man's pained breathing, the clanking of metal instruments, the footsteps of the attacker, shuffling now, bumping against the door as he left the lab. Kellhorn turned off the machine when the tape reached the second silence, which signaled the end.

"English," Kellhorn said. "He speaks *English*. And I think she wounded him."

"Yes, it sounds like it," Neumayer nodded. "And maybe he *is* English. Or American. Or Canadian. Or God knows what! We all speak English around here." He slumped back in his chair and rolled his arm to look at his watch. "It's late. Who's on tonight?"

Sergeant Kellhorn told him.

"When that man we've got posted up at Marlowe calls—"

"Suter," Kellhorn said.

"Yes. He'll be checking in soon. Have the officer on the desk tell Suter to be particularly sharp tonight. And get one of our men up to the school as support."

"It's the same man, isn't it? The one who broke into the Marlowe kitchen?"

Neumayer shrugged. "I keep thinking about what you can find in an M.E.'s lab. Something you can't find too easily anyplace else that isn't heavily wired with alarms after hours, as all the stores in Fernstaad are. Something you might find in a kitchen, too."

"Knives," Kellhorn said.

"That seems to be this fiend's preference. Ursula Freimann was stabbed, they told me before I left the clinic. And that knife the little Luzzatto girl picked up—she says she found it near the body of Sophie Karas. If there's any connection—" He cupped his hand over a yawn and looked at Kellhorn with eyes watering from fatigue. "Well, it's been a long day. I don't think there's anything else we can do tonight. May as well go home, get a fresh start tomorrow. We'll run tests on everything you picked up, first thing in the morning. Oh, that's right. I know you're supposed to be off, but I'll need you. Sorry."

"Of course, sir. I'll be here early in the morning."

"It's *already* early in the morning." Neumayer rose as if every muscle in his body were in protest. "Go get some sleep. I'll see you later."

Hans Kellhorn watched his superior leave the office. Then he closed the door and picked up the phone.

"Her condition is stable," the attending physician at the Leitner Clinic informed him. "But she's still in very bad shape. With this kind of blood loss, we can't give you a reliable prognosis. She's a very strong lady, though, and holding on. Do you want to check with us later, or shall we call you if there's any change? You won't be able to talk to her, in any case."

Kellhorn said he would like them to call him, and he left his home number. If he did not hear from the clinic, he knew he would call them himself.

On the way home, he thought about Dr. Ursula Freimann.

Then he thought about the dirty dinner dishes waiting for him in the sink.

In the middle of the night, Bianca rushed to the bathroom, just in time to throw up.

She had flung her bloodied jacket at Renato as they both stood, horrified, under the light on the road to town. She couldn't bear to have it on her body, to touch it. She had stripped it off as if it were on fire. Tears streaming down her beautiful face, distorted now with revulsion, she had babbled at Renato to rip it up, burn it, bury it—do anything, except try to return it! The jacket had been her favorite, one she saved for special occasions. Now she viewed it as something diseased.

She had hurried back to school, protected from the night cold by only the ski sweater she wore beneath her overalls. But the terror had followed her into her sleep.

As she bent over in the bathroom, retching emptily, she began to sob again. She had to tell *someone!*

CHAPTER
34

Lady Katharyn Patricia Nadine Sunynghame got her rangy good looks from her American mother, the countess, and her supercilious manners from her British father, the seventeenth earl of Prestwycke. Her taste for the kinky had been born on one of the family's annual visits to their castle in Scotland when, at the age of eleven, she began experimenting with cousins of both sexes and, subsequently, expanded her activities into the nearby village. Her porcelain complexion and piquant, heart-shaped face glowed with innocence, although her eyes had begun to take on a sly cast as she indulged her appetite for shocking people. She was used to moving about without much restriction—she had learned early that an outward show of obedience would win her freedom from the petty restraints that her less tractable brothers and sister suffered—so, when she was sent to the distinguished Marlowe School, over her most passionate protests, she found the rigid discipline painful.

Painful, but not hopeless. She was determined to enjoy herself. That meant calling on all her skills to present herself as a model student—good grades, a polite and cheerful manner, a cooperative spirit—in order to avoid scrutiny. It had been work, but definitely worth it. For three years, she had come and gone very much as she pleased.

Now, in her fourth year at Marlowe, she had been placed on detention for the very first time. She was more annoyed than upset at this one blot on her record, since she had no intention of honoring it. Nothing was going to keep her stuck on school grounds for the rest of the semester.

In the nine days since the detention had been imposed, Katharyn had paid particular attention to her studies and appeared calm and contrite. She was eager to re-establish herself as the least problematic pupil, leaving Miss Grimsby and the senior faculty to worry about Nicole and Mindy and whatever else might occupy their energies. It had worked. By Wednesday, she noticed that Miss Grimsby no longer glanced at her during mealtimes, checking for signs of rebelliousness, and Miss Temple didn't touch her shoulder in sympathy and encouragement when they passed in the fifth-floor hall. She could now come and go freely, as before.

All she had to do was pick the right time.

Nights were out. Every door and ground-floor window was bolted, and the night watchman who had replaced the still-ailing Sleepless was grimly serious about his job. It had amused Katharyn to stop him in the dark hall one night—an innocent inquiry about Sleepless, her robe hanging open, nightie draped to reveal. He had replied politely, wished her a good night, and continued on his rounds.

Late afternoon would be best, she decided. The doors weren't locked and there was no bustle in the halls. Everyone would be either out on the slopes, down in town, or studying quietly behind closed doors. She could leave without being noticed. She was ready for some excitement, and a whispered phone call to the barone had assured her that he, too, was waiting eagerly.

Now, if only she could convince Nicole that it would be perfectly safe—and fun. Bloody hell, wasn't *she*, Nicole, getting just as dotty being locked up? An outing, a bit of sport—who would know?

Nicole was adamant. Nothing could persuade her to endure the repellent Mookie and his sick games again. She just *might* accompany Katharyn to town, if it looked safe. But Mookie and his friends?—never again!

Katharyn gave up and made her own plans.

The next day, in the hushed calm after the rush of ski-laden girls had left the building, she tucked her hair under a fuzzy blue cap, bundled herself into a padded ski jacket, and slipped away from the school grounds unnoticed.

Veep had gone too far! Elvina was exasperated and frustrated. She had received the message on her return to the chalet from a late lunch in town. Here it was, only two days before the *Skimarathon*, and Veep had left word with the housekeeper that he was taking their Learjet to Val Triazzo for a few days, and the plane would return to pick her up if she wished to join him. Really! As if she could get away before the weekend was over. And why would she want to spend a minute in that dreary, over-advertised village in the Italian Alps when everyone interesting was here in Fernstaad? He *knew* she wouldn't come. As usual, Veep was making it look as if *she* were refusing his invitation! He always did that when he was off on one of his little adventures. For all she knew, he was sneaking off to some grubby ski lodge in the area with one of the local bunnies. Very well, she would shoulder all the hosting duties herself; it wouldn't be the first time. And if that grumpy Inspector Neumayer from the *Kantonspolizei* came sniffing around the greenhouse again, she'd send him off to Val Triazzo to ''inspect'' her husband.

Meanwhile, was there anyone new and exciting that she might now invite to the chalet for the weekend? Perhaps she could find out what had happened to Claude—what *was* his last name? An amusing man, such a wicked tongue! She wondered why Veep had banished him from the chalet after the death of the young schoolgirl. So what if rumor had it that he was heavily into hard drugs. Was he dealing or using? Oh, well, some of her very best friends. . . . She would have to ask some of those best friends if they knew where Claude was these days.

It was hours before dinner, and Nicole was already bored and restless. She had come to loathe these endless afternoons of detention in the deadly quiet of the school. She had finished her classwork, had even written a dutiful letter to her parents, knowing that they were probably away at some international science congress in Singapore, or Kyoto, or California, and wouldn't receive it for weeks. Now she wandered the silent halls, looking for company.

She couldn't find Katharyn, and assumed that she had sneaked away to town as she had said she would. Mindy, her other "coconspirator," as Miss Temple called them, was such a grouch these days that Nicole couldn't stand her. Still, she was better than nobody. She searched the gym and the cozy Ping-Pong room, but no one was around. With growing depression, she returned to the empty fifth floor, almost wishing she had agreed to join Katharyn.

As she passed Bianca's closed door, she heard snuffling inside. What was Bianca doing in the building at this hour? *She* wasn't on detention. Was she crying? Best not to interfere.

But loneliness and a surge of compassion moved Nicole. She knocked softly on the door.

"Bianca? It's Nicole." The sounds inside ceased. "Are you all right?"

She waited.

Slowly, the door opened. Bianca stood there in skimpy bra and panties, her eyes and nose red, cheeks wet-stained and upper lip glistening as she sniffed. Beyond, Nicole could see the rumpled bed, pillow lying on top of the *plumeau* as if it had been clutched for comfort.

"Are you sick?" Nicole asked. "Can I get you something?"

Bianca shook her head and sagged against the door, then turned and walked back to her bed. She flung herself onto the *plumeau* and wrapped her arms around the pillow, mumbling inaudibly.

"What's *wrong*?" Nicole followed her into the room.

Bianca turned her tear-streaked face to Nicole.

"I hate it here! I want to go home!" she cried.

"What happened?"

"S-s-s—I think . . . someone is trying . . . to *kill* me!"

"You're crazy!" Nicole said, aghast.

The story poured out, filled with anguish and terror: the note Bianca had found in her pocket, the blood deliberately smeared all over her jacket—*that* wasn't a joke, it was another warning; she *knew* it now! Maybe the deaths of Sophie and Anneliese *hadn't* been accidents! Maybe someone meant to kill them *all*, and *she* was going to be *next!*

Nicole listened, eyes wide, torn between incredulity and shock. Her friend's imagination had gone berserk. Still, it wasn't like the usually cheerful Bianca to be so morbid. And two of their classmates *were* already dead. And someone *had* tried to break into the school, although Nicole didn't add that to Bianca's list.

"Does anyone else know about this?" she asked.

"Mindy does, and I told Miss Temple—just about the note. I didn't say anything about the blood on my jacket. That just happened. Oh, I don't know what to *do!*" She pressed her face into her squashed pillow.

"Don't be an ass!" Nicole snapped, impatient with Bianca's weeping, and fighting her own fears. "Of course you must let Miss Temple know, about everything! Come on— get dressed, and we'll go find her. If you don't want to tell her, I will."

"She's not here," Bianca sniffed. "I looked for her earlier."

"Okay, I'll leave a note in her mailbox. We'll catch her before dinner. Only, for God's sake, stop crying!"

Bianca sat up and hugged her knees, calmer now. "Do you have a joint?"

"No, I was going to ask you."

"*¡Mierda!* Want to go down to town? We still have time until dinner."

"Mmmm, no, I can't," Nicole said evasively. She wasn't allowed to talk about the detention; the terms of her agreement with Miss Grimsby were very specific. "I'll just write a note for Miss Temple, and you meet me in the TV room downstairs. We can watch the local yodeling contests."

Bianca laughed first, then flashed another grim and fearful look at Nicole.

"Oh, grow up!" Nicole said. "Why in hell would anyone want to kill you? Or any of us?"

She stamped out of Bianca's room, wondering if she really felt as confident as she sounded.

* * *

Carla wasn't going to make the same mistake twice. Her on-again, off-again date with Eric was on again for dinner tonight, but this time she wasn't going to dress like Princess Goes to the Ball. Her light-grey cashmere knit would be casual enough, although she was well aware that the color was heavenly with her grey-and-violet eyes and dark hair, and the tight, high-necked, long-sleeved line spilled down her body with a fit as close as her perfume. Still, she convinced herself that she wasn't fussing. And, to be totally casual, she left Marlowe early to make a few shopping stops in town before she was to meet Eric at the bar of the Chesa Monteviglia. If he turned out to be a no-show again, she would at least have the satisfaction of accomplishing a few chores.

Actually, Carla loved shopping in Fernstaad. The stores were small and elegant, the attention polite and friendly, although sometimes a bit snobby if one was not known. On the main street, Cartier was next door to Revillon, and Revillon was next door to Hermès, and Hermès was next door to Chanel and Givenchy and a fine art gallery, and then came Grete's, Carla's favorite jewelry store.

Seated on a spindly gilt chair in Grete's lush boutique, Carla chose a birthday gift for her mother, a gold Audemars Piguet watch with a woven gold band, perfect for tailored or evening dress. Maybe it would convince her mother that not everything had to be crusted with diamonds to be beautiful. On impulse, she also picked a gold-hinged set of pipe tools for her father; his were always hiding when he needed them. She had both gifts sent together, then headed for the fine linen shop to buy herself the exquisite, flower-embroidered handkerchiefs that she had recently become addicted to. Delicate, old-fashioned in their charm, they made her feel wonderfully feminine.

The early Alpine twilight had caught up with Fernstaad by the time she finished her shopping. The snowbound streets were satiny blue, and warm lights glowed in the chalets on the mountainsides. She would be a little late, but she decided to walk.

When she reached the Hotel Chesa Monteviglia, Eric was already waiting for her in the bar. He rose and came toward her, smiling. Carla admired the masculine grace of his body in his dark-blue suit and pearly tie. She had never seen him look so formal and handsome—and happy to see her. He crossed the room and stood looking down at her for a minute, eyes shining.

"I'm forgiven," he said, taking her coat. "What a relief! I was afraid you'd decide I wasn't very dependable."

"Are you?" she asked.

"Count on it!" He glanced around the bar. "I've made a reservation in the hotel dining room—Fritz Leitner's recommendation—but if you'd rather just have a drink here and dinner someplace else?"

She *would* have preferred someplace without the associations of the Chesa Monteviglia, but decided she could make her peace with it. The dining room had an excellent reputation, and she didn't want to cause a fuss that she'd have to explain. They chose to skip the tumult of the bar and take their table right away. When Eric touched her elbow to lead her inside, she felt a spark that disarmed any personal objection.

They settled at their table, the chitchat between them easy, but screening an almost adolescent heart-thumping. Champagne to start, and a moment of distraction as the captain took their order for a dinner that would be leisurely and unobtrusively served. Flowers and candlelight and discreet musicians for mood. Carla sipped her wine, contented.

"Well," Eric said at last, "you seem much calmer than the last time I saw you. I'm glad. You spoke to your policeman, and he told you you were imagining things—am I right?"

"No, not really," she said slowly. "I mean, I did talk to him, but he seemed to take me seriously. He didn't come to any conclusions, though. At least, he didn't say so."

"What *did* he say?" Eric asked.

She took another sip of champagne, thoughtful. The urge to tell him everything was powerful. She was hungry for comfort. But *what* could she tell him? Suspicions? Fears?

Things oddly linked or misinterpreted? He'd only laugh at them, as he had before. And she'd feel like a reckless gossip—like Elvina von Wetzlar, lord help her!

A lightning frown flashed across her face.

"You can tell me," he prompted softly. "I won't laugh."

Reading her thoughts again? She felt herself weakening. She put her glass down, succumbing to need.

"No, there's nothing funny about it. You know, the two girls who died—there was a threatening note before it happened. Oh, not to either of them, as far as I know—it was to another girl. And the note *could* have been just a nasty prank, but—"

"What did it say?"

She shook her head. "Never mind. I never actually saw it myself. But I believe the girl who said she got it, and it *was* threatening. And Sleepless, Johann Bächli—"

"I'm so sorry we lost the old fellow—"

"Yes, of course. But, you see, someone was trying to get into the *school* the night he was hurt. They were after someone *inside!*"

"Maybe they were after some*thing*."

Carla leaned forward. "I don't believe that!"

"What does your policeman believe? If he really thought the girls were in danger, wouldn't he put guards at the school, or have it closed, or do something?"

She sighed in exasperation. "He *did* send guards, and you don't know Miss Grimsby, the headmistress. She'd never agree to an unscheduled closing, even if the building were on fire! And *my policeman* is an inspector, if you must know!"

Eric reached across the table for her fluttering hands. "Carla, what can I do to help you? Please, I want to."

Yes, what did she expect from him? This wasn't his problem, and she wasn't sure he really took her seriously. Still, it was a relief to share her fears with a—friend. She reached into her purse and pulled out one of her dainty new linen handkerchiefs.

"You're doing it," she said, smiling weakly, pressing the soft cloth to her nose. "Just listening to me. Really. I'm okay—only a little scared. God, I do get drippy when I'm around food and you together!" She laughed. "Don't let me spoil this evening. I feel better, just talking to you."

"Are you sure?"

She nodded, convincing herself that it was true. She looked around. The string ensemble near the dining room's fireplace had just finished their last number. The players smiled appreciatively at her and began their own arrangement of a Schumann romance, hoping to please. The captain gravely presented the fine white Dézaley, Philosophe, for Eric's approval, which he gave just as solemnly, with the flicker of a wink at Carla. Waiters arrived with their first course—fresh scallops from Ireland for Eric and a silky lobster bisque for Carla.

The mood turned light again—a relief for both of them.

Eric took a few bites and a sip of wine. "Okay, I will now ask you very prying, very personal questions. You're on your honor to tell the truth."

"Oh, for heaven's sake!"

"No, I mean it. I really know very little about you, except medically, and as a sports figure. And who your family is, of course. Just what everyone knows from reading the papers and sports magazines. I tried pumping Fritz Leitner, but it seems his lips are sealed."

"I pay him off regularly," Carla smiled.

"He said I should ask you myself."

"Sly devil! Okay, ask me what?"

He paused, his eyes linked to hers. "I don't know, really. Like, what have you been doing here? Why haven't you ever gone back to the States—since the accident? I would think with your, well, advantages, you'd be happier at home."

"Long story," she said, and turned her attention to the creamy soup.

"Those are the best kind, my favorites. So, tell me. You've been here for more than a year, all—alone?"

"Well, I didn't *come* here alone. Oh, I don't mean just the Olympic team. Naturally, we were all together. But there was—someone. On the men's team. Ski jump." For a moment, Carla could see Michael flying off the tip of the steep ski jump high above the trees, a single line, with his arms pressed to his sides as he soared over the ninety-meter hill, his beautiful body as close to parallel with his skis as humanly possible. A stitch of unexpected pain caught her. "But, um, he didn't hang around too long—after the accident." She shrugged. "Doesn't matter."

"Say that again?"

"It matters. So what. He just couldn't stand seeing me all smashed up. I didn't blame him; I understood. He was a winner, and entitled to all his chances. He had too much ahead of him to sit holding hands with anyone so—earth-bound."

Eric nodded. "It must have been very painful for him, too."

"Don't you dare take his side!"

"You're absolutely right. The guy was a perfect shithead, and everyone knew it."

Carla laughed and set the tiny dimples twinkling at the sides of her mouth. The musicians changed keys smoothly and launched into a peppy version of a Gilbert and Sullivan song. Carla changed keys abruptly by clattering her spoon on her plate.

"That's enough," she said. "Let's drop it. Your turn now, anyhow. What about you? Personal and prying, remember?"

"Divorced, no children," he said easily, but there was a fleeting look of pain on his face. "She left me, ran off with a high-flying ski jumper. I tried to warn her—"

"Eric, you are a very silly person!"

"Actually, she ran off with our lawyer—and our Apple Macintosh. I won't say that I missed the computer more. I didn't. It was very messy; also, not that long ago." With that, his glibness was gone.

Carla felt a chilly, unwelcome reality scuttle up to join the party. It was a fragile moment between them. She wondered if she was reaching out, getting attached, to someone still deeply in love with another woman. Was Eric missing his wife and just easing the pain by passing time with her? Was *that* what she was doing with *him?* Helping herself forget

Michael? No, she would know it! Eric was very different from Michael, more important. She wanted to believe that.

"I'm sorry," she murmured into her wineglass.

"It was worse than that, you may as well know. Fritz would tell you, anyhow—eventually." His voice was somber but steady. "There was a child, a little girl. Jenny. So beautiful. She was the most wonderful thing in my life. The marriage—well, it was becoming strained. I was working too hard, always busy. My wife and I rented a house on an island for the summer. I thought we might be able to relax together, at least on weekends. Jenny loved it there. I was teaching her to fish. She was only two, but she was such a joy to be with." He looked away for a minute. Carla caught her breath, wishing she could stop the story from unwinding to what she knew would be its inevitable, dreaded conclusion. He saw her anticipate it. "Yes, she died," he continued. "Drowned, in three inches of water in the bottom of an old rowboat. I was inside on the phone. My wife must have turned her back, for only an instant. I heard her screaming and ran out. I tried everything, but I couldn't save her. I knew it was hopeless, but I was still working on her when the ambulance helicopter landed. Do you understand? I was a doctor, and Jenny was the most precious thing in the world to me. And I couldn't save her." He spoke simply, but the impacted anguish was overwhelming.

"Oh, Eric, how cruel," Carla whispered. She was awed by his pain and felt diminished in its presence. "You didn't deserve such cruelty."

"No one does. I wanted you to know about this. For whatever it may mean to you."

"That you've suffered; that you're still suffering. And you go on, strong and caring about others. That's how it seems to me. That's special."

His look was tender. "*You're* special. And we both go on because we have to. But for a while back then I was pretty wild—you should know that. Both my wife and I were destroyed, she more than I. She wouldn't speak for months, not a word. Finally, she said, 'I don't think I want to be married to you anymore.' Just like that. In a daze. And I didn't make it easy for us. I fought her over the divorce. I had the crazy idea that if I could hold on to her I'd be holding on to Jenny. Without her, Jenny would be gone forever.''

There was nothing wild or crazy about him now. Carla saw only the moraine of a tragedy, and acceptance of that which couldn't ever be changed.

"God, how did you survive?'' she asked in a voice hushed by compassion.

"How did *you*?'' he countered. "I don't think life was too easy for you, either, a year ago.''

"I had Dr. Leitner to help.''

He smiled with the warmth of a better memory. "So did I. Fritz was in the States then; that's when I met him, in fact. I was working with him. He was very tough on me—he pushed me back into the business of living. I'm grateful that he did.''

Carla considered this. "Is that why you're here, in Fernstaad?''

"Partly. Maybe. Probably. I'm here on a trial basis. I didn't make any long-term commitment; Fritz knows that. His instincts are good, though. I'm glad I came. I'm glad I met you.'' His voice rose suddenly as his spirits revived. "I must say, I like a woman who can drink me under the table.''

She was momentarily puzzled until she glanced at the wine bucket and saw the bottle upended in the ice chips. Without intruding, the waiters had kept their glasses filled, and they had already finished the Dézaley. With it, they silently acknowledged, they had finished with a painful but necessary step in knowing each other, at least for now.

Eric signaled, and the serving of their next course began, starting with the uncorking of a light red Valais that would accompany the lamb they had both ordered. Carla was relieved that the mood of earlier in the evening, the excitement and anticipation she had felt when she first joined him in the bar, was returning. She felt that she had just come through white water and prevailed against the emotional current.

She tasted her wine and lifted the glass to him. "Meet you under the table!'' she said.

He looked at her for a long, appreciative moment. "You should always wear that color. It lights up your eyes. I think I'm going to prescribe it as part of your treatment."

"*Wirklich, Herr Doktor?*"

"Now, *that* reminds me. You were going to teach me some German, remember? I'm still waiting for my first lesson. What about it? I'm hopeless with languages, but very sincere, so go ahead."

"Okay. But I warn you, I'm a tough teacher."

"I'm warned." His fork hovered, and he leaned forward. "Go."

"First lesson, repeat after me: *Scheisskerl.*"

"*Scheisskurl.*"

"Wrong!" Carla laughed. "*Kerl, kerl!* Lighter on the tongue. Try it again. *Scheisskerl.*"

"*Scheisskerl!*" Eric said triumphantly. A woman at the next table pointed her nose at him with disapproval and looked away quickly.

Carla winced. "Great! You're on your way to becoming a real German scholar."

"What does it mean?"

"Shithead."

"I'm shocked! Is *that* what you teach those innocent little virgins at Marlowe?"

"No. I teach them *Finnegans Wake.* They teach *me Scheiss-kerl.* And they're not so innocent, if you want to know."

"You really like them, don't you? The girls, teaching."

"I never expected to live my whole life on a slalom run." She grew pensive. "That part was for fun, even though I worked hard at it. It surprised me that I was any good, actually. I mean, good enough to make the Olympic team—"

"You were the best!" he said. "They're still writing about you in the sports columns. Every new skier gets compared to you. You'll be back on skis again, I promise you. Not out to beat the clock, of course. But it'll be fun again. You'll see."

The light from the dining room candles flickered on Carla's face and blended with her own high color. She sighed and leaned back in her chair.

"Well, I always wanted to *do* something—useful, I mean. And I couldn't see myself trapped in the family business. I would have felt like a parasite. So Marlowe hasn't been a hardship for me. I'm near Dr. Leitner. And you're right, I do like the girls. That's why I worry about them so terribly."

"I know you do. But you haven't said why you never went home. Not even once this past year. How come?"

"I speak to my parents regularly. God knows they call often enough. They'd only make themselves crazy worrying about me if I were home, especially if they'd had to see me every day with that brace and those crutches."

He didn't look convinced. "I would think you'd want to see *them*."

She fidgeted in distress. Why didn't he just drop it? What difference did it make *why* she had stayed in Fernstaad? She couldn't explain what it meant to have doting, perfectionist parents, not when she hadn't sorted out her own feelings about it.

"I just didn't want to burden them, that's all."

"You sound like a very good daughter," he said.

A tiny alarm rang in her head. She looked at him sharply. "What did you say?" she asked.

"I said that you seem very considerate of your parents' feelings. What about your own? Haven't you *wanted* to go home at all? You might have— *Hey!* Where did you disappear to all of a sudden? Did I lose you?"

"Oh! No. I'm sorry. I was just thinking of something— odd. Not important."

"I hope not."

As their dinner plates were being removed, she saw Eric suddenly stiffen, listening intently. All she could hear was the music from the string ensemble.

"Something?" she asked, tilting her head at him.

"Ambulance. From the clinic."

Then she heard the siren's two-note seesawing drifting into the restaurant, challenging the music:

Whee-haw, whee-haw, whee-haw. . . .

"I'm on call tonight," he said. "Fritz tells me there's

always a heavy load of accidents during *Skimarathon* week, and not just off the slopes. Well, they know where to find me—but only if it's urgent.''

The siren faded underneath the music, and they turned their attention to dessert, a dark and sinful *Sachertorte*. Carla enjoyed the comfort that settled between them, with its edge of thrill. She loved reading the map of emotions on his handsome face; every glance flattered her. They lingered over coffee until the musicians finished their performance with a flourish and accepted the applause of the diners. A new sound floated into the dining room, loud and raucous, from the rock band in the popular late-hours club upstairs. Carla's hand tapped on the table.

Eric looked at his watch. ''It's still early. What would you like to do? I have no intention of letting you go so soon. Tell me what you like best, besides skiing.''

''Dancing!'' She cocked her head at the music coming from the club. ''How about it?''

''Forget it! You're not ready for that, either. Pick something else. Do you like the movies?''

''Sure, but how many times can I see *Dirty Harry kommt zurück?*''

''You're kidding! Is that really playing here?''

''Right down the street at the Cine Scala.''

''I think we'll give it a miss. So . . . no dancing, no movies.'' He reached across the table and took her hand. ''How about a drink at the bar? They're supposed to have a good jazz group in there after dinner—well, half jazz, half yodeling. What do you say?''

It wasn't what either of them was thinking.

Carla's eyes sparkled at him. His hand felt so warm, so strong as it caressed hers. A luscious, soft feeling spread through her body. She said, almost mischievously, ''How about a drink upstairs, instead, in the hotel. In private. Would you like that?''

She saw the fire leap in his eyes.

''Are you sure?'' he asked, his voice husky in his throat.

''Very,'' she said simply. ''My parents keep a suite here

year-round. I've never used it before—I never wanted to. But they're probably the only unoccupied rooms in all of Fernstaad this week.''

''I can't think of anything I'll ever want as much,'' he said.

She retrieved her hand. ''Okay, second lesson: *Zahlen, bitte*. That's the correct way to ask for the check. Why don't you try it out on the captain. He's heading our way.''

The captain bustled up purposefully without being summoned and leaned over toward Eric.

''Excuse me, *Herr Doktor*,'' he said softly. ''From the Leitner Clinic, they have just called—'' Eric started to rise. ''No, they are not on the phone anymore. They wish that you come as quickly as possible.''

''Of course. The check, please.''

He counted out the bills and handed them to the captain. He rose quickly, galvanized by professional energy, but his face was pale with disappointment. He smiled his regret at Carla.

''You can't possibly know how sorry I am,'' he said.

She smiled back. ''Raincheck. Promise. I hope this isn't anything too serious.''

''It may be—if they didn't even wait to speak to me. I'll have the captain call a taxi for you.''

''Please, don't worry about it. I'll take care of it myself. You'd better go. Really, I can get home without any trouble.''

''I'll call you later, if it's not too late.''

As he passed her chair, he stopped suddenly, bent over her, turned her face up to his, and kissed her mouth, quickly, but with pure hunger. For a second, his eyes explored the mystic grey depths of hers.

''You're so lovely,'' he whispered.

She watched him hurry across the dining room, saw him speak to the captain as he handed the man additional franc notes and accepted his coat. Then he rushed out of the restaurant, leaving Carla staring after him and feeling the tingle still on her lips.

I'm sorry, too. She sent the thought after him.

Eric had ordered a taxi for her, after all. It was waiting

when she stepped out of the restaurant. She breathed in the night air, welcoming its icy prickle on her overheated face. She settled inside the car and gave herself up to thoughts both pleasurable and frustrating as they snaked up the mountain to the accompaniment of grinding gears. She was unaware of the time passing until they swung into the courtyard of the Marlowe School and stopped in front of the steps.

The only light she could see in the upper floors of the building came from the tower—Miss Grimsby's suite.

CHAPTER
35

The funeral of Johann Bächli that morning had been simple and wrenchingly painful. Standing at graveside, the pastor read his benisons, the wind whipped snowy powder around the stones, and Felice Grimsby laid a comforting hand on Herr Blumen's arm as the stricken chef wept openly at her side. The other teachers huddled grimly in the cold, glancing at the headmistress to measure her grief. Her thin body stood straight, eyes dry, face composed for the sake of the others, but she felt the loss like a new wound.

Worse, she felt that she was losing control.

Unable to sleep that night, she stood at her window in the tower and watched Carla Temple return from her date in town. Twice this week, she thought, and it pleased her that the beautiful young woman was out in the world again, both physically and emotionally. But her pleasure could not push back the pain of the day for long.

Her beloved Marlowe was under seige—she believed that. Her precious school, which she tended with total commitment, was suffering one terrible loss after another. Its sanctity was being violated, and she was powerless to define or deal with the menace. She didn't want to express her fears to Rudi Neumayer and have him tell her that she was being foolish. Not that he would say it in so many words. But she knew that, aside from the deliberate attempt to break into the building, he'd never acknowledge that the recent plague of deaths was anything other than a tragic series of accidents. *That* she could not accept. After years of success and security, everything she loved was threatened.

She looked down at Carla climbing the front steps and tried to recapture those proud, early years. She remembered how happy she had been when she first came to Marlowe, a young woman, eager and confident.

Her father, Frank Grimsby, had been a powerful model throughout her childhood. The principal of Northmere High School in central New Hampshire—a school with a national reputation for excellence—he was severe in manner, demanding, but generous with compassion and encouragement. He was an old-fashioned educator, although he welcomed the whizbang electronics that served to stimulate his students. He believed in young people, and respected them. In turn, generations of students flourished brilliantly as they passed through his school, trusting and even loving him. Naturally, Felice adored him, even if she felt he was harder on her than on any of his other intellectual charges. Precocious and endlessly curious, she knew he delighted in her, his only child.

At nineteen, she graduated from Vassar with the commendation of summa cum laude; a year later, she earned a master's degree in education. She was filled with pride on the day she returned to Northmere to begin work as a teacher in her father's school. The only thing that puzzled her was that Frank Grimsby didn't seem to want her there.

At first, she doubted her perceptions. But as her father continued to urge her not to bury herself in the small town of her childhood, to explore instead a more sophisticated world, there was no question that he wanted her to leave. "To achieve your potential, to fulfill yourself," he said in uncharacteristically pedantic tones. When she argued that *he* had managed to fulfill *himself* in Northmere, his reply was simply that she was different and that he thought he knew what was best for her. "Although, God knows, your mother and I would miss you terribly if you left," he added. So Felice put aside her hurt—she didn't really doubt his love—and considered his advice with full trust.

On her twenty-first birthday, she sailed to Europe with two of her friends. They were to spend the summer vacation touring the great foreign cities she had long yearned to see. She never returned to Northmere again, except as a visitor.

That summer, restless and hungry for the adventure of personal discovery, she left her companions in Zurich and went wandering into the heart of the country. Switzerland! How she loved its shifting landscapes, the diminutive scale of its provincial villages, the breath-catching grandeur of the Alps!

Hiking for days up the steep mountain fields above Chur, she arrived, finally, at Fernstaad.

She had known the town only through its exotic reputation as a ski resort for the rich and fabled. Now, fragrant with summertime greenery, its high slopes speckled with delicate Alpine flowers, the imposing stone mass of its celebrated Marlowe School riding the midpoint of the hill near the funicular track, Fernstaad beckoned to her. It promised her a new home.

She started in the fall as an English teacher for the first-form girls, the youngest teacher ever hired by the Marlowe headmistress. Felice Grimsby had been inspiring confidence since she was a youngster; the doughty Miss Mary Adeline Marlowe never regretted her decision.

Felice never regretted hers.

The years that followed were totally satisfying. Marlowe was the focus of her life, and, although she couldn't remain celibate in a town filled with glamorous, attractive men, no lusty adventure ever tempted her away from her preoccupation with her work for long. She missed her parents, but Frank and Abby Grimsby visited Switzerland each year. And she, herself, made occasional trips back to Northmere.

Fifteen years after her arrival in Fernstaad, her parents were present at the ceremony when the elderly Miss Marlowe retired and Felice became the new headmistress and owner of the renowned school. She was respected, successful, wealthy—and content. She had attained her goal.

Now, watching from her tower window as Carla Temple disappeared under the balcony overhanging the front door, she felt suffocated by fear. With it came a passionate rage. She could *kill*—she was sure of it—destroy *anyone* who threatened Marlowe or her girls! She tugged her bathrobe close and stepped out onto her small terrace. Standing in the dark, blasted by the freezing wind, she whispered to the great stone walls stretched out on both sides and to the lives they sheltered: *"No one will ever harm you again!"*

The tears came, for Johann and Sophie and Anneliese— tears of grief, finally, and of anger, as well. She let their icy trickle burn her cheeks unchecked, as if she were doing penance.

She couldn't stand there for long. Shivering, she stepped back inside, emotionally spent but secure that everything and everyone was safe—for now.

Below, on the fifth floor, Nicole Robineau crept cautiously down the hall to Katharyn Sunynghame's room. It was after two in the morning. Katharyn hadn't returned to school for dinner. Nicole had tried to cover up for her friend, although her worry had increased as it grew later in the day. She reported that Katharyn wasn't feeling well enough to come down to dinner—just cramps, nothing serious, *vraiment*— and she, Nicole, would be happy to take up a bowl of soup. She didn't tell anyone that Katharyn was gone—not even Bianca, who had confided in her. How could she? They'd only ask if she knew where Katharyn had gone. She was quite sure she knew, but she certainly wasn't going to tell anyone about the barone, and all the rest!

When she checked before going to bed, Katharyn was still missing. She knew she ought to say *something*, but she just couldn't. Lying in bed that night, indecision kept her awake, and worry turned to alarm. She began to think about what Bianca had told her and she made a sudden, terrifying connection—first about Sophie and then about Katharyn. She *must* be wrong. She *had* to find out that she was wrong. Surely Katharyn was back by now. One more look, she decided.

She slipped into Katharyn's room, straining her eyes in the dark. She could see the soup bowl on the desk where she had left it, still full, and the neatly made bed, still empty.

Now what was she to do? It was hours until morning. She'd have to talk to Miss Temple tomorrow, anyhow; she had already left the note in her mailbox asking to see her. But she only wanted to speak to her about Bianca. And about Sophie; that was worrying her more and more. She wasn't going to say anything about Katharyn.

Back in her room, she huddled in a fetal curl beneath her *plumeau*. Maybe tomorrow Katharyn would return. She fell asleep, whimpering without hearing herself.

"Car-LAH! Car-LAH! Car-LAH!"

The dream always began the same.

Tense, she was racing tense at the start of the slalom run. Wreathed in the brume that misted over the top of the mountain, Carla could hear the rhythmic chant of unseen spectators far below, the cry of a ghostly crowd—calling to her, pulling her down to them. . . .

"Car-LAH! Car-LAH! Car-LAH!"

Now she was on the course—she never saw herself begin—spurting toward the first gate. She could not see it through the mist, but it was out there. Freezing wind deflected by her goggles stung her ears, and gusts battered against her body. She thrust herself forward, powerful legs bending and pushing, feeling out every caprice of the rutted terrain with microsecond responsiveness. Knees pumping to absorb each shock, body suspended as if on gimbals over her stiff-heeled Yamaha SRX Custom skis, she sped blindly through the fog toward the first pole. Now the dream mist cleared. She saw the red and blue flags ahead and flung herself down to meet them. The breath almost sucked from her open mouth, she bit the snow with the edge of her ski, whipped into a short-radius turn that bent the hinged fiberglass of the first breakaway pole, and plunged downward, jetting to the next gate. The chant below changed to a moan, like the keening of the wind—

"Car-LAAAAHH! . . . LAAAAHH! . . ."

Rising and falling, a wailing lament that howled in the icy air and chilled her blood. It would not stop! *She could not stop!*

Faster . . . faster . . . down the fall line, drunk with speed, an aggressive mass of totally concentrated energy, feeling the mighty edge-grip of her skis as she flew into the next turn, through the gate and on to the next. . . .

"LAAAAHH! . . ." The moaning rose.

And the next gate. . . .

"LAAAAHH! . . ." Higher.

Suddenly, horribly, she was out of control! *How had it happened?* She was flying, spinning through the air with sickening speed, flailing with useless poles gripped in clenched fists, a blur of spiky trees whirling over and over, the snow-covered track rising up to meet her—

Then the crash!

"Aaaagh! Aaaagh!"

The snap of her tibia was as loud as a rifle crack. She lay in the snow, writhing in unbearable agony, crying out, her hand trembling spastically as she stretched it toward her leg—

Her leg! That obscene protrusion of jagged, bloody bone —*that was her leg!*

She cried out in her sleep.

Now she would wake up. She would be drenched in perspiration and shivering violently in the cold of her bed, gasping. Her own cry would wake her. *Wake up!* It always did.

Wake up!

But, this time, she slept on.

The dream continued. . . .

She lay in a vast, high bed. She could not move. Around her, the dream light was blue-white, like the snowy slopes. But she was not outside, she knew. She was floating, alone, in that high ship of an endless bed. Through the mist of unspeakable pain, she felt that she was suffocating, *drowning* in the light. A sound drifted toward her. A voice murmured above her, unintelligible. A warm hand touched hers, held it lightly. Slowly, a face took shape, hovering over her. A kind face—Dr. Leitner, gentle Dr. Leitner, whispering comfort and encouragement. But what was he saying?

"You are a good daughter, my child. A good daughter. . . ."

Then Dr. Leitner was gone, and it was Eric who leaned over her, held her hand, and whispered softly:

"A good daughter—*and daughters die!*"

She cried out again—and woke.

Shuddering, soaked, Carla lay in confusion. The dream had fled. She knew that she had lived through the crash again, that the nightmare had violated her sleep as it had so often in the past year. But she did not remember it. All she knew was that something about it was different—something terrible and much worse than ever before.

It was still dark outside. Not even five o'clock, her digital clock told her. She listened to the pounding of her heartbeat as it throbbed in her ears and tried to recapture her dream, not sure that she really wanted to. Gradually, her pulse subsided. She was almost afraid to sleep again, but she was too exhausted to resist. Before the hour tolled on the town bells, she had drifted off again.

At six o'clock, the baker's van pulled into the small alley behind the *Konditorei* Klaus. The morning chef helped the driver unload great wooden trays of sour *Bürli*, the warm peasant bread steaming in the cold air. When the last loaf was stowed in the pantry, the two men shared a cup of coffee and a tidbit of local gossip. The chef watched from the doorway as the van backed out of the alley. As it maneuvered around a curve, its headlights flashed on a large, untidy sprawl of rags in the corner. *Rags?* The van braked sharply. The driver leaped out and reached the pile at the same moment as the chef. Together, in horror, they bent over the body, a piteous monstrosity. They could not tell if it was male or female. The hair was hidden under a fuzzy blue cap, and ribbons of blood-matted flesh crusted around the slashed face.

CHAPTER
36

Carla awoke early, drugged with fatigue. She showered and dressed mechanically, feeling weighted down by the effort. In her mirror, she saw the frown lines creasing her forehead. Something—*something* about *Eric* was troubling her, and it kept eluding her. She had been uneasy ever since she had awakened, and she thought it was because of the nightmare. It had come again last night, she remembered that same fearful, anguished dream about her accident. But she was used to it by now. Why was it tormenting her so much this morning?

She reached back through jumbled thoughts in search of the source of her distress. Something about Eric. . . .

She had a vague awareness that last night's dream had been different—worse than usual—and that Eric had been a part of it.

Eric. And danger.

The thought leaped to her mind: *Eric is the source of danger!* She rejected the idea with passionate denial, but facts started insisting. *Daughters die.* Eric had lived through the kind of catastrophe that could warp the healthiest of minds. And he seemed so interested in learning what was happening at Marlowe. Was he trying to find out what she knew? Also, he had been at the von Wetzlars' chalet the night Anneliese died, Elvina had told her. During the weeks since Anneliese's death, Carla had wondered how that not particularly brave girl had found the courage to jab a needle into her arm, without any previous experience. Another person might have helped, or done it for her—a doctor, with ease. And Sophie, and the break-in, and the death of Sleepless. . . . Everything terrible, all the trouble at Marlowe, had started since Eric had come to Fernstaad!

She was shocked by the realization and continued to fight it. Maybe it was triggered by stress, or by an irrational association of ideas that had taken over her dream last night. If only she could remember it, maybe she'd be able to drown her suspicions. *Drown*. What made her think of that word? She wrestled with her memory, but the dream remained beyond her grasp.

Stop it! You're making yourself crazy! Just cut it out! she ordered herself. *Next, you'll be suspecting Dr. Leitner!*

She fluffed out the collar bow of her black-and-white-checked blouse and straightened the waist of her black mohair skirt. A tug of the comb through her ebony hair and a tug on her high black boots and she finally felt ready to put aside grim fantasies and turn to her responsibilities. *Let's get this day on the road!*

It wasn't even seven o'clock yet, a half hour before breakfast. She sat at the desk in her sitting room and checked the day's schedule. Her first class wasn't until midmorning; she'd have time after breakfast to go over papers in her office downstairs. She didn't expect any interruptions, except maybe Nicole Robineau, who had asked to see her—a personal matter, the note had said.

Carla hadn't been too surprised to find Nicole's note in her mailbox when she returned to Marlowe after her dinner with Eric last night. In the past weeks, many of the girls on her floor had been suffering because of the recent deaths, even without knowing about Sleepless. Requests for personal meetings came almost daily now. It wasn't like the usually independent Mlle. Robineau to ask for a comforting word, but Carla assumed her request would have something to do with wanting help in getting Miss Grimsby to lift her detention for the *Skimarathon* on Saturday. She had penciled a reply at the bottom of Nicole's note—"*I'll be in my office after breakfast. Just knock. CT.*"—and decided she'd try to help spring Nicole and her friends for the special event.

She was surprised now, however, when the knock came on her sitting-room door and she opened it to find Nicole, bleary-eyed, still in her bathrobe, and two hours ahead of schedule.

"You'll be late for breakfast," Carla said, but she made the girl welcome.

"Bianca was too upset to speak to you herself, so I said I would," Nicole explained. She settled in the easy chair next to Carla's desk and tried to look at ease and in control. The puffed, bluish skin below her eyes, the tangled hair straggling down to her brows, the heavier-than-usual inflection of her French accent gave her away.

Carla waited patiently.

Nicole began with an attempt at a casual apology, dismissing Bianca's fears, but she became more tense as she continued. By the time she finished telling Carla about the blood-smeared ski jacket, her voice was shaking. Something else was coming, and Carla tried to keep the look of shock from her face for fear of alarming Nicole any further.

"I know what Bianca thinks," Nicole said, "about that note she found in her pocket—the way she told me about it—but what *I* think is that it was meant for me, not her. It happened while we were all together at the Klaus, when the storm began—the day that Sophie Karas was killed—"

"Did you get a note, too?" Carla interrupted.

"No, no, let me explain!" Nicole waved an agitated hand to drive away the confusion. "Sophie should not have gone over that cliff! *I* should have!" Her voice rose. "*I'm* the one who should have died, not Sophie, and *I'm* responsible for her death!"

"*Nicole!*" Carla cried, appalled.

"Listen! Please! You see, I talked the others into taking that cutoff from Piz Wolfram the day of the storm. I *always* ski that piste alone, and I know all its markers. But the flags on top of the cliff weren't there that day. Someone took them away! I don't care what the police say—that they were just where they should be. *No!* They were *missing*. I tell you, I know that piste by heart and I was looking for them. I would have been alone and I would have skied right off the edge because the *warning flags* were not *there*! You can ask Mindy and Bianca.''

Carla shook her head in disbelief. "The storm was so sudden, so heavy. You just didn't see them—''

"No, that's not true! You can't miss them. And it *was* my fault! They were all depending on me. I teased them into coming, and Sophie followed after us. If Bianca and Mindy hadn't been so slow and careful, maybe *all* of us would have gone over the edge. *They* steered us away from the cliff. Except Sophie was too far behind to see us through the snow. But I swear she would have seen those flags, storm or not. *Except, they weren't there!* And now she's dead, instead of *me*! Someone meant for *me* to die!''

"Stop that!'' Carla ordered, her hand reaching across the desk to subdue Nicole's rising hysteria, but her own voice was almost croaking with fear. Nicole turned away from her. Comfort refused. Carla withdrew her hand. *Think.* Hadn't the note Bianca received said "daughters''? Plural, more than one? Maybe someone *had* deliberately tried to force Nicole over the cliff below Wolfram—or *all* of the girls! She shuddered, then noticed her hands tightly clenched on her desk. *Think, think!* She would keep Nicole and Bianca as close to her as possible until she could reach Inspector Neumayer. And Mindy and Katharyn—and who else?

She'd have to put the entire fifth floor into a cage!

She forced herself to sound relaxed.

"Okay. I understand how you feel, all of you. These weeks have been bad, I know. And being on detention hasn't helped. I'll talk to Bianca myself. Meanwhile, I want *you* to calm down. Nothing's going to happen to you, I promise.'' Nicole scuffed her slippered feet and stared at the carpet, unconvinced. Carla brightened. "I have an idea. Tomorrow is the *Skimarathon*. I'll take you and Mindy and Katharyn up to the little footbridge at the base of Salastrina. We can see the race better from there. Bianca can come, too.''

Nicole looked up, yellowish-brown eyes peering from under her straggly bangs. Her normally sharp features were especially pinched this morning. She was a pretty girl in her own original, eccentric fashion; she might become a glamorous woman one day, a *jolie laide*. Right now, her appearance was that of a pale burrowing animal.

"We can't," she said. "We're not allowed to leave the grounds." It was a calculated appeal, with overtones of self-pity.

"You'll be with me," Carla said, smiling gently. She wasn't deceived, but she felt sorry for the troubled girl. She was also eager to end their meeting so she could call Inspector Neumayer. "I'll take the heat, if there is any. All you have to do is promise me you'll stop blaming yourself for Sophie's—accident. She was a good skier, even if she didn't know the trail well. And old enough to take care of herself. It *was* an accident, and as for the rest, nothing's going to harm you or Bianca. I'll see to that. Do you think you can stop worrying now?"

Nicole nodded reluctantly.

"One other thing," Carla continued. "I'm going to call the *Kantonspolizei*—about the missing flags."

"You believe me."

"Of course. And it could be important. They may want to talk to you themselves. Those pistes should be clearly marked at all times. It's nothing for you to be concerned about, though. You understand?"

Another nod.

"Good. I'll let you know if Sergeant Kellhorn wants to see you again."

Bright morning sun streamed through the windows behind Carla. Blue and red sparks glinted in her hair. She adjusted the bow at her throat in a gesture that should have meant the end of their conversation. She studied the pensive girl on the other side of her desk. Nicole was not moving.

"Was there something else you wanted to tell me?" she asked.

"Uh, no!" Nicole sprang to life again and jumped from the chair.

"Better hurry and dress, then. Breakfast in ten minutes. I'll see you there."

She watched Nicole scurry across the sitting room, her long bathrobe flapping.

As soon as the door closed behind the girl, Carla reached for the phone on her desk and called the *Kantonspolizei*. By now, she didn't have to look up their number. Officer Dominik Trivella politely informed her that neither Inspector Neumayer nor Sergeant Kellhorn was there, but could he be of any assistance? She hesitated, then thanked him and asked that her call be returned as soon as either man arrived.

After she hung up, she sat with her hand on the phone, undecided.

Outside her door, Nicole had already made her decision.

She hurried back to her room, dressed quickly, and pulled out the thermos she often filled with hot chocolate and carried on cross-country hikes outside Fernstaad. Without being observed, she entered Katharyn's empty room, messed up the neat *plumeau* and the rest of the bed coverings, and poured the cold soup into the thermos. Hiding the bowl and the thermos under a towel, she ran to the bathroom and flushed the soup down the toilet. It would be no problem to return the bowl to the kitchen unseen. If Katharyn hadn't returned by the time morning classes began, her absence would be known. They would surely question *her*. If they did, she hadn't seen her friend since she had taken her the soup last night before dinner.

God, she was frightened! Something terrible had happened to Katharyn, she *knew* it. But she didn't dare say anything or they'd all know what she had been doing—and how she had gotten Katharyn involved. She would never let that happen. It was one thing if she was to blame for Sophie's death—how could she have prevented it? But Katharyn! No one must *ever* find out! She didn't want to think about it anymore. She must concentrate on protecting *herself*. From now on, she would stay inside the school building, for the rest of the semester, in sight of others as much as possible. And when she went home for the Easter holiday, she would try to persuade her parents to let her finish her last term in France, near them. She would plead, knowing that they wouldn't take very much notice of her, even if she were there. All she wanted was to get far away from Marlowe as soon as she could—permanently.

* * *

By noon, the newest shock had hit the school. Miss Grimsby had reported to the *Kantonspolizei* shortly after breakfast that another Marlowe girl was missing, and it wasn't long before the grotesquely mutilated body found behind the *Konditorei* Klaus was identified. Dr. Lüthi, newly returned to Fernstaad, gave a cautious preliminary report: Death was instantaneous and came from a single slash across the throat powerful enough to sever the jugular vein and both carotids, with nearly complete severance of the musculature of the neck. The disfigurement was committed after death in random slashes, probably with the same weapon, a long-bladed knife. There was no indication on the body of any struggle. Until further examination, the time of death could not be pinpointed, although it was noted that the girl had been seen on the school premises by a classmate, the evening before.

Miss Grimsby waited until after lunch, then called Carla and the members of the senior faculty together for a meeting. The fewer who knew, the better; the less they knew, even better. Rudi Neumayer had given her all the details, but she would have been incapable of communicating them, even if she had wanted to. Seated behind her desk, her skin as translucent as tallow, eyes glazed and resisting contact, she told a story simplified to distortion, in a voice that was strained and uninflected:

There had been another accident to yet another senior Marlowe student. Lady Katharyn Sunynghame had apparently broken detention and had been found in Fernstaad early that morning. She was seriously hurt and was being returned home to London, accompanied by an emissary of the family who had just been sent up from Zurich. Miss Grimsby wasn't free to discuss the nature of the accident, but Katharyn would not be returning to school to finish the year, or to graduate. At this, the headmistress's voice choked slightly, and she covered it with a few dry coughs. She instructed the faculty that the only information to be given to the other girls was that Katharyn had been called home on family matters, and it was doubtful whether she'd be back before the spring holiday.

Miss Grimsby stressed the importance of not alarming the students any further, as they were already suffering from the recent loss of two of their classmates. Her eyes circled the room slightly above the assembled heads. She was certain, she went on, that she could trust them all to respect her wishes and refrain from discussing the matter any further once they had left her office—either with the girls or with other members of the faculty.

At first, there was blank puzzlement and shock in the room. Carla tried unsuccessfully to capture Miss Grimsby's eyes. Then a few hesitant questions were asked, but the headmistress simply repeated that she was not at liberty to tell them anything else. She apologized for the secrecy, but explained that it was at the insistence of the family—and in the best interests of the girl and the school. There was a brief silence. Felice Grimsby sighed and rose heavily, making it clear that the meeting was over.

Carla hung back after the others had left. Miss Grimsby had turned her back on the room and was standing at the windows looking out.

"I'm sorry, but something else came up this morning about—" Carla began.

Miss Grimsby turned, hardly seeing her.

The rest of Carla's sentence remained constricted in her throat. She had never seen age overtake a person so quickly. All snap and vigor had drained away, and the older woman actually looked smaller. Her bearing sagged, and her usually brilliant blue eyes were focused hazily someplace beyond Carla.

"Yes, Miss Temple?" she said dully and with unexpected formality.

"I wondered—I thought maybe there was something I could do? With the girls, I mean." There was no way Carla could bring herself to add to the present burden. Her news would have to wait until she could reach Inspector Neumayer. "Any special way I can help?"

"Just as we agreed. Nothing else. I think that will be for the best." Miss Grimsby crossed the room and stood over her desk, shuffling the few papers there without particular purpose. "Your next class is at two-thirty, I think," she said, without looking up.

Carla confirmed this. She waited, reluctant to leave.

"Miss Temple . . . *hmmmm*," Miss Grimsby said, considering the name. "I was just thinking that maybe it's a bit old-fashioned of me to insist that the girls call everyone Miss or Mister or Herr or Madame. Especially when addressing the younger members of the faculty, like you. Everything seems so informal these days, doesn't it?" She was rambling now as she avoided looking at Carla. "Maybe next year we can be a little more relaxed about the titles. . . . Well, just a thought. I won't keep you any longer." She sat suddenly and made a show of studying the papers on her desk.

Carla was stunned by the abrupt dismissal. Worse was the state of the headmistress, which only confirmed her deepest fears. The woman was clearly in some form of shock. Whatever had happened to Katharyn Sunynghame, there was no ambiguity this time—*it hadn't been an accident*. Carla had been right all along. Someone was attacking and *killing* the Marlowe girls! How badly hurt was Katharyn? Was *she* dead, too? Did Miss Grimsby know about the other two—that there were questions about their deaths?

Carla wanted to shake the answers from her, but a look at the stricken woman prevented her from any further prodding. She knew, too, that there was no comfort she could offer.

She fled the office, already late, and rushed down the hall. All she could think of was that she had to talk to Inspector Rudi Neumayer. She wanted to see him personally, not just try to describe what was happening in a remote phone conversation. Her immediate impulse was to cancel her class and hurry down to Fernstaad to the *Kantonspolizei* as fast as she could. But she had a powerful conflict: Until she spoke to Neumayer, nothing would get her to leave Marlowe.

CHAPTER
37

Inspector Neumayer was used to full cooperation from his old friend Fritz Leitner, and he expected the same from anyone on the clinic staff. So he was surprised when he called on Fritz's new associate, Dr. Sunderson, made his request, and was brusquely refused. All he wanted was to see Ursula Freimann for a few minutes, just to ask one or two simple questions. He would be most sensitive; he certainly wouldn't tire her. It was three days since the attack, and he understood that she was improving, that there were moments of lucidity. Maybe she could tell them something—*any* information was desperately needed.

"No, it's out of the question," Eric said.

Seated in the doctor's office, Neumayer tapped his burning cigarette into the makeshift ashtray Eric had reluctantly provided and repeated his request, thinking it hadn't been understood.

"I'm sorry," Eric said firmly, "but I can't permit it. Dr. Freimann had an unexpected relapse last night and went into coma again—in fact, I was called away from dinner to attend her. **She**'s better now, but still critical. I can't risk it. I understand your problem, Inspector, especially now. Fritz told me about the girl, *another* Marlowe girl, found dead this morning—" Neumayer frowned sharply at him. "—in confidence, of course. I realize that very few people are supposed to know about it. It's a terrible shock, I agree. But you'll have to understand *my* problem. Dr. Freimann was badly wounded. She's suffering from severe trauma, both physical and emotional. I don't have to go through the medical details; you've got my report. I believe she'll make it, but I won't allow anything to agitate her right now. You'd be asking her to relive that trauma. Even if she could, which I doubt, it would be the worst thing for her.''

Neumayer debated briefly with himself whether he should ask Fritz Leitner to intercede, but he quickly dismissed the idea. It probably wouldn't help, and he might need the young doctor's cooperation again very soon.

As if reading his mind, Eric added, ''You can count on my help any time, I assure you—as long as it doesn't endanger my patients. Dr. Freimann is my responsibility, and I'm not going to lose her.''

Neumayer nodded. ''Has she said anything these past days? Any words at all, even if they didn't make sense to you?''

''Nothing intelligible. Not that I heard. And I've asked the nurses, too. Your sergeant has been most insistent about that, and I'm telling you just what I keep telling him.''

''My sergeant?''

''Kellhorn? Hans Kellhorn, yes. He's stopped in several times in the past few days. I wouldn't let *him* see Dr. Freimann, either. I assumed that's why you came?''

''Oh, yes, of course. Just to follow up.'' Neumayer felt the heat from his cigarette burn his fingers and quickly stubbed out the last inch of the butt. He reached for a fresh cigarette, but the doctor's look of disapproval stopped him.

''Well, I haven't changed my mind,'' Eric said. ''I can't risk letting either of you see her and possibly upset her.'' He paused. ''Do you know, by the way, if Sergeant Kellhorn is a friend of Dr. Freimann's?'' Rudi Neumayer looked at him, puzzled. ''I was just wondering. He seemed personally concerned, as well. I wasn't sure if his visits were solely professional. *Are* they friends?''

''I wouldn't know,'' Neumayer answered, although he knew quite well. He hadn't forgotten that when he called Hans and told him of the attack on the pathologist, his sergeant first thought that Dr. Freimann was a man. The two had never met. How had Dr. Sunderson gotten the idea that there was a personal interest behind Han's visits to the clinic?

"Does it matter?" he asked the doctor.

"It might. Sometimes the voices of family or close friends can filter through even a deep coma and have a beneficial effect on the patient. But since Sergeant Kellhorn said he was here on official business, of course I couldn't let him see her. I've been sending him regular reports, though, just as he asked. You've seen them?"

"Certainly." He hadn't. Hans had simply told him that she was improving.

"I'm afraid that's the best I can do for you until Dr. Freimann's condition improves significantly. But I am hopeful."

Neumayer grunted as he rose from the chair. Nothing more he could accomplish here.

On the way back to his office, he considered the delicacy of the matter. He remembered the look on Hans's face when they listened to the tape of the attack on Ursula Freimann. The more they replayed it, the more pained his expression became. Perhaps Dr. Sunderson was right; some subtle vibration from Hans had triggered the impression of intimacy and personal concern. Neumayer was surprised, but decided there was no reason to ask his sergeant any extra-official questions. Hans Kellhorn would handle this situation with even more than his usual dogged, obsessive thoroughness. He was a perfectionist, anyhow, and if he had found powerful new motivation in the violence done to Ursula Freimann, that was for the best. With the discovery of the body of the murdered English schoolgirl that morning, they were now catapulted into crisis.

It was the eve of the *Skimarathon*. Fernstaad was so clogged with visitors and skiers taking part in the race tomorrow that it would be impossible to control any single individual's activities. Every private chalet, every hotel and guest house was filled up to the tiniest reserve rooms and attics, and the weekenders had spilled over into the surrounding villages. The SOS Wolfram had hired additional forces to monitor the crawling slopes, and already the accident rate had climbed. In town, Neumayer's men were issuing stern warnings to the more rowdy revelers. Tomorrow promised to be even worse. In the midst of all this chaos, Neumayer had to find a deranged killer who was systematically murdering innocent young girls—a diseased monster who was probably, at this very moment, stalking his next victim.

His throat burned from the gastric flux his belly sent up. He strode down the crowded corridor at the *Kantonspolizei* to his office.

"Kellhorn!" he bellowed as he walked, not looking around.

By the time he was settled at his desk, cigarette going furiously, Hans Kellhorn stood before him, eyes glinting with an anger that mirrored Neumayer's own feelings.

"I've seen a lot," Kellhorn said, "but this is the sickest. That girl's face. . . ."

They discussed the details known so far about the death of Katharyn Sunynghame. Then Kellhorn said, "I spoke to Miss Temple at Marlowe. She called you this morning when we were both out, and I rang her back. She had some new information, something one of the students told her. I think we may be able to narrow down the next target. It might be one of two girls."

For the next fifteen minutes, they reviewed Carla Temple's call and considered the signs of danger, to the two girls that Carla was particularly worried about, and the potential for danger to any of the other students. As expected, Felice Grimsby would not cooperate beyond permitting additional security people at the school. There would be no general detention; the girls would still range freely from town to slopes, and it would be impossible to watch over them. And, above all, no early closing; Marlowe would remain open until the end of the semester. The job of protecting the students through the *Skimarathon* weekend and for the next few weeks was staggering. And it was all Neumayer's responsibility.

He gave Kellhorn instructions, then dismissed the tense sergeant. With a heavy sigh, he turned to his next duty.

Katharyn Sunyghame.

A report of her murder would have to be made to his superior at headquarters in Chur. He'd have to do it by phone, with a paper follow-up, naturally. But the situation was too urgent for even a day's delay in the mail. There was one consolation, at least, he thought as he picked up the phone: He'd be able to summon more help from Chur. There was no way the limited resources of the Fernstaad *Kantonspolizei* could handle this alone.

CHAPTER
38

Elvina, Gräfin von Wetzlar, was proud of her good taste. She considered herself most stylish and demanding—in matters of dress and decorating, jewels and art, homes and household staff, cars and planes, and the right place to be seen at the right time. In matters of sex, she was just as demanding, but about as discriminating as a feeding shark. At the moment, she was feeding on the deliciously wicked, amusing Claude Griffith, who lay in a tangle of custom-made Porthault sheets on her empress-sized bed.

She knelt over him, cooing in the dimly lit peach and coral of her immense bedroom. Her body had been nipped and tucked as often as her face, and suctioned and built up so expertly that in the half-light it looked almost youthful. That was the only way anyone was going to see it without benefit of clothing—artfully lit and reflecting the rosy health of the room's walls and decor. The bedrooms in all four of her homes around the world glowed with the same youth-imparting color. She felt like a perfect jewel in a perfect setting. She felt in total control.

Trying to control Claude was fun. He was muscular and naturally aggressive, and she enjoyed the contest. She had assumed that he would defer to her after accepting her invitation to the bedroom—the privilege of her rank, after all —so she was delighted when he took the initiative and pounced. Flinging her to the pink and cream rug that covered most of the floor, he had half-stripped and mounted her, ignoring her pretense of protest. They had graduated to the bed after that, where she greedily wore him down. But only temporarily. As long as she didn't get too rough with those parts of his body that were bruised or taped—the result of a nasty spill on the slopes, he explained—she could play with him as hard as she liked.

She was playing with him now, in a coke-driven high that he had provided, although he declined to share its powdery pleasures. She raised her head to his chest and nipped wetly at his distended nipples while her hand massaged the bulging root below his testicles until his swollen organ jerked upright. She reached for the delicate stem crystal glass of champagne at her bedside and emptied its contents over his penis, making him start angrily, then took him in her mouth to lap it up. Controlling Claude was the game tonight, and she pressed his forearms into the sheets to emphasize her victory as she felt him thrust involuntarily against her tongue and teeth. *I win!* she exulted, but was instantly surprised when he freed himself with a growl, flipped her over, face down, and entered her from behind, pressing her head down on the oversized pillows. This she hated! She struggled, but he did not release her until he had spent himself with a final jolt that made her neck crackle. Then he turned her over, took his member in hand, and slowly wiped the sticky fluids off on the hairy nest between her legs.

"Any more champagne?" he asked, smiling down at her.

She looked at him through lids slitted with genuine outrage—then laughed.

"Bastard!" she hissed softly, but she was still smiling. She had already decided that he was more fun than the effete wimps who excused their poor performance in bed with tales of grueling days on the slopes. It was a lackluster crop this season, indeed. At least Claude could ski and chew cunt on the same day, she thought, and the idea tickled her. "Help yourself," she said, waving at the frosted bottle of Roederer Cristal next to the bed.

"I usually do," he said, pouring.

She pulled the embroidered voile sheets across her hard, improbably sculpted breasts and considered him. "Are you going to watch the start of the *Skimarathon* tomorrow?"

"Too early. I dislike being around my fellow man until well after lunch. Fellow woman included." He poured a second glass of champagne and handed it to Elvina.

"You're a night person," she said as she drank thirstily. "Like Dracula."

"Vlad the Impaler. I'm glad you noticed."

"Well, if you change your mind, I always give a luncheon for friends in town right after the start of the race. We take over the upstairs club at the Chesa Monteviglia, and you're welcome to come."

"Won't the graf be there? He's not too fond of me, you remember. Ever since that girl killed herself in your greenhouse. I think he blames me."

"You *were* supplying her, weren't you? A schoolgirl, after all."

"Who said? You shouldn't believe everything you hear. I was just taking care of a few friends of a friend. Your husband was one, in case you didn't know."

Her hand combed through her smoky hair and she shrugged. "Well, don't worry about him. He won't be at the luncheon. He's either off in Italy, running wild in Val Triazzo with his buddy the barone, or else sneaking around Fernstaad with one of his little playmates. He won't show himself for days. Who the hell cares."

"Ah, the joys of a happy marriage!" Claude said, raising his glass in a toast. "I can't imagine why I've denied myself the pleasure for so long."

"Mmm, did you say pleasure . . . ?"

Revived, they went at each other again until the gräfin fell asleep, exhausted. Claude dressed and let himself out of the silent chalet into the cold, black night.

CHAPTER
39

Carla had ignored three phone messages from Eric since yesterday. She was too confused to speak to him. She wasn't sure she could trust her voice, or trust herself to be careful of what she said. It was ironic that he had such a seductive way of making her feel secure. She had to remind herself that the trail of her terrified suspicions led to him, and she must be on guard, even if it made her feel silly and a little hysterical.

Still, she longed to speak to him. Yesterday, when she received the first of his messages, she rushed to the privacy of her sitting room, eager to return the call. As she picked up her phone, her hand began to tremble, and she didn't know why. Something about that damned dream! Eric *had* been a part of it, and she couldn't remember *how*. She only knew that thinking of it flooded her with fear. She hung up and let his messages accumulate throughout the day as she struggled with the elusive memory and a collection of surely innocent facts that she *must* be interpreting wrong.

When she woke in the morning, she was delighted that her sleep had been untroubled. She bounded out of bed, fresh with enthusiasm and a new resolve. She wasn't going to spend another day cowering with fright. She was being stupid, and it was time she stopped! Today was Saturday, at last, a glorious morning—perfect for the skiers in the marathon. Perfect for her, too. She wasn't going to sit indoors and miss the excitement. She'd collect Nicole and Bianca after breakfast and take them up to Salastrina to watch the start of the race—Mindy, too. That way she could keep her eye on them. And she'd be out on the snowy trails again—after a year of exile! It was just a short walk, but the thought of being surrounded again by miles of towering white mountains thrilled her.

Also, she'd stop being such a fool about Eric. After breakfast, she'd return his calls with an appropriate excuse. She felt cool and confident enough.

She looked for Miss Grimsby, to inform her of her plans for the girls, but the headmistress didn't come down to breakfast and wasn't in her office afterward. Carla didn't expect any objections, so she went ahead and spoke to Nicole and Bianca.

At first, Nicole was reluctant to accompany her. Bianca said she was too tired. That made Carla more determined to shake them out of their gloom, before it got any worse.

"You'll feel much better—you'll see," she told them, and they finally agreed. "When you find Mindy, tell her to meet us outside in two hours."

She spent the morning finishing some paperwork, then checked her watch. It was time to dress. She had delayed her call to Eric, telling herself she'd do it right after this, and as soon as she finished that. Light seeped through the windows of her sitting room, and a sunburst flashed on the shiny surface of her telephone. *In a minute! Don't nag!*

In the bedroom, she pulled out her favorite ski outfit, a jazzy Bogner jumpsuit splashed with brilliant silver-and-blue lightning bolts. The last time she had worn it was just a few days before her accident a year ago. It was a gift from Michael. "For my Lady Lightning," he had said, and she had loved it from the moment she first put it on. She remembered how thrilling it was to feel like the fastest streak on the slopes, to imagine that the outfit made her almost invisible against the glare of the snow, as if she were part of the mountain itself. Well, there was no more Michael now, and no more thunderbolt speed, but *she* had survived, and nothing was going to defeat her again. She was excited as she slipped into the suit and felt its sleekness hug her body.

At last, she settled at her desk and reached for the phone —just as it rang. She plucked up the receiver, surprised.

"Good morning," Eric said. "I can see you look incredibly beautiful today."

"Oh, I was just going to call you. Sorry I couldn't do it sooner. Yesterday was very hectic here." It pleased Carla to know that she sounded so composed, although Eric's voice was already stirring her longings.

"And I thought you were avoiding me. Never mind. I'm the one who's sorry. I wanted to call you Thursday night, to make sure you got back all right, but we had a bad time at the clinic." He mentioned vaguely a young woman who'd had an accident, was badly injured, and had needed his attention until the early hours of the morning.

"Do you mean Katharyn Sunynghame? Another of our students has been hurt—yesterday. Did you know?"

"Yes, yes, I heard," he said quickly. "No, this is a young doctor from town. She's been here for several days, but she had a relapse and went into coma again while you and I were at dinner. That's why they called me away."

"Oh, how terrible!" Carla said, not knowing how really terrible it had been. "How is she?"

"Not too good," Eric said. "But I think she'll make it. She'd better. I've been threatening her for days if she doesn't—just in case she can hear me."

Carla was silent as she worried the thought. *Threatening her?* Why did he put it that way?

"Are you there?" he asked. "I've been calling since yesterday to find out how *you* are."

"Fine," she said, recovering her composure. "I got home without any trouble. It was a lovely evening, and I thank you."

Eric laughed. "You sound so formal—and well brought up. I can almost see you as a proper, good little girl wearing proper little white gloves and learning to say 'Please' and 'Thank you' and 'I beg your pardon,' when you really want to say 'Go to hell!' and run off and climb a tree. Don't be so polite with me. It makes me nervous."

Carla couldn't help herself. He was charming her, as before. His voice warmed and relaxed her.

"Don't worry," she laughed back. "I assure you I'm pretty tough, and no one ever stopped me from climbing a tree if I wanted to. But I did enjoy our dinner, and I do thank you."

"It ended too soon—and I'm the one with thanks. I planned to ask you to be my guide this morning at the *Skimarathon*, but I'm not sure I can leave the clinic. Do you think they'll run another one again tomorrow?"

"Absolutely, for anyone who isn't too stiff to move or too hung over from celebrating to see. That should be about five or ten people in all of Fernstaad. Not your most thrilling race."

"Okay, next year's *Skimarathon*, then. Is it a date?"

"Got to check my calendar."

"While you're there, see if you're free tomorrow."

"What did you have in mind?" Carla said.

"Lunch? Dinner? Church? All of the above?"

"I don't think you really mean to go to church."

"Why not?" Eric protested. "I've gone on occasion. Besides, those damned steeple bells keep bugging me, reminding me of time passing, that I'm not getting any younger. Don't they ever turn them off?"

"You'll get used to them. I hardly hear them anymore, myself. And if you're just curious about seeing the inside of the church, I warn you that going with me on a Sunday morning and having almost a hundred snoopy little Marlowe girls staring at us is a very poor idea."

"Lunch, then?" His voice dropped to a more intimate register. "At the Chesa Monteviglia? Let's say it's the continuation of our interrupted evening."

Carla toyed with the zipper on the front of her jumpsuit and felt herself retreat. She didn't want to be trapped into a closeness she was no longer sure she could handle. Doubt and fear had clouded her desire.

"I—I don't think so," she said. "I really couldn't."

"Someplace else, then?" The way he said it told her that he had taken the measure of her reluctance.

"I don't think I'll be able to get away tomorrow at all. Miss Grimsby will need me here, I'm sure. She's been terribly upset—especially since yesterday."

"Yes, I can imagine. Maybe you'll change your mind, though. Will you think about it?"

She promised she would. Now she was eager to get away. The girls would be waiting for her outside. She tried to end the conversation, but Eric didn't want to let her go.

"What's your rush? You sound like you're in a hurry," he said.

"I just want to find someplace to watch the race. I thought I'd go for a little walk. You know, someplace where there's a good view." She said it casually, but got the reaction she expected.

"What do you mean, *walk?* Walk *where?*"

"There are beautiful trails up here. I just feel like being out on them."

"I'll bet they're beautiful," Eric said, "and they go up and down, and they're icy and slippery, and they have beautiful big potholes waiting to trip you."

"*Potholes!* In the Alps?"

"Whatever you call them. Your doctor forbids it, Carla!"

"Oh, yeah? Well, he's down there, and I'm up here. Honestly, Eric, thanks for worrying, but I'm only going for a short walk and I'll be *very* careful. I need to do it, believe me."

"I don't like it. Where are you going?"

"Just up to Salastrina. Maybe a little farther. I don't think I'll make it to Corsetti."

"Alone?"

Carla couldn't bring herself to tell him that some of the Marlowe girls would be with her. And she *was* annoyed.

"Of course alone!" she snapped. "Just like a grown-up! You really are on my case, aren't you!"

"Okay, okay. But don't do anything foolish. Be careful of that leg—of yourself. Do I have to remind you that I care?"

"I know," she said, sorry and impatient at the same time. "I'll call you when I get back, let you know I'm still in one piece."

"I'll be waiting to hear."

"'Bye, Eric. I hope your patient improves."

"You're my patient, too. Don't forget it."

She sat at her desk in the sunny sitting room for a while after hanging up. Conflict swirled through her head. She loved the way Eric sounded, so warm and so vibrant with sensual appetite. He *did* care. The tenderness in his voice told her as much as the concern in his words. She felt a shivering openness whenever she was within his orbit. Then why did she think now that she had heard him sound very different, almost cruel—

"A proper, good little girl . . ."

—his voice full of menace and clouded meaning?

"A good little girl . . ."

Was it in her dream that she had heard him—in that inescapable nightmare that seized her between its teeth and shook her mercilessly, night after night?

"A good daughter—"

She jolted upright in her chair. Thursday night's dream came flooding back. Now she remembered it. All of it. Eric, and what he had said—

"Good daughter, daughter, daughter—"

No!

"—and daughters die!"

No, that was wrong! It made no sense at all! It was one thing to speculate on those random coincidences that had led her to suspect Eric—that was just theorizing, and coincidences could always be explained away. It was only prudent to be on guard against anyone who came too close—to her or the girls. But to think that Eric might actually harm them! She shook her head in shock and rejection. Still, she had great respect for the submerged perceptions that the subconscious threw out in dreams. These were messages to pay attention to. Something about Eric had registered subliminally and become equated with danger, *mortal* danger. And yet—

And yet, she could be very mistaken. The danger could be a personal one, to her alone. Maybe it was no more than fear of the pain and loss, the grief Michael had caused her—that it could happen again. A fear that now became entangled with her budding feelings for Eric. She was misreading the message: The danger was emotional, not mortal—to her, not to the girls. Surely, that was the correct way to see it! She *wanted* to trust him. It hurt too much not to trust. . . .

Carla took a deep breath to clear her head, then stood and zipped up the top of her jumpsuit. It was time to shake herself free. Conflicts could wait; there would be time to resolve them later. Right now she had other responsibilities. The diamond-bright slopes were still out there, sparkling in the sun, waiting for her.

And so were the girls, she quickly reminded herself.

A scarred, metal-speared walking stick leaned against the wall in the corner. It was an old alpenstock that Carla had borrowed from Mme. Guinet. She crossed the room to pick it up, automatically checking her reflection in the small mirror on the wall as she passed. Oh, yes, she did look better now! And her leg *was* better, almost perfect again—she could feel it! For the first time since her accident, she had lost that pervasive sense of helplessness. She felt healthy and confident. Despite her growing dread, her protective fears for the girls waiting for her outside, she could see from her reflection in the glass that she was *strong!*

She tested her leg and felt a rush of joy. With a new buoyancy, an incipient spring in her stride, she closed the sitting room door behind her and walked down the hall.

She had just begun the deadliest walk of her life.

Eric's conversation with Carla kept ringing in his head. A short hike up to Salastrina, or maybe even Corsetti? Those trails were steep, the drifted snow unpredictable. She'd be alone and unprotected, her newly healed leg making her much more vulnerable than she realized. She could twist it and fall, out of sight of anyone else. Most of the town would be gathered around Lake Clemenza to watch the race. Fritz Leitner had told him that the trails and slopes were usually empty on the day of the *Skimarathon*.

Alone . . . unprotected. . . .

He went about his rounds efficiently but mechanically, his thoughts distracting him. When he checked on Ursula Freimann, his most critical patient, and found her improved, he made his decision. He called the senior physician on duty under him and gave instructions for the rest of the afternoon. Then he shrugged off his lab coat, zipped himself into his warm new parka, and left the clinic.

CHAPTER
40

Nicole and Bianca didn't notice Carla as she came down the front steps of Marlowe and started across the courtyard. They were too deep in argument. They stood at the lip of a hill in the far corner of the courtyard, their green and orange ski suits vivid against the snowy mountains behind them.

Carla stopped and jabbed her alpenstock into the snow. She was relieved to see the girls, safe, for the moment. But where was Mindy? Hadn't Nicole asked her to come, too? She shaded her eyes against the brilliant sun and looked up. Only a few specks dotted the Corsetti pistes and the lower trails around Salastrina. The high runs from Piz Wolfram flashed white and empty. Everyone was down at Lake Clemenza for the start of the great cross-country race. Ten thousand on skis alone!—and thousands more gathered to cheer them on. She hadn't seen the race last year; she had been in the Leitner Clinic, conscious of little else besides pain and terror. Now she was thrilled to witness the spectacle—thrilled just to be alive and walking on her own.

A cry rose in the air. Nicole and Bianca broke off arguing and looked down at the lake. There was a bustling at the far shore, where tiny dots of people were clustering around something that looked like a large worm. It was the giant alpenhorn—the wooden horn whose curved length stretched from mouthpiece to bell over thirteen feet—that would be sounded to start the race.

Carla called to the girls, and they hurried to her, both talking at once.

"What's the problem now?" Carla asked. "Where's Mindy?"

"*That's* the problem," Nicole said. "*Mindy!* She said she couldn't stand being shut up like a prisoner another minute. She took her skis and went up to Salastrina!"

Oh, the little boob! Carla thought. *She just can't stay out of trouble.* "Why didn't you stop her? Nicole, didn't you tell her I was going to take you off the grounds for a while?"

"I told her," Nicole said. "And I *did* try to stop her. She said no one would see her, that she'd only take one run down from Salastrina and come right back. But I don't believe her. I think she's going to take the T-bar up to Corsetti and ski down from there."

"So, after what happened in the courtyard later," Bianca said, "I thought we should both go after Mindy and warn her. But Nicole wouldn't—"

"What happened in the courtyard?" Carla demanded, alarmed. "Warn Mindy of *what*?"

"*Miss Grimsby!*" both girls answered.

"Miss Grimsby just went up to Corsetti with her skis," Nicole said. "She'll catch Mindy, I know it!"

"Ah, I see," Carla said. It was trouble, certainly, but not what she had first imagined.

"This time, she'll get expelled," Nicole said. "And it will be her own fault."

"What exactly did Miss Grimsby say?" Carla asked.

"That she was going up to Corsetti for a fast run before lunch," Bianca answered. "But she seemed very strange, you know? She kept looking up at the school while she was talking to us, studying the building, almost. Is she all right?"

"I'm sure she has a lot on her mind," Carla said, and Nicole gave her a hard, sidelong glance.

"We should warn Mindy," Bianca said. "But I'm not going alone."

Carla nodded in agreement. "Maybe Miss Grimsby will

change her mind and go all the way up to Piz Wolfram. It's such a beautiful day, I wouldn't be surprised if she decided to ski the whole mountain. That way, she won't be anywhere near the Corsetti or Salastrina trails—''

''No, she can't.'' Nicole shook her head. ''They've closed the pistes from Piz Wolfram today. There's a buildup of snow on the high slopes, Miss Grimsby told us. They're going to try to shoot it down before it gets too heavy. They've even stopped the cable car for the rest of the day, just in case of avalanches.''

Carla looked up at the highest peaks. That explained why they were completely empty. She turned back to the two girls, with decision and regret in her eyes. ''Okay, I'm sorry about our little expedition—it's been scratched. I want you both to stay here. On the grounds. I'll see what I can do about Mindy, not that she deserves any help.''

''What—what *can* you do?'' Nicole asked hesitantly. She and Bianca tried not to stare at the spear-tipped walking stick in Carla's hand, a reminder of the cane and crutches and brace they had never seen her without.

''Go after her, of course. When I catch up with Mindy at Salastrina, I'll send her right back. If I don't decide to kill her first. What was she wearing?''

''Blue,'' Bianca said. ''A dark-blue jumpsuit.''

''And Miss Grimsby, so I can try to keep them away from each other?''

''Just like me,'' Bianca said. ''An orange parka and ski pants. I made a joke that we looked alike, but I don't think she heard me.''

Carla pressed her lips together, troubled. She was almost as worried for Miss Grimsby as for Mindy. The headmistress was apparently so distracted that Carla wondered if her concentration could hold for a run down a tricky piste. She was suddenly aware that the girls were watching her, quietly shuffling their boots in the snow.

''Something?'' Carla challenged. ''Out with it.''

''Uh, it's pretty steep, the road up to Salastrina,'' Nicole said uneasily. ''Do you think you—?''

''It's not as steep as the back stairs at Marlowe,'' Carla

cut her off sharply. "And not dark, either." Bianca looked puzzled, but Nicole got the message. "Look, I *am* sorry to disappoint you about our walk, but you can complain to Mindy when she gets back. You'll have a good view of the race over there," she pointed with her alpenstock. "So go ahead, now. You don't want to miss the start. Go *on!*"

Nicole and Bianca heard the unequivocal end of the discussion. They turned and walked away without further protest. Carla watched them go, glad that they didn't look back at her. She wasn't feeling half as sure as she sounded, and she was afraid it showed.

She walked out of the courtyard, stopped for a second, and looked up at the steep rise of the Salastrina slope. Then she gritted her teeth. *Damn you, Mindy! I really could kill you for this!*

She dug her alpenstock into the snow and started up the trail.

CHAPTER
41

He had seen her!

Crouching in the snow behind the trees along the trail, he had been scanning the Marlowe School grounds, until his position became too uncomfortable. He rose and stretched, careful to remain concealed as he watched the excited schoolgirls scurrying down the road to Fernstaad. The *Skimarathon* would start very soon now. It was drawing them down to the lake, and they poured out of the courtyard in a happy stream. But *she* was not among them.

He grunted softly in discouragement as the stream dwindled

to a trickle. He must not give up. He was too close. Maybe she was so frightened now that she wouldn't appear. Maybe she *knew*. That last girl, two days ago—he hadn't meant to kill her. *She* wasn't the one. But he had seen her in the *Konditorei* Klaus and recognized the crest on her ski jacket. Another Marlowe girl! This one was behaving furtively, looking around every time the front door swung open. When she saw two women enter—teachers, probably—she rushed out, hiding her face as she went. He couldn't help himself. He followed her into the small back alley behind the Klaus, fondling the knife tucked into his waistband. She didn't know he was there until the last minute—too late! He *had* to do it. He *wanted* to. Afterward he lost control. *Wrong—one—. wrong—wrong. . . .* He heard himself snarling as he erased the face that wasn't the one he sought. Then, calmer, he wiped the splatterings off in the drifted snow. Only the wetness showed on his dark-blue parka. He would not do this again, he promised himself. He would wait for *her* only. . . .

He crouched again and squirmed restlessly. His new parka was a little tight, and the sleeve pressed on his wounded arm, the one that pathologist bitch had slashed. But the tape held it firm, the ache was receding, the arm was healing already. It hadn't given him any trouble in his most energetic activity, and it wouldn't stop him now. He felt the knife, rigid against his body. He hadn't brought the note, the last one. That would come later. Yes, he was prepared for this day, which he had feared might never come. He studied the courtyard below. Waiting . . . waiting. . . .

Then she appeared!

He held his breath. Which way would she go? Down to the lake? Or up?—to him? *Come to me. To me.*

She wasn't alone . . . she had stopped to talk to two girls in bright ski clothes. Maybe she would be with others . . . or change her mind and return to the school. *Come to me.*

Then she walked out of the courtyard, turned from the direction of the lake, away from the road to town, and looked up at the great mountains rising to the cloudless blue sky.

Up! She was heading up to the ski slopes. And she was *alone!*

Yes, come to me, child. Come to me, little one, little daughter. Hurry. I am waiting. . . .

CHAPTER
42

Pindar Breitel picked his way carefully through the ice-flaked slush of the narrow walkway bordering the road into Fernstaad. His metal-speared cane, white and banded with red, felt out the snow mounds and skiddy ice patches ahead. One gloved hand rested on the railing of the small wooden bridge that signaled he was approaching his first destination.

The morning sun was warm on his face. It heated the resinous pines along the road, releasing the rich fragrance of their oils. Pindar Breitel gulped the air greedily. He loved being outside, even in snowy winter when every trail and walkway was a minefield for the unseeing. And he loved having a destination, as he did this crisp Saturday morning. He would walk all the way down to Lake Clemenza for the start of the *Skimarathon*. Such excitement! He could hear the noise already, rising from the lake below—the shouts and cries of ten thousand *Langlauf* skiers as they milled around the shores and limbered up for the race.

He was close enough to town now so that tourists and villagers rushing to witness the spectacle surrounded him. They bumped into him as they brushed past and made his slow passage even more perilous. But he was too happy to care. He would join them in plenty of time to hear the blowing of the giant alpenhorn, the booming call that would begin the great cross-country race.

But first, he would stop off at the *Kantonspolizei*. It was on his way, after all, and if Rudi Neumayer wasn't there or was too busy to see him—well, he could come back on Monday. He'd be glad to do that; it would give him another destination for another day.

His hand slid to the end of the wooden railing of the bridge. He gripped his cane tightly. Now came the steep, rutted driveway down to the courtyard of the *Kantonspolizei* buildings. Carefully, he braced himself as he made his way down through the slush and crossed the icy yard. One shallow step up, and he pushed open the door.

A rush of warm air and a flurry of activity greeted him as he stepped inside. He stopped and loosened the muffler at his throat. A man jostled him in passing, and he had to plant his cane to regain his footing.

"Watch out!" the man shouted. "Oh, sorry, Breitel. Didn't know it was you. What do you want? We're pretty busy—"

"Yes, yes, I can see that. Corporal Trivella, isn't it? I just thought the inspector might be here. I could say hello for a minute?"

"This is a bad time for a visit. I don't think he can see you today, unless you've got some problem?"

"*Ach*, what problems would I have?" Breitel laughed. "No trouble, Officer Trivella. You think the inspector is too busy for a good-morning call, then I could come back, maybe Monday?"

"That would be much better. I'd rather not interrupt him now—"

The door to Neumayer's office opened suddenly, and Sergeant Kellhorn strode out into the hall.

"Trivella, there you are! Can you get us that file of guest registrations they sent up from Chur? They're in a big carton in the storeroom, I think. If not, look in one of the empty cells in the back. The inspector isn't sure where they were put." Kellhorn walked toward them. "Come, I'll help you look."

Neither officer paid any attention to Pindar Breitel as he

slipped past them and moved quietly down the hall. His fingers feathered the wall until he came to the open doorway of Rudi Neumayer's office.

"Put two men on it, Kellhorn," Neumayer said snappily to the footsteps that entered the room. He didn't look up from the papers on his desk. "It'll go much faster. Maybe we can narrow it down, check out anyone with a passport that fits. Then, I'll want you to try the clinic again—"

"So busy, Rudi?" Breitel said.

"Oh, Pindar! I didn't expect you. Excuse me, my friend, I couldn't call you back the other day. We've been terribly—"

"I know. I can see how it is with you today. I won't bother you, only to say good morning. I was passing by on my way to the lake. You aren't going? Tsk, you'll miss all the excitement."

"We've got enough excitement right here. You'll forgive me, but I can't ask you to stay. Next week, eh?"

"Of course. I invite you for a coffee. Monday?"

"We'll see. Now, you go and enjoy the race."

"I'll tell you all that you missed, next week." Pindar Breitel turned to the door and was roughly bumped by Sergeant Kellhorn as he returned.

"What are you doing in here, Breitel?" Kellhorn said, steadying the tottering man.

"He's just leaving," Neumayer said. "Did you find them?"

"Yes, sir. Don't bother, Breitel, I'll close the door. And watch your step going up the driveway. It's very icy."

"Up is easier than down," Breitel sniffed. "And I got down just fine, thank you."

"Sure you did, old fellow." Kellhorn patted the blind man as he ushered him out and closed the door. Then he turned to Neumayer. "I've got Dünner and Hess working on them now. They'll pull any card listing a passport from an English-speaking country."

"Needle in a haystack," Neumayer sighed. "The man could be from anywhere. Still, it's all we've got."

"Unless Dr. Freimann pulls through. She could help."

Kellhorn crossed the room and leaned stiffly against the back of an iron-runged chair next to Neumayer's desk. "Maybe I should run up to the clinic—?"

"Better call first. No point wasting time if they won't let you see her." Neumayer heard the sharpness in his voice and remembered too late Kellhorn's unexpected interest in Ursula Freimann. He continued, more softly, "Besides, I'll want you here to look over those guest cards with me."

"Do you really expect something?"

"Four weeks of tourists?" Neumayer snorted. "You don't have to tell me how impossible this is. We've also got private houseguests in every home and chalet in Fernstaad. There won't be any cards for them—or for all those dozens of guest houses that rent out a room or two during the season. Most of them never bother with the cards, anyhow, no matter how often I—"

Neumayer stopped in midsentence. His eyes turned to the closed door of his office. Kellhorn followed his glance and caught the thought immediately.

"You think—?" Kellhorn asked.

"What the hell," Neumayer shrugged. "Let's not miss anything, as long as he's here."

Kellhorn rushed to the door and flung it open.

At the end of the hall, Pindar Breitel had just finished tying his muffler around his neck and was feeling for the knob of the outside door.

"Herr Breitel!" Kellhorn called. "Could you please come back in here for a minute?"

Twenty minutes later, a bewildered Pindar Breitel sat in the back seat of Rudi Neumayer's car as they raced through Fernstaad *Bad* toward his house. He would miss the start of the *Skimarathon*, but that hardly mattered now. Something he had told Rudi and the sergeant had excited them—something terrible that had to do with their new boarder. All the questions they had asked!

They barreled up the icy highway at what felt like dangerous speed. In the front seat, Rudi and Sergeant Kellhorn weren't talking. The tension in the car frightened him.

When they were halfway to his house, Breitel heard a loud roar from Lake Clemenza, far below. The crowd started cheering. Then the booming of the alpenhorn rose up from the hollow like the primal bellow of a wild beast, reverberating from the mountainsides. The marathon had begun!

"*Faster!*" Neumayer commanded Kellhorn.

CHAPTER
43

Mindy Parson stood at the top of the Salastrina peak. It was a half hour since the *Skimarathon* had begun, and she could see a troupe of almost a thousand skiers in the rear still straggling across the ice of the lake. Cries urging them on floated unmuffled on the clear air. This was the fourth time she had thrilled to the spectacle, and it would be the last. Next year, she'd be as far from Fernstaad as she could possibly get, and she'd never come back.

She toed into her skis and pressed her heels down to lock the bindings. The beginners' slopes of Salastrina spread gently below her. She looked down without enthusiasm.

Baby stuff! What fun was that?

Nearby, the T-bar crawled lazily up to Corsetti. She shaded her eyes and stared up at the steep pistes below the Corsetti station. Above it, the breathtaking summit of Piz Wolfram sparkled in the sun. She was surprised that no skiers rode its high face today, but its very emptiness made the precipitous slopes even more inviting.

What the hell! If she was going to risk trouble, she might as well have a good time doing it. The beginners' trails just weren't worth it. She could skip lunch. Nicole and Bianca would cover for her at school, and she'd grab something at one of the snack bars up the mountain.

She dug her poles into the snow and skied to the T-bar.

The *Evangelische* steeple bells had already tolled two o'clock when Felice Grimsby reached the base of the main Corsetti piste. She had made several runs since noon, hoping to ease her sick tension, but each time she flung herself down the mountain she found herself more knotted than before. Instead of calming her, the activity was making her more frantic.

Katharyn Sunynghame had been murdered . . . and probably Sophie and Anneliese, too . . . and she had been powerless to protect them. Were other girls in danger? God, no! *What should she do?*

She stopped at the bottom of Corsetti to catch her breath. The noon meal at Marlowe would just be ending. She had told Lina where she was going and not to expect her for lunch; she was sure her secretary wouldn't volunteer the information unless it was absolutely necessary. She needed time to think. She would not return to school until she had sorted through her fears and either laid them to rest or put a name to them. Then she would know what she must do.

She adjusted her yellow-lensed goggles and looked around. The ski trails were almost deserted. To her surprise, she was fiercely hungry. She felt a compulsion to work her teeth around something, as if the act of chewing, the very sound of gnashing in her ears, could make her feel powerful and menacing to anyone who threatened—instead of the helplessness and terror she now felt. Her teeth clenched in anticipation. She would ride the chair lift back up to the Corsetti station and stop at the snack bar for a hot *Würstli* with bitingsharp mustard. And a beer. Yes, that was what she wanted. That, and *time*.

She tapped the clotted snow from her skis and slid to the chair lift.

Carla came out into a clearing just below the Salastrina peak. The climb hadn't tired her as much as she had expected. That was some satisfaction. And so was the terse, no-nonsense lecture she had rehearsed for Mindy's benefit on the way up.

She blinked against the snowy glare and scanned the hills for a glimpse of the truant girl. What was Mindy wearing? Blue—a dark-blue jumpsuit, the girls had said. It would be easy to spot a familiar figure on the nearly empty slopes.

She leaned into the incline and continued to push up the hill.

Suddenly, she saw her. There was no mistaking the jaunty, copper-haired girl traversing the smooth belly of the piste. Where the hell was she going?

"Mindy!" Carla called, but she knew the girl was too far away to hear her.

She called again, anyhow, and waved her alpenstock through the air. Mindy didn't turn around. She was heading for the T-bars! Frustrated, Carla watched her plant herself in the snow, look back toward the advancing bar, then lean her behind against it as it scooped her along and slid her up the hill.

Corsetti!

The dumb kid was going up to Corsetti, just as Nicole and Bianca had predicted. Straight into the arms of Miss Grimsby, who would surely spot her very visible and very delinquent student on those uncrowded runs.

Oh, damn!

Carla wrestled briefly with responsibility, anger, and concern for the foolish girl. At the very least, Mindy could get herself expelled. At the worst . . . *don't think about it*!

She gave herself the order: *Keep going*.

She stabbed the snow with her alpenstock and started across the spine of the Salastrina peak toward the wooded hiking trail up to Corsetti.

CHAPTER
44

Rudi Neumayer stood in the center of the small, clean guest room, turning, studying.

A flustered Minna Breitel trundled her stubby body around the room, clucking in distress at the invasion.

Pindar Breitel sat on the bed in a daze, face lifted and shifting toward each new sound.

Hans Kellhorn pulled at the drawers of the rough pine desk and pronounced each of them empty.

"Oh dear, oh dear!" Pindar said when he heard the new sound of the clothes chest opening.

"Would you like to wait downstairs?" Kellhorn asked sternly.

"Please, you mustn't touch anything! He might come back—"

Kellhorn ignored him. He held up a heavy ski sweater he had just pulled from the chest.

"The labels don't tell us anything," he said to Neumayer. "Mostly Swiss, or common imports—but this is his size. Medium to large, depending on how tight or loose he likes his clothes. And everything looks new. Underwear the same. Not very helpful." He replaced the sweater, neatly folded again. "I'll check the bathroom."

Neumayer nodded. He was frustrated. His patient questioning of Pindar and his mother together hadn't told them anything new of importance. Their boarder spoke English, when he spoke at all; his name sounded English to them, although they hadn't seen his passport and didn't know how to spell it. They mangled its pronunciation so badly that neither Neumayer nor Kellhorn could understand it. "It could be a phony, anyhow," Kellhorn said. The elderly Minna Breitel's description of the man would fit half the adult male population of Fernstaad, maybe even of the Western world. She hadn't seen him that often, she admitted. Although he was paying for the room by the week—"Yes, Rudi, in cash."—he would be gone for days at a time. She would knock on his door each morning to ask if he wanted breakfast, but most of the time he refused—or he wasn't there. He was quiet, not friendly. Yes, it was strange, perhaps, that he was here in Fernstaad without skis. But he was polite—and so *clean*! It was a pleasure to have such a clean guest, not like some of those young students, so rude and careless! She couldn't imagine that he had done anything wrong that Rudi and the sergeant should invade his possessions! A fine person like that!

Neumayer sighed and nudged her back on track.

The only thing unusual about the man was his comings and goings. Those days when he never appeared, and then Pindar would tell her that he had heard him arriving at four in the morning, sometimes five, more than once. "And if Pindar says so, then it is so. He is such a light sleeper—"

"*Mutti*, please!" Pindar squirmed in embarrassment on the bed.

Which days? Neumayer prodded him, then asked him to repeat it, to be sure. They seemed to match. One of them coincided with the early-hours break-in at Marlowe and another with the attack on Ursula Freimann—the same night the man had smeared blood on the jacket of a Marlowe girl.

It wasn't enough.

Neumayer asked Minna Breitel what the man was wearing when she last saw him leave the house. Pindar answered for her because it pleased him to speak of colors: "As always, his tan parka; he only had the one." His mother corrected him: "*Ach*, no, dear. Blue. He bought a new one. I *told* you." She described it for Neumayer.

Kellhorn returned from the bathroom, shaking his head. "Standard toiletries. Nothing special. But everything seems brand new, even his small toiletry case. Like the clothes. I find that odd, don't you, sir?''

"Hmmmm," Neumayer muttered to himself. His eyes swept the room. "His suitcases—they're not here. Did you store them someplace?" he asked the Breitels.

"Only one suitcase he had," Frau Breitel said. "I said to Pindar—"

"Did you put it away in some other room?" Kellhorn interrupted. "In an armoire someplace? Downstairs, maybe?"

Minna Breitel peered around the room.

"It must be here. He didn't ask us to take it out. You didn't move it, did you, Pindar?"

Her son thought for a minute. That object he had heard their boarder slide along the floor—the sound had come from the area near the bed, he remembered. He bent over and lifted the frilled dust ruffle.

Kellhorn knelt and pulled out the light canvas suitcase.

"Yes, that's it!" Frau Breitel cried, then she stiffened. "Oh! Rudi, no! You're not going to open his suitcase, too, are you?"

Neumayer motioned to Kellhorn, who lifted the case onto the bed next to Pindar and tried the lock. It didn't give. He inserted a small metal pick and turned it delicately. The lock sprang open.

Minna Breitel sputtered in protest.

Neumayer moved closer.

When Kellhorn raised the lid and the two men saw what was lying on top, Neumayer quickly blocked Frau Breitel's view and turned to Pindar.

"I want you to take your mother downstairs *right now!* Do as I say, old friend. No questions now."

There was no arguing with the urgency in Neumayer's voice. The Breitels left the room without a further word.

Slowly, Kellhorn lifted out the slashed and bloody tan parka that was on top of the pile in the suitcase. As he held it up, both men heard in their heads the replay of the tape made in Dr. Freimann's laboratory when her attacker had cried out in pain. They stared at the parka in silence, then turned back to the suitcase. There was a bundle of crumpled underwear and, below it, a large, metal-tabbed envelope. Kellhorn placed the clothing on the bed, wrapped a clean handkerchief around his hand, and seized the envelope.

Neumayer peered inside the suitcase over Kellhorn's shoulder. They both saw it at the same time—the black leather scabbard on the bottom.

Kellhorn dropped the envelope on the bed and reached for the black knife case. Cradling it in his handkerchief, he rolled it deftly so that they could see its markings. Pressed into the leather was the gilt signature design—an eye radiating sun rays—and under it the identification: *Carl Schlieper, Solingen, Germany*. It was the right size to hold a survival knife twenty-seven centimeters long.

"*Sir!*" Kellhorn hissed. "The knife the little Luzzatto girl picked up—near the Karas body—same markings!"

"Give it to me," Neumayer said gruffly, reaching for the scabbard with his own handkerchief. "See what's in the envelope. Quickly, man!"

Kellhorn emptied the contents out onto the bed.

"No passport," he mumbled, and spread the few papers and objects wider. "No plane ticket, either. He must have taken them with him. Some plain blank letter envelopes— *oh!*" He held up a yellow receipt from a clothing store in Fernstaad for the purchase of a ski jacket. The date was a few days ago, and the scribbled name of the customer approximated the mispronunciation the Breitels had given them.

"Name mean anything?" Neumayer asked.

Kellhorn shook his head and continued sifting. "Two small paperback books, a German-English dictionary, and a guide to Fernstaad . . . some Fernstaad booklets, the weekly listings of the latest events around town—seven of them. He could have picked them up in any hotel lobby—"

Neumayer gave a hurry-up wave of his hand.

"Postcards . . . panoramic views of the town and ski slopes with all the trails and their elevations and— *Look!*" He thrust one of the cards at Neumayer. "That building halfway up the mountain. That's the Marlowe School. He's *circled* it."

Neumayer grabbed the card. "We'll take all of this with us. What else?" He reached into the pile on the bed and drew in his breath sharply. He had flipped over a single creamy sheet of stationery with shiny black raised insignia and a familiar name and address at the top of the page:

> **MARY A. MARLOWE**
> School for Girls
> 7557 Fernstaad

In the middle of the page, he saw two handwritten words in shaky script: *Daughters die*.

"*Good God!*" His face was grim, his voice almost a whisper. "*We've got him!*" He studied the papers on the bed. "No passport? No plane or train tickets? You're sure?"

Kellhorn began to shake out the books onto the bed, one by one—dictionary, guidebook, each of the leaflets. . . .

A small, rectangular green-and-yellow card floated down. Kellhorn pounced.

The card was a computer-printed Swissair boarding pass. Flight 111, the date several weeks earlier, destination Zurich from JFK New York.

"The passenger!" Kellhorn said. "*Look at that!*"

Neumayer's head jerked as he read the card. His forehead bunched into wrinkles and he gaped, speechless.

"*The name!*" Kellhorn said.

"*I see it!*" Neumayer said. It didn't make any sense.

Then he was galvanized into action. "Put that stuff together, all of it," he ordered. "We're taking it with us right now." Kellhorn was already scooping up the papers and books and stuffing them back into the envelope. "*Let's go, let's go!*"

"To Marlowe?"

"We'll radio on the way. *Hurry!*"

Downstairs, Neumayer gave hasty instructions to the stunned Breitels in case their boarder returned before men from the *Kantonspolizei* could get to the house.

The car's motor was running, and Kellhorn was talking

into the radio when Neumayer hoisted his bulk into the seat next to him. They started rolling away before Neumayer had even closed the door.

CHAPTER
45

He shifted in his cramped position in the snow. He had anticipated her destination and gotten there ahead of her. From behind the dense tree trunks and snow-mounded bushes, he had a clear view of the crest of the Corsetti peak. He could see the funicular station, the outdoor snack bar, the T-bars, and the chair lift that mounted the rise where the ski trails fell away. Not far from his hiding place was the squat building that housed the ski shop and the SOS Wolfram—and the massive, almost primitive mechanism that drove the Piz Wolfram cable car.

That was how he would do it—with the help of that gigantic machinery!

He had studied it several days ago in wonderment. Its size was overwhelming. Corsetti was the main station of the cable car; its secondary control tower was perched at the peak of Piz Wolfram. But here, only yards away, was its nerve center. *And here was where her final journey would end*.

It had been surprisingly easy to wander through the station. He must have looked like a workman; no one had stopped him. In fact, no one was around. The entire system must be so automatic that it needed only the flick of a switch to activate and operate. He had moved cautiously around the powerful electrical drive unit, marveling at the giant, ten-foot bull wheel and the thick steel haul and track ropes. Most incredible were the colors: wheels and spokes of brilliant yellow, mountings of flaming red, engine housing of vibrant turquoise. The whole system looked like a Brobdingnagian toy.

Then he saw the partly opened door in the far wall. He circled the gleaming machinery and swung it wider. Sudden vertigo seized him, and he clutched the door frame to steady himself.

He was looking down a dank shaft more than one hundred feet deep. A moist, cementy odor rose from the gloom. Below were more enormous wheels and steel ropes lurking in the brownish, dust-speckled light. A metal ladder descended the wall beneath the door.

He turned to see if anyone had entered the room. He was alone. He swung himself onto the ladder and climbed down.

The bottom of the shaft was gritty and smelled of must. One wall was blank, with a narrow crawl space at its base. Opposite, the huge, oil-smeared wheels rolled gently back and forth, winding and unwinding their thick ropes only a foot at a time without dislodging any of the caked dirt. He stared at them, trying to understand their function.

The shaft was enveloped in eerie stillness. There was no rattle or clank, no whir or hum that he might have expected from such a mass of machinery. Only a faint breathing that came from the rolling wheels, their movement so languorous it was almost lazy. He strained to hear their whispering in the echoing silence of the shaft.

Suddenly, as he watched, the wheel closest to him rolled a full half-turn. Swiftly, it wound up its rope in one huge sweep, as if to swallow it. He sensed motion behind him. He turned, fearfully, and the sight made him stagger back against the wheel mount.

The wall—it was moving!

For an instant, he thought he would be sick. He stared, horrified, fascinated. The wall had lurched upward—then descended just as violently, but with only a tiny hissing sigh. Now he realized where he was.

He was standing on the floor of the pit room. In this chamber, the gigantic counterweights were housed—the cement blocks that hung from the steel track ropes surrounding the haul rope on which the cable-car cabins rode. The wall was not a wall. It was a block of cement weighing 300,000 pounds. *The counterweight*.

This was the stupendous device that maintained the tension of the ropes, that moved in response to the vertical motion of the cabins outside on the ski slopes. Up and down, gently up and down. As a cabin rose, its counterweight fell. A smooth motion of only a few inches, until the cabin rode up and over the crest of one of the metal towers that supported the cables. Then the counterweight danced downward to the pit floor—a swift drop of almost seven feet. The whispering counter rope wound just as quickly around its sheave, pressing against the great wheel, whose twelve-foot diameter rolled easily in its cement casing.

It was all so overpowering in size—but such an incredibly simple system.

He had scurried back up the ladder, eager to be out of the murky pit room. He didn't relax until he was out on the snowy slopes of Corsetti again. But already the idea was forming.

Now, huddled behind the bushes, he looked out at the Corsetti peak and reviewed his plans. The thunder of the cannon reminded him of his good fortune. They were shooting down the unstable snow on the summits around Piz Wolfram and had closed the high pistes until they were safe again. The cable car had been stopped, motionless—*all ready for him*! They were giving him the time he needed to accomplish what he had come for—and time to get away. He would escape to savor his success, to live in comfort and satisfaction for the rest of his life.

His plans were simple, just like the machinery that would execute them.

When she reached Corsetti, he had no doubt that he could lure her to him, close enough to use his knife, if he had to. Or better, just to stun her first. *Then to the pit room*. He could carry her, if necessary; she wouldn't be too heavy. Accidents were such a frequent occurrence on the pistes that no one would pay any attention to someone being helped off the slopes—if anyone was there to see. Once he got her down the shaft of the pit room, he would roll her deep underneath the concrete counterweight. She'd be hidden in a place no one would think of searching. There she would rest until the cable car started up again, resuming its slow passage over the slopes between Corsetti and Piz Wolfram. There she would lie, helpless, until the cabin bounced over the first high tower and sent the 300,000-pound counterweight plummeting down to *obliterate* her! She would be beyond identification—she might never even be found. And he would be *free!*

His eyes sparkled with excitement, his breathing was shallow as he scanned the white hills. In a few hours, it would all be done. He would slip away on the late train to Zurich tonight, losing himself first in the confusion at the Fernstaad station and then abroad. Just one last gesture—the note he had already prepared and left in his suitcase at the Breitels'. He'd mail it to the Marlowe School just before boarding the train. They'd understand, eventually, that she was never coming back. One day, *he* would return, to relish his triumph.

The chill of the lengthening afternoon penetrated his parka. His ears ached. He pulled his hood up onto his head and snapped it closed. Stretching to ease the cramp in his legs, he stared out at the snowy pistes.

There! There she was—at last!

CHAPTER
46

God, she was hungry!

It was way past three. Mindy felt in her pocket for her francs and began skiing toward the small snack bar on the crest of the Corsetti slope. Only one lone skier was there, a woman. It was Bianca! Mindy recognized her hideous orange ski suit. Great! She'd have company now.

When she was close enough to smell the steaming *Würstli* Bianca was eating, Mindy lifted her pole and started to call out—

Oh, Christ! It wasn't Bianca—it was Miss Grimsby! Her Grimness, herself!

Mindy braked and looked around frantically. Where could she hide on the open hill? What if Miss Grimsby had seen her . . . !

She hunched into her collar and sidestepped back up the rise toward a stand of pine fronted by snow-mounded bushes. As soon as she was deep enough behind the bushes, she looked out. No, the headmistress hadn't spotted her. She was still standing there, calmly biting into her roll and sausage. Mindy gulped with relief. She was lucky today—for a change! She unlooped the ski pole from her right hand and slipped it onto her left wrist, next to its companion. Crouching in her hiding place, she waited for Miss Grimsby to leave.

A heavy mound of snow plopped down at her side.

The bushes hissed behind her.

She turned and looked up.

A large man stood over her. His face, framed by the hood of his dark-blue parka, looked as startled as Mindy's; his eyes bored into hers. *Eyes . . . wild . . . menacing.*

Mindy gasped and jumped up. *His face—it was so familiar!* Where had she seen him before? Was she imagining things?

Fear seized her. She wheeled around to look out at the snack bar. Miss Grimsby was still there, finishing the last bite. Mindy wanted to call out to her, but she didn't dare. She turned to face the man, stupefied. He had flung off his hood and was sliding the zipper down from the neck, reaching inside the half-opened parka.

"*Who are you? What do you want*?" she croaked. "*What—?*"

Her voice choked off as she saw his hand emerge, clutching the big-bladed knife. She moved back and felt one ski slide over the other, rooting her in the snow. She twisted her captive body and opened her mouth to scream.

In one leap, the man was upon her, slamming her jaw with a swipe of his balled fist. Mindy started to fall. He yanked her close. With one hand he pressed on her throat—just enough to stop her struggling. His face was puffy with rage. As the blackness closed in, Mindy heard him growl, "*Wrong—one—wrong—wrong. . . .*"

Out on the hill, Miss Grimsby brushed the crumbs from her jacket, turned away from the snack bar, and glided off down the piste.

CHAPTER
47

Carla saw the two things almost simultaneously.

Rounding a bend in the hiking trail, she had an open view of the entire Corsetti peak up above. First, she saw a lone skier at the top of the mountain, a slender woman in orange, spring lightly onto the run, picking up speed on her first traverse down the piste.

Miss Grimsby.

Then she spotted the stumbling pair emerge from the bushes. They were both dressed in dark-colored skiwear. The taller one, a man on foot, half-supported, half-carried the smaller figure, a young girl on skis. She was swept along without any power of her own, her ski poles looped over one wrist and skittering in the snow.

An accident.

Carla blinked. The dark-blue belted jumpsuit . . . the short, coppery hair, visible even in the fading light. . . . *Oh, lord! It was Mindy!* Thank heaven someone was still there on the deserted peak to help her!

Carla pushed herself faster up the trail. It was late. The church bells in town started tolling the hour—four o'clock. The early winter dark would close in soon. Behind her, the Salastrina T-bars had already ended their crawl and hung like dead twigs strung out down the slope. She watched the attendant shutter the facade of the snack bar and depart, skiing down the trail.

How badly was Mindy hurt? Where was the man taking her?

Ah! They were heading for the low building that housed the SOS Wolfram. She knew it from last year, from her Olympic days. Inside was the ski shop, the first-aid station, and all the cable-car machinery. But, wouldn't it be closed already? *Hurry, hurry.* She bent her weight into the climb. She was almost there. *Thank God that man had been there to help!*

The first skeleton fingers of purple shadow appeared on the peaks and stretched down the mountainside. Lights flashed on in the buildings around the darkening bowl of Lake Clemenza. The Corsetti funicular was now on its evening schedule; the bright blue ascending car rolled up the track and into the station just as Carla reached the peak. Mindy and the man had already disappeared around the corner of the building. It must still be open. *Good.*

Suddenly, Carla thought: That man—who is he? Why isn't he on skis, as the rescue team usually is? A picture of Sophie Karas flashed through her head. Sophie! . . . Anneliese! . . . Katharyn? *That man!*

Oh, Mindy! Oh. God, no . . . !

She drove herself forward. Her hiking boots crunched in the snow, intolerably loud in the silence of the peak. She used the metal-speared walking stick for purchase on the icy flat around the building. She stopped at the front door. It was closed. She thought she heard a faint mewing cry—a whimpering, deep inside the building. She grasped the doorknob

DEADLY BONDS / 271

and turned. It wasn't locked! As she pushed open the door, she heard a loud crunching behind her. She spun around.

The man in the dark ski parka . . . alone. Coming around the corner of the building . . . coming toward her!

Eric!

"No!" she cried.

"Carla! Wait!"

She flung herself through the door and slammed it behind her. *Eric—it was Eric all the time!* Fingers trembling, she fumbled the heavy bolts closed. Locked! *Safe!*

A fist pounded on the outside of the door.

"Carla!" Eric shouted.

She recoiled and fled deeper inside the building. The pounding receded behind her. Now she could hear a girl sobbing. She ran toward the sound, past the glass display windows of the ski shop, past the closed room of the SOS Wolfram, down the dank cement corridor, through puddles of melting snow.

"Mindy?" she called. *"Where are you?"*

Beyond the first-aid station, she saw the room containing the cable-car machinery. Its door was open. Weeping came from inside, strangely distant, with the overtone of an echo. She pushed into the chamber.

A dim utility light shone on the immense shapes that filled the space. Shadows crouched to spring from the walls. Stunned, she moved around the giant wheels, peering behind the great drive engine and the thick steel ropes, calling. There was an open door in the far wall. Next to it lay a pair of skis and poles. She ran to the door—and almost fell down the hundred-foot shaft into the pit room! She staggered back a step and braced herself against the doorjambs.

"Mindy? Are you down there?" Her eyes traveled down the metal ladder to the base of the shaft.

A small, dark body lay huddled on the cement floor. A shimmer of red-gold hair stirred.

"Miss Temple?" The body rolled, a pale face looked up from the brown depths. "Oh, help! Please!"

"Are you all right?"

"A man . . . outside. . . . He dragged me here!"

"I know," Carla answered. "Are you hurt?"

"He's got a knife! He made me climb down!" Mindy pulled herself to her feet, using the bottom rungs of the ladder. "He's coming back . . . *to kill me!*" Hysteria echoed up the shaft.

"Stop that!" Carla shouted. "He's locked outside. He can't get in. Can you get up that ladder by yourself?"

"I—I think so. Don't leave me!" Mindy cried.

"I won't! But I want you up here—*fast!* Grab hold and start climbing." Carla looked over her shoulder fearfully. "I'm going to get us out of here, as soon as you're up that ladder. *Hurry!*"

Mindy started a slow, hand-over-hand crawl up to Carla. Her ski boots make it perilous going.

"Careful! . . . That's it! . . ." Carla talked the girl up the shaft. As soon as she saw that Mindy could make it on her own, she called down, "Keep climbing. I'll be right back."

She ran out into the corridor and back to the ski shop. She no longer heard Eric pounding on the front door. He must be looking for another way in. *Why . . . why . . . why?* She didn't bother trying the ski-shop door. Using all her strength, she drove the alpenstock, point-first, into the glass windows. They shattered inward, and she smashed out a safe space for entering. She found the phone and ran to it. *Locked!* A thick, silvery button jammed the dial! Terror-driven, she thought quickly. Then she searched out what she needed: the high-backed Lange boots, a display pair of Rossignol slalom skis with the bindings already mounted, poles—not the high-powered equipment she was used to, but she was desperately grateful. She crawled out through the shattered glass with her stolen treasure, almost slipping on the walking stick she had dropped in the corridor. It had been no more than fifteen minutes since she fled from Eric into the building, but it felt like a lifetime. She was sick with the pain of having her worst suspicions confirmed. *Why, Eric? . . . Why?*

She hurried back to Mindy.

The exhausted girl was leaning against the wall, panting. "He choked me," she rasped. "Who *is* he?"

"Never mind," Carla said sharply. "We've got to go!"

DEADLY BONDS / 273

She was frantic to galvanize Mindy. How much longer before Eric found a way inside?

"Go where? He's outside . . . *waiting!*" Mindy looked up and realized for the first time that Carla was carrying skis. "*No!*" she gasped.

"Listen to me! We're getting out of here, the fastest way we can. There's a tunnel under the building, built for the Olympics last year. It leads out to the far side of Corsetti—straight to the racecourses. I'll get us down to Fernstaad from there . . . on skis. He won't be able to follow!"

"A racing course? In the dark? *No! You can't!*"

"*Quiet!* I could ski those runs with my eyes closed. Don't be frightened, Mindy. I'll flatten out that course for us. You'll see. Now, grab your skis and *let's go!*"

Terrified, Mindy bent to pick up her skis.

They heard a rustling outside the door. Through the spokes of a giant yellow wheel, they saw the fuzz of a shadow swell up on the wall. A body burst into the chamber and rushed at them.

Mindy screamed at the top of her lungs.

CHAPTER
48

In Miss Grimsby's office, Rudi Neumayer turned to Hans Kellhorn with urgent orders. The two worried girls, Nicole and Bianca, who had just left the room, had stunned them with their information: Not only was their headmistress missing, but another teacher, Miss Temple, and one of their schoolfriends had gone up the mountain hours ago and hadn't been seen since.

"Two women and a girl," Neumayer growled. "This maniac may be after all of them!" A saucer on the desk spilled over with burnt cigarette stubs, and ash dusted the front of his jacket. He clutched the green-and-yellow Swissair boarding pass they had taken from the Breitels'. "The airline confirms their passenger. He could be gone by tonight. I want you up in a helicopter, Hans, right away. Fully equipped. Telescopic sight, infrared scope—you'll have to be prepared. You're the only one who can handle it. He's out there, I know it. You've got the description. If you spot him on the slopes, don't wait to ask . . . *just take him out!*"

"Too risky," Kellhorn protested. "Shooting from a helicopter, in the dark!"

"I know your record. You'll do it. Get going, now. I'll call Trivella and set it up."

"And you?" Kellhorn asked.

"I'll wait a little longer—just in case. Then I'll be at the station, in radio contact from the minute you go up. *Go on!*"

The door opened a second before Kellhorn reached it.

Felice Grimsby brushed past him and hurried into her office, unzipping her ski jacket as she crossed the room.

"What's going on, Rudi?"

"Felice! *Thank God!* At least *you're* safe!"

"Sir?" Kellhorn paused in the doorway.

"No change in orders," Neumayer barked, and waited for the door to close behind Kellhorn.

"What happened?" Felice Grimsby demanded.

Neumayer took her arm. "My dear, who is Claude Griffith?"

She shook her head, not understanding.

He held out the green-and-yellow card. "Maybe you know him better as Anthony Claude Grimsby?"

She sagged against the desk.

CHAPTER
49

Carla backed against the wall and froze. Mindy cringed at her side. They both clutched their skis, as if for protection.

The man dropped the coiled rope he was carrying and pulled out his knife. His face was bloated with fury. He swung the knife between them as he advanced.

"So—*two* of you. All right." He pointed the big blade at the door of the pit room. "Get down there."

Carla stared, stupefied. *It wasn't Eric!* Who was this man? He looked crazed. There was something so familiar about his eyes—those sapphire-blue eyes. They . . . could be . . . Miss Grimsby's! Only *these* eyes blazed with a fiery rage, the rage of madness.

"*Who—who are you?*" she sputtered.

"Shut up! I said *down!*" Light glinted off the knife blade and off the huge yellow wheel that framed him. "*Move!*" He stepped closer.

"Why are you doing this?" Carla choked out the words. *He's going to kill us, Mindy and me—down in that shaft!* "What do you want with us?"

His voice sounded almost reasonable. "You got in the way. You wanted to stop me, didn't you? Well, you won't. I can't let you—don't you understand?" It was a patient explanation. "She *will* die, you know. They'll never find you two, but *she'll* know about it—and I'll get to her later." A half-smile lit his face.

A sob burst from Mindy's throat.

Do something, Carla begged herself. "Do you mean Miss

Grimsby?'' *Keep him talking*. ''What did she ever do to you? Why would you kill her?''

His face puckered with hatred. ''She stole my life!'' he roared. ''She made them send me away and lock me up. All those years! It was *her* fault they wouldn't let me come back. All those terrible years, while she was free!'' Spittle flew from his lips. ''Now she's rich and smug. *But now I'm free, too!* I'm going to take away from her what she took from me! I'll have it all—the money, too. She'll pay for hurting me!''

''*We* never hurt you,'' Carla said softly. ''Let the girl go, at least. She won't say anything.'' She heard her voice tremble and knew it was useless.

He looked at her with contempt, then waved the knife at them. ''Down the ladder, both of you. I said, *move!*'' Without taking his eyes from them, he stooped to gather up the rope.

Stop him!

''Now!'' he shouted. ''Do you hear me?''

The faint sound of tinkling glass outside distracted him for a second.

Yes, now! Carla filled her lungs and rushed at him, pushing her skis flat into his chest. He grunted with shock as his back hit the yellow wheel. The knife flew from his hand and clattered to the floor. She pressed him against the wheel with the full strength of her body pushing on her skis.

''*Run, Mindy!*'' she screamed. ''*Run! Get away!*''

Mindy fled out the door, hugging her skis, clumsy in her heavy plastic ski boots.

Carla felt panicked tears stream down her cheeks. *God, give me time!* She jammed her body harder against the skis, pushing, pushing, already sensing the man's power. His thick arm reached around her and locked her neck in the crook of its elbow. The other arm pulled her close in a crushing embrace. The pressure sent black waves across her eyes. She . . . couldn't . . . breathe. . . .

There was a flash of sudden movement behind her. A dark shape hurtled at them. The choking arm was wrenched from around her neck, the other pulled free, the man dragged from the wheel and flung out into the chamber.

The force spun Carla around. Released, she dove frantically for the rest of her equipment, and raced from the room, too terrified to look at the two bodies crashing at each other inside. The sound of their violent struggle followed her out into the corridor as she ran.

She spotted Mindy halfway to the front door.

"Mindy! *This way!*" she shrieked. "Follow me!"

Breathless, she led the girl to the underground passage, down the rank-smelling tunnel. They didn't stop or speak until they were out on the dusky Corsetti peak at the lip of the racing run. In seconds, she had changed into the Lange boots, and both she and Mindy had their skis on.

It was a new feeling; it was a wonderful old and familiar feeling! *On skis!* She bounced several times, testing.

"Okay, honey," she said over her shoulder, "we have to do it. Slow and easy. Piece of cake!"

She pushed off over the crest, into a wide traverse across the snow, Mindy following.

At that moment, she realized: *That was Eric back there, Eric! He had saved them!*

In the cable-car chamber, Eric and Anthony Grimsby charged at each other. Grunting, they crashed around the room, bounced off the great wheels and ropes, feet scuffling on the gritty floor. The older man wasn't tiring, despite Eric's superior strength. As a young medical intern, Eric had seen the rampaging power of the insane in full fury, and he knew the danger he was facing. *Was Carla safe?* He was distracted for a moment, trying to catch sight of her, and realized that she was gone. Anthony Grimsby seized the opportunity and drove himself into Eric's body with a force that knocked him against a steel rope and down to the floor. Eric saw him poise to leap. He struggled to his feet, and his hand fell on the knife that Anthony Grimsby had dropped when Carla ran at him. Eric clutched it and swung furiously. The long blade caught Anthony Grimsby's wounded arm and slashed deeply into the still-open cut. He howled in pain. Blood spurted from the tattered, gaping sleeve, surprising Eric with its massive flow. *Had he cut that deeply?* The bleeding man staggered backward, toward the door of the pit room. If Eric could push him into that small, dark room, he could lock the door and go after Carla. He ran forward, arms outstretched, and shoved with all his force. Anthony Grimsby toppled backward through the doorway, screaming as he fell, the pitch of his cry changing as he hurtled down the shaft of the pit room.

Eric was shocked to see him disappear. It wasn't a room —it was a shaft! He ran to the door and looked down. He was awed by its depth and the size of the machinery below. With horror, he saw the injured man sprawled on his back across the twelve-foot wheel around which the counterweight rope was wound. One arm was pressed beneath him. The fall had wedged him into the angle between the counter rope and its enormous spoked sheave. He was pinned! Eric hadn't meant to cause that, but the man had given him no choice. Was he alive? As if in answer, Anthony Grimsby groaned softly. His free arm fluttered; the wet ooze glistened as it spread across his chest. He looked trapped, helpless. But he seemed to be moving consciously. Eric would have to get help.

But first, he had to stop Carla! She had been holding a pair of skis. *She mustn't try anything so crazy.* Whatever she felt about him, however much she disliked and mistrusted him, he was still her doctor. She could reject him as a man—he'd learn to live with that pain—but she couldn't reject his help. He couldn't let her hurt herself any further. *He had to stop her.*

He ran out into the corridor. It was empty, as he had expected. He raced out the front door of the building.

The Corsetti slopes were blue in the late twilight. The moon was visible but had not yet risen to significant strength. He scanned the trails straight down to Salastrina for any sign of movement. No one was out there. How could she have disappeared so quickly?

A sudden blur caught his eye.

There! Out on the farthest Corsetti run, he saw a streak of silver in the weak light. He recognized the flash of Carla's lightning-bolt ski suit as she leaped the edge of the run and started down. A smaller, darker figure followed her.

"Carla!" He shouted as loud as he could, but the wind carried his voice away.

She was going to ski an Olympic racing course in the near-dark! She'd kill herself—or permanently damage her newly healed leg. He had to do something. This was his fault. She had run from him, in fear, possibly in hatred, and he didn't understand why. All he knew was that he cared for her as passionately as he had ever cared for anyone in his life. *He had to do something.*

He heard a hissing sound and wheeled in its direction. Off to his left, the rising car of the Corsetti funicular was just gliding into the station. The lights inside the compartments showed that they were almost empty. With the meager evening traffic now, the funicular ran at only hourly intervals. He'd have to catch this train before it left. It was his only way down, and he couldn't wait. He would get the attendant at the controls to radio the *Bergbahnen* in Fernstaad and have them call the *Kantonspolizei* for help.

He began running toward the station.

A racketing helicopter suddenly lurched into view, shimmying above the mountain, angling in toward him. It hovered overhead. Eric could see the *Kantonspolizei* markings on its belly.

Great. His heart leaped as he ran. Maybe they could signal the helicopter directly.

Then the first bullet splashed in the snow near him.

In the helicopter, Hans Kellhorn swore. How the hell could he hit anything from here? The pitch and roll created an unstable platform that was a shooter's nightmare. He lay tethered in the open door and steadied his 9 mm Steyr Mann-licher. It was fitted with an infrared, heat-sensitive scope and had a flip switch to automatic, but he preferred its single-shot bolt action. *Goddamn*, Neumayer was asking too much! Yes, he had done it before, just like this, but only at practice targets. Still, that was a monstrous killer down there—the description fit. Was he running away? In pursuit? It didn't matter. He had his orders.

He took a deep breath and sighted.

* * *

Eric had been a medic in the service; he knew what was happening. Not *why*—but *what*. He swerved as he ran, hoping the maniac in the helicopter would realize his mistake and *stop*. Still, the bullets smashed against each tree he sought shelter behind.

He heard the bells of the funicular signal its imminent departure. He saw the doors close. He was fifty feet away when the train began to glide out of the station and down the track.

It was his only chance! With a mighty surge of energy, he charged forward, leaped at the moving train, and seized the outside handle of a closed compartment door. A bullet pinged off the metal near him. Using his powerful swimmer's arms, he pulled himself hand over hand, step by perilous step, down the funicular's length, slipping in the snow on the narrow ledge at the base of the compartments. Then he swung around to the far side, momentarily out of sight of the helicopter. The track curved. One hand lost its grip. He dangled to the side, frantic to catch hold again as they approached a narrow tunnel. His hand found a grip a second before they slid into it. In the dark, he edged down the train toward the control cab. The helicopter was waiting when they emerged. Another bullet struck the roof, just as he reached the front of the train.

"Um Gott's Wille! Was isch los da?" At the controls, Artur cried out in shock when Eric popped up outside his window.

"I'm Dr. Sunderson . . . from the Leitner Clinic. . . ." And again a bullet rang on the metal, so close he could feel the heat of its contact. "Let me in!" he shouted. He couldn't hear his own voice in the clatter of the helicopter blades. "Must get to the *Kantonspolizei*—Inspector Neumayer!"

Artur understood only three of the shouted words: "Doctor," "*Kantonspolizei*," and the name of his old buddy, "Neumayer." He also understood what was clanging on his roof. He motioned Eric slightly to the left and pushed open the door.

Eric tumbled in and squeezed Artur to the side.

"Emergency! *Radio!*" Eric panted.

"Rudi Neumayer?" Artur asked.

Eric nodded, and Artur turned to the radio channel that put the funicular in direct contact with the *Kantonspolizei* station in Fernstaad.

CHAPTER
50

Pinned between the wheel and the rope of the counter-weight, Anthony Grimsby floated back into semiconsciousness. His teeth chattered from the agony of his body. Blood from his arm spattered to the floor of the pit room below him. He looked up the dizzying height of the shaft, through endless brown shadow, up to the dim light shining in the open door-way above. The brown shadows . . . like those in the narrow hallway of his home . . . the light that Mommy kept on for him at night. . . .

He crept down the hall toward the light, tiptoeing on bare feet, hugging his pillow to his chest. His pajamas, a replica of a baseball uniform in just the right size for an eight-year-old, stretched on his robust body. The house was quiet now. *She* was quiet now. For once, the screaming had stopped. She screamed all the time, this new one, yelped like a dog. Like when he fed Sweeper the rat poison from the barn, and the big yellow dog bit at his legs and paws until they bled, and howled because it hurt so bad. This new one must be sick. Good! Then she would die soon, anyhow—only why was it taking so long? He hated her noise, the horrible dirt and smell of her, and the way Mommy fussed with her. So small and red and ugly! He was afraid of her, too, and that slash down *there*, where they had cut off her *thing*—just like with the other one! He'd never let them do that to him! He would stop her screeching for good, the same way he did it before, with the first one. *Now* was the time to do it, before she woke and drove away sweet peace with her terrible cries.

The light . . . the light . . . the light. The sweet nighttime creaking and ticking of his home. . . .

He tiptoed into her room. The light shone on the slatted cage of the crib. The lumped bundle inside did not stir. Maybe she was dead already—finally! He came closer. No, still moving. The tiny tremble of each breath caused the white blanket to shiver and swell gently. Still alive, belly down, in her pink night sack, face turned toward him. He could smell her sourness. This would be easier than last time. He was only six then, and he had to stand on his toes to reach inside the cage. *Now. Quickly. Before she wakes*. He leaned over the bars and stretched out his pillow. Quickly, with all his strength, he pressed down on the small face. The lump began to squirm; the blanket jerked. He leaned down heavily. . . .

The light. . . .

Suddenly, the hall light was blotted out. He turned. Mommy stood in the doorway, bathrobe loosely tied, hair tangled. Her voice came from far away:

"Anthony? What are you doing in here?" Sleepy. Puzzled.

Bright room lights snapped on. She looked at the crib . . . *and began to scream*. She was across the room with a tiger's force, plucking away the pillow, flinging it to the floor, seizing him with rough hands he had never felt before, hurling him out into the room—and *screaming*. . . .

"Frank! Frank! The *baby!*" The bundle was in her arms now, wailing, their cries mingling.

His father burst into the room, panic on his face.

"Frank! He—he had a *pillow!* In her *crib!* He was trying to *smother* Felice!"

Both of them stared at him, a new and terrible look of shock—and comprehension. . . .

The light at the top of the shaft grew dimmer. He heard a loud spattering on the floor of the pit room and realized that he had wet himself. Like then. He drifted away, unconscious again.

CHAPTER
51

Carla felt the thrill of speed. And fear. Her eyes had made the twilight adjustment, but the dark course was keeping its secrets. She tried to search out its ruts and threatening moguls. Too dark! The wind whistled around them, whipping up deceptive plumes of snow. She sucked in each icy breath and strained forward. The firefly lights of Fernstaad glittered far below. She edged into a long cruising turn to test her leg, then shortened up into the first of the giant, serpentine loops that would bring them down—if she didn't fly them over a cliff!

The leg was holding. She felt its strength and could have shouted with joy. She could do it, she *would* do it . . . she *was* doing it!

Down and down . . . heart racing . . . easing into the next gentle turn . . . and the next. . . .

She forced herself to concentrate totally on the terrifying task. The turbulent emotions that buffeted her would have to wait. She had been wrong about Eric. She had *wronged* him, and there could be no forgiving. She knew she had destroyed something she valued, and there would be no way to bring it back to life. The pain was almost physical. But as soon as she realized what she had done, that moment when she started down the run, she thrust it from her mind so that it couldn't punish her and the young girl who was depending on her.

She would not let her concentration break. There was nothing now but this course and her power to conquer it.

Hurtling down the mountain, turning to monitor Mindy close behind her, looping down through the dark—*she was doing it!*

"They're coming down the main Corsetti run," Neumayer's voice squawked through the helicopter radio. "Carla Temple and the girl. Find them, Kellhorn."

The pilot heard the orders and veered away from the funicular tracks toward the big slopes.

"Sir! Our man's getting away," Kellhorn shouted at the radio. "He's on the funicular, going down. If he jumps off before town, we'll lose him on the mountain."

"He's not the one. That was Dr. Sunderson. Our man is still up there, not going anywhere."

"Dr. Sunderson? My God! I almost hit him!"

"Forget it, Hans. Can you see them yet?"

"I missed! Oh, Gott sei Dank! I missed!"

Neumayer called tensely through the radio, "Find those women, do you hear me? *Fast*. They can't see where they're going."

The helicopter clattered through the dark. Kellhorn squinted down at the slopes below.

"Wait! I think—yes, there they are, up ahead. I can see them now."

"Lights, Hans," Neumayer ordered. "Flood that slope and stay with them—"

Kellhorn gasped. "They're heading for a blind cliff, too fast. They can't see it—!"

"Lights!" Neumayer shouted. *"Give them light!"*

The floodlights from the helicopter exploded onto the course.

Carla saw the fall-away cliff, banked by trees, and a sudden turn to the left. She swerved sharply, just in time, and looked back to see Mindy negotiate the turn, clumsily but safely. She shuddered. *That was too close!*

The helicopter swayed above them, throwing a blaze of light onto the run that illuminated every small mound and crevice. She could see ahead now—and plan. *If only the leg would hold. . . .*

She swept down the slope, heart thudding violently. The light from above was a living presence.

The radio crackled in the cable-car terminal at the top of Piz Wolfram. The attendant stationed there to monitor the unstable snow on the high peaks was surprised to hear Inspector Neumayer's voice: An accident at the Corsetti station, a man hurt down in the pit room. The ambulance was on the way, but he could get there faster. He was to take the cable car down to Corsetti right away and report.

Glad to be relieved of his boring watch, he left the small, glassed-in terminal cage and crossed the icy platform. He stepped inside the cable car, turned on all the cabin lights, and reached for the manual starter switch.

The cabin slid away from the platform.

Anthony Grimsby felt the first vibration in the wheel against his back. He sensed the shiver in the rope. He heard the gentle purring of the electrical drive system coming from overhead, far above the pit room. The information blasted into his brain. A tidal wave of hormones flooded his body. He was fully conscious now and he understood immediately:

Someone had started up the cable car!

In a frenzy, he kicked out with his legs. Frantic, blubbering, he fought to free himself from his trap between the giant wheel and the now thrumming counter rope. His eyes shot to the wall of the counterweight. It was shedding a delicate spray of dust in response to the tremor of the mechanism. Already, he could feel the increased press and pinch of the wheel, the tightening twitch of the rope.

He began to scream—a wild, animal bellow that roared up the shaft and echoed through its tunnel. . . .

On the high slope of Piz Wolfram, the lighted cabin of the cable car sailed down through the dark on its haul rope. Ahead was the first metal support tower, thrusting up above the snow and jagged rock of the mountain. Closer and closer. . . . The cabin lifted on its approach to the tower. Then it bounced upward as it rode over the support structure . . . and plunged down again.

Miles below, in the pit room, the counterweight responded. In one fall, it danced downward a smooth seven feet—a plummeting force of 300,000 pounds.

The huge wheel rolled. The counter rope wound around its sheave with a snap. Neatly, it sliced through the obstruction pinned against it.

The scream that was howling up the shaft ended in a sudden gasp and a gurgle.

Then silence.

The counterweight rose. The whispering counter rope unwound. The wheel rolled again and released its burden—two severed halves that fell with two distinct, dull thuds to the sides of the wheel's casing.

The body had been transected cleanly across the abdomen; the spinal column had been sliced through two of its lumbar vertebrae. On the gritty floor, the legs jerked in a reflexive twitch; the soft-soled boots drummed in a cottony rhythm against the cement. On the other side of the wheel, the torso lay on its back. Only one arm was attached. The head was angled in an impossible twist of the neck, and glassy, sapphire-blue eyes bulged from the contorted face like huge marbles. Twin trails of blood oozed from the nostrils and seeped out of the wide-open mouth. A torrent of body fluids began to gush from the abdomen, flowing through the dust and out into the center of the pit room. They washed over the other arm, which had been pinned against the wheel and thrown clear as it was severed. The arm lay in the open near the counterweight. The long bones of the radius and ulna had been crushed; the pressure on the tendons was causing the hand to clench and unclench its spastic fingers.

For almost thirty seconds, the quivering of the parts continued. . . .

Then the dead tissue relaxed. The only sounds were the whisper of the counterweight mechanism and the trickle of fluids.

Outside on the snowy slopes, the bright cabin of the cable car rode serenely down toward the Corsetti station.

CHAPTER
52

Eric Sunderson shivered in the cold. A tense group of men milled around him at the base of the Corsetti run. The spinning lights of the ambulance splashed blood red in the snow at his feet. The *Kantonspolizei* car waited near the rise, doors open. His eyes were fixed on the slopes far above where he could see the floodlights of the helicopter, wobbling as they descended.

Oh, baby! You fool! Slowly . . . slowly. . . .

The police radio sputtered. One of the officers leaped from the car and rushed to the ambulance. Eric followed, alarmed. There was a rapid exchange of German between the ambulance driver and the officer that Eric couldn't understand. The driver quickly translated: The body had been found in the pit room of the Corsetti station—he described its condition—and they needed another ambulance for the cable-car attendant who had found it. The man was hysterical, in severe shock. Eric was shocked, too, but he breathed in guilty relief: *It wasn't about Carla.*

He was still shaking when he returned to the group huddled in the snow. He stood, fearful and useless, his head raised to the mountain.

The helicopter lights were closing down on them now. He could hear the chop of the blades. Now he could see two dots on the face of the slope, growing larger as they came closer.

Now he could see *her*! Carla—wheeling in graceful loops down the lower piste . . . down . . . down . . . trailed by the girl. *Carla!* How elegant, how beautiful . . . !

Easy . . . easy! Don't push it!

Closer . . . closer. . . .

Come to me!

At last the helicopter swung overhead, rotors blasting, and stationed itself above the waiting men, whipping the wind around them as it threw its powerful lights onto the final sweep of the course.

Eric rushed forward and scrambled up the snowy rise to the bottom of the run. Two ambulance attendants with stretchers followed.

In a spray of snow, Carla braked easily on her stronger leg.

Eric ran to her—then stopped short, uncertain.

Carla turned, surprised to see him there. She was panting, cheeks red from the wind, droplets falling from her dark, curly hair. It really *was* Eric, standing there before her, his face a map of concern. Her eyes sought his, and the tears welled. She tilted her head, exhausted, eyes pleading. Softly, she said, "Forgive me."

In one step, he caught her in his arms and pulled her close. "Crazy, crazy! You fool, how *could* you!" he whispered. "What were you thinking? Didn't you know? If anything had happened to you—" His lips pressed her wet and sweaty curls, her cold cheeks, her eyes, her mouth.

"I'm fine," she gasped. "Honestly, Eric, I'm fine! Mindy . . . ?"

"She's all right. They're taking care of her. Stop moving! Let me have a look at you."

"That man up there . . . he looked just like Miss Grimsby! He was going to—"

"We know, we know. Don't think about him. He's dead—and you're *safe*!"

"Oh, Eric! I skied! I came down that whole run. *I did it!*" The words tumbled out in a passionate rush.

"Off!" he shouted. "Get those goddamn skis *off*! I want to see your leg!"

"I want to go home!" The tears spilled over and streaked down her face.

"I'm taking you to the clinic first. I've got to check you over. Only for tonight, just overnight. As soon as I'm satisfied, I'll take you back to Marlowe myself."

"No, I mean home! *Really* home."

She released the bindings and stepped out of the skis. She meant to pick them up but she was too tired. She leaned against Eric and let his strong arms hold her.

Overhead, the helicopter killed its floods, lifted up, and swung away into the dark sky. The last flicker of its lights sparkled on Carla's wet hair, on her tear-beaded lashes.

"Home? You mean it?" Now he understood. "For good?"

She bobbed her head against his shoulder, then looked up at him, grey eyes swimming.

"Maybe," she said.

CHAPTER
53

She had known and she hadn't known.

Rudi Neumayer couldn't wait for explanations when he confronted Felice Grimsby on the day of the *Skimarathon*. The details came later.

He sat next to her on the big leather couch in her office, ignoring the coffee she had poured for them. It hurt him to see his dear friend reliving a nightmare that began years ago and culminated in the horror of the past weeks. Her voice was small; she didn't embellish the facts as she knew them.

Felice grew up believing that her two older siblings had

died in an automobile accident before she was born, when her sister was only an infant. That's what Frank and Abby Grimsby had told her. It was obvious that the subject was so painful for them that she mustn't question them. She never even saw a photograph of the children until after her father died three years ago. Then Abby told her everything: about the death of the baby Elizabeth that was assumed to be from accidental suffocation in her crib; the terrible night they caught young Anthony in the act of smothering Felice; the shocking realization that he had killed their first daughter and was sick enough to kill again. Frank Grimsby had moved his family to Northmere, to escape the past, and sent Anthony to an institution, determined that he never be released. Several times throughout the years, the doctors felt that the boy was sufficiently recovered to be treated as an outpatient; they urged that he be returned to his family. Each time, Frank Grimsby refused. Anthony would never be permitted near Felice as long as he lived. But, as the years passed, Frank realized that he might not be able to keep Anthony, now a young man, locked up forever. His only desperate solution was to encourage Felice, herself, to move away, far away—somewhere Anthony could never find her. Her decision to settle in Fernstaad was both a grief and a blessing to him.

All this Abby told Felice on that bleak day in Northmere after they returned from Frank Grimsby's funeral. The one thing she wouldn't tell her daughter was what had become of Anthony. Felice realized that her mother was in deep widow's shock, so she didn't insist. She would ask again another time. But six months later, Abby, too, was dead.

Sorting through her parents' possessions, Felice found the only photo Abby had managed to save when her husband destroyed the others in a wild attempt to obliterate all remnants of Anthony's despised image. It was the photo in the blue-and-green-enamel frame that had sat on the end table in Felice Grimsby's office ever since.

The sun angled through the office windows and stippled her face as she leaned over to pick up the photo.

"I tried to find him, Rudi," she said. "I had a feeling he was still alive. I did manage to track down the institution, but all they could tell me was that he had been released some years earlier. They didn't know where he was."

She studied the picture.

"I understand he looked like me a little—around the eyes?" she said. Neumayer had refused her request to see the mangled body, and he sensed that she was relieved. "I imagine that's why Johann Bächli thought he saw me that night outside the kitchen."

Neumayer didn't respond.

"At least, we know why Bianca Gioianni found that note in her pocket," she said wearily. "We both have the same color ski outfits. He must have seen me going into the Klaus on a day that Bianca was there and thought he was putting the note into *my* pocket. He meant to frighten *me*! Oh, it's horrible!"

She tilted the photo to catch more light.

"If only I could have found him! I *did* try. I wanted to meet him, to know him, to see if he needed help. I never believed they would have released him if he were still sick."

"I'm sure he appeared reasonably normal, even to professionals. That's very common in cases like this," Neumayer said.

"Cases," she sighed. "I wonder how he was able to find me."

"It was his obsession. He may have been keeping track of you all his life."

"I'm responsible for what's happened here, Rudi—for all those deaths." She shuddered and placed the photo back on the end table, face down. "He was looking for me, to kill *me*. The others were meant as torment, a warning, and I didn't see it until Katharyn Sunynghame was killed. I just didn't see it! Maybe I could have stopped him if I had realized sooner."

Neumayer shook his head. "No, Felice, I doubt it. He may have seemed recovered for a time, years ago. A calculated, external adjustment. But he was probably determined to kill you ever since he was a child. And remember, when he started his rampage, the deaths looked like accidents. He may have planned that when *you* died—an accident, too, of course—he would not only have satisfied a lifelong obsession, but he would also inherit your money. He would have been your next of kin, yes? Compulsion and money. He was planning it all along.''

''And the others?''

''I don't know why he killed them, but the more he killed, the more frenzied he became—and reckless. No, my dear, the only way you could have stopped him would have been by letting him kill you first.''

Her sapphire-blue eyes were edged with pain. She had to look away. ''Is that supposed to comfort me?'' she asked softly.

''I don't have much else to offer. But I'm here to help, if you need me.''

Felice Grimsby knew that nothing would ever help. She'd be leaving for Northmere at the end of the semester. She would see that Anthony's mutilated remains were laid to rest, finally, with his parents—with *their* parents—and she doubted that she would ever return to Fernstaad again. She had already decided to sell the school. Hotel magnates had constantly approached her in the past—the magnificent, huge old building so beautifully positioned on the Fernstaad slopes would be a gold mine for them. She didn't want Marlowe to die, the last victim of Anthony Grimsby, but she couldn't imagine anyone caring about the school passionately enough to want to save it. In her heart, she had already said her farewells.

CHAPTER
54

At the Leitner Clinic, Hans Kellhorn was keeping watch over the small figure in the high white hospital bed.

She was sleeping now, freed at last from the lines of tubing and wire monitors that had bound her to the world of the living for almost three weeks. Her face was pale, and the freckles that spattered her nose were sharp against the hospital pallor of her skin. But the bluish swelling around her eyes was almost gone. She had been able to sit up for several days, even able to eat lightly. And talk.

Dr. Ursula Freimann didn't remember what had happened when the intruder dragged her back into her laboratory. Only fragments of the attack, of her wild struggle, occasionally burst through the protective cloud her mind had provided. Mostly, she remembered the man's sudden appearance beyond the glass door, his awkward speech—then the shock of his forcing the outer door and seizing her. This she explained to Hans Kellhorn, slowly, carefully, barring emotion from her voice.

He watched her as she rested weakly against the raised pillows. Her eyes were dulled by pain and medication. The short, straight cap of her sun-streaked hair was dull, too. But he could imagine both hair and eyes shiny and crackling with health. Battered as she was, he could sense her former vigor. She would be well and strong again, he knew it.

He told her about the tape recorder that had been left running. She was interested to know that he had heard it—all of it—but she didn't ask him any questions. What she had needed to be told was that the man was dead. Then she remembered:

"My notes . . . on the tape. . . . I was working on—?" She had lost the name.

"Johann Bächli," he said. She nodded. "That's been taken care of. We gave the tape to Dr. Lüthi. He has your notes." She was satisfied.

He came to visit her every day. Most of the time, she was asleep and didn't know he was there. Once she woke to see, in a water glass on the window ledge, five tiny spring crocuses whose pink and white blooms had popped out in a sunny patch of garden near his home that morning. The sight cheered her into a boyish grin.

She was sleeping now as Hans Kellhorn sat by her bedside.

A nurse stopped in the doorway when she saw him. She told him that Dr. Freimann had just been given medication to assure her a good night's rest. He couldn't expect her to wake soon. He might as well leave.

"*Ach, nein, ich warte,*" he told the nurse.

Ich warte!

Those terrible words! The words the madman had first spoken to her! They reached for her like claws—reached down to seize her as she slept. Ursula Freimann whimpered in protest against the nightmare that was beginning to take hold.

The nurse stepped into the room, concerned.

Hans Kellhorn rose and reached through the guardrail to touch the small hand on the bed. He understood.

"No, no," he whispered. "He's gone, he's dead. He'll never hurt anyone again. Sshhh. You're safe. You're safe now."

The sleeping figure relaxed, breathing evenly again.

He held her limp hand and looked up to nod at the nurse.

"I'll wait," he said again. He felt the soft fingers curl peacefully into his hand.

CHAPTER
55

Eric leaned across the tangled sheets of his bed and stared down at Carla, asleep in the gentle, curtained light of late afternoon. How, he thought, how will I ever convince her that I forgive her? As much as he tried to reassure her, she didn't really believe him—that he understood her fear and confusion, her suspicions, her not knowing whom to trust. It was the terror that had gripped Marlowe that had swept her into panic. Terrified or not, she had been so brave. Of course he forgave her!

They had been together for almost a month. Ever since the night she fled down the mountain and skied into his arms, they had rushed to the privacy of his Fernstaad apartment whenever they could. It was there that Eric had taken her that same night, after she pleaded not to be left at the clinic. Why not? She wasn't hurt, only exhausted. He could take care of her. If only she'd *let* him.

But she was leaving Fernstaad. She had gone ahead and made her arrangements, mentioning it only casually. He wouldn't try to change her mind. He kept hoping she would.

He studied her, his heart aching at the sight of her beauty, at the swell of pride he felt when he thought of her courage. Her eyes were closed, lips softly parted in sleep. Her dark, curly hair, grown longer and fluffier now, spread out like a cloud on the pillow. He already felt the melancholy pain of their separation, and saw it stretching out before him for a very long time.

"Stop staring," Carla said, eyes still closed.

"I'm not."

"Yes, you are. You know what happens to people who tell lies." She propped herself up against the pillows and smiled at him. A glorious sunburst of crinkles radiated around her twinkling grey eyes. "I'm still here."

"When, then?"

"You know. Next Tuesday. As soon as the semester ends."

He nodded. "Yes, I know. I'm going to take the day off, take you down to Zurich and out to the airport."

"It's such a long ride," she protested. "Hours both ways."

"I want to. I'll be the last friendly face you'll see in Switzerland. That should count for something."

"Are you thinking that I'll forget you?"

He didn't answer. "Have you started packing?" he said, just to be saying something.

"Why bother? I'm not taking much." He looked at her, head cocked. "Only a few things—enough for a week, if I can stand it that long."

He moved closer to her on the bed. "A week?"

"Listen, I've made up my mind, Eric, so don't say anything. Don't try to discourage me because I've already decided. *I'm going to buy Marlowe.* No, don't interrupt. I've spoken to Miss Grimsby—Felice—and she's willing. Neither of us wants to see the school close, turned into just another Fernstaad hotel. It *mustn't* close. I'm going home to arrange for the money from my trust. It won't make much of a dent, I assure you. Please don't give me any arguments. I can handle my parents if they try to talk me out of it, but not you!"

"You're going to run that school?" he asked, stunned.

She shook her head. "No, I don't have the experience. And I know myself. I'd be too restless with all the responsibility. And there's so much else I want to do. But I can hire the best people and see that it's run the way Felice managed it. I've learned so much from her this past year. I can do it, Eric, I can save Marlowe. At least, I can *try*. And it's a great investment! . . . Well, *say* something. Am I crazy?"

Eric burst out laughing. "Crazy, yes. And wonderful. Good for you, my darling—good for you!"

"You like it?"

"I love it. I love you!"

She reached for him. "Well, then, good for us. I'll be back. We'll be together, if you want."

He folded her in his arms.

"I want," he said passionately.

Carla tasted on his lips the sweetness of the rest of her life opening up before her.

CHAPTER
56

In Val Triazzo, late that spring, the police found the nude body of a very young woman wedged into a crevasse whose snow had begun melting. She had been dead for more than a month—strangled and buried in the deep winter snow. There had been no report of a missing woman to fit the body and no inquiries from abroad. The only clue was the body itself, and that the pathologist gave his most careful attention. The age was estimated at eighteen to twenty years, the semen found in the vaginal vault indicated that intercourse with at least two different men had taken place just prior to death, and the track marks on the arms told the tale of a heavy habit. Detective Bruno Abati of the Val Triazzo *Polizia* concluded that the young woman was one of the untraceable professionals who came and went through the fashionable Alpine ski resorts in season. Unless someone was looking for her, there was little chance of identifying her and possibly catching her killer. Still, Detective Abati couldn't just consign her to the permanently unsolved files without making an effort. He remembered hearing of a series of murders of young girls somewhere in the Swiss Alps that very season. Was it in St. Moritz? Fernstaad? Yes, in Fernstaad. Were those girls strangled? He thought there was some connection with drugs, a murderous overdose made to look like an accident. Weren't those cases solved? Had the killer been in Val Triazzo, too? Had *anyone* traveled between Val Triazzo and Fernstaad around the time the woman was killed?

He had no other leads. He might as well give it a try.

Without much hope, he sent an inquiry to the Fernstaad *Kantonspolizei*.